KILL DAY

ANDREW RAYMOND

HUNTERHILL BOOKS

ALSO BY ANDREW RAYMOND

GET EXCLUSIVE ANDREW RAYMOND MATERIAL

You can keep up to date with my latest news by joining my mailing list. You also get a free Novak and Mitchell reading pack with some very cool exclusive content.

Also, in the next few weeks, I'll be adding a free Duncan Grant prequel thriller, *Kill School*, that won't be going on sale anywhere. Ever.

If you would like to find out more about the mailing list, head over to:

www.andrewraymondbooks.com

"If you do not know yourself, you will be in danger in every single battle."

— SUN TZU, *THE ART OF WAR*

1

Interpol Detective Claude Pinot rushed up the steep stairs, winding up through the Renaissance buildings on the hillside of Lyon's Old Quarter. He had done well to make it so quickly across the city from Interpol's headquarters on the banks of the Rhône to the sharp rise of the *Montée des Chazeaux* – all two hundred and twenty-eight steps of it. Although darkness had descended on the city, the temperature had barely fallen since late afternoon: now thirty-three degrees Celsius.

Pinot was sweating and short of breath – and not only from the exertion required to meet his contact on time. He had been sneaking around for weeks, talking and sending messages on burner phones, keeping his real work secret from his colleagues.

He was now just one meeting away – one simple exchange of information – from all his troubles disappearing.

He paused near the top of the stairs, removing his suit jacket to air his loose-fitting linen shirt which was soaked with sweat on the back and chest. He may have been a born-and-bred Lyonnais, but an overweight one like Pinot still suffered in the heat of the French summer. He gathered his breath then checked his watch.

'*Merde,*' he cursed to himself, trudging up the final steps.

Halfway down the *montée*, two men were trying to keep Pinot within their sight.

The younger of the pair – Duncan Grant, codename Mobile Two – was thirty-seven, dressed in a smart cream slim-fit suit and crisp white shirt. Although an open-air opera suggested smart attire, he'd decided to forego a tie. In his line of work, they could easily become a liability. Too easy to grab, or use as a choking device. Instead, he'd opted for the continental look of opening his top two shirt buttons, hinting at the tanned, toned chest underneath.

His older, more experienced colleague – Fletch, code-name Mobile One – was scruffier by comparison. His shirt was creased, and his two-day stubble looked more like laziness than an active style decision.

Such sloppiness also extended to Fletch's physical conditioning, as evidenced by the way he'd been puffing for breath during their march across the city. The steep stairs were only making it worse. He couldn't understand how Grant was still looking and sounding so fresh.

Grant had been biting his tongue for the last mile as Pinot increased the gap between them. There was an etiquette issue: it wasn't Grant's mission, and he wasn't part of Fletch's crew. Grant had only been brought in to follow Fletch and gain some mobile observation experience. But he couldn't stand by and watch a simple purchase of intel be compromised by a senior officer's inability to climb stairs.

During training ops surrounded by almost all English colleagues, it became apparent that Grant would have to take off some of the rougher edges of his Hebridean accent so that they could clearly understand him in the field.

Grant got on his radio. 'Survey One, this is Mobile Two. Do you have eyes on the target?'

The reply came from a white surveillance van parked at the top of the hill. 'We have eyes, Mobile Two. Target is approaching the Roman theatre, joining the queue.'

Grant waited three steps up, glaring at Fletch. Urging him on, Grant's gaze drifted back down the stairs to a solitary woman trailing behind a group of middle-aged couples. As Fletch caught up with him, Grant put his arm around Fletch's shoulders with a fake chuckle. He muttered, 'We've got a tail.'

Fletch asked, 'Are you sure?'

'She's been with us since the riverside. We're only coming this way to follow Pinot. There are faster and easier routes to the theatre than following us.'

Once they summitted the stairs, making it onto the same quiet cobbled street as the surveillance van, Fletch radioed. 'Survey One. Female, early thirties. Green blouse, black trousers. About twenty seconds behind us.'

In the surveillance van, Ellen was poised at the left window, ready to snap the suspect with a telephoto lens. 'Bobbed hair. Glasses with clear frames. Got her.'

Grant checked behind using the blind-spot mirror on a concealed works entrance. He said, 'That's her, Survey One.'

A few seconds later the couples appeared.

'She couldn't have overtaken that group without running,' Grant said.

Fletch replied, 'But she's got her hands in her pockets.'

'Exactly. She ran when she knew we couldn't see her, and now she's trying too hard to look casual. Survey One, this is real.'

After getting a few photos of the suspect, Ellen said to her senior colleague Rory, 'I think Mobile Two has got rookie mirage. She looks normal to me.'

It was a common occurrence for recent graduates to see imaginary enemies.

Rory swivelled in his seat to his laptop where the pictures had been sent. 'She looks smart for the opera, Mobile Two. What's wrong?'

Grant said, 'She's wearing flat shoes, and she doesn't have a bag.'

Fletch muttered, 'We don't have time for this. I know that paranoia feels like the safest option, but it also means wasted energy and attention.'

Undeterred, Grant continued, 'No French woman goes to the opera in flats. Not even an open-air one.'

Ellen chimed in, 'This is a hilly city, Mobile Two. She can always change into...' She realised Grant's point. 'No bag.'

'Nothing to change into,' said Grant. 'Anyone dressed to move quickly like that is worth monitoring. Did you get any close-ups, Survey One?'

Ellen moved to the other side of the van to keep tabs on the woman. She told Rory, 'Number four looked clear.'

He sent it to Grant's phone. 'Coming through any second, Mobile Two.'

Grant elbowed Fletch with a laugh then showed him his

phone, as if it had something funny on there. Speaking quietly, Grant said, 'That's Édith Lagrange. She works in the "Antiterrorism Criminal Analysis" department. The same as Claude Pinot. This is officially a problem.'

'Control, can you check this?' asked Fletch.

Grant complained, 'I don't need it checked. I've studied the department face book. It's her.'

'It's closing night of the festival. It could be a coincidence.'

'That she shows up tailing us half an hour before we buy a cache of files from a crooked detective in her department?'

The stern voice of the team's director, Leonard 'Leo' Winston, broke in. He was overseeing the operation from the European Task Force Control room at MI6 headquarters in London. 'This is Control. Mobile Two, keep her in your pocket. Right now, I want our focus on Pinot.'

Rory flashed his eyebrows up. 'That's him told.'

Ellen said, 'I suppose Grant was bound to get jumpy at some point.'

Rory pulled up a screen showing the differing heart rates for Mobile One and Mobile Two. 'He doesn't seem jumpy.'

Ellen leaned across to see. She nodded, impressed. 'Seventy-two. I should go out there to check he's still awake.'

Rory said, 'There's a reason he's being groomed for Section Seven.'

Named after the section of the Intelligence Services Act 1994 that protects officers in the field who break the law in the act of service, it granted only the most promising MI6 operatives the opportunity to apply. Section 7 operatives acted under the direct authorisation of the Foreign Secretary, thus making them immune from prosecution back in Britain should their actions become known. The loophole that essentially gave legal sanction for murder had led regular field officers to christen Section 7's notorious training programme as "Kill School". Almost nothing was known about it, other than to those who graduated. Over time, only tiny – often contradictory – slivers of information had seeped out from the ninety-four per cent of applicants who failed, leaving Section 7 a mystery, even to twenty-year veterans like Rory Billingham. In an agency whose existence the British government hadn't even publicly acknowledged until nineteen ninety-four, Section 7 remained one of the true secrets of the Service.

'Is it because of what people are saying?' asked Ellen. 'That he was fast-tracked because of something that happened at Kill School?'

Rory squirmed in his seat. 'Don't call it that, Ellen. Leo hates when anyone calls it that.'

Ellen had a glint in her eye. Relishing the opportunity for some insider gossip on someone who had largely been an enigma since joining the team. 'That's not a denial.'

Rory checked the live camera feed, showing Grant and Fletch joining the queue for the opera.

'Target in sight,' Grant confirmed.

Satisfied that he had time, Rory shuffled his seat a little closer to Ellen. 'This is only what I've heard, okay. Grant was on his final training run for Section Seven. He tracked his target all day. I'm talking Waterloo at rush hour, Oxford Street at lunchtime – Grant was with him every step of the way. And they were running every interference they could throw at him. Waterfall runs, coat checks, bag snatches. Grant didn't blink. But after six months of background checks, and a year of field training, with barely an hour to go before passing the test, Grant veered off. Dropped his target.'

'Why?' asked Ellen.

'He said he had a terror suspect in sight.'

'What? For real?'

'For real. It turned out that MI5 had a man in play who was following a person of interest, but lost him on the underground.'

'How did Grant know?'

'He said he just knew that something wasn't right about him. So he pursued, waited for the right moment, and somehow disarmed the guy. He had a ten-inch butcher's knife hidden down his trouser leg, and his phone was showing directions to Trafalgar Square. The police found Grant kneeling on the guy's chest on the platform at Piccadilly Circus.' Rory enlarged the picture of Édith Lagrange. 'So if Grant says he's got a tail, then he's probably right.'

2

The closing night of the annual *Nuits de Fourvière* summer festival had attracted a well-dressed crowd to the ancient Gallo-Romain amphitheatre. Posters lined the cobbled street, advertising the open-air performance of Puccini's *Tosca*. White lights lit up the façade of the theatre that overlooked the city, seen from miles around. It was truly the highlight of the Lyon cultural calendar.

Once Fletch was inside, Grant peeled off into the crowd via one of the many snaking pathways. 'I have eyes on Lagrange,' said Grant.

It amused him how easily she gave herself away: up on her tiptoes, scanning the crowd a little too hungrily, making it obvious she was looking for someone. But it wasn't a methodical search. It was frantic. Eyes darting from one side of the venue to the other.

'Survey One,' said Grant. 'Is there anything in Lagrange's file about weapons training?'

Rory pulled up the information. 'She's on secondment from the Bordeaux regional office of the *Direction Centrale de la Police Judiciare*. Interpol agents aren't generally armed, but she's still technically operating as part of the National Police.'

'So she could be carrying,' said Grant.

'That's affirmative.'

Fletch had to speak up on his radio to be heard over the sound of the thousand-strong crowd. 'This is Mobile One, I'm inside and have eyes on the target.'

Pinot had gone straight for the wine bar at the rear of the venue, and was shakily draining a tall plastic cup of Merlot like it was a shot of whisky.

It didn't take long for the place to reveal itself to Grant as a flawed location for a meet. Apart from the stage, the lighting everywhere else was dim, and the informal nature of the seating meant that it was easy to lose a face in the crowd. Grant had also noted the lack of metal detectors at the entrance, which meant that weapons could easily be brought in.

In short, it was a spy's nightmare.

The plan was Fletch's, and on paper it looked simple enough. Pinot was to stand behind the last row of concrete steps of the amphitheatre. Fletch would stand beside him. Pinot would ask Fletch to hold his jacket for a moment while he took a photo of the stage. While Pinot did so, Fletch would reclaim a memory stick from the inside pocket of Pinot's jacket. Fletch would hand it off to Grant, who would make an early exit for Survey One's van, where Rory and Ellen would verify the contents of the memory stick. Once satisfied, Fletch would get the call, then show Pinot the transfer of cash to his account on his phone. And that would be that.

But plans aren't executed on paper. They're executed by

human beings. And sometimes that's all it takes for simple plans to turn into disaster.

From London, Winston put out a call. 'Mobile Two, you're my eyes. How's it looking?'

Grant had circled around the back of Lagrange, tracking her. He at least knew that she wasn't there to see *Tosca*. Her eyes were everywhere but the stage.

Grant kept his phone up to his ear, as if taking a call. 'Control, I think we should postpone until we find out why Lagrange is here. I can watch Mobile One, or I can watch her, but I can't do both.'

Winston said, 'Mobile One, it's your call.'

Fletch replied straight away, 'We're still go. Mobile Two: eyes on me.'

Grant pocketed his phone.

The orchestra completed their final tune-up, filling the night air with an expansive wave of bowed strings. The Romans could never have known how good their theatres would sound with an amplified orchestra. To Detective Claude Pinot, it was the sound of tension. Of being out of his depth. And not knowing what was to come.

Inside a standard opera house, the audience would need to be seated before a performance could begin, and no one could enter once the performance had started. The unique Gallo-Romain venue allowed for a looser set up: people were still finding seats on the concrete steps as the conductor took his place at the podium to delighted applause.

The lights on the stage dimmed, then the dramatic opening chords of *Tosca*'s Scarpia motif played as Angelotti, the escaped political prisoner being pursued by the Chief of Police, took refuge in a chapel.

Pinot knew basic Italian, but he wasn't paying attention to the tone and delivery of Angelotti's singing. All he could think about was his churning stomach and quickening heart rate.

What the hell am I doing? he thought. He just wanted it to be over.

'I'm going in,' said Fletch, sharking through the crowd towards Pinot.

Grant moved in sync with him, staying out of the glow from the lights strung across the bar area.

Having tailed him and Fletch across Lyon, Lagrange could picture Grant clearly. His strong, well-proportioned upper body. The easy way he carried himself, that was both genteel and masculine. What she'd heard of his voice had been resonant and warm. Yet there was still something of the "grey man" about him. An ability to shrink into the background.

Trying to pick Grant up again in a sea of silhouettes of men in suits, those other details became irrelevant.

Grant retreated to a spot in the crowd where he could observe Pinot and Fletch.

There was a sense of anticipation in the air as the languid strings of "Recondita Armonia" began: the most famous aria in *Tosca*, and arguably Puccini's most beautiful.

Pinot and Fletch were side by side now.

Pinot removed his jacket. 'You have the money?' he asked in English.

'Relax,' Fletch whispered in reply.

Pinot was sweating. His forehead bubbling. 'I want the money first.'

Fletch gave a fixed smile. 'That's not what we agreed.'

'No money. No files.'

'You'll get your money...'

The music swelled from the orchestra pit.

Pinot held out his jacket, but as he turned, he hesitated, looking beyond Fletch.

'Something's wrong,' said Grant. He pushed through the crowd to get a better view.

Pinot retracted the jacket.

As the tenor playing Cavaradossi prepared for his heroic long note at the aria's climax, the orchestra and PA system were punctured by the unmistakable sound of a gunshot.

Everyone standing around Grant instinctively ducked down, clearing his view towards Fletch and Pinot.

The shooter had his back to Grant, obscured in the darkness.

Pinot buckled over, clutching his stomach. As Fletch whipped around, the shooter moved in and fired a single bullet into Fletch's forehead. Then he finished off the bent-over Pinot with a shot directly into the top of his head.

The sound of the shots echoed around the amphitheatre, the acoustics playing havoc with the crowd's ability to tell where the gunman was.

For a country sadly well-accustomed to terror attacks, it didn't take long for the panic to spread. It was bedlam on the concrete steps, a mass of bodies climbing over each other to escape.

'Shots fired, shots fired!' Grant radioed, struggling to force his way through the dense crowd. 'The target and Mobile One are down.'

Édith Lagrange called out in horror, 'Claude!'

The shooter crouched by Pinot's body, his face obscured. He was wearing a dark suit, a grey shirt and black tie. All Grant could see was the shooter reaching into Pinot's jacket with latex gloves, taking the memory stick. He left the gun, then high-tailed it into the throng.

Police swarmed into the venue. In a terror attack, the gunman would be obvious: they wouldn't stop shooting until they were dead themselves. But now, the police had no idea who or what to look for.

Grant set off after the shooter, shoving clear anyone in his way. All he could see was the shooter's silhouette.

Édith Lagrange, closer to him than Grant, tried desperately to direct the police towards the man, but by the time she'd explained, he'd dipped his head down and disappeared again.

As Grant gave chase, he noticed the shooter's jacket and tie on the ground. He was stripping off. 'Survey One, I need eyes on a male, short hair, grey shirt, no tie!' Waiting for a response that didn't come, Grant repeated, 'Survey One?'

Control couldn't get them either. 'Mobile Two, it's all on you,' said Winston. 'Stay on the shooter.'

The street outside was too narrow to cope with a sudden exodus from the thousand-capacity theatre. With all the parked cars, it was a total crush.

Lagrange had climbed the boot of a car for a better view and caught sight of the shooter making for the stairs back down into the Old Quarter. Lagrange pointed him out to a *gendarme*.

The shooter noticed, and had an easy isolated target.

Grant could see the danger she'd put herself in and pulled her off the car.

The shot was so close that Grant heard it fizzle past his head on their way to the ground.

Lagrange looked up at her saviour in confusion, recognising him.

There was no time for accepting thanks. Grant scrambled to his feet and looked all around for the shooter. No amount of training can prepare a rookie recruit for such a moment.

There were so many people. Panic seized him. 'I've lost him,' he radioed.

He only had one option left.

Survey One was only a short distance back up the hill, away from the screaming throng.

Grant sprinted towards the white van. 'Survey One, this is Mobile Two. Respond!'

Through the front window, Grant could see the racks of tech gear, various screens lit up, and two empty chairs.

When he opened the rear door, Ellen's body slid down the inside then spilled out over the edge. She was flat on her back – two gunshots in her chest, one in the forehead.

Rory had been shot second. He lay in a crumpled heap on the floor, killed as he tried to defend Ellen from the onslaught.

Grant gulped. 'Control, this is Mobile Two. Survey One has been taken out. They're both dead.'

The Control room was chaos, with analysts and tech operators all clamouring while Winston tried to assess the situation.

Still staring at the bodies, Grant asked, 'Do you *read* me?'

Winston replied, 'This is a Level Two Abort, Mobile Two. Get to the safe house.'

Grant heard footsteps quickly approaching. Before he could close the van door, Édith Lagrange appeared, pointing a gun at him. She shouted at him in English, 'Who are you?'

She took one look at the dead bodies, then at Grant.

He didn't move. 'We need to talk,' he said in French. 'It's not what you think.'

Lagrange's eyes flitted from Grant to the *gendarmes* back down the road who were within shouting distance.

In Grant's earpiece, Winston repeated, 'Mobile Two, do you read me? What's your position?'

Grant replied into his mic, 'Complicated.'

3

'Who are you?' Lagrange asked.

The easy option for Grant was to take out his navy blue diplomatic passport, then stay silent until the police relented and let him go. It wouldn't matter if there were ten kilos of heroin in the back of the van. A diplomatic passport was unimpeachable. Sure, it would cause a mess for a few days. But MI6 would work it out with the French security services.

It reminded him of the Resistance to Interrogation phase of his training. Many candidates confused the idea of resistance with strength. Instead of trying to appear humbly innocent, giving away little without clamming up entirely, letting the interrogator think they were on top of them, the candidates wanted to flaunt their mental superiority. To appear tough. They'd smirk at questions or demands for information. In reality, such behaviour could get you killed.

Talented officers like Grant understood that appearing vulnerable and being vulnerable were not always the same thing.

He might have been able to evade legal repercussions for the dead intelligence officers lying in front of him, but it would rob him of the one thing he needed: a chance to dig deeper on Claude Pinot *in* Lyon, to figure out what had blown his op and why three of his colleagues were now dead.

Grant needed someone he could trust, to get more information. He decided to lay his cards out.

'I'm an MI6 intelligence officer,' he explained, slowly turning around to face her, showing her his hands. 'My name is Alex. I'm unarmed.'

'What did you want with Claude?'

Grant kept steady eye contact. 'He was selling us information. He wouldn't say what that information was. The files were taken by the man who shot him.'

Lagrange slowly lowered her gun. 'I think I know what this is all about.'

Grant looked worriedly up the street. The crowd was spilling out towards them.

Grant lifted Ellen's body back inside the van. 'We can't talk here,' he said, hurrying to the driver's door. 'If you know what Pinot was selling us, then you need to decide who you'd rather explain all this to: me or the police.'

Lagrange looked at the numerous *gendarmes* back at the theatre exit.

Grant added, 'You could be at risk too, Detective.'

'You know who I am?' she asked.

'I know your whole department.'

'I was just trying to protect Claude. I don't want to be a part of this.'

Grant said, 'The shooter got a good look at your face.

I'm afraid you're a part of this whether you like it or not. I can protect you.'

Lagrange shook her head, torn by the choice she was facing. Finally, she asked, 'Where can we go?'

'I have a safe house a mile down the hill from here.'

Lagrange mumbled to herself in French, 'God help me...'

She got into the van.

Grant had studied the winding narrow roads at the top of the hill during recon earlier that afternoon. A series of back roads and alleys steered them away from the blockage outside the theatre.

Grant consulted the sat nav. It was blinking with some kind of interference as he tapped in the address for the safe house at Place Saint-Paul. He gave the dashboard a firm thump with the heel of his palm.

Lagrange pointed right. 'This way is faster.'

Grant went as fast as the tight roads would allow, and without drawing any attention. If the police pulled him over, it would be lights out. He had to get the van to the underground car park at the safe house.

Grant kept a keen eye on the side mirrors, checking for tails. 'It doesn't make sense,' he said. 'He shot them before going into the opera.'

'He didn't have time on the way out,' Lagrange replied.

'It's risky, though. If anyone saw him he would have blown his primary.'

'Primary?'

'*Une mission*,' said Grant. 'His assignment: to steal Pinot's files. Shooting my colleagues could have jeopardised that.' He turned on the radio – not because he wanted to listen to music. He wanted to check the digital display. It was also flickering. 'Shit,' he said.

'What's wrong?'

He alternated between looking out the windscreen and stealing quick glances under the steering wheel column. He reached down and tore away the plastic cover. Louder this time, he repeated, 'Shit.'

Lagrange couldn't see what he had discovered.

He radioed Control, 'This is Mobile Two in transit.' He paused for a deep breath, staring at the electronic detonator that had been hooked up to the car. 'I need bomb disposal. Preferably not a trainee.'

Lagrange's English was excellent, but even a novice could have made out the word Grant had used that really mattered.

As she reached for her seatbelt Grant threw his arm out across her.

'*Ne touchez pas*,' he told her. 'I don't know what it's connected to.'

Lagrange stiffened, terrified of touching anything while every reflex in her body made her want to throw open the door and run.

By the side of the River Saône at the foot of the Old Quarter, Grant looked for a parking space as far from buildings as possible. He managed to find a space between the river and the cycle path. He pulled over, keeping the engine running.

His breathing turned heavy as he fumbled with his radio earpiece. 'Where are we?' he asked.

Winston replied, 'Randall's here.'

Grant paused, unsure that he'd heard correctly. 'From *forensics*? Is he getting a head start on IDing the victims?'

Winston said, 'He started in bomb disposal. He knows what he's doing. I'm patching him in now.'

A reassuringly calm voice came on the line. 'Can you show me what you're seeing?' Randall asked.

Grant quickly opened his phone's camera function. The flash light only highlighted the direness of the situation: a tangle of multicoloured wires were jutting out of a small metal box with a blank LCD screen.

'Okay,' said Randall. 'That's a remote receiver.'

Grant began, 'As in...'

'Someone could blow it at any second.' Watching the relay on a monitor in the Control room, Randall said, 'Right... it looks like it's connected to the OBD port. It's what accesses all the electronic elements of the van. Whatever you do, under any circumstances, don't turn anything else on or off. Even opening a door could trigger it if it's hooked up to the locks.'

'Don't worry,' replied Grant. 'I'll stay right here. With the bomb.' He looked at Lagrange, then nodded at her. '*Tout ira bien.*'

It's going to be alright.

Lagrange knew that Grant was just trying to keep her calm. But no words could quell the turmoil taking place in her body. Tension rose through her chest and into her throat. Breathing had become difficult.

She closed her eyes, muttering something in such rapid French that Grant couldn't make it out.

Randall had often practised flicking to random places in his thick A4 binder, trying to find fixes for various worst-case scenarios as fast as possible. What had been smooth and swift in practice was now a frenzy of fingers and laminated pages. Once he found the page he needed, Grant could hear him typing rapidly on his keyboard.

Impatient for a response, he snapped, 'What's happening, Randall? How do I stop this thing?'

'Okay, okay,' Randall replied. 'Sorry. Can you – very slowly – open your door and see under the chassis?'

Grant paused. 'You said not to open the door. Under any circumstances.'

'Yes, well, rather a lot has happened since then, Mobile Two...'

When Lagrange saw Grant move for his door handle, she extended a hand to stop him.

'It's okay,' he told her, pointing to his ear. 'They say it's alright.' He opened the door, aiming for zero vibration.

The moment the door cracked open there was a loud beep from under the steering wheel column.

'What's that?' Grant asked quickly.

'I need a visual of where the noise is,' Randall replied.

Grant showed him with his phone.

An LCD screen had lit up on the metal box.

It showed *1:00...*

Then *0:59...*

0:58...

Grant said with urgency, 'Randall–'

'Yeah, I know,' he replied. 'What I need you to do is get down to the metal box and pull out the black and white wire until you can see what it's connected to.'

0:53…

0:52…

With the door wide open, Grant got down on his knees outside for a better angle then made a "come here" gesture at Lagrange. 'Climb over me,' he told her, indicating behind his back.

'What about you?' she asked, holding the headrest for balance on the way past.

Grant angled the flashlight on his phone to see the wires. 'I'll be fine.' He gestured with a flick of his head towards a young woman with a pram walking towards them on the riverside pathway. 'Show her your badge. Tell her there's a gas leak and to get back. Do it quickly. *Allez!*'

Lagrange ran with her badge in the air, shouting to the woman who stopped in her tracks. The intensity in Lagrange's eyes convinced her that something was truly wrong.

All around, police sirens echoed through the city. Lagrange could only look on from a distance, ushering the woman with her pram quickly away.

Randall asked Grant, 'Can you see it?'

'Yeah.' He gently teased the black and white wire out. It seemed much longer than the others. He kept pulling. And pulling. But it wasn't going taut.

He pulled it until all that was left was an exposed, frayed end. He showed it to Randall on the camera. 'What now, Professor Oppenheimer?'

0:40…

0:39…

The sight of the frayed end stumped Randall for a moment. Then he flicked through his binder again.

'What *is* it?' Winston barked.

'Still counting down,' Grant reminded them.

Re-reading a paragraph, Randall looked up at Winston with a long, relieved sigh. 'It's fine. It's botched. They didn't hook it up right.'

Listening in, Grant said, 'The clock's still ticking down, Randall.'

0:33…

0:32…

'Let it,' he replied. Then he added, 'But to be on the safe side, why don't you back up a safe distance until it's run out.'

'How far is a safe distance?'

'Oh, I don't know. Maybe a hundred yards?'

'Christ,' Grant muttered to himself. He scrambled around the car door then ran towards Lagrange, who naturally feared the worst was about to happen.

She turned the woman's back, shielding the pram, waiting for the explosion.

'*It's okay!*' Grant called out to her.

He explained the situation to Lagrange, then counted down the remaining time on his watch.

Reluctant to go back, Lagrange checked, 'It's safe?'

'Yeah,' Grant confirmed, looking with concern at the increasing visibility of blue flashing lights across the river. 'I need to get this van off the road.'

4

The service station at the foot of Mont Blanc in the French Alps – five miles from the Italian border – was customarily quiet for midnight. Few people made the journey through the Mont Blanc tunnel at such an hour.

The man parked his Renault Clio a few spots along from a black Audi S8. After the tension of the job in Lyon, the cold air and serenity came as much-needed relief to the man. Goosebumps formed on his arms almost immediately as he went to the boot. He had rolled up the sleeves of his grey shirt. Not through choice but by necessity: some of Pinot's blood had spattered him from the head shot.

He put on an insulated down jacket along with a plain baseball cap, pulling it slightly lower than normal down his forehead. He stretched his arms above his head, using the moment to scout the location for cameras before approaching the service station forecourt.

In the shop, a lone man in business attire finished paying for his diesel and a takeaway coffee.

Satisfied that cameras were his only concern, the

shooter raised his hand to the peak of his cap, pretending to adjust it slightly. The subtle motion was enough to fully obscure his face as he came into the path of the globe security camera outside the shop door.

The businessman mumbled a fatigued apology in German as he attempted to exit the shop at the same time as the shooter was entering. The men made the briefest of eye contact – a cold, fleeting exchange of recognition – pausing slightly as the businessman held the door open. As they squeezed past each other the shooter took a car key from the man's hand.

It was a flawless motion that someone standing right next to the men would have been hard-pressed to notice.

The businessman yawned extravagantly as he returned to his BMW, then set off in the direction of Italy.

The shooter picked up an early edition of *Le Monde* and a machine takeaway coffee. He used a wooden stirrer to make his selection on the push buttons. Even knuckles leave distinct biometric traces.

Using a self-service checkout – despite the cashier being free – meant that the shooter didn't even have to open his mouth.

When he returned to the small overflow car park behind the shop, he used the car key from the businessman to open the Audi that had been left there half an hour earlier.

He rifled through a black holdall in the boot containing several nationalities of registration plates. After deftly removing the Clio's French plate, he swapped it for a Swiss one. Then he took a rucksack from the Audi with various bits of hiking gear, and left it in the back seat of the Clio.

It would be at least another twelve hours before anyone

even noticed that the Clio had been sitting unattended. And another six before the authorities made any efforts to trace the owner. The Clio had been stolen weeks earlier in Paris, and now bore all the hallmarks of a hiker that had gone missing. Given Mont Blanc's deadly reputation, it wouldn't take long for the local police to make their easy assumption.

By then, the shooter would be long gone.

Speeding towards Geneva in the Audi, the shooter received a message from the solitary contact on his prepaid phone:

'*The bomb failed. I want a plan in place for handling Grant and Lagrange.*'

5

The safe house was on a back street off Place Saint-Paul, a small cobbled square on the edge of the Old Quarter. The apartment was on the second floor, above a traditional café and a wine shop that had been there for fifty years.

Cover for the apartment was that it was a short-term rental, much like an Airbnb. If a curious resident went looking for it online, they would find a genuine listing that looked like any other property on the website. From what anyone could tell from the blurry pictures, it was relatively overpriced for such a dingy-looking apartment. Even if someone happened to enquire about renting the property, all they got was a bot response from MI6's mainframe, apologising that the property was undergoing renovation for the next several weeks.

Grant was confident that the safe house hadn't been compromised: he'd been working with an experienced team who would have flagged any suspicious activity around the building before the mission. But he wasn't sufficiently confident to bet Detective Lagrange's life on the fact by spending the night there.

In the hour since the attack, there had been no updates on the shooter.

As Grant waited for the metal shutter on the residents' underground car park to open, Lagrange asked, 'Do you think he's still in the city?'

'I doubt it,' he replied. 'He'll probably be heading for the Swiss border.'

'Is that where you would go?'

Too coy to answer directly, he said, 'A fast car, night-time, and no border controls are a good combination for someone in his position.'

The fluorescent overhead lights in the car park were harsh after the relative darkness outside. As Grant parked the van, the subtle twinkling lights of the Old Quarter at night seemed far away.

'What now?' asked Lagrange.

He switched off the engine. 'Now we walk.'

With the bomb safe, Grant's priority was safeguarding the van until the forensics team could safely remove it.

Under the clinical lights, a small blood stain at the back-door footboard was noticeable. Grant wiped it away, then covered the van with a tarpaulin.

'Where should we go?' asked Lagrange.

'Somewhere that you can explain what this is all about.'

'I don't know if I can explain it,' she said. 'But I think I know what Pinot was trying to sell you.'

The nature of Interpol's work was hardly a nine-to-five enterprise, but it still surprised the guard at the security barrier to see Detective Lagrange after a full day, entering with an unknown male so close to midnight.

Lagrange didn't appear to know the guard's name. Which fit with the shy, cagey demeanour Grant had observed in her so far.

'I'd like to sign in a guest,' she said.

The guard turned the register around for her to sign, keeping eyes locked on Grant.

Grant said nothing. His French was excellent, but no foreigner can fake it so well that they wouldn't give themselves away as a non-native. And Grant didn't like giving anything away.

Beyond reception, Grant assessed the security to be nominal at best. Although Interpol didn't detain suspects or keep evidence on the grounds, there was plenty of information in the building that would be valuable to some very dangerous individuals.

The marble reception opened up to an expansive quadrangle, with windows to offices on all sides, six floors up to a glass ceiling. An abundance of potted plants around the edge of the large Interpol seal in the centre of the floor looked like an attempt to fill up empty space.

The building may have been impressively modern when it was built in the late eighties – all glass and brushed aluminium railings – but its architectural style had aged poorly. The overly large sans serif font on the signage made it feel like a hospital reception rather than the headquarters of an international police organisation.

As Grant and Lagrange entered the Antiterrorism Criminal Analysis department on the third floor, evidence of Interpol's limited funding became starker. The agency's €140 million annual budget left little spare cash for décor or furniture. The offices were lit by stark overhead fluorescent lights, and the telephones and computer equipment looked like the cheapest available models. There were wires and cables everywhere.

'This is me,' Lagrange said, showing him to her shared office space.

The cramped room had nearly a dozen computer terminals squeezed into it.

The other officers' desks were a mess of paper stacks and old coffee cups, chaotic desktop-filing systems known only to the officers themselves. Lagrange's desk was diligently organised, a cheap wire letter tray with neat piles carefully arranged in related batches.

Grant noticed the only other similarly tidy desk, at the end of a row next to a window with the blind pulled down. 'Was this Pinot's?'

'How did you know?' Lagrange asked.

The monitor had been turned slightly towards the window, away from prying eyes. Grant squared it up. 'Corrupt officers are generally very tidy. They like order. It helps them keep track of anything incriminating.' He stood directly over Lagrange's shoulder as she booted up her computer.

She looked up at him as her password screen appeared. 'Would you mind?' she asked.

Grant turned his back. He waited for Lagrange to hit the keys for her password. 'How well did you know Pinot?' he asked.

She answered over a flurry of keystrokes. 'Not as well as I thought.' Her password screen now clear, she turned in her chair, laying her hand on Grant's lower back. 'You can look now.'

Her touch disarmed him. He thought about how long it had been since he had last felt someone else's touch. Weeks? He found it strange that he had stopped thinking about such things since joining the Service.

Lagrange clicked and tapped quickly through her files to a folder marked "*INTERNE*".

Internal.

'Pinot was always kind to me,' she said. 'I know he had his flaws.'

Grant nearly chuckled. *Flaws?* Pinot had been suspended twice in two different divisions of the National Police. The first time on suspicion of bribery – not proven. The second on a charge of perverting the course of justice – also not proven. He had faced multiple disciplinaries for tardiness, missing reports, and smelling of alcohol while on duty.

Lagrange continued, 'That doesn't mean he wasn't a good person. This can be a tough place to work if you're not good at playing politics. Claude always reminded me to let my work do the talking.'

Grant said, 'I'm not here to assess his morality. I just need to know what he was selling us.'

Lagrange pushed a chair out for Grant to sit next to her. She lifted herself out of her seat slightly to check the corridor outside was clear. It was. The nearest lights were far down the hallway behind a closed door.

She hunched slightly at her desk. 'I've had access to more than most other officers and agents have here. It wasn't a coincidence that I ended up in this department.'

It all made sense to Grant now. The thirteen-digit password. The impersonal relationship with security outside.

Her presence at the opera. The diligently neat work spaces like Pinot's.

'You weren't following me earlier,' he said. 'You were following Pinot. You're internal affairs.'

Lagrange looked relieved to discuss it. 'Claude Pinot might have been corrupt, but he wasn't stupid. It's also no accident that a detective like him secured a place at Interpol. The organisation has been mired in one corruption scandal after another. Agents have been abusing the Red Notice warrant system for some time now. Normally, a country's police force puts in the request for a fugitive to be caught and arrested wherever they're found internationally. Except, some states like Russia have been using the Red Notice system to persecute political opponents. For a fee, you can get rid of your opponents, no questions asked. And it's all deniable, because the only evidence presented to Interpol comes from the accuser. It's totally one-sided. Which begs the question that's plagued Interpol for years: who polices the world's police?'

'That's what you were doing at the opera,' said Grant.

'I knew he was up to something. He'd been acting strangely all day. Leaving the office to take calls. And I saw him swapping phones twice. I went to the opera hoping to identify his buyer. To help build my case against him. I had no idea that he was intending to sell to MI6.'

Grant asked, 'What was he selling?'

She pulled up the first piece of evidence. 'These files are from Interpol's wires service. Every day we get hundreds of communiqués from police agencies around the world: sightings of fugitives, details of plane flights, bank transfers. It's all saved on the mainframe, organised by country. Not long after coming here, I noticed a number of files had been removed from the mainframe. He tried to cover his tracks, but I found logs that confirmed files had been downloaded to Pinot's computer.'

'Files on what?' asked Grant.

She held up a finger. 'On who...' She opened up a still image sent by the New York bureau of the FBI. The image showed a man exiting a real estate brokers in the Hamptons in Long Island, New York, captured by CCTV from the bank across the street. The man had on a pair of sunglasses. The face was indistinct. 'This was taken two weeks ago and forwarded to us for circulation. As you can see, Pinot removed it from the mainframe before that could happen.'

'Why would he do that?' asked Grant.

Lagrange opened a PDF bank statement. 'A month ago, ten thousand euros appeared in Pinot's personal bank account. Two weeks ago, another ten thousand.'

Grant nodded. 'We knew he had gambling debts. Nearly fifty thousand euros.'

'I think that Pinot was being paid to keep that man in the Hamptons out of Interpol's hands.'

'Then what was he selling us?' Grant asked.

Lagrange had one more file to show him. 'Abuse of the Red Notice system can work both ways,' she said. 'Senior officers like Pinot can issue warrants on people they want to be arrested. But they can also make genuine Notices go away. Not just Red ones.' Lagrange clicked into the final folder and opened a blank template.

It looked like a typical Interpol "Wanted" document. Except, instead of the Interpol logo appearing in white against a red background, it was set against a grey one. The square for a suspect's photo was empty, and the description filled with placeholder text.

'Not many people have even seen one of these,' Lagrange said.

Underneath the Interpol logo it read "GREY NOTICE".

Grant couldn't hide his fascination. 'What *is* this?'

Lagrange said, 'Red Notices are public. They're loud. They're visible. They're sent to every police force in our charter. Interpol lists them on their website and they're updated every day. Some of them are for the worst crimes imaginable. Everything from paedophilia to war crimes. But there are also lots of relatively minor criminals. Hit-and-run drivers who flee their native countries. Class-B drug offences. Then there are Grey Notices. Arrest warrants that aren't made public.'

'Why aren't they made public?' asked Grant.

'The individuals wanted in Grey Notices are only for the consumption of intelligence agencies. Most are classified eyes only. I believe that the files Pinot wanted to sell you were on this man.' She clicked into another folder, showing a log taken from Pinot's computer.

The Grey Notice showed "PHOTO NOT AVAIL-ABLE". The suspect's face had been removed, but it still listed the name and description.

Family name: MARLOW
Forename: HENRY
Gender: MALE
Date of birth: 9/3/1974
Age: 47
Place of birth: LONDON, ENGLAND
Nationality: BRITISH

Agency: MI6

Status: DISAVOWED

Charges: HIGH TREASON, MISPRISION OF TREASON, MURDER,

ILLEGAL ARMS SALES, FORGERY, CONSPIRACY

Lagrange pointed at the screen. 'What is this word?'

Grant answered, 'Misprision is deliberately concealing knowledge of treason.'

He had never seen such a laundry list of crimes attributed to a single individual. *Who the hell is this guy?* he thought.

Lagrange said, 'The strange thing about this Grey Notice, is that the only place it exists for Interpol is on Pinot's computer. There's no sending history of this Grey Notice on the mainframe.'

'What does that mean?' asked Grant.

'It means, MI6 filed it with Interpol, but it wasn't distributed to other foreign intelligence agencies as it should have been. The only way that could have happened is if someone stopped it. Pinot buried it. Why would he do that then try to sell you the same information?'

Grant had no answer.

Lagrange scanned his face. 'I cannot find any record of this man. Yet Pinot's computer history was full of searches for his name. Who is this Henry Marlow?'

Grant shook his head. 'I have no idea.'

6

A few hours before dawn an extraction team arrived at Place Saint-Paul. They were to remove the surveillance van under the cover of a call-out mechanic whose company name would be found in no public listing, website, or phone book – one of a long line of phantom companies created by MI6.

They towed the covered van to the industrial area of Chassieu, inside a secure lock-up where the forensics team could carry out their examinations in private.

With the sun barely risen, the extraction team picked Grant up at a misty Rhône riverside, then he was flown by private plane from Saint Etienne to take him back to Vauxhall Cross – MI6 headquarters in London – for his debriefing.

Meanwhile, Winston was in the Control room with a dozen analysts and operators – all exhausted and overcaffeinated. They were problem solvers, number crunchers, digital trackers – the brightest minds that MI6 could find.

The Pinot op should have been wound up by nine

o'clock London time the previous night. It was now six a.m. and there was no end in sight.

European Task Chief Officer Leo Winston stood at the front console – one of the most respected, and intimidating, presences in the Service.

Out of a suit and into army fatigues, he would have made a convincing SAS operative: tall, shaved head, trim beard, thick arms. If anyone asked him, he'd say that the U.K.'s last line of defence wasn't the Prime Minister, Parliament, the SAS, or Trident. It was the Secret Intelligence Service.

His skin was deeply black, a tone inherited from his Sierra Leonean father. It was also perfectly clear because of his monk-like diet. He had been a heavy drinker for a spell, but not anymore.

Even frequent gym-goers would have classed Winston's exercise regime as obsessive – which he still sustained at fifty years old. He brought an ex-field officer's gritty determination to operations. Anyone on Winston's crew knew that they weren't dealing with purely intellectual exercises. The European desk dealt with real-world implications for large numbers of civilians. The idea that the Control room wasn't on the front lines was simply a matter of geography.

Winston held his phone out, pointing at each area of the room in turn. 'Personnel, I want all your grids up on the wall. Anything out of the ordinary, you call over Miles.'

In contrast to Winston's imposing physicality, was his deputy, Miles Archer. He was forty-one, and looked like he'd been forty-one for the past ten years – and would continue to be so for another ten, such was his anonymity. He would have made a formidable grey man, as everything about him was utterly forgettable: normal eyes, normal nose, and a rakish build. The one thing that didn't recede into the background was Archer's brain. As long as he could remember, he'd been the smartest guy in any room he'd been in. Having struggled his whole life with making eye contact, it was often hard to tell if he was talking to you or to himself.

Despite that, his intelligence and closeness with Winston guaranteed the team's respect.

Winston clapped his hands once. 'Ears and eyes open. Let's go.'

It might have been dawn, but the room buzzed with energy and determination, the sound of intel flowing. Getting the intelligence wasn't the issue. The team's talent lay in selecting what was pertinent.

Winston and Archer watched on the screen as the lead investigator – an explosives expert – streamed live video from the Lyon lock-up.

Behind him, someone in white overalls raised their arm and announced, 'I've got a print!'

It was quickly dusted and transferred onto plastic film for scanning. The fingerprint appeared in the corner of the video wall.

'Scanning now,' Archer confirmed.

Possible results streamed in, a blur of headshots from international police agencies and intelligence agencies.

It didn't last long.

Winston's face was tinted red by the accompanying flash on the wall. There was an agent's photo and name, beneath a digital stamp in bright red that said DISAVOWED.

The room fell silent. Heads turned towards the unfamiliar face.

The name was unfamiliar too: HENRY MARLOW.

Winston stared at the screen. When he spoke up, his deep voice easily penetrated the busy murmur of the team. 'Everybody except senior staff, clear the room.'

Phones hung up. Typing stopped. Silence.

'*Now*,' he added, making a rapid loop in the air with his hand. 'Let's go, people.'

The room stood up collectively save for Archer and two of Winston's most trusted analysts: Ryan and Samantha. Both in their early twenties, they had met during a training seminar at GCHQ, and proved to be a perfect team. There was no problem when they informed Human Resources that they were in a relationship together: MI6 preferred it when employees dated in-house, as it meant that they didn't have to run a costly and time-consuming background check.

Winston stood with his hands on his hips, sucking in his bottom lip as he considered the name and face staring back at him.

He pointed. 'Miles, lock that door. Samantha, the blinds.'

With one switch, the glass walls looking out into the packed corridor turned black. The LCD screen beside the door said, "STRAP ONE LOCKDOWN."

Winston turned to Archer. 'Are we absolutely sure that's him?' he asked.

Archer confirmed, 'It's definitely him.'

Ryan stole a nervous look at Samantha, then showed her the question mark he'd drawn on a pad.

She gave a micro-shrug.

The air in the room was tenser than anything the pair had ever experienced before.

Winston picked up his phone. 'This is Winston at the Euro desk. I need to speak to her.'

There was a long pause before the assistant replied.

Winston took a second to process the response, then asked, 'Do I *sound* like my schedule is flexible?'

7

Before Winston got into the lift, he checked with the four other occupants, 'Going up?'

Only one of them answered, looking up from their early edition *Financial Times* and nodding yes.

Of course they were going up, Winston thought. Everyone on six or higher was either a director or a Hannibal.

Unlike his, their suits were tailored. He could feel them looking down on him, their air of superiority.

Typical Hannibals. Winston knocked the button for six with a knuckle. They hadn't been up all night. They weren't paid as little as he was.

The sixth floor was home to the Anticorruption and Internal Investigations department. In an agency as sprawling as MI6, with two and a half thousand employees, and offices and substations on six continents, there were always a few people who abused their position – whether for power or money. That was where the sixth floor came in.

They went by many names, depending on who you asked. But the one that had stuck was the Hannibals: one mistake, and they'd bite your face off. Winston had once found himself on the wrong end of a Hannibal investigation. They had a way of making you think you had committed treason just by asking you for your date of birth.

One of the first offices outside the sixth-floor lifts belonged to the Director for Anticorruption and Internal Investigations: Imogen Swann.

Swann was on the phone when she saw Winston through her blinds, haranguing her dutiful assistant, Justin Vern, for access. Swann tried to continue with her conversation, turning her chair away slightly from the commotion. But Winston kept on with his demands, thrusting a file towards Swann's office.

Justin got to his feet, physically blocking Winston's path, but he was young and slender, and couldn't provide much resistance. He complained in a reedy voice, 'She's on a call.'

Winston marched right past.

He threw the door open, the whites of his eyes bulging, standing out against the darkness of his skin. 'Henry Marlow,' he announced.

'I'll call you back,' Swann said into her phone, hurriedly hanging up.

Justin stood in the doorway, hand out in apology. 'I'm sorry, ma'am. He barged right—'

'It's fine, Justin,' Swann replied. 'Close the door, would you.'

Visibly rattled, Justin did what he always did: whatever Swann told him.

Winston said, 'I hope you didn't put him on your door for security, Imogen.'

Swann said, 'He's been with me from day one in here, Leo. He might not look like much, but he's loyal. That's like gold dust around here.'

'If I hurt his feelings, I'll get him some flowers or a machine coffee.'

It was already clear that Winston had no intention of sitting down.

Swann placed an elbow casually on her armrest and rested her chin in her hand, a picture of stubborn intransigence: there was no way she was moving to shake his hand, or get out of her chair. Her red hair was almost aggressively straight, with a severe fringe that fell low on her forehead. It looked like someone had cut it with the aid of a spirit level. Nothing was messy or out of place. Everything about her was by the numbers. The power suit. The air that whatever you were bringing to her couldn't be nearly as important as what she already had on her desk. She had two mobile phones in front of her, both of them pinging and lighting up with emails and messages.

As Director of Anticorruption, she had dealt with a lot of dishonest spies in her time. She was so used to hearing lies in her daily life that disbelief was now her default setting.

She wasn't arrogant or naïve enough to believe that the Anticorruption department was the most important at Vauxhall Cross. But there wasn't a doubt in her mind that she was the only one who could run it the way it should be.

'You look like you've had a rough night.' She headed for the sideboard. 'Coffee? The kettle's not long boiled.'

He replied, 'We need to talk about Henry Marlow.'

Swann poured herself a cup of peppermint tea, then returned to her chair. 'Was there a question there? Because all I heard was a name that, much to my chagrin, this entire agency has tried very hard to forget.' She took a sip of tea.

'Last night, he killed three of my team during an op in Lyon.'

Swann nearly dropped her cup. 'Are you sure?'

'A fingerprint at the scene.'

'Marlow would never be that careless.'

'He didn't think it would survive the explosive device it was attached to. But for some good fortune and faulty wiring, I would have lost four guys and an Interpol detective.'

Bracing herself, Swann asked, 'How much do you know?'

'As much as the other task chiefs. That an operative went off the reservation a few years ago. I know the name. Now I want to know the rest.'

'You'd better sit down.'

'I'm fine standing, thanks,' he replied. His body language suggested he was in need of a punching bag.

'He was one of mine,' Swann said. 'Before I moved to Anticorruption. He went AWOL five years ago. He was disavowed.'

'What did he do?'

'It's complicated. We put out a Grey Notice for his arrest. We chased everything we could for years. Then I was told to stop.'

'By who?'

She hesitated. 'By someone worth listening to.'

Winston didn't show any sign of outward frustration. But he wasn't going to leave the room until he had answers. 'Three of my guys are dead because of Marlow. Who gave the order to stop looking for him?'

Swann sighed to herself. 'Leo, at a certain level in this job, things happen that we don't agree with. We go home, take a shower, pour a whisky, go to bed. What we don't do is barge into each other's offices throwing around blame. You lost three of your people? I lost plenty more tracking down Henry Marlow. Welcome to the Premier League, where sometimes you're beaten. Deal with it.'

Winston surveyed the room with disdain. The wall behind Swann was decorated with her various accolades and commendations, the way a doctor displays their framed qualifications. In the corner was a large Union Jack, hanging limply from a six-foot-tall pole.

He gave a sardonic chuckle. 'You know, I could never figure out how you ended up here. We came up together. You never wanted this. You wanted to be a field officer.'

Swann replied, 'One look at you tells me I made the right decision. You seem to forget that I know how you dealt with being a field officer.' She peered at him. 'Glug. Glug.'

Ignoring the dig, Winston said, 'I want to know why one of our field officers went rogue.'

'Then you want something no one else knows the answer to.'

'I want the truth.'

'The *truth*?' She said it like the concept was some quaint anachronism, like sending a letter or watching something on VHS. 'You really want to do this? Because most people, once they actually see how the sausages are made, tend to lose their appetite.'

'Try me,' Winston dared her.

Swann pushed her tea aside. 'You seem to be forgetting that one of the first things I did when I joined Anticorruption was to bury a report detailing your *alleged* alcoholism.'

'That was ten years ago,' he said. 'I haven't touched a drop since.'

She retorted, 'Which would make it all the more unfortunate for it to resurface now. That would be a terrible fall for the European Task Force Chief. This Service used to sack gay officers because it was thought they couldn't be trusted with secrets. That they were easily blackmailed. The same as alcoholics and drug addicts. The only people we shove faster out the back door are thieves and traitors. So don't come in here and try to hold Henry Marlow over me.'

There was a knock on the door. It was Justin, holding a mobile phone in the air. He said, 'I'm sorry, ma'am. I've got the Chief on the line. She's called everyone in upstairs.'

Winston feigned a look of innocence. 'Oh, I'm sorry. Did I forget to mention that when I came in?'

Swann forced a smile at Justin. 'Fine. Thank you.'

Winston did up his top button and tightened his tie.

'Okay, then,' said Swann, getting to her feet. 'Let's make some sausages.'

The group had assembled in the seventh-floor conference room, the lights dimmed to aid the clarity of the video wall at the front. Winston felt like he was behind enemy lines: there were familiar faces of various higher-ups in the Service on both sides of the large oval table. By some distance, Winston was the lowest-ranked official in attendance.

Looming over the room was a large picture of Henry Marlow from his personnel file. It showed a hardened intelligence officer with eyes so dead they were in need of resuscitation. He was the greyest of grey men.

Chief of MI6 Olivia Christie was last to arrive, rushing in with an armful of paperwork and a tablet, her phone clamped between her cheek and shoulder. She was in midsentence: '...I know. I've never met such a collection of bell ends in my life. But in politics, stupidity is never a handicap.'

Winston shared a knowing glance with a deputy director across the table: Christie had just returned from a breakfast meeting at Downing Street.

She was a little over five foot, but she had no Napoleon complex: unlike the Little Corporal, Christie had never lost a battle. She reminded Winston of a Yorkshire terrier that, from a distance, seems small and cute and innocent, until someone tries to tell it what to do and it turns into a snarling savage.

The first head of MI6, Mansfield Cumming, used to sign his correspondence as "C" with green ink. The title of "C" had been bestowed on every Chief since. It was a part of MI6's history that, like many others, Christie took seriously. She even kept a pot of green ink on her desk, to remind herself of his legacy. As Cumming before her, Christie had been a surprise and initially unpopular choice for Chief. But she eventually won over the intelligence community, by sticking to her life motto: be so good that they can't deny you.

She made no apology as she took her seat: the only person Christie ever apologised to was the Foreign Secretary – the Minister responsible for MI6.

She straightened her paperwork while thanking

everyone for coming at such short notice. She then looked to Winston. 'Leo, why don't you bring us up to speed.'

Winston had his laptop in front of him, connected to the video wall. 'Thank you,' he said, clearing his throat. He pulled up an image of Claude Pinot on the wall. 'Two weeks ago, Interpol Detective Claude Pinot contacted our European desk. He claimed to possess files that he said would be valuable to us. For a fee, he agreed to sell them.'

'A dirty Interpol detective,' remarked Swann. 'What a shock.'

'Pinot was certainly no angel,' Winston conceded. 'He had gambling debts, and a questionable reputation with the French National Police. Nonetheless, GCHQ found out that Pinot had been trying – and failing – to access records associated with some of our French agents. In the hope of protecting them, I arranged a meet in Lyon for last night. As some of you already know, it went south quickly. Pinot was shot, along with the team's primary, Mark Fletcher, and both members of our Surveillance team, Rory Billingham and Ellen Chang. Pinot's assassin stole the files and is currently at large. The sole survivor of the ambush, Duncan Grant, made it out and was extracted earlier this morning. He's being debriefed downstairs.'

Christie squinted at the video wall, at the part showing Grant's personnel record. 'I remember this one. He collared some psycho with a knife during a Kill School training op.'

'That's correct, ma'am,' said Winston. 'Because he technically didn't complete the op, I took him into my unit to build up some more experience.'

'It sounds to me like he was born for Section Seven. What idiot signed the four-D denying his application?'

The silence that followed gave Christie her answer.

She gave a rueful snort. 'It was me, wasn't it?'

Winston pursed his lips.

'A denial was your only option, Olivia,' said Swann. 'Section Seven isn't the place for officers to go off on flyers like Grant did.'

'That *flyer* saved dozens of lives,' replied Winston. 'And without him in Lyon last night, Interpol would have had twice the casualties.'

'Maybe,' said Swann, consulting Winston's interim report. 'But would a true Section Seven officer have prioritised sparing some Interpol detective over his primary objective: securing the files your unit was there to buy in the first place?'

Eager to move on, Christie asked, 'Do we know who's behind this ambush?'

Winston tapped to forensics photographs taken in the lock-up on the outskirts of Lyon. 'There was an explosive device found on the Survey van. Faulty, thankfully, or Grant might not have made it home either. Our clean-up team found a partial print on the device. It belongs to Henry Marlow.' He added pointedly in Swann's direction. 'Previously one of our own.'

The wall switched to Marlow's updated file, showing a digital DISAVOWED stamp across it.

Christie muttered under her breath, 'That's a face I hoped to never see again.'

Winston leaned forward, hands clasped together. 'Ma'am, I understand that this falls outside my clearance level. But if I'm to capture this guy, someone's going to have to give me the unvarnished version of who he is and what he did.'

Swann was the first to speak. 'Olivia, I–'

'Ma'am,' Christie corrected her. 'This isn't cocktails in the Belfry, Imogen.'

Humbled, Swann said, 'Excuse me. Ma'am. But there are certain details I'm not sure I can discuss with Leo here.'

'Imogen, three of Leo's people are dead. He needs to hear this.'

Everyone in the room apart from Winston knew what Swann had to say. Winston could sense their unease. It wasn't a pretty story.

Swann began matter-of-factly, 'Henry Marlow was an operative in our Albion programme. It was something of an extension to Section Seven. The difference being that Albions worked alone. Clandestine operations. Black on black. We never had more than three operating at any time. Henry Marlow was the best we ever had. We'd been running him without issue for three years. His psych reports were always clear. Then he started to miss call-ins and failed to file his mission reports. When he did file them, they were sketchy, lacking basic details. Eventually, he stopped filing them at all. That was when things escalated.'

While Swann paused for a drink of water, the tension around the table was palpable to Winston.

Swann continued, 'He started running his own missions. Assassinations. Completely unsanctioned. He was off the grid for months. We tried everything we could to bring him in, but he was unreachable. We sent another Albion after him – Dominic Lacey. He initially appeared to have located Marlow. Then Lacey went dark. A few weeks later we found him at his home. He'd cut out his own tongue then hung himself, leaving this note attached to his body.' Swann put it up on the wall.

It was a single line, written in a manic scrawl in black marker over the top of an old MI6 commendation letter:

"WORDS NO LONGER MATTER. ONLY ACTION."

Swann said, 'GCHQ found that someone had been talking to Lacey on the phone for three hours before he killed himself.'

'Was he talking to Marlow?' asked Winston.

Christie answered, 'We can't be sure, but we think so. The timing suggests Marlow may still have been on the line when Lacey did it.'

'Mother of... Who the hell is this guy?'

Swann almost looked embarrassed. She had personally selected Marlow for the Albion programme: his failure was a reflection on her, and her judgement.

She said, 'We sent another three guys after Marlow. All Albions. All our best men. He killed them all. We had no option but to disavow. The official charge is murder. We shut the Albion programme down, and I took over at Anticorruption to head up the search for him. He'd been completely in the wind. Until last night.'

Winston could barely believe what he'd heard. 'And now he's killed another three of our own. Unprompted and seemingly without motive.'

Christie rose from her chair, walking slowly towards the video wall. 'What does Marlow want?'

Winston answered, 'Last night, he wanted whatever files Claude Pinot had. Apparently they were worth killing for.'

Swann said, 'I'm sure they've got a sizeable resale value on the dark web. He's a rogue agent, Leo. This is his line of work now.'

Christie asked Winston. 'If you were in my position, who would you put on this?'

He didn't even have to think. 'Duncan Grant.'

Swann scoffed.

'Have you seen his charts, Imogen?' he countered. 'His heart rate didn't go over ninety even when he was working on that bomb. Look at Marlow's scores when he was in SAS training. Grant's got an extra fifteen per cent on him across the board.'

Christie checked the relevant section of Marlow's file. 'We're not chasing Henry Marlow when he was thirty-five, Leo. We're chasing an experienced veteran. There's no way Grant can match him for tradecraft.'

'Exactly,' said Winston. 'Marlow's my age now. If he's anything like me, he'll be up at least once a night for–'

Imogen didn't want to hear the rest. 'A weak bladder is surely the only thing you have in common with Henry Marlow, Leo.'

'My point is,' he went on. 'Let's use what we have to our advantage. If Marlow's been around for forever, we need someone he doesn't know. Someone he doesn't understand. Someone whose next move he can't predict.'

'It's a risk,' said Christie.

'I've been watching Grant since we took him out of the SAS, ma'am. He's the real deal.'

Christie thought about it. 'Imogen?'

Her answer was emphatic. 'Walk away.'

'Walk away?'

'From all of this. I know how Leo is feeling right now. But I also know what Henry Marlow is capable of when backed into a corner. If we start down this path there will be no going back. When I was posted to Beirut in the early nineties, an American diplomat described to me the suicide bombing of the U.S. embassy there in eight-three. The first major Islamist terror attack against the West. There were seventeen coffins draped in American flags. Congress was desperate for vengeance. The whole country wanted to see Iran carpet bombed. But Ronald Reagan could see the reality of who he was dealing with. He knew the jihadis were nuts, so he dusted his hands and said, we're out of here. It was a brave decision. And one that probably saved tens of thousands of lives. There's a lesson there that we should respect.'

Winston said, 'I wasn't aware that capitulation was an official MI6 strategy.'

'Sometimes,' replied Swann, 'it has to be. Particularly in the face of someone like Henry Marlow. It's too soon for Grant. And without being insensitive to Leo, the anger he feels at the loss of his team is nothing compared to the body count we could be looking at if we pursue Marlow.' She turned, pointedly, to Christie. 'There are also political considerations here. We're lucky that there's still a lid on Marlow's identity. What if next time we aren't so lucky? We can issue all the D-notices we want to the British press, but we can't do a thing if Marlow's face shows up in a French newspaper.'

Winston asked, 'And what happens when another Claude Pinot stumbles across him?' He turned in appeal to Christie. 'If we do nothing, we are guaranteeing that a month or six months down the line someone else will be sitting here, wondering why we didn't stop him when we still had the chance.'

Christie kept facing the video wall, as if staring down Marlow himself. 'Winston, debrief Grant. I want him up to speed on everything we discussed here. Marlow has a twelve-hour head start on us. I want an operational plan on my desk in an hour.'

'Ma'am, if I may,' said Swann. 'Surely this falls under the purview of Anticorruption? My investigation on him is still open.'

Christie replied, 'That's why you're going to be working with Winston. No one knows Marlow better than you.'

Swann barely masked her contempt. 'Ma'am,' she replied.

Understanding the gravity of what they were facing, Christie's voice grew louder with determination. 'I want to make one thing clear. Henry Marlow knows our every protocol, backup, and failsafe. I want him brought in.' She eyed each of them in turn. 'Imogen. Leo. Make this happen.'

Miles Archer was waiting for Winston in the corridor.

'Grant is downstairs, sir,' said Archer. 'He's been debriefed.'

Winston led him aside. 'Not fully, as it turns out.'

'Sir?' Archer noticed Swann approaching.

'We're going to have company.'

8

Winston returned to the Control room with Swann and Archer, the video wall blank.

Winston announced to the dozen analysts at their desks, 'Here's the situation...' He tapped the space bar on his laptop, making Marlow's original personnel file appear on the wall. 'This is our target. Previously one of our own. Henry Marlow. He will be, without a doubt, the hardest target you've had to find. But we absolutely must find him. For Fletch. For Rory. For Ellen. And whoever else gets in his way.' He motioned to the various international clocks above the video wall. 'Twenty-four hours. That's how long we have before the trail goes cold and we lose him for good, along with the contents of those stolen files. You have your grids.' His ominous tone suggested a very long day ahead. 'Let's get to it.'

The room immediately came to life – everyone was either on phones or typing feverishly at their keyboards. The video wall and computer monitors represented the

Control room's entire world. In many ways, the screens were more than a figurative representation.

They had personnel and operational files on the key players of the operation: Henry Marlow; Claude Pinot; and the fallen MI6 officers. The wall had uplinks to GCHQ, which had hooked the Control room up to the ECHELON system giving them access to global phone and internet metadata.

A large bank of keywords and -phrases filled the screen, relating to previous missions of Marlow's, and any others the team had assembled since dawn. The words and phrases were specialised, unlikely to appear in regular conversation online. Each and every utterance on any phone that GCHQ could tap into – which was almost every phone in the world – and any online hits prompted a background search by the team. They were to chase down any lead that came their way.

There were satellites and surveillance drones in position over western Europe, ready to target and transmit.

There might have been no one in military uniform in the Control room, but there was no doubt that MI6 had gone to war with Henry Marlow.

Swann scanned the video wall. 'What am I looking at?' she asked Winston, daring him to give an underwhelming answer.

Winston pointed at different sections of the wall as he explained. 'Grid one is Europe outbound. Marlow hasn't used any of his cover passports since he disappeared. I doubt he'll start now, which means air travel is likely out. We're up on train and bus stations, and all major road networks.'

Swann surveyed the dizzying array of CCTV images

being analysed on the computers around the room. Brussels. Milan. Berlin. All crowded. 'A needle in a haystack the size of a continent... We taught this guy to disappear, Leo. How are you going to pare this down?'

Winston said, 'A few hours ago, I had Interpol issue a Red Notice.'

'You want to broadcast to the world that a former MI6 officer is responsible for shooting up a French opera?'

'We haven't named him,' said Winston. 'There's no point. He'll have a hundred aliases we don't even know about. We've done picture only. It gets his face out there, and applies a pressure he hasn't experienced before.'

Swann wanted desperately to find a hole in Winston's logic, but she couldn't see one.

He went on, 'Two of my senior analysts, Ryan and Samantha, are on grid two.'

Swann scoffed. 'Who, Ken and Barbie over there?'

'Do you know how they ended up on my senior staff?' he asked. 'Because ever since they joined the Service, people have been underestimating them the way you just did. They're two of the best analysts in the Service. When they graduated university, every investment bank in the City wanted them. But they both knew that their skills could be put to better use than assessing some trading algorithm designed to turn fifty pounds into fifty-five. They're here because they have a sense of duty. You're not the only one around here who cares about loyalty, Imogen.'

Chastened, Swann moved on to another part of the wall. 'What about this?'

Winston said, 'That's all of Marlow's past connections: contacts, agents, informants, safe houses. Anywhere he went, any time he went there. Any potential connections with Fletch, Rory, and Ellen. Now, I don't believe for a second that any of them were involved in this, but right now there's nothing I'm willing to take off the table. Not yet.' Winston led Swann over to Grant, who was working on a laptop. 'Grid three is Grant. He's working on Claude Pinot.'

Grant buttoned his cream jacket as he stood up. It had flecks of blood on the right sleeve. He said, 'Ma'am.'

Swann shook his hand. 'Grant.' Her immediate reaction, based on nothing but instinct, was that he would never catch Marlow. On appearances, she could find another ten Duncan Grants in the Brecon Beacons participating in SAS training. She wanted to find out if there a mind at work underneath the granite exterior.

'How does Pinot lead you to Marlow?' she asked.

Grant pulled up the photo of the man in the sunglasses. 'This was captured by CCTV from a bank in the Hamptons. It was on Claude Pinot's computer.'

Swann leaned down for a closer look. It was the first photo of Marlow she'd seen in three years. She had thought she'd never see him again. 'When was this taken?' she asked in awe.

'Two weeks ago, ma'am,' Grant answered.

'That's him alright. Where did Pinot get this?'

'All taken off Interpol's mainframe. He had been suppressing the Interpol Grey Notice on Marlow, as well as all information and possible sightings of him.'

'No wonder my investigation kept hitting brick walls.'

'Is this what he was going to sell to us?' asked Winston.

'That's what I thought,' said Grant, bringing up Pinot's bank statements, zooming in on two separate transactions. 'Except, he'd already received these two payments. I believe that, until last night, Pinot had been working with Marlow. To help keep his name off the grid.' Grant waited for any dissension, but none came. 'When you think about it, it makes sense. A detective with a history of corruption and gambling debts. It wouldn't have been hard for Marlow to sink his teeth into someone like that.'

Always quick to spot a grift, Swann said, 'Marlow paid Pinot to suppress the intel.'

Grant said, 'Yeah. Pinot was on the hook for fifty thousand euros of debt. But I think he got greedy, and tried to get paid by Marlow for making any intel on him disappear, and also paid by us. Marlow was too smart to trust him. He found out about Pinot's deal with us and took him out before he could make the exchange, then he stole the memory stick with the evidence. The cash to Pinot had been sitting in escrow. Last night, every cent of it was retracted. GCHQ traced it to the British Virgin Islands, where it disappeared into a labyrinth of shell companies. We could spend weeks unravelling them in the hope that Marlow is waiting for us at the other end...'

'Or we get you to the Hamptons,' said Winston.

Grant zoomed in on the Marlow photo to see the name of the real estate firm he was walking out of.

The Southampton Group.

Grant said, 'Call me cynical, but I doubt he's buying a holiday let.'

Swann nodded. 'It's a starting point.'

Winston snapped his fingers at Ryan across the room. 'Grant needs a flight to East Hampton airport—'

Grant cut in, 'Actually, sir... I was thinking. If Pinot was using this photo for leverage, then Marlow knows we'll have got into Pinot's Interpol computer by now: he knows we'll be onto the lead. He'll be monitoring East Hampton air traffic for at least another week.'

'He's right,' said Swann.

'Make it commercial,' Grant said. 'To LaGuardia. He'll never be able to track me coming in.'

Winston told Ryan, 'Do it.'

As everyone got to work, Swann folded her arms as she surveyed the video wall. She said to Winston, 'You should savour this part, Leo. Because I don't think you have any idea what's coming your way. You or the Scotsman.'

Once Swann had left them alone, Winston pulled Grant aside. He lowered his voice. 'Duncan, next time I give you a priority you stick with it. I'm sure that Édith Lagrange appreciates you saving her life, but doing that lost you our suspect.'

'I was preserving life,' replied Grant.

'You're a spy, not a paramedic. You get your priorities from me, not your instincts.' Winston rubbed his hand over the top of his head. He could feel stubble coming through. 'There are people who think this is too soon for you. That you don't stand a chance against an Albion operative like Marlow.'

'That's exactly how I'll catch him,' said Grant. 'To him, I'm an unknown quantity. He won't know how to play me.'

Winston considered the answer. 'How do you know?'

'I've read the file.'

'And?'

'He's everything I'm not: privately educated; has at least a dozen kills under his belt; a legend. It was his entire life, and he walked away from it. If I'm going to catch him, I need to find out why.'

Winston was cautiously impressed with the analysis. 'He

also killed the last three operatives the Service sent after him. Be careful, Grant. Don't let Henry Marlow get in your head and don't be reckless with who you trust. You'll need to make sure no one gets too close to you. Something tells me I won't have to worry about that, though.'

Amused by the observation, Grant said, 'Yes, sir. If you'll excuse me, I need to see about a bomb.'

Grant checked each of the many offices that lined the corridor outside, each the same as the last: grey, lit with pale light, dark blinds tilted almost fully closed.

Eventually, he found a man sitting at a desk in a corner where excess office furniture had been stacked.

Grant recognised the man from the video call that he'd remember for the rest of his life. He knocked on the doorframe. 'Excuse me. It's Randall, isn't it?'

Randall looked up from his paperwork in surprise. He didn't receive many guests throughout the day. 'Grant,' he replied. 'I'm glad you're still in one piece. Though I'm not sure I can take full credit for that.'

Grant put out his hand.

Randall shook it, trying not to wince at the strength of his grip.

Grant said, 'I don't know how you guys cope with that kind of pressure.'

Randall flexed his fingers in relief. 'You either get it right, or the problem goes away quite quickly.' Pausing for laughter that never came, he added, 'Sorry. Bomb disposal joke. I don't get many opportunities.'

Grant smiled. 'I can only hope it stays that way. I was wondering, about the device...'

Randall reached eagerly for the report he'd already completed, sitting atop a large stack of papers. 'It's all in here. My reports generally go unread. Unless, you know, the worst has happened.' He chuckled nervously then realised Grant had paused at something on the front page.

Grant squinted. 'I thought your first name was–'

Randall put out his hand, 'No, it is. That's just, well, *legally*, yes, my first name is–'

Grant fought to keep from smirking. 'Achilles.'

'Only in the "officially on your birth certificate" kind of way. My parents were both historians.'

'Achilles Randall,' said Grant. 'School must have been fun. Eton?'

Randall balked at the suggestion. 'Thank goodness my parents aren't alive to have heard that. Lord, no. Harrow. *Stet Fortuna Domus*, and all that. You assume that because of my accent?'

'That, and it's the only way you could have survived adolescence.'

Randall said, 'Yes, well. Teenage boys are very under-standing about these things.' He opened the file in Grant's hands, eager to get back to work. 'Unfortunately, there wasn't anything too exotic about the device itself. Nothing we'll be able to track anyway. Still, it's somewhat surprising.'

Grant turned to the relevant page. 'Surprising?'

'It's a pretty sophisticated piece of hardware. I've seen them used in the Middle East, and a few incidents on Italian judges in the early two-thousands. If someone had connected that one black and white wire, I doubt you would have made it beyond turning on the radio or even the engine. So it seems surprising that whoever fitted such a sophisticated device didn't take the care to fit it properly.' Randall added hastily, 'Although, I'm relieved that that was the case.' He sat back in his chair, spinning a pen up and down his fingers with consummate ease and speed. He said with great amusement, '*Donorum Dei Dispensatio Fidelis.*' His smile vanished when he realised Grant didn't have a clue what he'd said. He clarified, 'It's an old Harrow motto. It means the faithful dispensation of the gifts of God. I meant that it was lucky.'

'Randall,' Grant said, closing the file. 'I'm sure we're going to get on, and there's every chance you're the smartest person in this building, and possibly the country. But if you can use one word instead of four Latin words that translate into eight other words, it would really make me more likely to come down here.'

'Got it,' Randall said.

Grant handed back Randall's report, a quizzical expression on his face.

Back down the hall, Ryan was holding a cover passport and a mobile phone aloft. 'These are good to go, and wardrobe's waiting for you.'

Grant set off towards the lifts.

Randall called after him, 'Is anything the matter?'

'We got lucky.' Grant turned, still on the move. 'I don't like that.'

9

It was so hot in the study that sweat was dripping from the man's face, off his chin, onto the computer keyboard as he typed. It was the only room in the crumbling mansion that he spent much time in. Through small gaps in the shutters that were keeping the scorching sun at bay, he could see the wild and overgrown garden that was full of spiders and snakes typical to most central African plains.

The door to the study was closed, but he could still hear voices chattering on the landing. They were speaking Lingala, a local Congolese dialect.

The man shouted in the same language, 'Be quiet out there.'

There was a large oak desk covered in classified MI6 files – marked "EYES ONLY" – and surveillance photographs.

One photo showed a man of Saudi descent, wearing a suit and crossing a busy street in Manhattan. The file named the man as Kadir Rashid, a journalist. Next to that were various news clippings reporting his assassination five years earlier.

There was a satellite uplink connected to the man's computer, giving faster internet speeds than most Western cities. The computer made a single beep, and a notification flashed on his screen.

'IMAGE-LIKENESS ALERT – Click to view.'

He sat up sharply and clicked the alert. It took him to a link listed as: **Interpol.int / red-notices**.

The page showed an active Red Notice on a fugitive with no name. The accompanying picture showed Henry Marlow.

They must have brought someone else in, he thought. *A change in strategy.*

He had prepared himself for the eventuality, and knew what to do.

Interpol made it easy for the public to contact them regarding Red Notices. All someone had to do was fill in the contact form that's underneath every individual listing. The comment was then sent to the officer leading the investigation.

The man opened up the online form under the Henry Marlow Red Notice. He entered his name as *"RICHARD CARLTON"*.

Message: "I saw this man in London on 20th September. He was carrying a file marked AC180."

He checked the box saying that he agreed to allow his data to be passed onto the relevant national authorities.

He had no issue with his data being passed on. In fact, he was counting on it.

10

Grant arrived at New York LaGuardia airport mid afternoon, just another face from one of the two hundred and fifty flights that would arrive there that day.

Staying off people's radar was easy. All he had to do was stare at his phone, pretending to type something every so often. Only half an hour in the field was enough to remind Grant how talented spies had to be decades ago. It staggered him how many people went about their day on autopilot, completely unaware of their surroundings or who was near them, lost in screens and noise-isolating headphones. The three remaining senses that hadn't been completely nuked were so tuned out that it took quite an effort to actually be noticed by someone.

Since his SAS training, Grant had taken to applying five key principles of jungle training to the everyday urban world: personal discipline; situational awareness; positional awareness; blending in; and the importance of training.

Most people have a single field of vision when in public:

that which is immediately in front of them. Grant kept three: foreground, middle distance, and far distance. The risks of being tailed were always greater at the start of each section of a journey. Leaving an airport terminal, Grant had a clear picture of anything in any of the three areas that looked wrong. If it was the far distance, he had time to divert. In the middle distance, he could assess and formulate his options. In the foreground, instincts kicked in.

Staring at a phone or listening to loud music in public places guaranteed that your chances of anticipating danger were basically nil. Being able to maintain such situational awareness whilst looking like you had none was a skill in itself.

MI6 had provided him with options for a wardrobe in keeping with his legend. 'Not exactly James Bond,' Grant had remarked, surveying a long rack of navy and grey suits bought by MI6 for their durability.

They pointed out to him that the Treasury was of the opinion that £4000 could be better spent on a civil servant's parental leave than on a Tom Ford suit tailored to Grant's physique. For officers at the upper level in Section 7, limited extra resources were given for wardrobe. At Grant's level, he would have to improvise.

Grant had built his legend around being an assistant to an angel investor from London. It was not only perfect for his practical means. It also seemed appropriate, given Grant's experiences in his first weeks of training at Vauxhall Cross.

They were the same issues as throughout his childhood, of never truly fitting in with a crowd. MI5 had made great strides in bringing in recruits from working-class backgrounds as it fit their brief well: a lot of their operations centred around deprived areas. In MI6, some officers' accents and demeanours cultivated in public-school education made them stand out. For Six, progress had only been made behind the scenes, on the analysis and translator side. On the front lines of recruitment there was still a tendency to favour candidates based on their background. The nature of MI6 operations abroad meant that officers were more likely to spend time at diplomatic receptions, cavorting with ambassadors, than infiltrating Islamist terror cells in the dangerous *banlieues* of northern Paris.

Grant had grown up dirt poor on the Isle of Skye, an only child to his father Alasdair, a sheep farmer, and his mother Mairi, a primary school teacher. There were plenty of farmers in Scotland who made a very good living, but Grant's father wasn't one of them. There was a subtle but crucial difference between farmers with crops and a traditional shepherd like Alasdair. A crop farmer can diversify what he sells, and doesn't have to worry about his livelihood being stolen in the middle of the night. Thieves generally don't have the patience to harvest crops by moonlight. But in the dead of night, sheep bleats cannot be heard in a far-off field as they're led onto the back of a truck. That distinction necessitated an aggressive nature in Alasdair. Without a fearsome reputation, word would get out that the Grants were a soft touch. Everyone on Skye knew better than to mess with Alasdair's herd: if they took him on, they would lose.

The Grants owned a small patch of pastureland that rolled down to the sea on the island's ruggedly exposed northern peninsula. With each passing year, seeing his profits shrinking, Alasdair sold off more of their land until it left the Grants with little more than a white stone cottage surrounded by a peat bog, edged with sparse hazel and birch trees.

When Mairi died Grant was eleven. It left him and his father bereft. Duncan spent increasing amounts of time at the local library. By the age of fifteen he had read the major novels of Dickens and Dostoevsky – becoming a voracious reader like his father, as most Skye natives of his generation had been. It became routine for Duncan to be asked to leave at closing time. The walk home, knowing what was awaiting him, was the lowest point of any day.

Alasdair's attitude to life shifted. His drinking, which in the past had been a by-product of merriment and singing, became heavy and morose. His ambition waned, giving way to nihilism and depression. Duncan knew it was serious when his father stopped reading books: often abandoning them after half a page. Alasdair would sit at the breakfast table, forlorn, three days of stubble on his face. He looked at Duncan like he was a stranger. 'The thing is,' Alasdair explained, 'life's not just about what you can do. It's about what you can take. And I can't take it anymore, Duncan.'

As the condition of the farm deteriorated, and the Skye bridge linking to the mainland was completed, Alasdair faced new and increasing threats from herd thieves.

Then, one morning, Duncan woke to find the entire herd gone. An empty field. Facing ruin, Duncan raged at his father, blaming Alasdair's weakness for the theft.

The pair managed to survive thanks to Duncan's enterprise, working various jobs around the island. But it wasn't uncommon for him to come home at seven in the evening and find that there was literally nothing to eat in the cottage. He would go to bed so hungry that he couldn't sleep.

That hunger stayed with him. Creating a fire in him, to every day do something that would help him escape that place.

When Alasdair died, it left Duncan with a cottage to pay for. He was eighteen. He needed a full-time job. Somewhere that would take almost anyone. That was when he saw an advert for the British Army pinned to the library noticeboard. It was as if it was speaking directly to him: "*BE THE BEST.*"

Grant flourished in the rigid routine and guidance of his superiors. There was nothing they could throw at him that he didn't take by the scruff of the neck. In the pursuit of "being the best", SAS selection was the logical next step for him.

When Leo Winston recruited him from the SAS, Grant got his first taste of cosmopolitan luxury in London. The sheer scale of the city was intimidating, but that was nothing compared to the culture shock of MI6 training. Grant could speak with greater authority and articulacy about politics and history than any other recruit, despite their infinitely more expensive educations. What Grant couldn't do was figure out who he was. But that began to work in his favour on field ops. While the others were too comfortable in their own skin to truly commit to a legend, Grant enjoyed being someone else. It was acting. He could be anything he wanted.

Even on training ops in the City, Grant relished them, blending in perfectly with people who had grown up in a different world to him. The instructor would give Grant directions via an earpiece to convince a stranger to let him borrow something valuable like a phone – a tough ask, as most people assumed such a request was a prelude to being robbed. The recruits had to respond on the spot, with no time to create a convincing backstory. Where the others fumbled and stammered, Grant excelled. It didn't matter what the instructors threw at him. It became a game to them: *what outrageous thing can we get Grant to do next?*

Within minutes, he could blag his way inside someone's house and leave with a coffee mug, or a £20 note. That stuff was too easy. So they told him to talk his way into the Foreign Office in Whitehall.

They were convinced that it would end with Grant being thrown out of the building by security. Instead, he left with a photo of himself sitting in the empty office belonging to the Minister for International Trade. That was when MI6 knew they had a real asset on their hands: someone with the much-coveted ability to get into places they're not meant to be.

The mistake the other recruits made was in believing that a convincing legend relied on an accumulation of facts and data – whereas Grant understood that it was about making yourself human. While everyone else tried to bludgeon their way past security by blustering about positions of importance and privilege – *"Don't you know who I am?"* – Grant simply told them a story that felt real. Of being a helpless, slightly scatterbrained intern who had left his boss's phone in a conference room. He had built a relationship with the guard based on mutual empathy: they were both in service to people much more powerful than themselves. Grant based it on what he had been instructed was a spy's number one asset: make yourself the sort of person people want to help.

A recruit could have a legend blown out of the water by a single question from a target or mark. Without the ability to adapt and improvise, a spy was useless, because the world doesn't conform to set patterns or learned behaviour. It shifts and morphs. To keep a legend intact, you had to be whoever you needed to be in any situation. And the other recruits liked who they were. Their lives at home had been comfortable. They didn't know what hunger was. They didn't want to change who they were.

Duncan Grant was more than happy to be anyone but himself. He created a motto around the notion: the more genuine you are, the more you can be someone else.

As he strode through the airport, Grant's confidence in his legend was reflected in how he walked, how he carried himself. His easy bearing.

He was to be Edward Parker: assistant to an angel investor from a private equity firm in London. Once he was in the Hamptons he would have to improvise from there: what he projected would largely depend on what information he could extract.

The twenty-five-year-old real estate broker quickly got to her feet when she saw Grant pull up in his Tesla Model S outside the Southampton Group shopfront. Big-tech money had flooded the Hamptons of late, and Southampton represented most of it. A single sale of their high-value properties could net a broker commission in six figures.

For the warm climate, Grant had opted for a light grey suit with the quintessentially British touch of a Prince of

Wales check – a subtle detail recommended by the MI6 wardrobe assistant.

The broker hovered near the front door, smelling money in the air. 'Well, hello there,' she said, flicking her blonde hair off her shoulder. 'My name's Amanda. Beautiful day, huh?'

Grant removed his vintage tortoiseshell sunglasses and slid one of the arms inside the front of his open shirt. The weight of the glasses pulled his neckline down, which Amanda's gaze followed momentarily.

'Yes, lovely,' Grant said, then paused, waiting for her to be fascinated by his English accent.

She was.

From Grant's research, he'd gleaned that there were two typical real estate clients in the Hamptons: the New York stock trader looking for a vacation pad, or old men trying to keep up with the new generation. Firms lived or died based on how well they satisfied the superficial demands of those two types. Which in itself required a little superficiality: there wasn't a brokerage firm in the Hamptons that didn't hire based on looks, and it was unthinkable for a prospective young broker to send out a CV without a headshot. If Grant was going to get what he wanted, he would need to buck the trends of Amanda's typical clientele.

Grant took out his phone and showed Amanda a picture of Henry Marlow – taken from his MI6 file. He said, 'I'm actually here on someone else's behalf.'

Behind Amanda was another broker, sitting at a marble desk. Although she was on the phone, she seemed more interested in the picture of Marlow.

When Grant caught her staring, she turned away quickly.

Amanda said, 'Oh yes, I remember him from a few weeks ago. Mr Nigel Jones.' She looked to her colleague. 'Maddie spoke to him. Unfortunately, she's on a call with a client right now. Would you like to wait until–'

'No, that's okay,' he said. 'I'm following up on the property he was here about...' Grant trailed off, pretending to be searching for its name in his phone messages.

'Yes, Dune Beach House.' She looked towards Maddie again, who seemed eager to get off the phone.

She held up a finger, asking Amanda to hold on.

While Amanda had her back turned, Grant glimpsed some business cards on her desk.

All he could make out was the writing in bold: **DUNE BEACH HOUSE** and **VIEWING PARTY**.

The time was set for later that evening.

Grant turned his palms up. 'The thing is, Mr Jones has asked me to come along tonight as well. So I can get a better understanding of what he's looking for.'

Amanda paused, trying to restrain a wince. 'Mr Bloom has asked that we restrict the viewing to buyers only. As you can imagine, a property like this attracts a lot of interest from asset managers such as yourself.'

'Gosh...' Grant chuckled.

Amanda worried that she'd said something to cause offence.

Grant said, 'As Mr Jones is always reminding me that I'm a mere "asset assistant", I should probably thank you for the promotion.'

Amanda smiled in relief.

At the upper end of the Hamptons property market, high-value buyers didn't scour listings themselves. They had people to do that for them, creating shortlists before committing their busy schedules to viewings.

'The thing is,' Grant said, moving closer, 'Mr Jones appears to have got the wrong end of the stick, and believes I have already secured an invitation. It's my fault. But if you knew Mr Jones like I do, you'd know that that's not a mistake I'll get away with. People in my job... well, let's just say we don't exactly have a long shelf life. I mean, *you* know how it is, right? It's cutthroat.' Grant leaned in for the killer blow. 'Could I possibly add my name to the list? I promise to remain incognito, and not be so gauche as to discuss the property while standing around drinking cocktails *in* the property.'

Amanda smiled knowingly at the unspoken Hamptons rule. 'This isn't your first rodeo.' She handed Grant one of the invite cards. 'I'll add your name to the guest list. My number is on the back of that. Should you wish to follow up.'

Grant could see that Maddie was on the verge of wrapping up her phone call. Before she could, Grant took the card. 'Very kind,' he said. 'Thank you ever so much.' He turned half in profile, as if about to leave. 'Tell me, will it be Maddie or yourself there tonight?'

'Sadly, I have another viewing. Maddie handles all of Mr Bloom's properties.'

'Ah, what a shame,' he lied.

As Grant turned to leave, Amanda gave the instruction so beloved of Americans: 'Have a great day!'

During his exit, Grant spotted Maddie in the reflection of his car door window. She was hurrying through the office to watch him leave.

Grant knew one thing for sure: Maddie knew more about Mr Jones than Amanda did.

Grant was on his way to the viewing party by the time Samantha at MI6 had compiled a briefing on Lawrence Bloom, the owner of Dune Beach House.

He pulled over at the side of the road to answer his phone, as gentle waves lapped up on the beach beside him.

'Cutting it a little fine, Sam,' said Grant.

In the Control room, Winston huddled over Samantha's shoulder, listening in. Swann stood passively within earshot.

Grant switched to speaker so he could view the dossier. Short as it was.

'Bloom is a pretty elusive man,' Samantha explained. 'These are the most recent pictures we have. It's him landing in Saudi Arabia two years ago.'

The first slide showed Bloom in the middle distance. There was nothing ostentatious about him, apart from the fact he was stepping off a private jet. He wore blue jeans with loafers, and a zip-front sweater with his initials on the chest, the sleeves pushed up. His tan accentuated a shock of short bleached hair on his head. He would have looked equally at home on the deck of a private yacht, or shopping on New York's Upper East Side at the weekend.

Samantha read from her notes, 'Born in New York City. Fifty-seven years old. A financier but the details are sketchy to say the least. He graduated from Harvard Business School, then worked for various venture capital firms. He disappeared off the map in his mid-twenties, but reappeared in his thirties with his own firm, The Bloom Group.

Their assets have been as high as one point seven billion dollars.

'Dune Beach House is one of dozens of properties he owns around the world. A townhouse in London; apartments in Paris, Rome, Madrid; various chateaux in France; there's a castle in Switzerland... but he's a virtual recluse. The last interview he gave was nearly a decade ago, and that raises more questions than it answers. To call his social circle elite would be an understatement: as you can see in the attachments, he's been pictured with movie stars, pop stars, various figures in publishing, the media, and he's in deep with a lot of Democratic politicians, and even an ex-president or two. A huge contributor to the contemporary New York art scene. The only constant through all of this? No one can really say for sure what he does in finance. He has no stock trades in his name, and no one on Wall Street seems to have done any business with him. I've estimated his personal fortune to be anywhere from five hundred million to two billion dollars. There's no way to be certain.'

'What about links to Henry Marlow?' asked Grant.

Samantha clicked through her summary. 'There are no overlaps on assignment locations or dates. No known association with any of Marlow's agents, contacts, or targets.'

'Marlow and random don't belong in the same sentence,' said Grant. 'There's a link. We're just not seeing it yet.'

Winston said, 'It's got to be the house. If Marlow wanted Bloom dead, it would have happened already.'

Swann broke in, 'Grant, give us a minute.' She leaned over Samantha to hit the MUTE button.

'What are you doing?' asked Winston.

'A word,' said Swann. 'Your office.'

When they got there across the corridor, Swann raised her arms in confusion. 'What are we doing here?' she asked. 'It's been two weeks since Marlow was in the Hamptons. Do you really think he's going to show up to a house viewing?'

Winston replied, 'The only way to find him is by working backwards.'

'And once you figure out what he wants with Lawrence Bloom, what next? A shanty in the Bahamas? Maybe a shipping container in Rotterdam. Or how about a bank transfer in Geneva? This is what Marlow wants you to do. To get bogged down in where he's been, rather than where he is and where he's going.'

'What's the alternative, Imogen? We can spend the next three days looking for a six-foot white male in his late forties, with short hair, or we can try to get ahead of this. Doing both only dilutes resources.'

'Then don't do both. Do what I'm telling you. This is a manhunt,' Swann spat, 'not a fact-finding mission. I might also remind you that this is still my department's investigation.' She pointed an accusatory finger. 'I'm starting to think that we want different things: I want to find Marlow, but you want to understand why he's doing what he's doing. Just so you know: only one of those strategies solves our problem.'

She marched past Winston, brushing his shoulder.

When he returned to the Control room, Swann wasn't there. He took Grant off mute.

'What's going on?' Grant asked.

'Creative differences,' Winston replied, eager to change the subject. 'Grant, there's a lot of hazy intel here and I don't like it. You should be prepared for anything at that house. I mean, if the devil himself shows up, I want you to not be surprised.'

Grant said, 'Understood.'

He hung up.

The devil might have sounded like hyperbole to Grant, but he was about to find out that Lawrence Bloom wasn't far off it.

11

The viewing party had been timed for sunset, the golden hour when the immense property looked its most magical. Perched on the coveted banks of Mecox Bay, the five-acre estate of rolling lawns and wetlands was one of the most sought-after private waterfronts in the Hamptons. For its $35 million asking price, the buyer would have their own bulkhead dock, tennis court, outdoor swimming pool with spa and waterfall, and a manicured lawn with spectacular views of the Atlantic Ocean.

Properties like Dune Beach House didn't come around often, and the clientele that had shown up for the viewing party reflected the exclusivity of what was on offer.

Grant parked on the main road outside, worried that his Tesla wouldn't quite fit in with the Lamborghinis and Ferraris already parked in the enormous driveway.

A fresh but gentle breeze coming in off the ocean wafted the soft tones of a string quartet from the garden as Grant walked up the curving driveway. Using the time to assess the building's layout, he noticed a subtle extension to a wall on the second floor. Grant thought it strange, as it almost looked like an architectural mistake.

The string quartet grew much louder as the front door opened, bringing with it a buzz of conversation, chinking glasses, and the sight of a doorman holding a tablet.

The setting sun cast a warm golden light from the rear of the house all the way through to the driveway.

The doorman was burly, with thick arms bulging in the sleeves of his black polo shirt. As Grant approached, it was like he had two volume dials in his head. On one side was the dial projecting the inner voice, telling him he was an intruder. On the other, a dial projected that he belonged there like everyone else. It had taken a lot of practice, but Grant could now simply dial down the volume he didn't want to hear, and turn up the one that he did. Confidence flushed through his body, extending all the way out to his fingertips. There wasn't a doubt in his mind when he handed over his invitation and gave his name.

'Mr Parker. Edward Parker.' Grant was already looking beyond the doorman, figuring out what his first move would be inside.

The doorman handed him the tablet. 'Just sign here, please.'

While Grant signed the screen with his finger, he asked, 'Could you tell me if Mr Jones has arrived? I can't get an answer on his number.'

'I'm sorry, sir. The guest list is private.' The doorman took back the tablet then stepped aside.

Dune Beach was classic Hamptons beachfront architecture. Lawrence Bloom had spared no expense. Huge arched windows filled the rooms with light. Large, modern abstract paintings covered the walls.

It was only as Grant wandered to the bar area in the open-plan living room that he realised he was walking across the biggest Persian rug he'd ever seen, stretching over one hundred feet.

On his way past a group of young women in cocktail dresses, Grant heard them exchanging gossip in hushed tones.

'I heard he isn't even going to show up. He's on his island.'

'He has his own island?'

'Ninety acres in the Virgin Islands.'

'What do you expect? The guy won't even eat out in restaurants...'

They took their drinks out to the garden, where the string quartet was playing versions of Beatles songs.

Grant headed for the bar. There was something temporary and bereft about someone wandering a party with no glass in their hand.

When it came to drinks, Grant was a simple man. Whisky. Neat. Never with ice. And certainly never with water or soda. Grant considered it a crime what many people did to drinks. Not least James Bond. His martini, shaken not stirred, was little more than gin and vermouth sitting in cold water. Shaking it only bruised the gin and chipped the ice. Any experienced barman would tell you that no one has done more damage to cocktail-drinking than James Bond.

The dresser at MI6 had given Grant a maxim to live by for navigating exclusive social gatherings: "a man should look as if he has bought his clothes with intelligence, put them on with care, and then forgotten all about them."

When Grant sized up the other men at the viewing,

they appeared to be masters of that maxim. In contrast, Grant had never been so aware of everything he was wearing. He caught himself in a mirror that had been distressed with flecks of black: he looked like an actor in costume on a stage for the first time. By comparison, the other men were on a whole other sartorial level. Suddenly, all the little details had a much bigger impact than Grant had ever considered. In a two-button suit jacket, you never button both as Grant had done, as it created a more flattering silhouette.

Grant then became aware of something else: no one else had a matching tie and pocket square like he had. Grant had ignored the dresser's advice on the issue; it seemed only sensible to Grant to match them. What he didn't understand was that a pocket square was there to complement a look. Not add to it.

Grant undid the lower button on his jacket, and slid down the square into his top pocket – figuring it was better to go without one than advertise a mistake.

Glass in hand, Grant turned from the bar to scope out the sprawling living room. There was no sight of Marlow, but Grant was curious about a number of men emerging from the periphery of the party. Each standing on their own, paying close attention to the guests. They wore tailored suits with dark shirts and no ties. Grant was sure they were security. Their broad shoulders suggested they were tougher than they were agile. Their suit jackets might have been slightly wider in the chest, but Grant could tell they were armed.

They each conferred on lapel mics, then one of them let their gaze drift up towards the long sweeping staircase.

Grant raised his glass to his mouth, letting the whisky

merely lap up to his lips. As he looked towards the stairs, he saw Bloom descending. He had the air of someone who knew that by the time he reached the living room everyone's eyes would be on him. That was the reality of being Lawrence Bloom. A sighting in person – let alone a sighting in a magazine or on TV – was a rare thing. Even in the hallowed social circles of the Hamptons.

He was wearing a white Oxford shirt with his initials stitched onto the chest, tucked into his blue jeans. As far as billionaires went, he couldn't have looked more unassuming.

Maddie from the Southampton Group greeted Bloom at the foot of the stairs. She made eye contact with Grant, but before he could deal with her inevitable conversation, he needed to see what he was up against with Bloom's security.

A smashed glass on the tiled floor wouldn't cut it. He needed something bigger, louder, without causing an actual panic.

Then he spotted it: a door leading towards a den that looked out to one of the many ocean views – being kept open with a weighted doorstop – and the tall grass on top of the dunes at the end of the garden. It was barely noticeable inside, but some of the women's hair was blowing ever so slightly in the opposite direction from a competing breeze.

A perfect wind tunnel effect.

Grant ditched his glass on the way to the den door, where a waiter was standing with a silver tray of champagne glasses. In a deft move, Grant turned the waiter away from the door with a gentle hand on the back.

'Excuse me,' he said, 'can you tell me if there's any whisky around here?'

With the waiter distracted, Grant slid the doorstop away from the frame with his trailing foot.

The waiter pointed Grant to the bar at the other side of the room. Grant paced quickly away, his eyes set on Bloom's heavies.

A few seconds later, the den door started to move. Slowly. Then gathered pace. Grant felt a rush of wind from the open French windows leading to the garden.

At peak momentum, the door slammed with a loud, deep thud, prompting guests nearby to reach for their chests in fright. It sent a jolt through the security detail some distance away. Two of them instinctively went for their holsters, stopping short of drawing their weapons once they realised it was a false alarm. The others were much slower in their reactions, unable to place where the noise had come from and no sense of where their principal was.

It was as Grant had suspected: they might have looked impressive, but technically they were weak. They had likely been with Bloom a long time – neutered by the glacial pace of social gatherings. With each round of cocktails, or charity auction, or gallery opening, their reactions blunted.

Nervous chuckles broke out as the waiter repositioned the doorstop.

Grant took his opportunity to move in on Bloom and Maddie. She was Grant's only lead, and now he had her somewhere that would be harder to shut down his enquiries.

'Mr Parker,' she said. 'I was wondering if you were going to show.'

Bloom was holding a salmon canapé in each hand, and showed no interest in being introduced to Grant.

Grant said, 'Mr Bloom, it's a pleasure.'

Bloom turned straight to Maddie. He voice was deep but soft. He didn't need volume. Anytime he spoke, everyone listened. 'I thought I made it clear that there were to be no asset managers here. If someone wants to buy this place, the least they can do is show up.'

There was an anxious pause. Bloom might have been smiling, but there was malice behind it. He did a double-take at Grant's squashed-down pocket square.

Grant knew that Bloom had spotted it, but he tried not to show that he was rattled. 'That's the second time someone has promoted me today, Mr Bloom. If I can keep up that rate I might have an offer for you in about...' Grant pulled his sleeve back to read his watch, 'oh, fifty years' time.'

Bloom laughed weakly, his eyes sticking on Grant's watch. 'Well, that depends on whether any of these people here are actually interested in buying this place, or if they just want to tell their friends they stood several yards away from me for a few minutes.' He laid a hand on Maddie's back and kept it there.

She was obviously uncomfortable with it, but didn't want to wriggle away. Not with her commission on the line. She tried to smile, but it was closer to a grimace. 'Mr Parker represents Nigel Jones.'

'Has he bothered to show up?' asked Bloom.

'Yes, he signed in earlier,' she replied, looking for him.

Grant tried not to gulp. He smiled at Maddie, then gave the room another once over.

Marlow was there. Somewhere.

A waiter appeared with a tray of champagne glasses. 'Sir?'

'I might as well,' said Bloom. 'This is all coming out of my brokerage bill, anyway.'

The waiter handed a glass to Bloom then moved on.

Bloom drained the glass then handed it to Maddie. 'Enjoy my party, Mr Parker.' He then reached into Grant's top pocket, and pulled out his pocket square, fluffing it up. 'That's better.'

Grant was dying inside. All he could do was stand there, smiling vapidly, and wait for Bloom to leave.

Once he was gone, Maddie shook her head like she'd forgotten something. She took out her phone and started tapping on the screen. 'Mr Parker, I seem to have lost your number.' She showed Grant what she'd typed into her phone:

"Make up a number, then ask to see the garden."

Grant needed just a brief beat, then made up a number. 'I was wondering about the garden.'

'Of course,' Maddie replied, opening one of the many French windows leading to a terrace. Once they were outside, she didn't have to speak too quietly as the string quartet was giving a rousing performance of "Eleanor Rigby".

Maddie asked, 'Who are you. Really?'

'I don't understand,' replied Grant.

'If I can see it, then Lawrence Bloom definitely can. It's the suit, the watch, everything.' She reached for his top pocket and squashed his pocket square back down. 'You don't work for an angel investor.'

With no option but to dig in, Grant blustered, 'Excuse

me, if I don't take fashion advice from a man who wears jeans and an Oxford shirt to a cocktail party.'

'He's Lawrence Bloom,' said Maddie. 'He doesn't have to follow the same rules as everyone else. But he still understands them.'

'Is this some sort of sales strategy? Because these are pretty cheap shots you're throwing. Well, maybe not cheap. But they're certainly inexpensive.'

Despite the bluster, all Grant could picture were the people in MI6 who believed it was too soon to entrust him with such a mission. His confidence was crumbling. He'd never felt so out of his depth.

Maddie said, 'You don't realise it but you're in terrible trouble.'

'What are you talking about?'

'It's not safe for you here. You have to get out.'

'I don't–'

'They know,' Maddie explained. 'They know that you're not Edward Parker, and whoever else you're working with isn't Nigel Jones. I heard Bloom talking about it on the phone before you arrived. I don't know who you really are, or what you're doing here, but you have no idea who you're dealing with.'

Allowing the mask to drop a little, Grant asked, 'Who am I dealing with?'

'You don't get it,' she said. 'These people can do whatever they want. And they're very good at making problems disappear. Just leave. While you still can.'

'I can't do that,' Grant replied. 'Not without Nigel Jones. I need to find him.'

Maddie shook her head. 'What is this? Some kind of corporate espionage, or something?'

Nearly half a dozen evasive answers sprang to Grant's mind. All of them convincing. And each one of them would result in him walking out of Dune Beach with nothing. Feeling Henry Marlow slipping through his fingers, Grant decided he had to take a risk. The biggest risk a spy can take: tell the truth.

Grant pointed vaguely towards the dunes. 'We're going to stand here pretending to talk about the amazing ocean views that this property affords.'

'And what are we really going to talk about?' asked Maddie.

'My name isn't Edward Parker and I don't work for Nigel Jones. I work for British intelligence.'

She paused. 'A spy.'

'Something like that. The man here presenting himself as Nigel Jones is very dangerous and I need to find him. When he visited your office, did he leave a phone number?'

Maddie looked down, her eyes darting all over the place. She fumbled slightly with her phone as she navigated to the contacts. 'He called the other day and left a number... hang on.'

Grant took out his phone and dialled a number from memory.

Ryan picked up. 'Control, go ahead.'

Grant pressed his finger on the screen.

At Ryan's end, his screen showed a message:

"*DUNCAN GRANT. Incoming call... fingerprint accepted.*"

'You're confirmed,' said Ryan.

'I need you to locate a number for me,' Grant told him.

Maddie showed him her phone screen while Grant read it out.

'Scanning now,' Ryan confirmed.

Maddie couldn't believe what was taking place in front of her. That spies were real. Just walking around, pretending to be normal people.

A few seconds later, Ryan had a live GPS tracker on the mobile. 'He's there,' he told Grant. 'He's in the building.'

'Okay,' Grant replied. 'I'm hanging up but keeping the map live.' He hung up his phone and checked the map. The signal was coming from somewhere inside. 'You should stay out here,' he told Maddie.

'Is there going to be any trouble?' she asked. 'Like, danger?'

There would be many moments in his career when he would have to lie. And this was no exception. 'No,' Grant said. 'Nothing to worry about.'

12

Grant made his way briskly through the crowd, following the signal on his phone. The viewing party was in full flow, the crowd dispersed widely across the property. There were so many rooms, giving them all names was redundant. They were simply multiples of other rooms: foyers, reception rooms, living rooms, hallways – the open-plan spaces bleeding into one another.

When Grant went up the stairs, he was able to ease into the slipstream of a group of four a few steps above. The first floor revealed an even greater labyrinth, but everything above was off limits. A brushed-steel barrier blocked the stairs leading to the second floor.

Grant checked the phone map, which had morphed to a three-dimensional view as he'd climbed the stairs.

Henry Marlow's phone was up there somewhere.

A security guard crossed the second-floor landing. He was dressed like Bloom's other heavies downstairs. There was something about his demeanour, the way he carried himself, his hunting eyes, ready posture, that told Grant he was a cut above his colleagues.

Grant waited until the guard had finished his pass along the landing above, then he pushed the barrier aside. He had barely made it two steps when the guard raised his hand.

'Excuse me, sir,' he said, attempting to keep his voice low to avoid a scene. 'You can't come up here. This area is off limits.'

Grant turned the dial in his head – the one that said he had every right to be on that second floor – all the way up to ten. There was simply no doubt in his mind.

He wore a pained "don't-give-me-that" expression. 'Come on, mate.' He motioned at the empty stairs behind him. 'I can buy this place, but I can't look around? Who has to know? It's just you and me.'

The guard's patience quickly evaporated. 'Sir. Go back downstairs. Now.'

In his snippiest tone, mimicking a phrase he'd heard around Whitehall numerous times, Grant snapped, 'Do you know who I am?' He reached into his inside jacket pocket for his wallet while he took the final steps up to the landing.

The guard backed up a few feet. A critical mistake.

Now he was out of view of the guests below.

Grant held out his wallet, showing his British driver's licence for Edward Parker. While the guard took half a second to process what he was looking at, Grant flicked the guard's jacket open and grabbed his Beretta 92X pistol from the holster.

In barely a blink, the guard had gone from intimidator to hostage.

Grant pointed the gun at him, then backed up a fraction: he could see that the guard had a good few extra inches reach on him.

'Turn around,' Grant told him.

As soon as the guard turned his back, Grant slammed his head into the wall. The guard collapsed to the ground like a sandbag.

Grant dragged him into the adjoining empty bedroom. He took the guard's covert earpiece out and put it in his own ear. If things went south, he would at least get a heads up about it.

The map signal was still flashing, somewhere at the end of the long hallway. Grant made himself a slim profile as he crept towards the signal.

There was no getting away from the fact that less than fifty feet away was a spy who had proven himself capable of killing his compatriots, willingly and without mercy. Marlow's abilities and skills were greater than Grant's. That was just the reality of Marlow's experience. Only one thing could give Grant an edge on that: positional superiority.

He knew from the property layout that he was heading towards the master bedroom, but the muffled voice he could hear sounded farther away than that.

That was when Grant remembered the sight from the driveway: the sloping wall extending out from under the roof. It was no more than twenty feet long, but there was nothing on the layout plan on the Southampton Group website that legislated for it. Either the room dimensions were totally wrong, or there was another, unlisted, room at the back of the master bedroom.

In a $35 million mansion that meant one thing: a panic room. Bloom's had been fortified with stainless steel and was just a few steps from his enormous Alaskan King-size bed.

As Grant edged nearer the bedroom, one voice became clearer. From the bedroom doorway he could now see a large David Hockney original – one of his swimming pools in his iconic azure palette – pulled aside from a hinge on the wall.

It was now apparent that there were two men in the panic room. By their shadows stretching out across the carpet, Grant could tell that one was standing. The other was on his knees.

One more check of his phone confirmed it: Marlow was no more than twenty feet away.

Grant took a position behind a large white pillar, which gave an angle through the gap between the wall and the edge of the Hockney painting. With limited latitude, Grant could just about make out Lawrence Bloom on his knees, his hands behind his head.

'You're making the mistake of your life,' Bloom said.

The gunman was out of sight, except for the gun and the end of his shirtsleeve, which Grant could make out as being the same as the ones worn by the waiting staff.

The gunman spoke. He was English. 'And you're making the biggest mistake of yours, Larry. By my watch, you've got about ten minutes before you fall into a coma.'

Grant thought back to the waiter downstairs. How odd he'd found it when the waiter made a point of handing Bloom his drink.

As methods of infiltration went, Grant grudgingly admired the gunman's invention. No one ever pays attention to the help.

But it did mean one thing: Henry Marlow wasn't there;

Grant would have recognised the waiter's face instantly. And if he wasn't Marlow, why had this man called the Southampton Group pretending to be?

Grant stole another peek from behind the pillar.

The gunman was showing Bloom a small glass vial.

'There's still time,' the gunman said.

'For what?' asked Bloom. 'If you want money...'

The gunman got rougher, shoving Bloom by the back of the neck. 'I don't want your *money*. I want you to open the safe.'

'I promise you, there's nothing valuable—'

Bloom couldn't finish his sentence. His mouth was too full of blood from the pistol whipping the gunman had just given him.

The gunman growled, 'You know what I want. The Rashid file.'

Bloom drooled blood down the front of his shirt, leaving a stain over his initials. 'He took it already,' he groaned.

'Who?'

'Who do you think? Marlow. He broke in two weeks ago.'

'There was no police report filed.'

Bloom held the bleeding gash across his cheek. 'I wasn't exactly keen to have them snooping around.'

The gunman wasn't convinced. 'Open it,' he said, indicating the safe with his free hand.

Bloom didn't need to be told twice this time. He struggled to his feet. His shirt had become untucked, leaving him looking dishevelled. Drained of his usual power.

The men moved deeper into the panic room, allowing

Grant to move up directly behind the painting – still out of sight. Now he could hear better, and see more.

The luxury Döttling safe was covered in brown leather and set into the stainless-steel wall. Even if a robber were to penetrate the panic room, without the safe's code they might as well be standing in front of a Swiss bank vault. There was no technology or hacking or hardware to get around it. There was quite simply no breaking into a Döttling.

Bloom entered his code, trembling at the thought of what would happen once the gunman realised he was telling the truth.

He opened the door then stepped back. 'See?'

The gunman pushed Bloom back into the corner of the room. He pulled out leather drawers one by one, his disgust growing. He spat venomously, 'The hell is wrong with you people?'

Bloom cowered on the floor. 'My hobby,' he said meekly.

The gunman dragged him by the hair to a steel table drilled into the concrete floor, then handcuffed him to one of the legs.

'Do you realise the jeopardy you've put us all in now?' the gunman said. He placed the vial on the table top, frustratingly out of Bloom's reach.

'Please!' Bloom implored him. 'Give me the antidote and I'll do anything for you. You know I can make it happen. Whatever you want!'

The gunman's parting words were, 'You should have told someone that the files were stolen. Now you're no good to us.'

Grant dived behind the pillar once more to stay out of the gunman's sight as he exited back through the bedroom.

As soon as the gunman had cleared the room, Grant dashed inside the panic room, his gun poised.

Bloom lay stricken on the ground, desperately grasping for the vial. Seeing Grant and the gun, Bloom cowered once more. 'He's already gone,' he cried.

Grant grabbed hold of him. 'Who was that?'

Sensing that Grant could be his saviour, he immediately said, 'Haslitt. Martin Haslitt.'

'Is he working with Henry Marlow?'

Bloom laughed despairingly. 'Next time you want to blend in, get a better watch.'

Grant squeezed Bloom's throat, wiping the smile from his face. 'What was he looking for?'

'A file,' Bloom croaked, his face reddening. 'Marlow stole it.' He looked towards the vial then back at Grant. 'I can help you get it. I can help you. If you help me.'

Grant was focussed on the safe. He let go of Bloom's neck then pushed him away. He approached the safe cautiously, almost afraid of what he would find inside.

Bloom was sweating profusely from the poison that Haslitt had slipped into his champagne. He said through heavy breaths, 'I can get you anything you want. Money... women...'

While he paused, Grant looked inside one of the leather drawers that Haslitt had left open.

Bloom then added, with sickening zeal, 'Girls.'

The drawer was full of photographs of naked children.

Grant closed the drawer in disgust. He felt like throwing up. In another drawer there were photographs of a film star who had won an Oscar just two years earlier. She was passed out on a bathroom floor with cocaine around her nose. There were also pictures of an American senator. He was tied to a bed, surrounded by ten men wearing leather gimp masks.

It was Lawrence Bloom's personal blackmail stash.

When Grant looked back into the bedroom, he recognised the bed where the children had been made to pose.

Grant couldn't help but wonder: *can I shoot this bastard in the face and get away with it?*

Bloom coughed, feeling his airway closing. 'I can get you Marlow.' Encouraged by Grant's reaction, he added, 'Oh yeah, I can help you find him. I know where he's been.'

Grant marched back to him, grabbing his throat again. 'Where?'

'A safe deposit box in Estonia,' Bloom choked. 'It's Henry Marlow's. Everything you need to know is in there.'

'What bank?'

Bloom shook his head. He could only manage one word. 'Antidote.'

Grant looked at the safe, then back at Bloom. 'Why do you do it?' he asked. 'Some of those children can't be over ten years old.'

Feeling Grant's grip tightening, Bloom shrugged as best he could. Unapologetic. 'I can afford it.'

Grant let go of his neck, disgusted by the feel of Bloom's skin. He took the vial and smashed it on the ground.

He stepped towards the panic room door. 'Soundproof, right?' he said. He rapped his knuckles on it. 'Yeah. Definitely soundproof.'

Bloom knew what was on the cards now. 'You pathetic piece of shit... You goddamn *peasant...*'

Grant checked his watch. 'Probably about three minutes left, I'd say, Lawrence. I could have saved you. I just don't know how I would live with myself.'

Bloom kept hurling insults, even after Grant shut the heavy steel door behind him. But no one could hear him. He was shouting into an abyss.

13

Charging down Dune Road, Grant took advantage of the long expanse of empty highway in front of him, getting the Tesla up to sixty miles per hour in under three seconds. He called the Service switchboard and was patched through to Control.

'Bloom's dead,' said Grant, eyeing the rear-view mirror. 'He was poisoned.'

'Was it Marlow?' asked Winston.

'No. Another professional. Run a check on a Martin Haslitt. I'm not sure of the spelling but he's English.'

Swann dragged a seat over and collapsed into it. 'Shit...' She looked up in despair. 'He was one of ours.'

'Someone who worked under you?' asked Winston.

'No. Investigated by.' Swann shook her head. 'Before my time. If there's ever been a filthier officer in the Service, I've never encountered them. Haslitt was an animal. A total crook. We disavowed him long before Marlow.'

Winston's demeanour was similarly dire. 'And now they're working together.'

'I don't know about that, sir,' said Grant. 'Marlow was at Bloom's two weeks ago. Why would he send Haslitt back for something he already stole?'

'What do you think Marlow has?' asked Winston.

'Haslitt called it the Rashid file.'

While looking at Swann, Winston said, 'Kadir Rashid?'

'I can only assume,' Grant answered. 'The timing makes sense. Rashid was killed five years ago, right around the time Henry Marlow turned.'

'Why would he steal files on a murdered journalist?'

'Maybe Marlow and Bloom were in business together.'

Swann, who'd been stewing in frustration, finally snapped. 'Am I the only one here who actually cares about *catching* Marlow? Is there *any* actionable intelligence from all of this?'

Grant said, 'Bloom told me about a safe deposit box in Estonia belonging to Marlow.'

Swann scoffed, 'Oh great! That's very helpful. If you could narrow it down to something smaller than an entire country, Grant...'

Winston snapped his fingers at Ryan, who was already bringing up search results on the wall.

On the grid was every mention and connection to Estonia in Marlow's file.

While Ryan pared the results down, Swann said, 'What if Bloom's wrong? Or was lying? We'll have wasted another twelve hours chasing a shadow. Meanwhile, you could be sending Grant straight into a trap.'

It was an assessment that Grant didn't necessarily disagree with. Bloom would have said anything to save his own life. But the information seemed too particular to have been plucked out of thin air.

Winston asked, 'Are you still suggesting we walk away from all of this?'

Swann replied, 'You started with Henry Marlow. Now we've got Martin Haslitt in the picture. I don't buy for a second that they're not in this together. Do you really expect Grant to take down both of them? And what are we going to do with the Estonia lead? Stick pins in a map?'

Samantha raised her hand. 'I think I've got something,' she said. She enlarged what she'd found: a covert photograph taken by Marlow of a black metal drawer with a gold "24" on it. 'It's from an old mission file in his records. He once used a safe deposit box in Estonia. He left the passcode, and coordinates.'

Winston turned to Ryan, too, now. Both he and Samantha were on the edge of their seats, ready to crack open the next link. 'You two,' he said. 'I need you to break open Marlow and Haslitt's files. Every possible connection between them. Even before they joined the Service. Duncan, I'm going to get you on a plane within the hour. But we're going to have to play this one carefully. Marlow's been two steps ahead of us since Lyon, and he still is.'

Grant hung up, watching carefully as police cars sped past, heading towards Dune Beach House. He checked his mirrors. The police kept on their way.

It was an unwelcome reminder of Lawrence Bloom's demise. Not that he had any regrets about what had played out. He might not have actually poured the poison into Bloom's champagne, but there was no avoiding the fact that he had let him die. He'd had the power to stop it. Sometimes doing nothing could still be a violent act.

What surprised Grant the most was how fine he was with his choice. Bloom was a monster. And no one would grieve his loss for a second.

Martin Haslitt killed Bloom. That was a fact.

But deep down, in a place he would be digging to for a while, Grant knew that he had crossed a line. He just didn't know yet how far past the line he was capable of going.

14

BRECON BEACONS, WALES

THREE YEARS AGO

Selection for the U.K. Special Forces was widely regarded as one of the most demanding processes in all military training. With a typical pass rate of under ten per cent, it was a test of almost unimaginable endurance, grit, and strength that covered a period of six months that began in the Welsh Brecon Beacons and Elan Valley, and ended in the jungles of Belize.

Selection took place twice a year without exception: no quarter was given for even the most extreme weather conditions. You either met the criteria or you didn't. You were tough enough or you weren't.

When Duncan Grant was confirmed for summer selection, it appeared to be preferable over winter. But summer was still no easy ride: recruits had died on marches in heatwaves. Grant's experience also told him that you can warm yourself up on an exercise, but cooling yourself down can be almost impossible at a certain level of exertion.

When the summer recruits reached the Elan Valley to find the most freakish weather the area had seen in nearly a century of weather recording, Grant was the only one unperturbed. Temperatures had plummeted to barely five degrees Celsius, and with a wind chill. The rain had been incessant for a fortnight, turning the normally parched and brittle fields at the foot of the monstrous mountain climb of Pen Y Fan into a marshy swamp.

The attrition rate was abnormally high in the opening weeks. Many couldn't cope with the conditions, which would have been rough-going for winter blocks, but quite a few dropped out because they had shown up with a set of expectations for the weather, and faced something entirely different. It messed with their heads and they couldn't adjust. The recruits had been soaked through since an hour into day one. They simply couldn't get dry.

Soon, what had started as forty became twenty-two. The 'High Walk' had seen to that – the most infamous and feared test in selection. Commonly referred to as the 'Fan Dance', it was a gruelling beast of a march over Pen Y Fan, the highest peak in south Wales.

The Dance took place on Pen Y Fan's west slope, along a well-worn ridge that led across its peak, then descended the far side, commonly referred to as Jacob's Ladder. The rest followed the old Roman road, a broken and dangerously steep brick path, which turned back on itself for the return leg.

Recruits had just four hours and ten minutes to complete the trek: fifteen miles with a twenty-seven-kilo Bergen – a camo rucksack that was so heavy it required a stiffened aluminium spine.

Not satisfied with wiping out nearly half the recruits in

one day, the DS (Directing Staff) had set up a new challenge on Jacob's Ladder: the cruellest, biggest lung-buster section of the Fan Dance. The recruits were to carry their Bergens up the steep slope, then meet one of the DS at the summit before going back down.

Provided the recruits hadn't broken their necks on the descent, when they reached the bottom they were sent straight back up the hill by another DS. The foot of the climb brought little respite. The uneven brick road wound its way through open marshland that was battered by driving rain and brutal crosswinds.

Ninety minutes into the exercise, three recruits had already quit. There was no drive back to a nice warm cottage somewhere for a hot bath and a bowl of soup. They had to sit in a cold Range Rover, waiting for the others to give up too, or for the DS to bring the madness to a halt – whichever came first.

The recruits were strung out all over the hillside. Each in a different world of pain. The words of encouragement from the stronger ones to the broken had long since ceased. It was a matter of survival now. There was no time to think about the weak.

As Duncan Grant began his third ascent of the Ladder – comfortably ahead of the next-fastest recruit – he started to think about agony.

To say that a man is in agony is easy. What the recruits were experiencing was so much worse than that. Grant could see that in their faces. He felt it too, but he was burying it better than they were. He thought about how he might describe the pain to a civilian once the hell of it was all over. He thought about telling someone to think about the earliest they had ever got out of bed. Then imagine getting up an hour earlier than that. But you don't get to stumble to the kitchen in warm pyjamas to make a coffee. Instead, you have to pack up a sleeping bag in the pouring rain, shine your shoes (still in the rain), put on a bag that's heavier than most dumbbells, then walk with it for six hours. When you return to base you get to sit and listen to an hour-long lecture (still in the rain), then do one hundred push ups, followed by fifty pull ups. Not doing them is not an option. You have to do them because your DS has told you to do them.

You do them, or you quit.

Simple.

Most people can't do ten push ups without a lot of discomfort and shaking arms. If their lives depended on it – literally with a gun to their head – they couldn't reach thirty. Even if given an hour to do it.

To Duncan Grant, being that person who couldn't do the thirty, that's what agony really was.

As he stomped back up the Ladder he heard the recruits still on their second ascent complaining to each other. Hoping to find some solace in someone else feeling as rotten as them. Knowing they weren't alone would make it easier somehow. No one voiced it, but it occurred to some that it might be a good idea to sprain their ankle, or experience some other painful injury. At least that way they would have an excuse to quit, rather than knowing they had simply given in. That their wills had broken.

Grant knew what their problem was. Unlike the Fan Dance, they didn't know when it would be over. The Dance was over when they had gone from point A to point B. Going in an open-ended loop created a whole new level of torture. A level that many couldn't get their heads around.

There was no end. The pain would never stop.

Grant was in the process of lapping two other recruits, Smitty and Barnes.

Smitty was the only one of the pair capable of speech. He muttered to himself, 'What is the point of this shit?'

Breathing heavily, Grant replied, 'The same reason they give us random punishments. Tying then retying your laces. Take off your Bergen and empty it, then pack it up again and put it on. The point is to not question orders.'

Smitty complained, 'Dunc... Why are you going so fast?'

'Albert Camus,' he replied.

Smitty paused. 'I literally... don't know... what you just said.'

Grant repeated it, then spelled it for them. 'He was a French philosopher. He wrote a book called *The Myth of Sisyphus*.'

Smitty looked at Barnes, who shrugged.

Grant explained, 'In Greek mythology, Sisyphus was forever condemned to push a boulder up a mountain only to have it roll back down again.'

Smitty wheezed, 'That sounds about... as meaningless... as what we're doing.'

'That's the point,' Grant replied. 'Camus said that we live our lives on the promise of tomorrow. Doing things we don't want to do, all in the hope that tomorrow, or years later, things will be better. The irony is that we spend most of our lives waiting for that time to come, during which death only gets closer and closer. It's absurd.'

Smitty asked, 'Did Camus have a solution to all this?'

'The same as Sisyphus: to find meaning in the absurdity

of life. Like the seemingly meaningless task of pushing a boulder up a mountain.'

'Or walking up one... with a Bergen.'

'Though I suspect the DS are just looking to maximise pain and suffering, rather than guide us to a deeper understanding of the meaning of life.'

Barnes finally summoned adequate breath to speak. 'I don't know... how you can smile right now, Grant.'

Grant gestured at their bleak, cloud-blanketed surroundings. 'Because this is what life's all about. It's about how much you can take.'

'Torturing yourself? Like some kind of sadist?'

Smitty asked, 'Is that why you want to be in the SAS?'

Grant thought about it for a moment. 'I'm not interested in living a life based on what tomorrow might bring. Because to do that means sacrificing today: it's like telling yourself, "I can't live today. Not yet. I'm not ready".' He shook his head. 'I want to do something valuable *today*. Every day. Maybe that means stopping some bad guys from doing bad things. Or keeping a country safe.'

There was a long pause.

Smitty said, 'Has anyone ever told you... you're quite intense?'

He replied, 'It's been said.' Then he picked up the pace and marched ahead.

By the time the DS were done, Grant had made a full two ascents more than any other recruit.

In that time, ten more recruits had quit.

Including Barnes and Smitty.

The exercise had been hard as hell on them.

More than anything, Duncan Grant had taken part of their souls.

. . .

Back at base in the Directing Staff log cabin, chief DS Forrester was sitting with Leo Winston. Forrester had on an insulated down jacket. Winston: a grey suit and black overcoat.

Two cups of coffee sat steaming on the table in front of them, an array of recruit headshots scattered around.

In front of them was a whiteboard, with three head-shots attached to it.

'So that's all the possibles?' said Winston, sitting back to appraise the candidates. 'Bit of a lean year, Mikey.'

Forrester ran a huge hand through his thick beard which was flecked with grey. 'You know me, Leo,' he said in his Geordie accent. 'I don't bother with the timewasters. I only give you the ones that have a real chance of working.'

In a career with many candidates, Forrester was by far the toughest, hardest man that Winston had ever encountered. Over the course of three months many moons ago, Winston had experienced Forrester's toughness first-hand during his own selection block.

As Winston was now doing, someone had plucked him out of the process, having won Forrester over. In a time when being a black recruit was still problematic for some, Forrester had treated Leo Winston, the skinny lad from East London, the same as everyone else. In selection, recruits were all equally worthless until respect was earned.

Winston had earned Forrester's, and then some.

He took a sip of coffee, walking to the board. He tapped a knuckle under the recruit headshot marked '24'.

Duncan Grant.

'What about *him*?' asked Winston.

A grin betrayed Forrester's true thoughts, unable to hide his enthusiasm. 'He's an interesting one.'

Winston knew that for Forrester, that was high praise.

Forrester slid Grant's file down the table to him.

Winston skimmed the basics. 'Alcoholic dad... Loner. I've heard that before...' He looked up. 'He's a bit sheltered, isn't he? Not much world experience. London will scare the shit out of him.'

There was a twinkle in Forrester's eyes. 'You might like the psych questions.'

Winston read aloud. '"Confuses impulsivity with bravery, and obsessiveness with dedication."'

'Remind you of anyone?' said Forrester.

'This is a new one: "Lies that the recruits believe about themselves."'

'We brought in a new psychologist,' said Forrester. 'She does sit-downs with some of the recruits we think have potential. Based on their conversation, she writes statements that she thinks sum up the recruit. Bear in mind that most of these guys aren't even aware of what's going on past the end of their nose. They're tough as shit, but the doc's observations are only as complex as the man sitting in front of her. It's pretty predictable, like, "I will never be good enough", "Money will make me happy", and other broken home-type stuff. No one else had more than a few lines from the doc.'

'There's a full page here on Grant,' said Winston, lifting it up.

'Yep.'

'"Typical lies that Grant believes about himself include: I could cope with having to kill people as part of my job. Extreme isolation and loneliness are necessary to protect others around me. Disconnecting from society will protect me and make me a better operative."'

Forrester said, 'We've done that test with three hundred and thirteen recruits now. Grant's the first one where the doc ran out of time.'

'She says that he couldn't cope with killing people,' said Winston. 'Why is that good?'

'The doc doesn't think he's ready, but Grant thinks he is. That's what matters. Ability comes later. That comes with training. The doc says Grant is light years ahead of the rest as far as mental strength goes.'

Winston peered out of the cabin window. The recruits were in rows across a concrete quadrangle, dressed down in green t-shirts clinging to them in the rain, alternating between push ups and planks. Winston could feel their arms and abdominals burning just watching them. Grant was visibly straining, but he was by far the fastest, knocking out every rep with perfect form.

'Have you ever seen *Lawrence of Arabia*?' Winston asked.

Forrester joined him at the window, admiring Grant's effort. 'When he holds his hand over the candle?'

Winston nodded. 'Grant gets it. It's about not minding that it hurts.'

Forrester passed him Grant's test scores. 'His psychometric tests and physicals are off the charts. He sailed through his BFT...'

Battle Fitness Test.

'...same with the Fan Dance.' Forrester then played an audio recording from his laptop. 'The exercise today wasn't just to weed out the ones who thought they could relax when the Fan Dance was done. The new doc thought it could be valuable for the DS to take out parabolic microphones. You can learn a lot about a recruit from what they say during an exercise.'

He pressed the space bar to play the clip.

Through some wind interference, it was Grant talking to Barnes and Smitty.

"I want to do something valuable today. Every day. Maybe that means stopping some bad guys from doing bad things. Or keeping a country safe."

Forrester stopped the clip. 'He's got Initial Continuation Training next. Four weeks of combat skills, weaponry, demolition and patrol tactics.'

'But you don't want to do that.'

'He's tough as nails, but he doesn't know how to operate in a team. Not yet.' Forrester said archly, 'Remind you of anybody?'

Winston chuckled. 'Yeah. A little bit.'

'He can switch off the part of his brain that makes him question every order he's given, because he wants to pass the course. He wants to do anything that's required to get to the end. To *win*. With training, he'd get there as a team player. But I don't think he'd like it. He's a better fit for you. It's early days, but I honestly think you might have a potential Albion operative here. If you don't mind handing over Grant to Imogen Swann.'

'Albion's been suspended, apparently,' said Winston. He had already made up his mind. 'He could be a good fit for Section Seven, though. Pack him up. Let's get him to London.'

15

Grant's overnight flight from New York got him to Helsinki for three p.m. local time. The twelve hours on board were more than ample to review the Kadir Rashid case on his encrypted tablet.

After comprehensive enquiries by the United Nations and various human rights groups, a lot of the details of the story had already been made public. Rashid's murder had sent shockwaves around the world.

A Saudi national and respected international commentator, Rashid had transcended the Arabic news world by breaking into English-language media. Editors loved him because he produced immaculate and punctually delivered copy, and readers loved him for his unique insight into Middle Eastern affairs. But in the classic tradition of my enemy's enemy is my friend, Rashid's popularity in the Western world triggered a resentful response in his homeland. Particularly the upper echelons of the Saudi Royal Family.

Rashid had always stopped short of directly criticising

them, but his published opinions had been deemed too liberal, too polarising, and a threat to Saudi sovereignty.

There had been no definitive proof on who made the final call, but the international community largely accepted that at some point Crown Prince Mohammad bin Abdul ordered Kadir Rashid to be killed. Or to give him his full title: Crown Prince of Saudi Arabia, Deputy Prime Minister, and Saudi Minister of Defence.

A hit squad from the Saudi secret police was assembled, and together, all ten of them made a total pig's ear of the assassination. Rashid had travelled to Athens on business. In his hotel, the killers waited to pounce. During which time they did everything a hit squad shouldn't do: some booked in under their own names; made calls home on the same mobile phones they used to talk to each other; they gathered in groups outside to smoke cigarettes, in full view of security cameras.

Then there was the hit itself: several eyewitnesses saw a suspicious-looking Saudi talking on a mobile phone, moments before Rashid was bundled into a van on a street corner. They tossed his body on a remote country roadside, the electrical wire they'd garrotted him with still wrapped around his neck. The same electrical cord that was later found to be missing from a lamp in a hotel room booked under the name of a Saudi national.

Once they found that one member of the squad the others fell like dominoes. The Greek police ran a trace on all of the mobiles used at the rough location and time of the Rashid kidnapping. It wasn't a long list. Once they had matched one of the mobile numbers to a Saudi, they were able to link ten other numbers to it from the days surrounding the murder.

To be generous, the killers had been naïve. To be accurate, they had been utterly inept.

When news of Rashid's assassination broke, the international uproar was deafening. Emergency hearings were declared at the United Nations. Sanctions were mentioned. Ambassadors recalled. Headline followed headline for weeks.

And through it all, the Crown Prince claimed innocence, even as the evidence against him mounted. The members of the hit squad put on little more than a show trial in Riyadh: it was conducted entirely behind closed doors, and the results never made public.

It had been five years since the murder, and even reacquainting himself with the material across numerous news websites, Grant was mystified as to why Henry Marlow would have any interest in Rashid.

The Crown Prince was too smart to leave any kind of paper trail proving his involvement. The killers had been captured and paraded in front of news cameras. All the enquiries came to the same conclusion. It was beyond reproach.

But whatever was in the Rashid file was important enough to drag Henry Marlow out of hiding, and out of retirement.

Grant caught a ferry from Helsinki to Estonia's capital of Tallinn, using a passport that had been carefully maintained over the past two years. All MI6 had to do was swap out the photo and name to match the field officer.

Anyone who had seen him on the ferry, standing on the deck in a ribbed sweater and insulated jacket, wearing round glasses as he consulted various maps, would never have guessed that they were looking at an international spy rather than some outdoor adventurer.

The two-hour ferry ride across a desperately cold Gulf of Finland gave Grant some necessary time with Marlow's file. What he'd been told by Winston seemed at odds with what Grant was reading. This was no out-of-control rogue officer. This was a hero.

Every job they had given him, every country they sent him to, Marlow excelled. Not only was he a brilliant operator in the field, his analysis had proven impressively prescient.

Everything about his record showed someone capable, mentally strong, intelligent. He'd turned around the Service's fortunes in places where most other operatives just hope to survive. Beirut. Kiev. Hong Kong. It was as if the hairier it got, the more he thrived.

In Section 7, Christie had loved him because he never caused a mess. And Swann had loved him because he always carried out orders – maybe even a little too well. There was a problem, though, with operatives as good as Marlow: eventually they get their own ideas about how things should be done.

It was only a matter of time before someone made him station chief somewhere. Berlin? Paris? New York? He could have had his pick of them when the time came.

Then an opening in the Albion programme came up. He had just turned forty, which would have made him the oldest Albion recruit in the programme's history.

The directors did everything they could to dissuade him, but ultimately they had to let him in to training: he was too qualified. His eight years in Section 7 had been immaculate. Perfect, really.

Grant knew all too well what was required to pass Section 7. The Albion programme was harder still. For Marlow to get in at his age must have taken real guts. Getting in also put paid to any chance of a station chief job. Not least because Albions didn't seem to last very long.

Grant couldn't understand it. Why did Marlow want to go out in the shit on his own? Lying under a camo blanket for eight hours in the baking sun, waiting to take out some bombmaker with a sniper gun.

Whatever his reasons, one thing was clear a few years into his Albion career: Henry Marlow was the best operative the programme had ever had. He had every commendation, every medal going.

Then, four years in, Marlow got his first feel for hot water. The trouble started with his memos to the director level, criticising the tactical strategy of his assignments.

Without Swann's intervention, the directors might have recalled Marlow from the programme. His memos were nothing if not candid.

Grant scanned some of the more choice excerpts:

"Our position of influence on the international stage is now largely untenable. Our enemies have an endless supply of weapons – i.e. guns, bombs, suicidal devotees – and a completely fearless attitude to death. Our worst fear is their dream. Their fantasy. That distinction not only ensures the impossibility of victory. It guarantees it..."

"Until we start to understand the nature of what we are facing, strategically, what we are attempting to do in targeted assassination is quite utterly absurd..."

"We can shoot and poison and drown all the 'high-value targets' we want. We can do this for years. Lord knows there are enough able

officers willing to fill the boots of the last dead Albion. But the reality is that we are losing the world and our place in it. To continue fighting as we have done, for the pitiful results we have accrued, would be borderline treasonous. We keep fighting in accordance with our rules and laws yet we expect different results. So we changed the laws to give us greater powers, and they haven't helped. They didn't go nearly far enough. We cut deals with people who have killed one hundred because we want to stop someone who's about to kill one hundred and one. Where has this tactic got us? We must change how we fight. We must be as ruthless as our enemies. We must kill them all."

Two weeks after the memos, Marlow assassinated two Mossad agents in Vienna. With the help of the Austrian authorities, MI6 managed to clean it up, but no one at Vauxhall Cross had sanctioned the hit. It was Marlow's way of telling them that he was splitting. He was done with Albion, MI6, the whole lot.

Grant looked up from the file and exhaled. He needed a moment. No wonder the directors had wanted to recall him.

What the hell happened? What changed?

Marlow had proven himself tougher than every other guy in the Albion programme.

What breaks a man like that? What does it take?

After the ferry, Grant drove from Tallinn into the empty north-Estonian countryside. The road had been arrow-straight for the last twenty miles – an endless highway lined with thick trees on either side.

He was driving a mud-spattered green Range Rover full of metal crates of geological equipment in the boot and back seat to fit with his legend.

He peered ahead at the surprising sight of two vehicles pulling out of the trees. A spot where Grant's Sat Nav suggested there was no road.

He had seen all of five cars in the last forty-five minutes, and they were all top-tier models from premium manufacturers. A strange coincidence hundreds of miles from the nearest city.

There had been much disagreement in the Control room as to where they were actually sending Grant. All available maps showed that the coordinates in Marlow's file would land Grant in the middle of a forest. Until Miles Archer decided to check a live satellite overview rather than an existing map.

What he found stunned everyone.

There was an entire town. And it wasn't on any map.

It had once had a proper name, but with the collapse of the Soviet Union all record of it had long been destroyed.

Like dozens of other locations, it was part of the Soviet closed-city network – although most were no more than villages or small towns. They housed sensitive military and nuclear facilities, whose work was deemed so secretive that their towns and cities were guarded with perimeter fences and watchtowers. Getting out was a nightmare, and getting in was almost impossible without the express permission of the KGB. In exchange for their silence and discretion, residents were rewarded with nicer housing, access to higher quality goods, and some even received salary bonuses.

The existence of the closed cities was classified and all listings wiped from every map. There were no road signs, and divulging so much as the existence of a closed city or town would land you a lengthy prison term.

The town had once been home to a jewel in the Soviet

crown – a nuclear-testing facility. It had functioned perfectly until nineteen eighty-one, when a suspected radiation leak led to the entire town being evacuated. Given its rural location and the firm muzzle that Moscow held over leaked intelligence, it was easy to keep a lid on things. By the time the authorities realised it was a false alarm nearly three months later, the residents had already been relocated, new jobs secured, schools found. In the end, it was decided in Moscow to simply abandon the town.

When the Soviet Union collapsed in ninety-one, the new Estonian government faced a real dilemma about how to handle the closed-city network. Most of them were military complexes. Even though the nameless town's radiation leak had been a false alarm, in light of the Chernobyl disaster, and the scandal of lies and denial that had slowly dripped out since nineteen eighty-six, the Estonian government didn't think anyone would believe the truth. So they covered it up, turning a closed town into a hidden one. Even now, few knew of its existence.

Grant watched the coordinates ticking over on his dashboard. 'I'm getting close,' he told Control.

Samantha watched him on a satellite view and could see the right turn he had to make. 'Right in about two hundred yards,' she told him.

Even though Grant had just observed two Mercedes pulling out ahead, he didn't believe that there could be a clearing to drive through until he reached it himself.

He stomped on the brake.

Through a tiny gap in the trees was a dirt road.

'Ten miles,' Samantha said. 'Straight on. Then you should be there.'

After a few minutes the trees became sparse, opening

out to a pan-flat plain, a bleak landscape of dull browns
and stale yellows. In the distance stood two tall chimneys on
the edge of a town.

There was no way of sneaking in. The dust trails
behind the car could be seen a mile away.

Grant was now finding the town exactly as it had been
left by the last evacuee over forty years earlier.

The main road through the once-quaint centre was
completely overgrown, with weeds sprouting out of cracks
in the pavement, and trees growing out of concrete
balconies.

Foxes and wild horses roamed through back streets and
alleys, scared off by the noise of Grant's car. Despite the
wildness, evidence of humanity persisted. The front
windows of shops were filled with goods that had been so
bleached by the sun over the years that everything had
turned white: clothes; tins of food; toys.

On the outskirts of the town, houses had been swamped
by tall grass. Gardens were covered in ivy, protected by the
soil which made it resistant to Estonia's bitter winter frosts.
Cars had been left by the roadside when the authorities had
moved in, the cars now rusty shells, some with the doors still
hanging open.

The only thing that had changed in the town was what
caused the evacuation in the first place: the nuclear facility.

The Russians had called it *Otverstiye*, which translated as
"the Hole", as most of it was housed underground. Good
for a nuclear facility. But also for what it had been repur-
posed to provide: security. Of the most private kind
imaginable.

16

It was largely true that the world of the ultra-rich was created and protected via a system of offshore accounts and shell companies, resulting in a near-zero rate of income tax. It had never been easier to hide earnings from the authorities. But the various tax scandals that had rocked the financial world since two thousand and eight had caused the pendulum to swing back – however momentarily – in favour of the regulators.

Tax havens in the Cayman Islands, Barbados, and the Virgin Islands might have protected huge corporations from having to pay their fair share of tax on billions' worth of assets, but once probable cause of criminal behaviour had been demonstrated, the accounts holding those assets were no longer so secret.

Under huge international pressure, even Switzerland's banking secrecy had been weakened, meaning that the ultra-rich could no longer shovel cash into their accounts without it being noticed.

It was a problem that Russian oligarch Fyodor Stam-

parov had considered after an exhausting three-hour interrogation in a conference room of the exclusive private
bank, Frères Van de Velde. At the time, it was thought to be
the most secretive institution in Geneva, which placed it
near the top of the most secretive in the world. After
enduring a true grilling from the Swiss authorities, Stamparov could see that Switzerland was heading for greater
regulation. In a world where Stamparov's bribes didn't buy
the same guarantees as they once had, he decided that
there had to be a better way.

That was when he saw it from his helicopter on the way
to Tallinn. The empty town below. *Otverstiye.*

When he got the pilot to set the chopper down and he
entered the Hole, Stamparov at first saw an opportunity for
himself. Then realised he was thinking much too small. It
was a solution to not just his problems, but many others.
And that would be worth a premium.

His contacts in the oil trade secured the services of
several ex-KGB officials who had worked at the facility and
knew the security protocols inside out. They started small in
the first few months, keeping only the assets of trusted
comrades. Once the concept had proved itself, Stamparov
spread the word.

His operation wasn't without trade-offs: customers'
money was simply locked away, neither earning interest nor
being reinvested elsewhere. But then the idea wasn't to keep
all of your money in the Hole – merely for that rainy day
when you found yourself on the run, or your assets frozen
by an unsympathetic political opponent. A real danger in
the Russian criminal world, that was built and sustained on
informing on your enemies. There wasn't much danger of
Stamparov disappearing with your money. There are finite

places in this world for a man who rips off billionaire criminals to disappear to. Stamparov was making so much money just from the Hole, it was wasn't worth risking it all to steal a few million more.

To the criminal underworld, the off-the-grid nature of the Hole provided a unique kind of security. The sort of place that a disavowed MI6 agent might turn to should he need a safe deposit box, far from prying eyes.

This much had been gleaned in advance by Grant and the team at Vauxhall Cross. But what awaited inside, no one really knew for sure – other than Henry Marlow, and Stamparov's men.

Grant pulled up outside the facility, an anonymous grey concrete block. Weeds were growing out of the window frames of the offices above. Stamparov's men only inhabited the underground area, where all the vaults were.

The Hole wasn't the kind of place that took phone calls in advance of a customer's visit. The nature of its clientele demanded a twenty-four-hour operation. And Stamparov had brought in the best muscle he could find to secure it: led by his head of security, Ramm Volker.

Volker and his crew had the steely expressions of men with a significant interest in protecting their boss's private bank. Stamparov understood that the best way to keep the loyalty of the best men is to pay them better than anyone else: he offered them direct financial stakes in the very property they were protecting. Volker and company were trained and prepared for every eventuality, and would think nothing of unloading their weapons on anyone deemed a threat.

But the Hole's main security advantage was also in some ways its weakness. One fatal flaw that would allow

Grant to access Henry Marlow's safe deposit box: geography.

The men and women in a position to use the Hole's facilities were not always amenable to making a trip that could take multiple days for some, all to retrieve a simple object from a safe deposit box, or withdraw cash. When the flaw started costing him clients, Stamparov introduced a biometric identity card system that allowed trusted advisors and assistants to access their boss's accounts on their behalf.

Practically, it was no more a risk than a Swiss account with a private firm. If sufficient data was compromised, then so was your identity. The likelihood of that happening, as well as someone even learning of the existence of the Hole? It was considered so unlikely – and by the sort of people who don't take chances with their money – that the Hole now held over €1 billion of clients' assets.

As Grant approached the front security barrier, Stamparov's men gradually stood to attention, flicking away cigarettes that somersaulted through the air. They readied their AK-12 assault rifles, the latest generation of Kalashnikov used by the Russian army. There was no need for suppressed rounds out there. If things turned nasty, there was no one nearby to hear.

Grant exited his Range Rover, hands aloft. 'Unarmed,' he shouted in Russian. He pulled up his sweater to show he wasn't hiding anything.

Ramm Volker called out in English, 'You speak good for a foreigner.' He waited until he was standing in front of Grant before asking his next question. 'Vault or box?'

'Box,' Grant answered. 'Number twenty-four.'

'Whose box?'

'Henry Marlow.'

Holding eye contact with Grant, Volker took out a handheld biometric card reader. Any doubts Grant may have had about the sophistication of the operation quickly vanished.

'Scan card,' Volker said, still staring.

Stamparov may have put his trust in technology, but everything Volker needed to know was in the eyes.

Grant took out a small plastic card and held the barcode under the infrared beam.

For anyone looking to rip off a Stamparov client, the hard part in copying a biometric card was accessing the data necessary to fool the Hole's system. For MI6, that was less of a problem. They had a whole catalogue of biometric data belonging to Henry Marlow.

The card reader gave an affirmative beep.

Volker still hadn't broken eye contact. He held out his hand to a subordinate, who placed a digital number pad in Volker's hand.

As blankly as he had said everything else so far, Volker said, 'Enter passcode.'

Grant stared back at him, giving no quarter. 'Do you mind,' he said, glanced down at Volker's feet.

It wasn't a question.

Volker took one step back, somewhat reluctantly. He turned his head, then spat.

Grant keyed in the code from Marlow's file, and a green light flashed on Volker's console. The security barrier lifted.

As Volker trudged back to his hut, he pointed at the guard emerging from the Hole's main doors. 'He will show the way.'

The architecture inside was a seventies time warp, with

typically Communist décor made up entirely of muted browns and beige.

Grant was taken across the hall to a staircase leading down. All hints at modernity – the seventies version of it – soon gave way to concrete Brutalist architecture. It was architecture designed to withstand bomb blasts, tank hits, and missile strikes.

The air turned chilly, and the lights above flickered.

The guard walking ahead said nothing, and didn't check to see if Grant was keeping up.

It wasn't hard to see why Stamparov had chosen the Hole for his private bank. Every wall and vault that Grant passed looked impenetrable. Easily the equal of anything Geneva's banks had to offer.

The guard stopped outside a thin corridor and pointed Grant to the safe deposit box room. It was a converted laboratory with a thick steel door, allowing total privacy. The walls were lined with various sizes of drawers, each individually marked by pristine gold numbers and with digital keypads on the front. Grant recognised their design from the photo in Marlow's file.

The guard shouldered his Kalashnikov and opened the door. 'Ten minutes. Knock when you are ready.'

Once he was alone, Grant entered the passcode to drawer twenty-four. The lock mechanism inside gave way with the subtlest of clicks.

He took out a short length of wire and slid it along the inside of the drawer to check for any latches or booby-traps. It was clear. Or so it had seemed.

Opening the drawer fully, Grant noticed a slight tug beneath the felt underlay. A tiny pinhole camera was attached to the rear of the drawer, looking up at whoever was standing over it. It was now recording.

Better a camera than a bomb, thought Grant. He pulled the camera out and broke it in two, but the damage was already done. With no idea where the video was being streamed to, and who was watching, he had to move faster than planned.

The drawer was long and wide, only six inches deep. Inside were passports for various legends Marlow had cultivated over the years – several not listed in his official MI6 file – along with credit cards to match the names on the passports. There was also £2000 in cash, and the equivalent in U.S. dollars and euros; contact lenses to match the different eye colours on his passports; a MacHasp USB security key (now useless, as it only accessed MI6 databases on site at Vauxhall Cross); a memory stick; and a mobile phone.

As Grant rummaged deeper, it became apparent that there was a thin false bottom to the drawer. No more than an inch. Grant removed the rest of the drawer, revealing a manila folder underneath. Inside were dozens of surveillance photos.

All of Édith Lagrange.

The photos covered her entire daily routine. Leaving her apartment building in the centre of Lyon at the crack of dawn; leaving Interpol headquarters late at night; reading a book alone at a riverside wine bar.

Grant had only one thought: *Lagrange is next.*

Like all reputable Geneva banks with safe deposit box rooms, there was a stack of red canvas bags with drawstring openings, marked on the side with the Russian Cyrillic for 'burn'. Burn bags were where clients could leave sensitive documents to be incinerated on site. No one could accuse Stamparov of skimping on the details.

Grant poured the contents of the drawer into one of the bags. But as the mobile phone spilled out, it startled him to see the screen light up with an incoming message. The sender was listed as "*UNKNOWN NUMBER*".

He instinctively checked the corners of the ceiling, wondering how a mobile was even receiving a signal down there. There was a black Siemens antenna attached to the wall above the door.

The message said:

"*MARLOW KNEW YOU'D GO THERE. IT'S A TRAP. GET OUT OF THERE NOW.*"

Grant replied to the number: "*Who are you?*"

While he waited anxiously for a reply, Grant looked towards the steel door, wondering who might be on the other side of it now.

The phone vibrated in his hand. This time it was a call.

Grant answered before it could even start ringing.

'Who is this?' he whispered.

A voice spoke over him almost immediately. Digitally masked. 'They know you're not meant to be in there. You'll be asked for a code upon exiting. Get it wrong, they'll shoot you on the spot.'

'I have the code,' Grant replied.

'Not this one, you don't. Check your phone and get out. Now.'

The caller hung up.

Grant's own phone pinged with a message:

"*STALKER.*"

Someone started banging the side of their fist on the steel door.

Then Grant heard a lock being turned.

The guard appeared. 'Come with me,' he said.

Burn bag in hand, Grant asked, 'What's wrong? It's not time yet.'

The guard simply repeated his demand.

The caller must have been right. Before, the guard had been practically comatose. Now he was alert and threatening. Something had changed.

He walked behind Grant now, his weapon lowered, with his finger resting across the trigger guard. Ready.

When they reached the lobby, Volker was perched on the edge of the reception desk, holding a tablet device. On the screen was a profile page showing a photo of Henry Marlow, provided for security purposes.

The profile had a list of codewords to cover almost every eventuality: to alert a guard that he had been followed; or if he had been forced to enter under duress – usually because of the kidnapping of a loved one somewhere thousands of miles away. The client could reply with a codeword that meant everything was fine. Or a codeword that confirmed to the security staff that they were indeed under duress, and help was required.

There was a certain word that Volker was about to quiz Grant on. They called it 'interference'.

If for any reason a client's biometric data and/or passcode had been compromised and it was feared that an imposter was accessing an account, the security team would ask for an interference code, confirming their association with the client. It was the equivalent of a website asking security questions for verification.

There was nothing in Marlow's file that had suggested such a system was in place.

Volker got off the desk, assuming a wide stance in front of Grant, leering and menacing even without a weapon in his hands.

'I must ask you for the interference code,' said Volker.

Showing no fear, Grant answered, 'Stalker.'

Volker checked his screen, making a dissatisfied pout.

It was only then that Grant realised how much trust he had put in the word of an anonymous stranger.

Volker said something to the guard, but Grant's Russian wasn't advanced enough to know what it was.

The guard began to laugh.

Figuring if he was going to be shot, he might as well die with a smile on his face. Grant joined in with the laughter.

Volker stepped back, clearing the path for Grant to exit the building.

He had said, 'Damn it. I was hoping he'd get it wrong.'

With every step that Grant took towards the Range Rover, he was convinced they would shoot him in the back. Once he had tossed the burn bag onto the passenger seat, he let out a long exhalation.

The moment he shut his eyes, his phone buzzed with another message:

"*If Édith Lagrange dies, so does the truth.*"

Grant immediately tried to call back, but only got a recorded digital voice:

This number is no longer in use.

17

Grant eyed the rear-view mirror carefully until he had passed the outer edges of the town. He only felt safe once he reached the cover of the trees lining the road.

He called Control on his phone. He said, 'You've got to get Lagrange out. Marlow's security box was full of surveillance photos of her. I think he's going to go after her next.'

Winston gestured wildly at Ryan to get his attention. Covering the mouthpiece, he called out, 'Find out where Lagrange is.' He uncovered the mouthpiece. 'This is good, Grant. We can finally get ahead of him.'

'It was a trap,' said Grant.

'How?'

'A codeword that wasn't in his file. Marlow knew we would go there. And anyone who did would be killed.'

Winston could hear the malice in Grant's voice. It worried him. He was reminded of the SAS psychologist's note about him: "confuses impulsivity with bravery, and obsessiveness with dedication." He didn't want Grant flying off the handle in search of retaliation.

'How did you get out?' asked Winston.

'A guardian angel,' said Grant. 'Why would Marlow risk going back to Lyon for Lagrange?'

'He clearly believes she's worth it. Get to Tallinn, Grant. I'm putting you on a flight to Lyon.'

It was early evening in London, which meant that it had been nearly three days since Winston had last left the Vauxhall Cross property.

Operating on a regimen of caffeine and protein bars, he was rapidly running out of gas. As soon as his call to Grant concluded, Winston did a quick three-sixty of the Control room.

'Where's Samantha?' he asked with irritation.

'She went home, sir,' replied Ryan, his only senior aide still standing. Realising that Winston needed an explanation, Ryan added, 'To sleep. She's coming on to night shift in a few hours.'

Winston nodded, remembering. Time had lost all meaning in a world without windows.

Half the team were on long-overdue breaks. The rest were diligently cracking on with their grid work.

Ryan said, 'GCHQ have got Lagrange's mobile signal at Interpol headquarters.'

'Okay, good,' replied Winston. 'Tell her that we need to get her to a safe house.'

Swann, who had been locked in her own battle with exhaustion, as well as a growing frustration with the mission, sprang up out of her seat. 'Leo, we're finally catching up with Marlow. Do you really want to hide the one person that's going to pull him out into the open?'

Winston asked, 'What do you suggest we do? Dangle her for Marlow like a live piñata?'

Swann didn't even have to think. 'Yes. Get her out in the open with a big spotlight on her and let's finish this thing.'

'Imogen, you're talking about exposing a foreign national to a risk she can't possibly be aware of.'

It might have been the lack of sleep. The stuffy air and smell of stale coffee pervading the Control room, but Swann had had enough. She threw an arm up in the direction of the video wall. 'What do you need? A bloody invitation with Marlow's signature on it? Don't waste this, Leo.'

An aide had appeared at the Control room doors, terrified to interrupt. Latching on to the brief silence, she said, 'Sir. The Chief has asked for you at the Belfry.'

Winston asked, 'Did she say why?'

The aide replied, 'Sorry, sir.' She turned quickly, relieved to vacate the tension in the room.

Winston whipped his suit jacket off the back of his chair. He told Ryan, 'Tell Lagrange that Grant is on his way. And while you have her, find out if there's been any movement on that Red Notice.'

Before Winston left, Swann said, 'I tried to warn you, Leo.'

'What is that supposed to mean?' he asked.

Swann almost appeared apologetic. 'When you're talking to C, I want you to remember that I tried to warn you.'

Winston waited in the doorway as Swann came past.

Under her breath, so only he could hear, she muttered, 'Someone had to take charge of things.'

18

Édith Lagrange was at her desk at Interpol headquarters, listening to a briefing from her captain who was droning on about some interminably boring fraud case.

With no one behind her, she was free to work away on her computer, making sure to appear alert whenever the captain looked her way. She was scrolling through the logs of the Henry Marlow Red Notice.

Almost every notice received messages in the opening days. Mostly from lonely sorts, depressives, trolls, the troubled. Sending in false leads was their way of feeling connected to something powerful in their lives. They were rarely malicious. Just misguided. Some genuinely believed that they had seen a fugitive, or someone who looked vaguely similar. Sifting out the cranks from the genuine was one of the hardest challenges for an Interpol detective. They lost entire days at a time to chasing rainbows, with no pots of gold at the end of them.

Lagrange had spent many hours of her Interpol career getting a feel for genuine leads, and in the Henry Marlow feed filled with all-caps, typo-ridden messages, one of them stood out a mile.

It was from a "*RICHARD CARLTON*".

The IP address had been blocked. Which wasn't strange in itself. Most of the cranks had the good sense to at least hide their location. Easily done via a VPN server that could bounce your IP address to almost any country in the world.

But Richard Carlton had gone a great deal further than that. His level of encryption was far beyond anything available to the general public – and had been bouncing around various international servers for the past twelve hours. It was either a private contractor, or intelligence/military-grade, and he'd used it to get Interpol's attention.

Lagrange re-read the message. Even with her excellent English, she couldn't understand its meaning:

"I saw this man in London on 20th September. He was carrying a file marked AC180."

At the front of the room, Captain Marcuse repeated for the third time, 'Édith!'

She snapped out of her daze. 'Sorry, sir.'

'I know that this must seem pedestrian to you now, but I've got some actual police work for us here...'

Lagrange didn't see much evidence of that in a case concerning counterfeit t-shirts being smuggled in from Belgium. They were only investigating it because the owner of the company whose goods were being copied had a buddy on the Budget and Fundraising Board.

Choosing the option to '*Edit as Administrator*', Lagrange clicked on the settings icon for the Henry Marlow page, then highlighted the message. She brought the cursor to the foot of the page and selected '*QUARANTINE*'.

A drop-down menu appeared, showing the names of all

her department members. She clicked on her own name, and the message disappeared. If anyone wanted to see the Richard Carlton message, they'd need to break into her password-protected folder.

The captain's monologue was interrupted again, this time by the piercing ring of Lagrange's phone.

Feeling the heat of everyone's eyes on her, she fumbled with her phone as she rose from her chair, making a loud screech on the linoleum floor. 'Sorry, sir,' she said, showing him the phone. 'I have to take this.'

Marcuse tutted, and motioned her dismissively out the back door of the room.

She found a quiet spot in the corridor to answer. 'Detective Lagrange.'

It was a young English voice. 'Detective, this is Ryan Matthews at SIS in London.'

Almost immediately, Lagrange felt her head turn light.

Had they been monitoring the page somehow? Had they seen what she'd just done?

Ryan said, 'Has there been any progress at your end?'

The more she told herself to calm down, the more she panicked. 'Progress? With what?' she asked.

'Well... the Red Notice.'

She held the phone away from her mouth for a second so she could take a calming breath, unheard at Ryan's end. 'No, there's been nothing. Nothing important, anyway. Is anything wrong?'

'Actually,' said Ryan. 'I'm afraid we've come into some information concerning your safety.'

19

Once Grant reached the busier highways to the west, he pulled over at a layby. He'd been eyeing the burn bag for the last hundred miles, but didn't want to take his foot off the accelerator until he had reached some semblance of civilisation.

He was almost certain that Lawrence Bloom had set him up by sending him to the Hole. He would have banked on Grant not having the interference code. Which begged the next crucial question: who had helped him escape?

He opened one of the metal boxes in the back seat and took out an air-gapped laptop: it had never been connected to the internet, or to any other unsecured network. From a remote location, it was the definition of unhackable. A hacker might as well try to infiltrate a brick.

Grant took out the memory stick from the burn bag, and opened the solitary folder on it on his laptop. The folder was named "HM".

There were hundreds of documents in it. It would take days to comb through them all.

He clicked on the first in the Recently Modified list. What he saw on the screen made him freeze.

The digital stamp on the document said, "STRAP Three clearance."

Not even Winston or Swann had clearance to see such material.

It didn't take much scrolling around the rest of the folder's contents to work out what it was: the complete, unfiltered, classified history of Henry Marlow, Albion operative. There were operations listed in countries that Grant didn't even know Marlow had ever been sent to. Liberia, the Philippines, Congo... all black ops. All with one thing in common: they'd been wiped from the official MI6 archives.

He opened up a search window and typed: "*Rashid*"

He waited with hope rather than expectation. It was soon punctured:

NO RESULTS FOUND.

Overwhelmed at the amount of material, Grant filtered the folder to 'Type' and scrolled down the page. The vast majority were PDFs and various other kinds of image files. But there was also a long list of audio files. Unnamed. Just numbered.

Grant clicked on the first.

The media player opened, and an English male voice came out of the speakers. It was languorous, steady. Like he was really contemplating what he was saying. Thinking aloud.

Grant clicked to the middle of one of the clips.

"I was kneeling over a man on the ground. There had been a struggle. My gun slid across the tiled floor. As I flipped him and over-powered him, I tried to reach for the gun. It was too far away. But I didn't want to get off him, because I had fought so hard to get into a

superior position. That was when I knew: I'd have to strangle him. As I gripped his throat, I could feel his windpipe collapsing under my thumbs, being pushed in. It felt like... nothing I'd ever felt. I had never really contemplated how fragile we are. These machines made of flesh and blood and bone. How easy we are to break.

"I didn't want to keep feeling it in my fingers. So I gripped harder, to get it over with sooner.

'The life drained from his eyes. He made a kind of... gurgling sound. I can still hear it. When people die peacefully, it comes out as a soft exhalation. Like a spirit, or a soul, exiting the body..."

There was a long pause, then the sound of a cigarette being lit.

"When people die because their life is taken, it sounds very different. It's only when you hear that sound, that you realise how unnatural it all is. What we're asked to do. To take lives. For reasons unexplained. We take them because that's the job."

Another pause.

"I used to understand what the job was. What it was for. I kneeled over that man and took his life from him. I was the last thing he would ever see. His killer. His assassin. I'll never forget that day. No one ever does. The first time you kill someone."

There was a faint sound of ice dropping into a glass, then someone taking a sip from it.

"I walked into that room one man, and left it a totally different one. I knew I would never be the same again."

Grant knew the voice because he'd listened to his recorded interview for joining the Albion programme.

It was unmistakably Henry Marlow.

20

There wasn't time to sit by the side of the road and listen to more, so Grant queued up a list of audio files and got back on the road. For the next two hours, he drove the monotonous National Road 1 route to Tallinn, listening to Henry Marlow's personal history.

The dual carriageway was lined with trees almost the whole way, giving no indication of what the countryside looked like. All Grant had to focus on was Marlow's voice, and the road ahead.

Some of the files ran for upwards of thirty minutes, others were no more than thirty seconds. They ranged from detailed mission run-throughs to scattered philosophical musings.

If Grant turned the volume all the way up, he could make out various audio artefacts in the background – a birdsong; waves lapping; traffic noise of a major city. One of the Service's army of forensic tech analysts would have a mountain of material to work with.

Marlow described missions that weren't in any files or archive. On paper they didn't exist, and never would.

What intrigued Grant most were the recordings where Marlow didn't talk about missions. He talked about his childhood. How he saw the world. What he wanted from his life. It all sounded very familiar to Grant.

They had both grown up in rural, isolated areas – Grant, the Isle of Skye; Marlow, a village in Cornwall. Both had lost their mothers by the age of eleven, and their fathers had been heavy drinkers.

His first impression from Marlow's official file had been of someone who couldn't have been more different to him: Marlow was a product of the English public school system, then Cambridge; Grant had gone to a decrepit rural school and bypassed university altogether. The Marlows had been decorated Army stock, a long line of heroes stretching back to the Boer War; the Grant family tree was little more than a stump.

Now it appeared that they had far more in common than Grant had realised.

Timelines aside, Grant was struck by their shared sense of isolation growing up, and a sense of being different – something of a theme in MI6 operatives. Even before his first experience with grief, Grant had been a solitary child. The only sports that interested him were individual pursuits. That way, he only had to rely on himself, rather than faltering teammates. The sports he played, he threw himself into fanatically. But with each, there always came a point where he realised he wasn't going to be as good as his competition.

In the years following his mother's death, Grant turned away from competitive sports in favour of personal improvement: weight training; reading every book he could find on psychology and history in the island library; being rigorous about his diet.

He was no longer competing against others: he was competing against himself.

Listening to Marlow's story was like listening to his own. It unsettled him.

When he reached signs displaying twenty kilometres to Tallinn, Grant thought about shutting off the recordings, but the next audio file in the queue was only five minutes long. He decided to let it run.

It was a decision that would prove to have far-reaching consequences.

21

'You can never anticipate the missions that will really stay with you. And Charles Joseph was no different.

'I was coming off some rare downtime, which amounted to sitting around my flat in central London waiting for the phone to ring. I packed and re-packed my go bag. I watched the phone. I checked my messages. I did bodyweight exercises in my living room. I sat on my sofa and watched the light gradually change outside. The idea of doing normal things after ending another life was impossible to me.

'The moment I dreaded most was standing in my hallway, one hand on the door handle, about to go outside and face reality. People walking around with takeaway coffees, chatting on phones, going to offices, or yoga classes, or picking up children, dropping off children... I had no place in that world. It got so that I stopped going out altogether. What was I supposed to do? Go to bars with friends? I didn't have any. What on earth could I possibly do with a friend? Talk? About what? Work?

'Sometimes I'd go out at night, walking alone. Piccadilly was my favourite. Around three a.m. when the rubbish collectors were in full operation. They were the only people I felt any affinity with. Working the jobs that no one else wanted. The councils don't make them work at night because it's more convenient. It's so that when the streets are busy during the day, no one is confronted with the dirty and necessary work that needs done.

'Most of all, I liked the quietness of the streets at night. It meant fewer faces to keep track of. Remembering car registration plates. And always looking out for a pair of shoes you recognise: jackets are easily reversed and quickly changed. The one constant in an operative that you can count on is that they won't change their shoes. It takes too long, and draws too much attention.

'My sleeping patterns had got so lopsided that I was waking up at four in the afternoon and going to bed at nine in the morning. So when the call came in the middle of the night, I picked up halfway through the first ring. I was on the sofa, watching *Apocalypse Now* with the sound off. "Promenade. Sixty minutes," they said.

'I was picked up on the Mall thirty minutes later. If anyone had been monitoring the call, I'd have been long gone. Swann handed me the dossier in the back seat. She looked like they'd woken her up not too long ago. I hadn't seen her without makeup before, and it wasn't obvious what she was wearing underneath her long black coat. From her neckline, I presumed it was a creased t-shirt. She had on jeans and black boots. It was like that first time you bump into a teacher not in school. They look so strange outside of the only world you know them from.

'The target was one we'd been tracking for a while. Charles Joseph. An arms dealer, warlord, whatever you want to call him. Insane was a fairly reasonable assessment, though. He'd been one of the few child soldiers in the Congolese War of the nineties to avoid getting shot, or strung out on heroin. There weren't many that managed both, which allowed him to ascend the ranks quickly. By twenty-one, he was general of an army division.

'Not even he could have told you what he was fighting for or why.

There were so many factions and tribes. What they all wanted or were fighting for hardly mattered. All Charles Joseph cared about was guns. And money.

'Weapons were streaming in from all angles, funded by the West as countries raced to take charge of the Congo's numerous and valuable natural resources. See, the country had this problem: they decided to have a civil war right around the time that global demand for coltan was skyrocketing. Why coltan? Because you couldn't make mobile phones without it.

'It wasn't the first time the Congo had been cursed by its natural resources. King Leopold of Belgium was the first to make a success of exploiting the country, killing any and all who stood in his way. Right at a time when global demand for rubber – which the Congo had in abundance – was peaking. Millions were enslaved and murdered to fuel Leopold's insatiable desire for riches and power. A trend that changed little through the twentieth century.

'Charles Joseph was Europe's best friend. In between his many shopping trips to Paris, he took lunch with the French president. He dined at the most exclusive private clubs in London. All because his weapons ensured that coltan, and gold, and copper, all flowed in the direction the Europeans wanted it to.

'So when he decided to run for President on a programme of reforms and education, it was only natural that he be assassinated. The first attempt was a Frenchman. He was captured sneaking through Joseph's compound one night. French intelligence officers found his head on a spike at the Rwandan border a week later. That was ten years ago. I was to be attempt number two.

'The decision to kill him wasn't totally out of line, you know. His proclamations about democracy were an obvious smokescreen for his true desire of tyrannical power. In a way, he went crazy with it. The power. There was nothing his army wouldn't do. Joseph told them that drinking the blood of their enemies made them invincible. Which led,

inevitably, to the conclusion that eating their flesh would be a further improvement. Cannibalism was soon rife on the front lines of the war.

'By the time I reached him, his soldiers were so strung out I could have marched into his compound wearing a one-man band. Even the lowest class of soldier had more money than they could spend. More drugs than their bodies could process. The entire compound was a monument to excess. There were tigers prowling in cages, emaciated and dehydrated, too weak to growl as I sneaked through the gardens on a cloudy night.

'The clouds were crucial to the success of the mission. If you've never seen the stars in Africa, you can barely imagine how bright they are. The sky almost looks more white than black, and even a half moon can light up the ground like a spotlight.

'Some soldiers were in the living room, surrounded by naked, doped-up, sleeping prostitutes, watching *Rambo* on a giant TV downstairs with the volume up painfully loud: the constant chug of AK-47 gunfire had blown out their ears. How Joseph could sleep upstairs was a mystery. When I reached his bedroom I discovered the answer. He had the contents of a small pharmacy on his bedside table, with more downers than a Cure album. He didn't even stir as I put the suppressed Glock to his forehead. No one downstairs knew I was there.

'I was fully aware of the impotence of my mission. Warlords and arms dealers like Joseph were like whack-a-mole in Africa. And they'd stay Britain's friend until they were no longer useful, or following orders.

'Back home a few weeks later, I got out of the shower and caught myself in the mirror. I'd lost so much weight. Then I remembered that I hadn't eaten in almost thirty-six hours. I'd just been drinking water and coffee. When Swann saw me, she faked concern for my wellbeing. It had nothing to do with that. She was protecting her investment, and in turn, the country's. She needed me functional.

'Intelligence agencies have it rough in the twenty-first century. Gone *are the days when you can just send operatives on psychologically draining missions and let them fend for themselves when it's over. There are protocols to follow, paperwork to file. Everything has to be done above board. There's no mention of whatever atrocities you've been told to carry out, of course, but they offer you the usual modern solutions: talking to psychologists, drugs. Talking is supposed to cure everything these days. Feeling low? Life not going in the direction you want it to? Just talk about it. Open up. Get it off your chest. You don't want me doing that. It's the last thing you want. Trust me. The scariest thing you'll notice when someone asks you to talk about your feelings is when you realise you might not have any.*

'These people actually think the goal is to make people like me less anxious. That it will help me do my job better. But that's not a solution. That's like trying to fix a broken vase by moving it to a different room. You don't deal with the reality of the world by having others make it feel safe for you. You step into the thing that causes you pain. You make it bigger. And hold it really close in your hand. Until it burns. You don't run away, or try to make your pain or grief or anxiety small, or trick yourself into forgetting about it by watching ten episodes of a TV show in a weekend. You make the pain bigger. And you learn to live inside it. Until it can no longer hurt you. You haven't escaped your pain. You've made yourself stronger.

'That's the discipline it takes. Our brains are different. They have to be. As soon as we talk, we lose our discipline. We were hired because we are capable of withstanding what no one else can. The secrets. The lies. The loneliness. Never being able to love somebody. Never being available to be loved. Because here's what's true about someone in my shoes: sometimes it's better to not talk. You don't make yourself stronger by dwelling on all the things that turn you inside out. You make yourself stronger by confronting the brutal truth of who you really are. Who I am. And the things I've done. I don't need to talk about the things I've done to help me get out of bed in the morning. I need to take

a brutal, honest inventory of the things I've done. And accept responsibility for who I really am.

'*They say that sometimes the best thing for a forest fire is to let it burn. It clears dead trees and leaves, and stops competing vegetation from taking over. It returns nutrients to the soil, and releases seeds allowing new plants to grow.*

'*The Service's answer to what I live with is stopping a forest fire by pouring water on the embers. But as soon as that spark becomes a fire, and the fire takes over, it's already too late. There's no going back. What they don't understand is, sometimes, the most humane thing you can do is to let the world burn.*

'*And that's exactly what I'm going to do. They have no idea what's coming. That's what's so beautiful about it. I'm going to burn the entire system down.*'

END OF RECORDING

22

Winston was still doing up his tie when he reached the Belfry restaurant on the ninth floor. A large iron bell on a concrete plinth was the centrepiece of the elegant layout, though Winston had never understood why it had been put there.

The windows were tinted for security reasons, but they still provided a magnificent view across the River Thames, past the Tate Modern and towards Westminster. The setting sun cast a lovely light over the panorama, ushering in one of those London summer evenings where you can stay out deep into the night and not need long sleeves.

Chief Olivia Christie was already tucking in to a dinner of salmon and asparagus. She pointed at the empty chair opposite with her knife. 'Take a seat, Leo,' she said with a half-full mouth.

The nearest diners were far across the room, safely out of earshot.

As he took his seat, he said, 'Ma'am.' He couldn't help

noticing the manila file on the table beside Christie's sparkling water.

'When was the last time you ate?' she asked.

'I've got a box of protein bars in my office that–'

Christie held up a hand to stop him, then called out to a waiter. 'Philip. Steak and chips for Leo, please.'

'Right away, ma'am,' came the reply.

Winston insisted, 'Really, ma'am, I'm fine. I should probably get back quite soon.'

Still chewing, Christie said gently, 'Bollocks. You've got to eat something that's not in a wrapper. Consider this a well-being intervention. You haven't even left the building in forty-eight hours.' She met Winston's eyes. 'Yes, I did check. I have a duty of care these days – so it's been explained to me several times by the Service's army of lawyers. I can get away with droning a wedding party in Pakistan, but the greatest threat to my pension is a sternly worded email from Human Resources. I'm not sure what that says about our political system.'

Winston said, 'I'm pretty sure I do, ma'am.'

Christie chuckled. 'That's why I enjoy our chats, Leo. I always get the truth from you.' She dabbed her mouth with a napkin, then relinquished her cutlery. She sat back in her chair.

Winston braced himself for whatever was to come.

'Kadir Rashid,' said Christie. 'Why am I hearing that name with regards to Henry Marlow?'

Winston replied, 'There seems to have been something relating to Rashid in Lawrence Bloom's safe. Something that Marlow stole from Bloom two weeks ago. Martin Haslitt was looking for it too.'

Christie snorted with disgust. 'There's a name I hoped to never hear again.'

Winston said, 'Imogen showed me an old Hannibal file on Haslitt. He was a real piece of work.'

'It was a different Service back then. We didn't know where our field officers were half the time. Do you remember?'

Winston nodded. 'I'd have to wait until my station chief answered a landline phone.'

'The truly scary thing is that what we actually know went on with men like Haslitt is likely the tip of the iceberg.' She paused. 'Transparency – at least within the walls of Vauxhall Cross – is vital. Don't you agree?'

'Of course, ma'am.'

'Then let me be transparent right now: I want any mention of Kadir Rashid kept out of your updates and any subsequent reports.' She leaned forward, resting her fore-arms on the table in a conspiratorial pose. 'I know how this might sound. But believe me, Leo. It's for your own protection.'

'My protection? Why would mentioning a reporter that was killed by a Saudi hit squad five years ago be dangerous?'

Christie checked around the room, ensuring no one else was listening in. Even so many years after the Cold War, she was still wary of lip readers when talking business. 'Leo, who was in charge of Henry Marlow and the Albion programme?'

'Imogen,' he answered.

'Who answers directly to me,' she added. 'And who do I answer to?'

Wondering where she was going with her line of enquiry, he said, 'The Foreign Secretary.'

'I'm telling you to remove Kadir Rashid from the investigation for your own protection.'

Winston glanced at the manila file. 'Ma'am, we've always been very candid with each other.' He took a breath.

She gestured for him to continue.

'The Albion programme was terminated after Henry Marlow went AWOL. He wasn't the first field officer to be disavowed in our history. It doesn't fit that it would cause the termination of such an elite programme.'

'Ask your question,' said Christie.

Winston didn't waste a beat. 'Did MI6 have anything to do with Kadir Rashid's murder?'

Christie gave a hint of a smile. 'There are about five hundred people in this building right now. Do you know how many would have the balls to ask me what you just did?' She pointed at him. 'And that scares me. Because I like you, Leo. But there are certain forces that even I can't protect you from.'

Winston reached for the file, but didn't try to open it. He already knew what it was. 'If this is going to sit here like Chekhov's gun, it's probably about time to fire it.'

'That was left on my desk an hour ago,' said Christie. 'You already know what it is, don't you?'

'I have an idea.'

'What is it?'

'A classified Hannibal file, detailing reports of my excessive drinking while in the Service.'

'There's only one person who could access such a file.'

'The same person who classified it,' Winston replied. 'Imogen Swann.'

'I don't like politics, Leo. I never wanted this job. That's why I'm good at it. Imogen left this file on my desk because she wants to play politics. And I think I know why.'

'Why?' asked Winston.

Christie paused. 'If anything else about Rashid comes up, I want you to come directly to me with it.'

'For my own protection.'

'Precisely,' replied Christie.

The waiter approached, putting down a plate of perfectly cooked rare steak and triple-cooked chips. Winston felt uneasy, the hazy sense of having been threatened and protected at the same time.

As Christie prepared to leave, she motioned towards the large bronze bell in the middle of the dining room. 'I can't imagine what a task it was to get that thing up here. It was part of a church nearby, from the seventeen hundreds. They only put it in here to add some gravitas and a bit of local history to the place. But I decided to do some digging. Turns out, they didn't only ring the bell for mass on a Sunday. The watchman of that bell tower had the best view in all of Vauxhall. He took it upon himself to ring the bell if he ever saw a crime committed on the streets below, to alert a nearby policeman. What the police never realised, however, was that the watchman wasn't as altruistic as he seemed. It turns out that he was actually in the pay of local criminals to ring the bell whenever a policeman came near. They'd hightail it before the police could reach them.' Christie stood up, collecting her phone but leaving the Hannibal file. 'Makes you think, doesn't it: if only someone had been watching the watchman.'

As she turned to leave, Winston picked up the file. 'Ma'am. What about this?'

'As I said: I don't like politics. And I don't like those who play at it. They always say that everyone has a breaking point. As Chief of this Service, I'd rather our officers broke once they got home like you, when they're no longer in an interrogation cell in foreign hands. Your strength, your silence, kept this country safer, Leo. If anyone had a reason to be pissed off and go AWOL from this place, it was you. As of right now, I have officially expunged that file from the Service archives. Human Resources has a good shredder if you need it.'

Humbled by the gesture, Winston said, 'Thank you, ma'am.'

'Henry Marlow was one of our watchmen. Let's not be looking the other way when he rings that bell again.'

On her way out, Christie caught the attention of the waiter. 'Box that up for him. He has work to do.'

When Christie reached the door, Miles Archer nearly ran her over.

'Pardon me, ma'am,' he said on his way past. He was out of breath, having taken the stairs in lieu of waiting for the lift.

Winston flicked his head up. 'What is it?' he asked quietly.

Between breaths, Archer managed to say, 'We've found him, sir. We've found Henry Marlow.'

Winston got straight to his feet, leaving his steak and chips behind.

23

As soon as Winston reached the Control room he tore off his suit jacket and threw it aside. His eyes darted hungrily across the video wall, trying to take in everything at once. An alert flashed in red over a map of Italy:

"*MILAN STATION* – **PROPERTY BREACH**."

As soon as Swann burst in, Winston picked up a random stack of reports and shuffled the Hannibal file in his hand underneath.

Swann's eyes were wide with anticipation at the wall. 'What is it?' she asked Winston.

'I just got here,' he replied.

Ryan fielded it. 'There was a flag at our Milan substation, sir. Someone tried to enter the house using an invalid access code on the alarm panel. Two minutes later the power went out.'

'Why is it flagging here?'

Ryan had an almost fearful look in his eyes. 'The alarm code was invalid because it expired, sir. It was a code assigned to Henry Marlow.'

Swann was definitive. 'No one else could have that. It's him.'

Winston looked at the screen, mulling it over. 'Surely he didn't think that that would work.'

'He's on the back foot, that's why. He's run out of places to hide.'

Ryan offered, 'Maybe he wants us to know he's there.'

All eyes turned to Winston for a decision.

He asked, 'Do we have any personnel in there right now?'

Ryan answered, 'No, it's empty.'

Winston turned to Archer. 'Miles, get a raid team over there. Ryan, I want a fresh pull on everything in Marlow's files. This time, every connection to Milan. There are twenty-seven substations in western Europe, and he picked that one. I want to know why.'

'Who are you sending?' asked Swann.

'Who am I sending? It's a substation in a Milan suburb, and our orders are to bring Marlow in. Who do you think I'm sending?'

She pulled him away from the rest of the team. 'Leo, you can't waste a raid team on this. We've got to be decisive.'

Winston said, 'I thought you were in favour of walking away.'

'That was before we had a solid lead on Marlow's location.' Swann now raised her voice to the extent that it was impossible for anyone in the room not to hear. 'Let's end this thing now. Make the call!'

Winston pushed past her, heading for the phone. 'I'm not sending in an aux. We're not there yet.'

Aux was short for auxiliary. The most Orwellian of euphemisms. By any other name, they were assassins.

As Swann backed off to her laptop, Winston started dialling the Italian desk.

'Look!' Swann called out, as if proven correct about something. She projected her laptop screen onto the wall, showing the current Milan substation op schedule: a blinking dot gave the location of current resources, including raid teams.

She pointed at the wall, 'The nearest team is an hour away. If you think Marlow will still be there in an hour, then be my guest. Maybe Ryan can put Netflix up on the wall until they get there...'

Winston turned to Archer, who grudgingly gave his approval.

Winston relented. 'Fine,' he said. 'Miles, get the Foreign Secretary on the line. If his secretary stalls you, tell her we need aux authorisation.'

Swann put her hand on Winston's shoulder, trying to reassure him. 'Just so you know, this is what opportunity looks like. We're doing the right thing.'

Winston shrugged off her touch. 'Nice try with the Hannibal file,' he replied quietly. 'It says a lot about your judgement of character that you actually believed Christie would use it against me. Now I think I understand how you got into this Marlow mess in the first place.'

Swann didn't have time to stew on her plan backfiring. Her assistant Justin was calling for her across the room.

He had an op schedule for the Milan station on his screen, but there were some differences between his and the one on the wall. 'Ma'am, I thought you should see this. There's actually a raid team twenty minutes away.' Justin was about to get to his feet, but in five years of being Swann's assistant, he had never once defied her or gone over her head. The most assertive thing he could think to say was, 'Maybe I should tell Leo...'

Swann pushed him back down into his chair. 'I see you, Justin. Palling around with Leo's guys. Don't forget what you're here to do.' She reached for his mouse and closed the window. 'You work for me. Remember that.'

24

Milan centred around three key things: fashion, football, and finance. Despite a reputation for being a buzzing metropolis, where beautiful people sit in cafés, drinking obnoxiously strong espressos, and sharp-cheeked young women stride through the iconic Galleria Vittorio shopping arcade carrying Prada and Louis Vuitton shopping bags, there was a political dimension to the city that made it a key European intelligence site.

Its position at the very north of Italy should have kept it far-removed from the migrant crisis in the south. But if migrants wished to proceed to the fabled lands of France, Germany, or the United Kingdom, whether by foot, vehicle, or rail, they had to go through the north – which, for the most part, meant Milan.

To the east of Italy, there was a jihadi and people-trafficking problem to contend with, as thousands of undocumented people streamed over from Albania and Greece. Where they had been before that was anyone's guess.

Turkey. Syria. Iraq. It might not have seemed like it but, from northern Italy, the entire Middle East was in play.

As the CIA and MI6 toiled to control the situation, the city became their post-Iraq War-era Casablanca. All roads led there.

For someone like Henry Marlow, getting in and out of Milan by plane was not as easy as it had been in the early days of his career. For the entire intelligence community, the game had changed. The age of flying in one day, then visiting an MI6 substation or getting a new passport via dead drop the next, was over. Any non-official cover officer operating in the modern age could no longer rely on a stack of fake passports hidden away in a train station locker or safe deposit box. Second-rate gangsters could no longer dole out passports. All because of something that no one had seen coming.

In the spy game – much as in life – the most painful changes occurred when something that had been taken totally for granted suddenly became a problem. For spies, it was the assumption that they could always travel in and out of countries using fake passports.

As a system, it should have been faultless. The forgeries were so good it would take hours of analysis to even raise doubts about a passport's authenticity. The customs agencies operated in such an isolated manner, it was easy to travel anywhere you pleased, under any name. Then technology started to catch up, and agencies began linking to each other via computer in real-time.

Travel to one country under an assumed identity, and all the biometric data associated with it – fingerprint, date of birth, face, and, increasingly, iris – was forever linked to one passport and one person. You couldn't simply change one detail and keep all the others. It was a package deal. Which meant that you couldn't enter a country again with a different name. And for a spy, it didn't get more fundamental than that.

Changing your identity in-country presented a variety of new risks. Hotels and car rental firms now routinely provided passport data to immigration services.

For agencies with multi-billion budgets like CIA, MI6, NSA, and GCHQ, creating perfect copies of new fake passports wasn't the issue. It was getting the data uploaded into the target country's databases. Which was why the Americans had been spending increasing amounts of their budget recruiting agents in foreign border-control agencies who can physically access the computers that hold and process the data, then either alter or delete it. But recruiting such people takes time, and is high-risk.

For someone in Henry Marlow's position, that wasn't an option. He didn't have access to GCHQ's malware programs that could remotely manipulate biometric data. Which left him only one choice: he'd have to sacrifice one clean alias to get into Italy undetected, knowing that after he was done, it would be torched for good.

It was a sacrifice worth making. For what he was planning, he didn't need any identity other than his own.

Marlow had taken the Malpensa Express train from the airport to the Milano Centrale station. Even though it had been a long time since he'd last been in the city, its familiar beats soon came back to him: the sound of buskers playing mandolins in the Piazza Argentina; the rapid, animated conversation between friends; the smell of zingy San

Marzano tomatoes and fresh dough seasoned with sea salt emanating from the open shopfronts of takeaway pizzerias.

At its centre, Milan was unmistakably grey. Not just the concrete architecture, but even the light, especially after sunset as Henry Marlow found it. The rest of Italy considered the city an exception to their *bel paese* ('beautiful country') image, seeing it as unwelcoming, and far less colourful than its famous coastlines and countryside. Such attitudes had forced Milan to constantly reinvent itself, giving it an energy found in few Italian cities. An energy that, as darkness fell, Henry Marlow could feel himself thriving on – stalking towards the Buonarotti district to the west of the city centre. That was Marlow's kind of place. Low-key trattorias and budget hotels. Dirty bars. Men in leather jackets hanging around on steps, smoking cigarettes.

Nestled among the residential blocks and vacant shopfronts was the intentionally vague-sounding *Contabile Agenzia Milano*. If you were genuinely in need of an accountant as "*Contabile*" suggested, then you'd be fresh out of luck. There were no phone numbers listed on the outside. Just a metal plate on the pillar outside advertising the firm, which also stressed that they were "*Solo su appuntamento*" – "By appointment only".

The *agenzia* took up the first floor, but also owned the surrounding floors – all empty. From the outside, it appeared to be just another middling business which deserved barely a glance from the street. Behind its heavy, wooden front doors was a security system light years ahead of the building's appearance. A system that Henry Marlow knew inside out.

Bypassing the locks required only a simple electric pick gun, but everything after would require precision.

He could tell from the status on the alarm code panel in the foyer that the building was empty. He'd suspected as much after making a brief pass across the road fifteen minutes earlier. The panel beeped, awaiting an entry code. Without one, the system would start wailing, and prompt an auto-response to the local *Carabinieri*.

Marlow entered his old code – knowing it would prompt an alert at Vauxhall Cross – then followed it up with a correct one. Once it was accepted, he pressed a button on his watch, starting a countdown of three minutes – the quickest that a raid team could arrive.

Having flown in, Marlow had been unarmed. He still had an active contact in the city, though. A contact who cared little about Marlow's current disavowed status. Marlow had met him on *Viale Papiniano*, making the hand-off between the double rows of parked cars in the middle of the street: out of sight at street level, overhanging trees blocked them from the view of the many apartment balconies above. Marlow had waited until he reached a quiet alley, then waistbanded the Glock 48 he had just purchased for a very competitive price.

Taking no chances, he drew the weapon while ascending the gloomy staircase to the first floor. He took his time, letting his fingers get used to the dimensions of the gun, which was a little on the slim side for his liking.

The lock on the first-floor office door was even easier than the front door, but he didn't open it yet. The substation had a back-up alarm that ran from an off-grid electrical source. Unlike downstairs, he had no code for it. It required a brute force solution: cutting off the power supply.

Following the run of the wire from the back-up alarm

panel along the wall skirting, he found the connection to the building's two electrical sources and cut them both.

In the darkness, the set-up appeared normal. What could have been any accountancy or administrative office. Several desks were covered in paperwork. Filing cabinets lined a wall.

A closer inspection of the office revealed a curious emphasis on security, with a bank of CCTV screens which would have shown all entry points to the building had the power not been cut. There was a conspicuous and heavy-duty safe. And the windows – barely visible to the apartment blocks next door – had been whited out with paint. Not even shadows could be seen from outside.

Marlow checked his watch.

One minute twenty left.

He found the hidden cupboard door he remembered, and opened up its false front. Inside was another safe, where the agency kept its most important documents and secrets. There was just enough space for someone to stand with the cupboard door closed behind them, which made a perfect hiding spot. But Marlow had no intention of getting in.

He took off his shoes, being careful to line them up as near to where the door closed as he could – shoes pointing inwards towards the safe.

He checked his watch again.

Under a minute now.

He stopped the timer and took his hiding spot under a desk across the room. He chambered a bullet while he could still get away with the noise.

Then he waited.

. . .

The aux had smiled warmly when he received the picture of his target on his burner phone. Anyone in his position knew Henry all too well. Most of MI6's auxiliaries had spent the better part of a year chasing his shadow around Europe until the trail finally went cold. The opportunity to redeem himself was welcome.

He was the same age as Marlow, a veteran of the auxiliary business. He wore black boots, black trousers, and a plain dark t-shirt under a casual jacket. He looked like he'd chosen them from the budget range of a supermarket. Zero ostentation: zero attention drawn. He parked his scooter a street away, then radioed to Control:

'Approaching the building now.' He muted reception on his radio so nothing could be transmitted. He could only be heard. The last thing he wanted was any sudden feedback or distraction in his ear. Against Marlow, that would be a death sentence.

With their comms to Milan muted, the tension in Control was palpable. All phone calls suspended. Everyone silent, listening only to the sound of the aux ascending the stairs, one creeping step at a time.

The office door was unlocked. Off the latch.

Using the barrel of his gun, the aux nudged it open a few inches. His heart was in his mouth as he stepped inside, knowing that if Marlow was there he'd do his firing early. In the darkness and with no backlighting, Marlow would aim at torso height and hope for the best, so the aux crouched down at first, taking in a view of the office from ground level, checking under desks.

It was clear.

At the back of the office, Marlow had a vice-like grip on the edge of a desk, hanging underneath with his feet off the

ground, perched on a rail. His plan was certainly unortho-
dox, but if he wanted to control the situation against a
trained aux, something outside the norm was required.

Watching on the wall back at Vauxhall Cross, Winston
shifted his weight from foot to foot. 'I don't like this,' he
said.

Across the room, Archer called out, 'Sir, I just
rechecked the grid. That raid team schedule is old. There's
a raid team ten minutes away.'

Swann didn't even try to appear innocent.

He shook his head in disgust at her.

She said, 'Now you know how the sausages are made,
Leo.'

Winston barked, 'Get them there, Miles. Now! And tell
the aux to stand down.'

'I can't do that,' he replied.

'What do you mean?'

'If they're going in heavy and silent, they switch their
radios to transmit only. We can't stop him.'

'Christ...' Winston turned to the wall, watching a
decibel meter showing the tiny deviations in noise picked up
by the aux's radio.

On a map of the area next to it, a flashing dot showed
the location of the raid team.

Winston exhaled. 'They're not going to make it.' He
directed his anger at Swann. 'You better pray that Henry
Marlow doesn't die in there, Imogen.'

The aux was aware of Marlow's history with the substation,

and knew all its processes and hiding spots. Convinced that there was nowhere else to go, he crouched down by the false front on the cupboard, and then shone a pocket torch towards the bottom of the door.

The aux held the light there, then leaned forward. The moment he saw the shadow of a pair of shoes under the door frame, he shut the light off.

Having taken the bait, the aux stood up and pocketed his torch. He took aim at the cupboard. There wasn't a doubt in his mind that Henry Marlow was behind the door. He couldn't hesitate. Before Marlow could burst out, the aux unleashed five bullets at the door. Three high, then two low to make sure he caught him as he fell.

Using the noise as cover, Marlow dropped his feet to the ground to get ready.

The aux waited for the inevitable thud of Marlow's body hitting the cupboard floor.

It didn't come.

The second the aux opened the door and discovered the empty cupboard, Marlow grabbed the underside of the desk and picked it up, rushing the aux. All he saw was an upright table charging towards him. Before the aux could get a shot off, Marlow had slammed him back against the cupboard.

The decibel meter in the Control room showed a sudden spike in activity. The commotion played out through the speakers.

For a moment, Winston thought that the aux had somehow subdued Marlow. 'There weren't any shots,' he said. 'Why weren't there shots?'

Before Swann could answer, two different voices came through the speakers. One snarling with effort, the other groaning in pain.

Winston snapped his fingers at Ryan. 'I need that team there now...'

When the aux landed on his back, his gun fell out of his hands and bounced away. Marlow stood over him, grinning. He took aim at the aux's face.

'I was hoping they'd send you, Rafferty,' said Marlow, kicking his gun out of reach. 'I see you're still under the impression the Service pays you by the bullet.' He backed off, motioning for him to get up.

Rafferty struggled out from under the desk and raised his hands.

Marlow tossed a cable tie at Rafferty's feet. 'You know what to do with that,' he said.

Rafferty tied his hands in front of him, then tightened the cable with his teeth.

Marlow said, 'Tighter.'

After tightening the cable, Rafferty slumped against the cupboard, the wind knocked out of him. He sighed, resigned to his fate. 'You're wasting your breath and your time if you want safe codes. You might as well get this over with.'

'I don't want the safe,' Marlow replied. 'I want information.'

'What kind of information?'

'Why they're after me.'

'I think you know why.'

'Not that. I'm talking about Lyon. This. *You*. Why did they send an aux instead of a raid team?'

'I've no idea.'

'You're lying.'

'Am I?' asked Rafferty. 'When you were in my position, how many times did you ask why?'

Marlow didn't reply.

Rafferty went on, 'I don't know. I don't *want* to know. And I don't care.' He looked up, suddenly hopeful. 'Any chance of a smoke?'

Marlow wasn't going to let Rafferty derail his questions. 'Who's Duncan Grant?'

'Never heard of him,' Rafferty said.

Marlow took a forceful step forward and punched him in the gut.

While Rafferty flopped to the floor, Marlow took aim at his knees.

'You can still walk out of here. As long as I get answers. Who's Duncan Grant?'

'Winston's new protégé.'

'Any good?'

'So they say.'

'Is he dirty?'

Rafferty laughed. 'He's as pure as the driven snow. Remember what that was like, Henry?'

'I need to know I can trust him.'

'Trust him? Grant is in charge of bringing you in. If you want to spin a tale to get out of this Lyon thing...'

For the first time, Marlow made the shift from being aggressive to losing his temper. He grabbed Rafferty by the front of his jacket. 'Hey, look at me.'

With his life on the line, Rafferty decided to go down swinging. 'You killed three of our own. Go to hell.'

'Look at me!' Marlow yelled. His eyes were wide, piercing through the darkness. 'I didn't kill anyone…I was never in Lyon!'

The sentence sent a shockwave through the Control room, Marlow's words clearly spiking the decibel counter.

Swann shook her head, complaining to Winston, 'Leo, he knows we can hear this.'

Winston stepped closer to the speaker, raising his arm. 'Quiet!'

Marlow continued making his case: 'This is the first time I've been in Europe since they tried to kill me. After a while, I let that slide. Because I was done. I was out. And if they hadn't set me up over Lyon I would have stayed out. That's what I realise now: it never stops. The lies. The killing. You give them your life, and they keep on taking. Not anymore. I want to set up a meet.'

Rafferty asked, 'With who?'

'Duncan Grant.'

'Then you're talking to the wrong person.'

'I'm not talking to you.' Marlow slammed Rafferty's head against the wall, knocking him out clean. Marlow then held Rafferty's lapel up to his mouth to ensure that Control could hear him. 'Look, you're going to try and keep me on the line until the back-up team gets here, and that's not going to happen. So I'll keep this simple: I want to talk to

Duncan Grant. Place Bellecour, Lyon. Tomorrow. Ten a.m.'

Winston asked Archer, 'Can we get their phone lines–'

Before he could finish, the audio signal flatlined on the wall.

'He's gone,' Archer confirmed.

Still hopeful, Winston asked, 'How far out is the back-up team?'

'Two minutes.'

Swann backed away, disconsolate. 'Forget it,' she said. 'He'll be long gone by then. If we're lucky he'll have left Rafferty alive.'

Winston was dumbfounded. '*That's* your takeaway from that exchange?'

'Come on, you don't really buy all that innocence crap, do you? The guy's been off the reservation for five years. There's no telling what sort of crazy shit he's been telling himself.'

'It doesn't make sense,' said Winston. 'If he wants Édith Lagrange then why ask us for Grant?'

'Because he wants Grant *out* the way, with all of our back-up teams so he can get to Lagrange. Christ,' she exclaimed to herself, 'it's like watching a child playing draughts with chess pieces.'

Winston said to Archer, 'Get Duncan Grant on the line. His Lyon assignment just got bigger.'

25

There were no available flights from Tallinn's small airport to anywhere in France let alone Lyon, so Winston had called in a favour from 'a brother at Langley'. Catching the private plane had saved Grant a potential layover in Germany and a loss of at least five hours.

A CIA Learjet had been on its way to Madrid from Helsinki, which made the slight detour a breeze. After Grant had explained his situation, the CIA staff on board insisted they take him direct to Lyon instead of Paris as initially planned.

Grant felt like he'd aged ten years since he was last in Lyon. MI6 had thrown him into not just the deep end, but a wild, rolling ocean. And so far, he had stayed afloat.

When the call came from Winston that a meet had been set for the next day, the thought of coming face to face with Marlow instilled a fear in him that he hadn't felt since the first day of SAS training. Not a fear of being hurt or killed, but a fear of the unknown.

In a way, he was relieved to have Édith Lagrange's

safety occupying him that night rather than Henry Marlow. He'd got sucked into listening to more of the Marlow recordings. He told himself that he should switch them off, but each new entry seemed to promise some kind of answer to unlocking the mythology of Henry Marlow. An hour passed. Then another. Before Grant knew it, it was nearly midnight, and they were starting their descent into Lyon.

Winston had warned him, and now there was no denying it: Marlow was getting inside Duncan Grant's head.

As instructed, Lagrange hadn't left Interpol headquarters all evening. She met Grant at the main security gate, giving the sceptical guards the okay to let him in.

It hadn't been long ago that Interpol only kept regular business hours. If a request from a police force came in late on Friday, it could be Monday afternoon before it was spotted. They didn't even open at weekends. The days of Interpol being a retirement home for police officers were long gone. Now the lights were on around the clock, even if the offices were still largely empty. The only obvious sign of activity was an occasional figure backlit at one of the many internal office windows.

Lagrange walked Grant across the deserted lobby, the lights turned down. 'It's nice to see you again, Alex,' she said.

She knew that his name wasn't really Alex, but she also knew that there were many things she would never find out about him.

Grant kept his voice low, as sound carried far in the

cavernous greenhouse-like lobby. 'I only wish the circumstances were better, Detective.'

'I can't imagine what all this is about. You really think I'm in danger because of some photographs?' She waited for him to answer, but he didn't. 'You can't talk about it. I understand.'

'Not here,' he said. When he realised she was heading towards the lifts, he reached for her arm, redirecting her. 'Stairs, please.'

'You know, we are in Interpol headquarters. It's safe here.'

'Then you're a lot more trusting than I would be right now.' His eyes were everywhere as they ascended the stairs. And they needed to be. The building offered plenty of opportunities for physical observation. Hundreds of office windows and balconies above overlooked the lobby.

'I don't expect you want to stay here all night,' said Grant.

'Is there a safe house?' she asked.

'There is, but we shouldn't use it. Our suspect has inside knowledge. I'd rather we went somewhere he doesn't know. There were no pictures of the inside of your building or apartment. If he'd taken them, they would have been there. It's our safest option.'

'Is this man in Lyon?'

Grant had already done some calculations on the plane. He said, 'He was in Milan earlier tonight. So, about five hours away by car. If he had got on a flight somehow, he could be in Lyon before the night's out. We're tracking every flight in and out of Milan Malpensa Airport, as well as Parma, and any other Italian airport servicing France.

It's doubtful that he would risk the exposure, but I don't want to mess around.'

'What is the saying?' asked Lagrange. 'I am in your hands.'

Grant was impressed with how she was handling the situation. Also surprised. She might have been a detective, but she was pretty green even for regular police. Yet she hadn't long found out that a hardened intelligence operative suspected of gunning down one of her colleagues, and three of Grant's, could be hunting her next. For someone with that kind of knowledge, she was either being extraordinarily brave or recklessly naïve.

Grant checked his watch. Marlow could conceivably enter French territory in just a few hours. 'We should get out of here as soon as possible.' He eyed her with a forensic intensity as she packed up her things.

As she typed in her password to log off from her sleeping computer, it reminded him of how quickly she could do it considering its length.

Trying to lighten the mood a little, Grant asked, 'Do you know the most popular password in the world?'

Lagrange logged out of all her databases, then shut the computer down. 'One two three four five six.'

'The world would be much safer if people were as scrupulous with their passwords as you are.'

'Most people are morons.' Lagrange tried to look unshaken as she picked up her bag. Inside, she felt like a guilty person playing the part of an innocent person. Being careful with every word, every action, was stressful and exhausting. Breezing past Grant, she added, 'I'm not like most people.'

Once they had cleared the security gate outside,

Lagrange paused to rub one of her feet. She leaned on Grant's shoulder. 'I don't know if we will get a taxi at this time,' she said.

'Sorry,' replied Grant. 'We can't do that. I'm not putting our trust in random taxi drivers who happen to pull up just when you need them. Once you're inside a taxi, you've handed over all your control to them. Where they go, when they stop. What if the doors lock? If we walk, I stay in control. I can see what I need to.'

The message was getting through to the detective. 'And we can run.'

Grant nodded. 'If we have to.'

26

Lagrange lived in a loft apartment in a traditional Lyonnais block overlooking the River Saône. There was only one way in and one way out: the front door. Although it limited options in an emergency escape, it also simplified securing the building.

The coolness of the stairwell was a welcome relief. Even approaching midnight, the air outside was warm and humid. The tension and unpredictable nature of the situation had brought Lagrange out in a light sweat. Not visible. But she was keenly aware of it under her arms. The relief didn't last long as they climbed the narrow winding staircase to the fifth floor.

It was at the end of a corridor. *Not ideal*, thought Grant. *Only one way out.*

He'd chosen Lagrange's apartment because in a formula of places that both he and Marlow didn't know, versus places he knew but Marlow didn't, the latter seemed the logical choice. Now he felt like he'd been too hasty in his selection.

When they got inside, Lagrange kicked her shoes off and headed for her computer while Grant stayed in the kitchen. It didn't take long to find the one item he expected any French household to have: a bottle of wine.

She was about to point him towards the cupboards for glasses, when he opened the bottle and proceeded to pour the contents into the sink.

He held the bottle upside down, turning it in rapid circles, then stopped, creating a whirlpool inside. The bottle went from full to empty in a matter of seconds.

Before she could protest, Grant said, 'I wouldn't have let you drink it, anyway.' He took the empty bottle to the front door. 'A single glass of wine can reduce your reaction time by ten, fifteen per cent. Factor in how tired you'll be at this hour, and you could be looking at a loss of nearly a quarter. I can't have that if it's me hauling you down a staircase at three in the morning.'

She looked over the computer monitor in confusion until it clicked what he was doing.

He balanced the bottle upside down on its mouth, placing it just an inch away from the inside of the door.

'What if they break it down?' asked Lagrange.

Grant shrugged. 'We'll hear that too.'

While she took a shower, Grant took his chance to recce the apartment. Not that there was much of it beyond the tiny kitchen and living room. Lagrange's bedroom could barely fit a double bed, and the en suite was little more than a cupboard with plumbing.

No one gets into police work in France for the money, he thought.

He closed the curtains near her computer desk, and noticed the expensive equipment she was using. The hard drive was top tier, super-fast, and she had a stack of external hard drives.

For personal use – backing up photos, music, or basic documents – it was surely overkill. And she didn't seem like the online-gaming type.

Can't be for Interpol Internal Affairs use.

She was far too exacting and cautious to take chances with official police data off-site.

He paused in the kitchen, taking in the full view of the apartment. Officers were trained to look closely, then pull back and take in the bigger picture. It was easy to get bogged down in minutiae and rush to conclusions about someone because of how sparsely their kitchen was stocked, or what computer equipment they owned. Taking in the apartment as a whole, it was clearer for Grant to see that Lagrange spent most of her time at the computer desk: the sofa didn't have indentations from prolonged sitting; the TV remote control was next to the TV rather than on the sofa, and it was dusty, with little to no wear on the buttons.

By contrast, the chair at the computer desk had worn arms, and there was a lighter, well-trodden path on the wooden floor leading towards the kitchen. There were no photographs. Anywhere. The books on her shelves were all worn and cracked, almost nothing from the last ten years.

She used to be a reader, but not for a while now. She spends most of her time at the computer. Doesn't go out much. Lonely. A lot of used coffee mugs in the kitchen, which means late nights and long computer sessions: whatever she's wired into, she won't even stop to rinse a mug after using it. And it's the first thing she went for when she got home.

Lagrange reappeared in the living room in a towelling

bathrobe wrapped tightly around herself. When her eyes met Grant's she pursed her lips. Although her glasses had clear frames, she felt naked without them.

Grant got the impression it was the first time anyone had seen her like that for a long time.

She dumped the many coffee mugs into the sink. 'I'm sorry about the mess. I didn't know I was going to have company.'

'Just pretend I'm not here,' said Grant.

She rolled her eyes at the absurdity. 'Of course. No problem.' She tried to sound casual as she asked, 'How much do you know about this Henry Marlow?'

'He was one of our best. For a long time.'

'Until what?'

'You work Internal Affairs, Detective. Do you always understand people's reasons for doing what they do?'

'Not really. Sometimes we never find out.'

Grant said, 'There are three things that make people turn: pressure, opportunity, and rationalisation.'

Lagrange bobbed her head. 'The fraud triangle.'

'There must be a lot of temptation in your field,' he said.

'There is temptation in every field.'

'When I was recruited they warned me about it. That certain people might try to turn me. I've never had any money, so there will never be a financial pressure on me. Opportunities, you can resist. That's a matter of discipline. Rationalisation? Maybe that's what got Henry Marlow. If you stick around long enough, learn the game, see all the angles... it's easier to tell yourself that what you're doing is okay.'

Lagrange stopped washing the mugs, zoning out as she

spoke. 'I keep thinking about Claude. His family. How heavy the guilt must have been for him. Walking around every day with this terrible secret that no one else knew about.'

'Except for you.'

She turned the tap off and gave a Gallic shrug. 'In a way, only Internal Affairs can understand these people.'

'You have to,' Grant agreed. 'It can't be easy, though.'

'I'm an outsider wherever I go. It's always been like that. It's so stupid. I know I'm an adult, but sometimes I still feel the way I did when I was a teenager. How everyone else seems to have it all figured out. What's funny is if they knew I was Internal Affairs I would be even more of a...' She tried to think of the word. '*Étrangère.*'

Grant nodded. 'An outsider.'

'It's okay, though. It won't be long before I'm sent some-where else. To infiltrate.' She paused, thinking about the wine Grant had poured down the sink. She desperately wanted a glass. 'You always have to be on the outside, you know? Close. But never too close. And when the job is done, you're on your own again. I'm sure you know all about that.'

It wasn't a stretch for Grant to see the parallels. 'I knew what I was getting into. I chose this.'

She asked herself quickly, 'What is the expression...? This is what you sign up for.'

'*Exactement,*' Grant replied.

'Why did you choose this?'

After thinking for a moment, he said, 'Because a solitary life is the only kind I can bear.'

'You can't be alone all the time. There are things that everyone needs.'

It was still Grant's baritone voice, but there was a fragility, a vulnerability there now. 'You'd be surprised what you can live without.'

'I don't believe that.' Lagrange considered his statement further. 'And I'm not sure you believe it either.'

The moment that followed lasted no longer than a second. But they both felt it happen.

Lagrange suddenly became keenly aware that she was standing in front of a strange man in her kitchen wearing only a bathrobe. 'I should go to bed,' she said, a diffidence in her eyes and body language. 'I'm sorry there's only...' She gestured towards the sofa.

Grant waved it off politely. 'Thank you. But I'll be staying up.'

The last thing she did before turning in for the night was shut down her computer. As she typed her password, Grant recognised the familiar pattern on the keyboard, the same cadence and rhythm.

If there had been a gun to his head, he would have sworn that it was the same password as Lagrange's Interpol terminal.

It wasn't entirely faulty logic. Lagrange believed – rightly – that a complicated password was a good one. But in order to remember it, she had to use it for multiple accounts and computers. Trying to remember multiple complex passwords was a recipe for getting locked out at a crucial time.

While Lagrange slept next door, Grant got to thinking about her manner. The timbre of her voice. Her behaviour. Everything about her. Her life was apparently at stake, yet she hadn't made a single phone call or sent a text – not to anyone at Interpol, or asked a single question about whether the French interior security agency was aware of her situation. She had even neglected to attach the internal door chain. In her position, Grant would have been demanding that heavy furniture be placed in front of the door. Instead, she seemed satisfied with putting her life in the hands of a British spy that she'd spent barely a few hours with.

It wasn't merely that she believed an attack from Henry Marlow was unlikely. She was acting as if she knew for certain that it was impossible.

He searched for his GCHQ contact on his phone, then tapped out a message:

"*I need a favour...*"

27

Lagrange rose at seven the next morning, finding Grant standing in the kitchen making coffee.

'Good morning,' he said. 'Would you like some?'

'Thank you,' she replied. 'I don't know how you stayed awake.'

'Practice,' he answered. He was still a full two days away from the longest he'd spent awake. He poured her a cup. 'It's good that the French won't take coffee with milk. There's only so much damage I can do to black coffee.'

'Thank you,' she said with a smile, taking the mug towards the living room.

'I was wondering,' he said, tentatively following her. 'I thought I should check for any malware or phishing emails.'

She waved it off. 'I never fall for those.'

'All the same. There might be something you've over-looked. Even from a few days ago. I can almost guarantee that Marlow will have tried to gain access to your calendar.'

Lagrange stared impotently at the computer. Saying no to such a simple request would raise suspicions. There was nothing else for it. She made her way towards the computer.

Grant assured her, 'I promise not to look at anything personal.'

He made a show of hanging back while she entered her password. She offered him the chair but stayed right behind him.

He scrolled casually through the inbox. 'No red flags there...' he said to himself, drinking the last of his coffee. He then held his empty mug out. 'Would you mind? I'm starting to feel like a man who's not slept.'

Satisfied that there was nothing in her email to worry about, Lagrange took the mug. 'Sure,' she said.

The few moments while her back was turned were all that Grant needed. He opened an email in the Junk folder with the subject line "*FINAL NOTICE!!! Subscription cancelled*". The English made it stand out from the native French spam.

The email contained a single link, a long string of numbers. When Grant clicked on it, the page refreshed, then returned to normal.

By the time Lagrange returned, Grant had already deleted the email and purged the recycle bin.

He had completed the hardest part of his plan, but it would all have been for nothing without the final detail.

Instead of announcing that he was done and relinquishing control of the computer, he used a combination of keys as a shortcut which logged off the current user.

'Ah, sorry,' Grant said. 'I'm not used to Windows...' He stood up, offering her the seat. 'I'll take that if you wouldn't mind signing back in.'

Lagrange handed him his coffee, then sat down, but didn't type straight away.

After considering her options, she decided that there was only one way to figure out what he was up to. By playing along.

To instil confidence that there had been no foul play, Grant stood back as she reopened the email window.

He pointed her around various messages, before concluding that all was well. He went back to the kitchen with his coffee.

With Grant out of sight of the screen, Lagrange quickly clicked around the internet history, file history, and recycle bin. Everything important on the hard drive was protected and encrypted. If Grant had even tried and failed to open anything she would know about it.

'I better get ready,' she said, retreating to her bedroom. She wondered if paranoia was getting the better of her.

Grant poured his coffee down the sink. For what was to come, he needed to be free of any nervous energy. It wasn't long before he needed to get to Place Bellecour.

The mere thought of Henry Marlow being out there somewhere, waiting for him, brought Grant out in a cold sweat.

28

The entirety of Winston's staff had been called in for the Henry Marlow meet. Nightshift stayed on, dayshift came in early to prep. Someone had convinced Winston to go home for some sleep, but he was gone barely four hours, reappearing at six a.m. when the cleaners were still vacuuming the corridors.

All the things that made Place Bellecour ideal for Henry Marlow were what made it bad for MI6. First was scale. It was one of the biggest open spaces in Lyon, and the third-biggest square in France. That meant personnel eaten up for surveillance, when Winston wanted as many available bodies for grab teams as possible. The next issue was seasonal: Lyon was still at the height of summer, which meant crowds. It didn't rule out marksmen entirely, but it complicated matters, and meant that strategy would need to be more fluid than planned.

Setting up on rooftops didn't bring any guarantees for sighting. If they set up on one roof and Marlow led Grant to another part of the square, he could easily be out of range – or at least make the shot so long that it was too risky. The last thing MI6 needed was the blood of an innocent tourist on its hands.

During his briefing, Winston elaborated on a further point of difficulty. Namely, access.

He pulled up various surveillance shots taken that morning, showing the extent of what the operatives on the ground faced. He said, 'Three entire sides of the square open up to the pavements. If you factor in tram stops as well, then Marlow has between fifteen to twenty options. And we simply don't have the manpower to control them all. Then there's this problem...'

Archer switched the photos to screenshots from various Facebook feeds of Lyon residents, all sharing the same post.

Winston explained, 'Twelve hours ago, this post appeared on the Mayor of Lyon's Facebook page, declaring the Ferris wheel as free of all charges, from ten to eleven a.m., for one day only.' He paused. 'Today. The mayor knows nothing about it. Someone hacked his account last night.'

Swann said, 'Marlow.'

'The mayor's issued a statement assuring the city that the post was a hoax, but there's no putting the toothpaste back in the tube now. Our survey teams on the ground are already reporting large queues at the Ferris wheel and a square packed full of children and families.'

Swann asked, 'We have grab teams in place, right?'

'We do,' replied Winston. 'In such a setting, they're going to be our priority option. Our first contact on the ground is Duncan Grant whose call sign will be Mobile One. He is unarmed. If there is a kill shot and I deem that we have no other alternative, then we have Increment snipers in place. The Foreign Secretary has signed the Section Seven, so be aware: this is a life-critical operation. We have DGSI helping us on the ground, but I make the final call on a kill order.'

Olivia Christie stood silently at the back of the room. MI6 hadn't openly assassinated anyone since nineteen sixty-one, when deputy director George Kennedy Young had ordered a hit in Iran without consulting his chief. Christie didn't relish the prospect of being at the helm should that fact need updating.

Winston finished by saying, 'Let's look alive.'

Christie took him aside while everyone else got feverishly to work with the teams on the ground.

She said, 'The Foreign Sec has cleared his lunchtime for me to update him.'

Winston was adamant. 'We'll have good news for him, ma'am. I'm sure of it.'

'Is the area locked down?'

'The surrounding streets,' said Winston. 'DGSI is helping us out.'

Direction Générale de la Sécurité Intérieure was France's version of MI5, responsible for security on domestic soil. Bringing them in had been a necessity. But with cooperation came inevitable conflict. MI6 might have wanted to bring in Marlow, but the DGSI's priority was ensuring the safety of the French people. Those were not necessarily mutually beneficial outcomes. What MI6 was willing to risk could be unthinkable to the French. There was no way to know until Winston had to make the call.

The digital clock on the wall showed ten minutes to ten, Lyon time.

Winston did his last checks around the room. Senior

staff were ready to go. CCTV and Survey teams were already transmitting. And GCHQ was monitoring every active mobile signal in the square. Field officers had been prepping on the ground since dawn.

In his head, Winston felt as ready as he could be.

Ten minutes to go.

There was no going back.

Little did Winston know that a simple takeaway coffee was about to turn the operation on its head.

29

Grant wouldn't trust anyone else to protect Detective Lagrange during the Marlow meet, so he had decided that the safest place for her was inside Interpol headquarters – provided she didn't allow visitors, or take any calls. She gave strict instructions to both security and the reception team to deny any knowledge of her whereabouts should anyone enquire. Regardless of the outcome at Place Bellecour, Lagrange swore that she wouldn't leave with anyone but him.

Throughout Grant's training, it had been repeated time and again: details matter. It matters when you talk to the person sitting next to you on a plane. On a transatlantic flight, that means nothing you say for five hours can contradict or raise doubts about anything else. If you claim to have studied literature but your eyes go glassy at the mention of James Joyce, you're blown. If you claim to be in finance but can't contribute in a discussion about Bitcoin and cryptocurrency, you're blown. Every lie out of your mouth must balance perfectly with every other lie you've told.

Because details matter.

That message hadn't got through to Fabrice Gasquet of DGSI. If it had, then Gasquet wouldn't have got out of his surveillance van that was parked off a side street, wearing his black fatigues with a medical-emergency pouch holstered to his belt. The pouch had a red cross set against a black background (so that it didn't hinder the camouflage of his dark clothing on night ops), and was unique to the DGSI.

It was a detail that Henry Marlow immediately clocked as he passed the intelligence operative in the street.

He could smell stale beer on Gasquet as he exited a coffee shop, carrying a badly needed espresso.

That one coffee told Marlow a number of important things. Firstly, that the French officers assisting were poorly briefed, as Gasquet should have been on the lookout for anyone even remotely fitting Marlow's description. Gasquet hadn't even reacted, immediately put off by Marlow's disguise: he was wearing dusty, backpacker clothes and carrying a large rucksack. He held a map out in front of him to confirm his tourist status, an archetype that Lyon was full of.

Gasquet's actions also told Marlow that if one of their team was heading out for coffee ten minutes before a target's ETA, the DGSI were uncommitted, ill-prepared, or both.

His confidence swelled. Now he knew the best street to use for an escape.

As he boarded a tram a few brief stops from the square, Marlow smiled, remembering his training.

Details matter.

Grant was in the centre of the square, wearing a white shirt with the sleeves rolled up. He could feel individual beads of sweat trickling from his armpits, down his sides.

There were two scenarios he was determined to avoid: a foot chase, and a shooting. In either situation, he would lose Marlow for sure.

He tried his best not to react to everything that moved. Which meant trusting the Survey teams. He'd been focussing on the trams, but they were almost all full when they arrived at the square. Far too many people to keep track of.

The sun was high and already blazing hot. Even as word leaked out from the baffled Ferris wheel operators that there was indeed a charge as normal, the families were still hanging around. Promises to kids had already been made. Most were going to queue and pay as normal. The reward for parents that stood their ground on principle was a chorus of wailing and screaming children.

At Winston's request, the various posts all sounded off, giving the all-clear on their positions.

'He's going to come in by tram,' Grant said.

'Are you kidding?' Survey Two countered. 'A three-hundred-pound gorilla could wander in here unseen.'

Grant looked up at the marksmen on the roofs overlooking the west side of the square. They were barely noticeable under their grey camo sheets. Rumours of the Increment had circulated for years, but only sporadic mentions of their missions had ever been reported. They were a cadre of operators working within MI6's General Support Branch, leading clandestine insertion and extraction missions, secret military assistance to foreign powers, and covert intelligence gathering. They were all, to a man, crack shots.

If a mission went south and they were caught, the British government would deny all knowledge of them. There would be no emotional appeals via the media for their return. Just lengthy prison sentences wherever they'd been found. Their ranks featured SAS and SBS operatives who were at the very top of their class. If Marlow was spotted on Place Bellecour, there would be nowhere for him to run.

Grant continued peering around, his back to a young boy cycling towards him on a BMX bike, smoking a cigarette.

Survey One saw him first. 'Mobile One, watch this kid. Your six o'clock.'

Survey Two: 'He's just a kid, Survey One...'

The boy braked by pressing the sole of a battered trainer onto the tyre, stopping himself in front of Grant. He was no more than thirteen and already had the attitude of the early twenties gangbangers from his neighbourhood.

'*Tire-toi*,' Grant said, still concentrating on the trams. ('Beat it.')

The kid took a drag on his cigarette, then slid off his backpack.

The Survey teams called over one another, 'What's in the bag...' 'Eyes open, Mobile One...'

The kid produced a brown Jiffy bag and shoved it into Grant's chest. He cycled off into the crowd without a word.

The rooftop snipers followed him on their scopes towards the tourist office, but by the time the Grab teams got there all they found was the kid's bike, along with the hoodie he'd been wearing, discarded on the ground.

The call went out, 'He's gone.'

At the edge of the square, having seen it all transpire as planned, Marlow took his cue and called the number pre-dialled into his phone.

Grant heard the ringing inside the bag before he could open it. He said, 'Control, I need a phone trace. Eyes up on anyone talking on a phone.'

Survey One's team leader muttered to her crew, 'Where the hell does he want us to start?'

Archer, Ryan, and Samantha on comms looked at their screens in dismay. Phone signals were popping up and disappearing faster than they could track.

Archer said, 'I've got three hundred and twenty-eight active mobiles in the square, Grant. This is going to take some time...'

Marlow had gleaned everything he needed from Google Maps on the overnight train from Turin, scoping out all the angles where snipers would set up, all the red zones they'd target. There was a good reason Street View visibility around government facilities was limited. For a public space like Place Bellecour, Marlow couldn't have learned much more from visiting in person.

Grant took out the phone from the bag and answered.

There was a strange steady drone running from Marlow's end. It was a background isolator. It played white noise anytime Marlow didn't speak. Whenever he did, the noise cut out like a radio DJ talking over the closing bars of a song. It stopped MI6 getting a read on the atmospherics of background noise that could give away his position.

Grant spoke first. 'I'm unarmed.'

'I know,' replied Marlow. 'But the Increment snipers overlooking the square aren't.'

'That's how it's got to be, Henry.'

'I want some privacy. Drop your earpiece on the ground, then step on it. Do it, or I walk.'

Winston told Grant, 'Do it.'

Grant took out his earpiece loop, then mashed it into the ground under his heel.

The only radios that Control now had were the Survey and Grab teams on the ground and the snipers. Grant was on his own.

'Good,' said Marlow. 'Now we can talk.'

Grant did a quick one eighty, knowing that Marlow would have made sure he had a visual to check that Grant had definitely destroyed the radio. All he could see was a crowd of faces, most of them hiding behind sunglasses.

Marlow chuckled. 'I was about to remark on how cool you look in that white shirt, then you start flapping around the place. I need your attention, Duncan.'

There was something beguiling and hypnotic about hearing Marlow's voice live – the voice that had been consuming his thoughts so heavily. Knowing that he was so close, it was hard for Grant not to be intimidated.

For all the relative intimacy, Marlow might as well have been on Mars. Grant kept getting tantalising flashes of potential suspects: a man with a disarmingly deep suntan, dressed like a fashionable local, wearing a blue polo shirt under a navy blazer, Persol sunglasses, canvas shoes, and carrying a briefcase. Then a man in baggy shorts and a sunhat seemed to be a match…

'If this is going to work,' said Marlow, 'I need you to focus on what I have to say.'

Grant made his way purposefully through the crowd. They had planned for this eventuality: he was going to cover off the square one sector at a time. 'And what do you have to say?' he asked.

'I didn't kill those people at the opera.'

'I know you didn't,' Grant replied.

For a moment, Marlow didn't know how to respond. 'The transcript of me and Rafferty in Milan didn't convince you of that.'

Grant said, 'I think that someone went to great lengths to place you at the opera. In order to be convincing, it couldn't be too obvious, like a print on a gun. But prints on a bomb that's meant to explode? That's a little more believable. Except, the killer at the opera was wearing latex gloves. I saw them. Why would you have set up the bomb and *then* put on gloves? The implied assumption, of course, was that you shot Rory and Ellen when you realised the bomb had failed. In which case, if you hadn't been wearing gloves and knew your prints could be on it, why would you have left the device behind?'

Marlow said, 'If me being framed is so clear to you then why are you chasing me?'

Grant replied, 'You're still a disavowed officer, Henry.'

'And you don't find it mildly absurd, charging an assassin with murder?'

'That's not up to me. But I think we can help each other.' Grant drifted out to the west border of the square.

'You're going to have to trust someone. You've got me. Or you've got the snipers.'

Marlow paused. 'You should look for a man called Martin Haslitt.'

'I know about Haslitt. Some would say that there's solid evidence you two are working together.'

'Such as?'

'How about the surveillance photographs of Detective Lagrange in your safe deposit box? Or the information that Claude Pinot wanted to sell us. Or Haslitt killing Lawrence Bloom two weeks after you'd been there.'

Despite the accusations, Marlow remained perfectly composed. 'Haslitt could have driven all of that. They had to set me up with something so serious that there was no other option but to issue a Section Seven on me. To make sure that I don't leave this square alive. That's why you have to protect me.'

'Protect you? Why would I do that?'

'I helped you escape the Hole for a reason, Grant.' Marlow paused to let it sink in. 'You'd be lying in a shallow grave in the Estonian countryside if it hadn't been for me. If I wanted rid of you, I would never have made that call.'

'Then why did you?' asked Grant.

Marlow didn't reply.

Grant went on, 'I want to know who was really responsible for the opera shooting, Henry. And I think you do too. I can protect you, but you have to come in and tell me what you know.'

Marlow puffed. 'You really have no idea who you're dealing with. The things I know would give you nightmares. You're talking about a world that you can't understand. You're not ready.'

'I'm ready,' Grant insisted. 'You risked your freedom to show up at Milan to make this meeting happen. Give me something, Henry.' He picked up his pace, sensing that Marlow would try to tie off the conversation soon; the longer he stayed out there, the greater his chances of being found. 'What about the files you stole from Lawrence Bloom's safe?'

'No,' Marlow replied. 'That's something I can't do. They're my insurance.'

'Give me something, *anything* that I can point to that either proves you're innocent, or points to someone who isn't.'

Marlow fired back, 'I gave you AC one eighty, what more do you need?'

Grant stopped in his tracks. AC stood for Anticorruption – a Hannibal file.

'What is that?' Grant asked.

Marlow replied, 'Are you telling me you didn't even follow up on the Red Notice? Don't they teach you *anything*?'

'Marlow,' Grant said carefully, '*nothing* came through to Interpol. I checked.'

'Then check again, because I sent it. It's everything you need.'

On the pavement, a man in his sixties was walking alongside someone who appeared to be his wife. The man gave the tiniest head flick towards Grant, then showed a spare radio earpiece in his palm. One of Winston's contingencies.

With Marlow about to run anyway, Grant figured it was worth the chance.

After giving the man the nod, they made the hand-off with the radio.

Grant crouched down, then waited to hear if Marlow had spotted it.

All Marlow said was, 'It's time to pick a side, Grant.'

Confident that he was out of Marlow's sight, Grant inserted the earpiece and heard full comms again.

The first thing he heard was the Increment snipers confirming that they had found a possible target.

Until he got off the phone, though, Grant couldn't offer any guidance on the target. He could only listen.

One of the Increment snipers was on the line. 'Control, this is Sniper Three. I have a positive ID.'

30

'How sure are you?' asked Winston.

He then got the answer that every task chief with kill-order authorisation dreads:

'Eight out of ten.'

Winston replied, 'Then you'd better clean your scope, Sniper Three, because I'm not issuing a kill order on anything less than ten.'

Sniper Two spoke up. 'I've got a ten, sir.'

Sniper One then cut in. 'It's not him, Sniper Two. Stand down.'

'It's him!'

Winston stared at the satellite image of the square, and the Survey teams' live feeds. All showing hundreds of people. He had nothing to go on but the snipers' word.

Swann stepped forward, taking control of the mic. 'Is your shot clear, Sniper Two?'

'Affirmative,' replied Sniper Two.

All eyes fell on Christie. She took no pleasure in issuing

it, but she couldn't see any other way out. 'Winston,' she said. 'Take him.'

Winston felt his breath quivering as he exhaled. 'Sniper Two, *only*,' he stressed. 'You are a go.' He shook his head and said away from the mic, 'God help me.'

Marlow said, 'Grant, find AC one eighty.'

Hearing the go order in his other ear, Grant said, 'Henry, wait...'

'I'd worry more right now about the ten Increment snipers taking aim at an innocent man's head. I'll let you get back on that radio.'

The phone line went dead.

Marlow had hung up.

Grant said to himself, 'He can see me...' He looked straight to the rooftops overlooking the east side and got on his radio. 'This is Mobile One! Abort!'

Before Grant could finish his sentence, a series of small explosions were set off in the flower beds at the other end of the square. Dirt and soil were thrown into the air in sync with what sounded like the cracks of gunshots.

Grant covered his head as he ran towards the blasts, shouting at everyone, '*Get down!*'

The public reacted just as Marlow had intended: with a chaotic scattering across the square.

The radios for the Survey and Grab teams went haywire, as frantic calls of gunfire were called in.

'*Shots fired! East of the square...!*'

'*Sniper team, is that you?*'

'*Negative, Control! Sniper team is inactive.*'

'*Where's the shooter? Does anyone see the shooter...?*'

The people nearest the explosions covered their heads as they ran. But no one dropped. No blood was spilled, because no bullets had been fired.

Grant stood back up.

The Survey and Grab teams surged into the east end of the square.

They were a cluster of confusion, huddled around the destroyed flower beds.

Grant fought through the scattering crowd, terrified that someone on his team was going to panic and shoot someone. He yelled, 'It's squibs! Stand down!'

The Grab team leader pulled out what remained of the offending device from the flower bed: a long cable hooked up with six small squibs rigged with blank rounds.

Lyonnais police flooded in to the square, looking in all directions for a shooter that didn't exist.

Grant reached the Grab and Survey teams. 'It was Marlow,' he said. 'He was on the roof, Leo. He saw me get the radio and he could see who the snipers were aiming at. He must be on a north roof. He was watching the square the whole time.'

In a cool stone stairwell, the screams and shouts from the square were distant but audible. Henry Marlow descended the stairs with quick feet, stripping off the same camo gear worn by the Increment snipers, one item at a time. It didn't matter if MI6 found it. He'd be long gone by then.

By the time he reached street level, he was in cargo shorts, a baggy shirt, and carrying a large rucksack that he'd stashed under the stairs on his way in. Adding sunglasses as the final touch of his backpacker look,

Marlow blended into the crowd that the police were directing away from the square.

He smiled as Fabrice Gasquet of DGSI ran past, oblivious for the second time that morning.

Grant set off running north.

Winston could see his position on the wall, and how fast he was going. 'Mobile One, where are you going?'

Picking his way through the middle of the stalled traffic, Grant spoke while he ran.

'Édith Lagrange,' he managed to say. 'I know why she wasn't scared of Henry Marlow finding her.'

'Mobile One, Marlow is still out there and you are unarmed,' said Winston. 'Return to Place Bellecour for back-up.'

Grant shook his head at his own impulsiveness and the impossibility of going back for a weapon. All he could think about was protecting the detective. Grant's voice shook with the vibrations of his body on the road. 'There's no time...'

31

Winston leaned over the console, trying to get a simple answer on his channel. 'Sniper One, confirm no shots fired from Sniper team!'

'Sniper One, that's confirmed.'

Winston sighed in relief.

Swann barged past to reach the senior staff who were monitoring personnel trackers. 'Where the bloody *hell* is Grant going?'

Archer was tracking him on his screen. 'He seems to be heading north-east. It must be to Interpol.'

'But Lagrange is safe there.'

Winston said, 'He's the one on the ground, Imogen. We've got to trust him.'

There wasn't time for him to make sense of what had just transpired. He had an overwhelming amount of data on the video wall to process. Every street linking to Place Bellecour was packed. Someone on the Survey team described it as 'a shit show'.

Swann stormed past Christie out of the Control room.

She rushed up to her office and locked the door. Her hastily closed blinds were still swaying when she opened her safe. She took out a burner phone and hit "CALL" against the sole number in the history.

At the other end, Lagrange answered with a whisper. 'Hello?'

'Can you talk?' asked Swann. Her heart was thumping like a jackhammer.

'Hang on,' replied Lagrange, rushing out of the shared office space. Once she was clear, she confirmed, 'Go ahead.'

'I need to extract you,' Swann said. 'Right now.'

Lagrange's stomach turned upside down. 'Are you sure? What's—'

Swann cut her off. 'The man we sent, he's figured it out, and he's on his way to you.'

Lagrange took a steadying breath. She could feel her entire life falling apart, like theatre scenery collapsing around her. 'Where should I go?'

'Are you at Interpol?'

'Yes.'

Swann took out another burner from her safe and began tapping a message. 'I'm sending someone you can trust, Édith. He'll meet you outside in five minutes.'

Lagrange paused. 'I don't understand. He's ready for me?'

'I don't take chances, Édith,' Swann explained. 'I had him on standby.'

'Okay,' Lagrange replied. 'I'm leaving.'

Once Swann hung up, she finished writing the message to her asset:

"Interpol HQ. 5 mins. Grant is coming."

. . .

Grant was still en route when he tried Lagrange's phone. The stream of emergency vehicles towards Place Bellecour had turned the city centre into a car park. With Interpol over three kilometres away, a run in thirty-four-degree heat and high humidity was far from ideal. Within a few minutes his shirt was clinging to his back, and sweat was falling freely down his face.

After trying Lagrange's mobile and her work extension – getting voicemail on both – Grant reached out for help. He got Archer to patch him through to GCHQ's Global Telecommunications Exploitation division, who confirmed that Lagrange's mobile phone was on the move. Heading for her apartment.

Grant told Archer he needed a live track there, and he set off running again, receiving directions for a shortcut through a maze of alleys and one-way roads that a car would have taken twice as long to get through.

Grant tried not to dwell on what could have caused Lagrange to have left Interpol headquarters. He at least knew that she couldn't have been taken by force. Which, in a way, was worse: only someone she really trusted could have convinced her to leave.

Lagrange didn't mess around with excuses to her colleagues before sneaking out. After shutting her computer down, she simply grabbed her bag and headed straight for the lobby. For years now, she had been prepared to walk away from everything at a moment's notice. The time had now come.

She didn't even wait for the lift – instead, she barrelled down the stairs, straight past Captain Marcuse.

'A little early for lunch, isn't it?' he suggested.

Lagrange replied, 'I'll be back soon.'

She felt calmer once she had cleared the security barriers outside. She hunted for Swann's asset, looking for a lone male figure. But there was no one around.

When she turned onto the main road, clear of the security cameras covering Interpol's entrance roads, an old Volkswagen came haring up alongside the pavement.

The man in the driver's seat was stocky and had a wispy beard. It was light ginger, the same colour as his receding hair. His complexion was pale. Everything about him looked tainted by nicotine.

'Get in,' he growled.

Lagrange had never seen him before, but Duncan Grant had.

In Dune Beach House in the Hamptons.

It was Martin Haslitt.

32

With Archer's live tracking in his ear, Grant charged out of an alleyway at full speed. The directions were spot on – the only thing Archer didn't have on the map was the delivery van coming the other way. The driver slammed into an emergency stop. Grant turned his body in profile, his shoulder absorbing the brunt of the impact, slamming into the flat front end of the van.

Before the driver could so much as open his door, Grant was off again, squeezing between the van and the wall. Once he was clear, Grant gently windmilled his arm, relieved to find that his shoulder wasn't dislocated.

An elderly man sitting on a wooden stool outside his front door with his shirt wide open looked on in bewilderment. He chuckled to himself. '*Crazy fool..*'

Grant charged on, sweat pouring down his face as he reached Lagrange's riverside street.

'I'm there,' Grant told Archer on the radio, then clicked off.

Inside, a woman in her seventies was boisterously singing a Jacques Brel song while brushing the stairs. She looked up with a start as Grant clattered through the front door.

'*Mademoiselle Lagrange*,' said Grant. '*L'as tu vue?*' ('Have you seen her?').

Miffed at Grant's unintentionally casual phrasing, the woman pointed upstairs, telling him Lagrange was in her apartment.

He didn't want to panic the woman or raise suspicions, but he needed answers. Quickly. He asked if anyone else was with her.

The woman said there was a man. They had gone up together five minutes ago.

Grant thanked her, then rushed past. He hurled himself around the turns on the landings, gripping the banister with his callused hands.

He slowed when he reached Lagrange's floor, approaching her door at the end of the hallway with caution. A few feet away, he held back, but heard nothing from behind her door.

He sneaked a quick look at the lock, seeing a key in it on the other side. Under the door, he noticed that sunlight coming from the attic window was being broken by something near the door. The shadow was too wide to be feet.

He gripped the door handle, turning it gently, not wanting to raise even a single decibel. The lock gave way, but there was a weight against the door.

He pushed – harder this time.

The weight on the other side started to move, sliding away. It felt like the weight of a body.

Before the door was even half open, Grant could see what had been blocking it. He recognised the legs and shoes.

Édith Lagrange.

Grant squeezed through the gap.

There was no sign of anyone else in the apartment. He crouched down and closed the door behind him.

Lagrange was slumped forward, forehead against the door, on her knees as if in penitent prayer. Blood was sprayed all down the inside of the door, from the peephole to the floor.

Grant pulled her back slightly by the shoulders, releasing yet more blood from the gaping wound across her throat.

She'd been locking the door. Locking someone in with her.

Her throat was slit from behind.

Whoever killed her is still inside.

There was a steady hum from the kitchen: the microwave. Someone had filled it with computer hardware – the motherboards, her Interpol RFID smartcard for accessing her department, as well as MicroSD cards and Lagrange's mobile SIM card – all inside, throwing out sparks.

He looked with alarm towards Lagrange's computer. It had been gutted, the keyboard upended on the floor. The hard drive platters ripped open with screwdriver holes smashed through them. The exposure to air and dust would probably have been sufficient, but Lagrange's killer wasn't leaving anything to chance. Whatever had been on the hard drives must have been important. Now they were destroyed.

Grant felt horribly exposed without a weapon. Against

an armed professional, he'd be lucky to last a minute in the confines of the apartment.

The killer had been focussed on the computer. With such singular attention, it was unlikely they'd have gone to the bedroom.

By Grant's calculation, that left only one place for the killer to hide.

The cupboard behind him.

Grant raised a forearm, bracing himself for the inevitable impact. The weight of the door took him by surprise as Haslitt drove it into his back with vicious force.

Shards of wood shattered over Grant's head, splinters of varying size piercing his sweat-covered shirt. The moment he turned, he recognised his attacker.

Haslitt's eyes were wild, brandishing the still-bloody knife with which he'd killed Lagrange. He swiped wildly across Grant's torso.

Grant jumped clear, but the tip had caught enough of his shirt to rip it open and draw blood from his chest.

All the training and one-on-ones can't prepare an officer for the reality of facing down someone determined to kill you.

Grant's past experience with death had resulted in an excessive contemplation of mortality that most don't confront until middle age. Even so, the power and intensity of feeling flooding through him was overwhelming. A voice that implored him to stay alive at all costs.

Haslitt swiped again, aiming for the thighs this time. The realisation that Haslitt was aiming for arteries for a quick kill only aggravated Grant further.

It was clear in his mind: there was absolutely no way he

was going to let himself be killed by someone like Martin Haslitt.

He was clearly out of shape, but his knife-handling technique was elite. The knife was a KA-BAR 1213 – the same combat knife used by U.S. Marines. The sight of fresh blood on the jet-black eighteen-centimetre blade made it look even more intimidating than it already was.

Haslitt taunted him, 'Come on, then.'

Grant backed up sharply to the kitchen, throwing one of the wooden chairs at him. Haslitt simply turned his back and kept coming.

Grant cursed his luck. The only utensils left out were wooden or plastic spatulas and spoons. The only option he could see was on the coffee table: a copy of *Le Monde*. He leapt into the living room and picked up the coffee table, hurling it at Haslitt.

He turned his back again, but the table hurt considerably more than the impact of the chair. He was knocked to the ground.

While Haslitt was down, Grant rolled up the newspaper diagonally, then folded it in half. It didn't look like much, but Haslitt knew what it could do.

It was called a Millwall Brick, and Grant was about to show why newspapers were still banned from British football grounds.

With the rise of football hooliganism in the sixties and seventies, it became harder for thugs to smuggle in weapons to games. Then someone realised that a rolled-up newspaper folded in half makes for a stunningly dense blunt weapon. They might have been thugs, but when it came to weapons, they were ingenious. They favoured broadsheets as they made lengthier, more dangerous weapons. Grant had adapted it into something sharper by folding from the diagonal.

The finished piece was like a miniature baseball bat, and just as hard.

Haslitt got back to his feet and squared up to Grant.

There was now no furniture between them.

Haslitt's grin grew wider at the sight of blood changing the colour of Grant's shirt from white to dark red. The adrenaline of the situation was pumping Grant's heart harder than he'd ever felt it – pushing blood with increasing speed out of his chest wound.

With a solid grip on the newspaper, Grant threw heavy blows at Haslitt's joints, working on him from the knees up to destabilise his base.

Grant sidestepped a forward thrust of the knife, but he couldn't evade the backwards swipe Haslitt made as he retracted his arm.

Grant's upper arm took the brunt of it. The slash was much deeper than the wound on his chest. Blood came spilling out at a frightening pace. He tumbled away, clutching his arm.

With a few metres between them, Haslitt thought about taking off. He had achieved his objective: kill Lagrange and destroy the evidence. The front door was within reaching distance. But the sight of Grant on one knee, clutching his arm, was too tempting to walk away from.

Determined to land a fatal follow-up before Grant recovered, Haslitt stalked towards him.

Grant struggled back to his feet. There was nothing else he could do about the bleeding. If he didn't stop Haslitt, it would be the least of his problems. Grant let go of the wound, hoping he could finish off Haslitt before he bled out.

Haslitt was overconfident, striding far too readily inside Grant's impact zone.

Grant landed his first blow on Haslitt's left knee, then quickly backed out before he could retaliate.

The blow elicited a slight tightening around Haslitt's mouth. His first sign of anger. Grant evaded each of Haslitt's slashes and swipes with agile moves up and down and side to side.

Grant's speed allowed him to land a further blow to the right knee, which prompted a groan: Haslitt's first audible sign of pain.

The momentum on his side, Grant didn't let up. He drove the sharp end of the Brick directly on top of Haslitt's thigh. It was so thunderous it sent him down onto one knee. The pain somehow got worse a few seconds later, spreading through his nerve endings. A dead leg.

Haslitt's lack of conditioning was also beginning to show in his slovenly reactions. His breathing was heavy and gravelly.

Grant could smell Haslitt's cigarette-breath from a few feet away. Grant teased him, 'Smoking will kill you.'

That he was capable of coherent speech made Haslitt feel like the tables had turned. Grant looked like he could go at it for hours.

He followed up with quick, heavy blows to Haslitt's hips and kidneys on both sides, but they didn't have nearly the effect they should have. Grant looked down in horror at his weapon: it had buckled under the force of impact.

The sight of Grant without a weapon gave Haslitt a second wind. He lunged at Grant with the knife overhand. Grant barely got his head out of the way.

Haslitt had stabbed down so hard, he had knocked himself off balance. While he regained his footing, Grant got around behind him and pulled a forearm up around Haslitt's neck.

He had a solid hold, but Haslitt was still flailing the knife around.

Grant grimaced as he tightened his grip around Haslitt's neck. If Grant let go, he would be well within stabbing range, and he had already lost a lot of blood. He couldn't afford to weaken any further.

Sweat stung Grant's eyes. The tighter he squeezed Haslitt's neck, the faster the blood poured from his wounds.

His heart rate was now pounding well above two hundred with a ferocity that no exercise could duplicate. His bleeding intensifying.

There was now only one way out: he had to kill Haslitt.

Grant tried to put all thoughts out of his mind, other than squeezing as hard as he could. It was life or death, plain and simple.

Haslitt relinquished the knife, dropping it on the ground. But Grant couldn't stop. He was already on the verge of passing out. To stop now would be suicide.

Haslitt's back stiffened against Grant's choke.

Grant kept on, telling himself that it was almost over. He pulled Haslitt backwards, arching his back to gain even more leverage on him. Haslitt threw his arms around and kicked desperately, unable to grab anything but fresh air. He kicked so hard his heels dragged down Grant's shins.

Grant didn't relent, gritting his teeth and shutting his eyes on the pain. Haslitt dug his heels in ever deeper, then started to weaken. Life was leaving his body, his oxygen depleting.

Even after he went limp, Grant resisted letting him go. Was he trying to trick him into releasing his grip a few moments too soon?

Grant pushed Haslitt away.

The body dropped with a thud.

Grant's breathing was as manic as his eyes were. He remembered about the wound on his arm, and clutched it again.

He stared at Haslitt's dead body, thinking of Marlow's audio diary, talking about his first kill.

"I was the last thing he would ever see. His killer. His assassin. I'll never forget that day. No one ever does. The first time you kill someone."

Grant looked towards the front door.

Someone was knocking urgently. The woman who had been singing Jacques Brel. She was calling Lagrange's name.

Grant hobbled to the kitchen, grabbing a towel that he tied around his upper arm. In a few seconds, it was covered in blood. He told the woman that he was sorry about the noise. He was moving furniture for Édith.

The excuse seemed to mollify her for the moment. The knocking stopped, and she said nothing further. Grant fancied that she might call the police anyway.

With two dead bodies in the apartment, hanging around wasn't an option.

He opened the microwave door, finding only a charred,

smoking jumble of hardware remains, some of it still on fire. All of it melted together.

His next thoughts flowed quickly. One part of him was in shock:

I've just killed someone and I'm bleeding badly.

Another part told him to strip Haslitt of his black shirt and suit jacket.

Both were a size too big in the chest. What mattered, though, was that they would cover up his arm and chest wound for what he had to do next.

He ripped off what remained of his bloodied shirt. He was a long way past worrying about leaving DNA evidence behind. What mattered most was getting out.

His torso was slick with sweat and blood, making it a struggle to get Haslitt's shirt on. He could feel Haslitt's sweat under the arms, and the smell of cigarettes was overpowering. But it beat the idea of running across the city in a white shirt covered in blood.

He ran to the bathroom to wash his face. It was spattered with blood.

He looked down at the bloody handprints he'd left on the edge of the sink. The more feverishly he tried to wipe them off, the more blood he continued to drop.

Catching himself panicking, he stopped. He looked at himself in the mirror, dabbing with toilet roll at the remaining drips of blood running down his arm to his wrist.

When he was satisfied with his appearance, he left the bathroom to pat down Haslitt. He had already tossed his burner and had nothing else on him.

Grant breathed heavily as he realised he would have to move Lagrange's body in order to get out.

Having cleaned his hands already, he didn't want to get blood on himself again.

He pulled her away from the door by her feet.

Closing the door behind him, he thought of something else Marlow had said about his first kill:

"*I walked into that room one man, and left it a totally different one. I knew I would never be the same again.*"

33

Grant called Control on the move, sticking to the quieter streets he'd taken with Lagrange the night before.

'Lagrange and Haslitt are dead,' he said.

Winston paused a moment. 'What happened?'

'She was already dead when I got there. Haslitt cut her throat.' Grant waited until he'd passed a group of men drinking coffee outside a café terrace. 'I killed Haslitt. There wasn't any other way. There was a woman on the stairs. She heard noise in Lagrange's flat. I told her I was helping her move. But we should get a clean-up team in there ASAP. Removal men might be a good cover for them.'

It impressed Winston that Grant was thinking about such things. 'Where are you now?' he asked.

'A few minutes from Interpol.'

'Interpol? Grant, get back to the meeting point. Our guys are still there.'

'I can't,' said Grant, picking up speed from a jog to a

run. 'Interpol's the one place that might still have the answers we need. I'll call you when it's done.'

There wasn't time for Grant to explain everything he had done the previous night, when his suspicions about Lagrange were snowballing.

He had asked GCHQ to send her the email containing a malware program. Once installed, it recorded every keystroke on her keyboard. With Grant having created the false premise for her to enter her password that morning, GCHQ had been able to log Lagrange's keystrokes. Grant had already called GCHQ, and memorised what could prove to be a vital password. One that he was certain would give him access to the files that Lagrange wanted so desperately to protect. Haslitt might have destroyed the backups, but there was a chance that the originals were still on Lagrange's Interpol computer.

Interpol might have looked impressive – the concrete anti-ramming barriers, the checkpoints manned by armed guards in their little huts, the cameras – but those were just window-dressing. Beyond the façade, at its core, it was not much more than a moderately well-protected office block.

Grant's plan to get inside was simple, but it wasn't easy. It would all rely on one vital piece of the puzzle. The only thing working in his favour: no one at Interpol knew yet that Édith Lagrange was dead.

The guard at the first security barrier recognised Grant from his first visit.

'I'm here to see Édith Lagrange,' Grant said.

The guard checked his computer and frowned a little. 'I'm sorry, she's not currently in the building.'

'That's impossible,' said Grant. 'I've just spoken to her.' He took out his phone, giving the guard the necessary prompt.

The guard was quick to raise a hand. 'No, no. I'll call her,' he said, dialling Lagrange's extension.

The plan was going just as Grant had hoped. It wouldn't have worked if he had been the one calling. Social engineering hacks – manipulating people into divulging confidential information or getting them to do things that will benefit the hacker – are based on faulty assumptions.

So when a French woman answered Édith Lagrange's phone extension, sounding weary and distracted, the guard heard what he was expecting to hear. His faulty assumption was that the woman *must* be Detective Édith Lagrange, because that's whose number and extension he'd just called.

It was actually a woman called Yazmin, a multilingual operator at GCHQ's Social Engineering desk which specialised in supporting tasks like Grant's. She had temporarily routed Lagrange's extension to her desk at GCHQ's headquarters in Cheltenham.

Yazmin had been a specialist in "physical penetration" before a car accident had left her wheelchair-bound. Before she lost the use of her legs, a private bank with gold bullion vaults hired her to break into their property in order to highlight weaknesses in their security systems.

It was a reasonable assumption that if breaking into a bank would be hard, a gold bullion vault would be next to impossible without automatic weapons and a team of ten plus. That was only true, though, if you went in the front door where security was airtight. Being a business-to-business bank, there were no tellers sitting behind counters protected by armoured glass. The back of the building was a different story. Physical penetration testers get the most success from simply trying doors until they find one unlocked, or wait for others to be opened. Once inside, there was still the problem of accessing the vault. It wasn't as if banks left their vaults wide open.

During the night, that would be correct. But in daytime, business-to-business banks routinely left their vaults open. And for the simplest of reasons: laziness. Employees were in and out of the vault dozens of times a day.

Having sneaked inside through an unlocked back door, all it took for Yazmin to reach a restricted floor was a high-viz vest over a smart suit, carrying a handbag and a clip-board. Then it had simply been a matter of walking in and out of the vault. If one bar hadn't been so heavy, she would have taken more.

In less than twenty minutes, armed with nothing more than a phone and clipboard, Yazmin had walked out of a gold bullion vault with a kilogram bar worth £50,000.

For the bank, the point had been made.

Yasmin stuck to her script, answering the guard, 'Yes, I've been waiting for him. I'll meet him in the lobby.'

Having heard everything he had expected to hear, the guard raised the barrier.

As Grant walked into the lobby, he sent Yazmin an encrypted text message, instructing her to dial out of Lagrange's number. He was worried about any other calls coming through to Yazmin, requiring answers to Interpol-specific things that she couldn't know about. Grant thought it better to let Lagrange's phone just ring out.

The guard, however, had seen Lagrange leave head-quarters barely an hour earlier, and he hadn't seen her return. He then did what Grant hadn't planned for: he called Lagrange's extension again.

The guard was persistent, letting it ring for so long that one of Lagrange's colleagues picked it up.

A male detective answered. 'Hello?'

The guard paused. 'I'm looking for Detective Lagrange. I was just talking to her.'

'Not on this line,' came the reply.

'Yes, this line,' the guard insisted.

'I've been here for the last ten minutes. She left about an hour ago and hasn't been back.'

The guard hung up and told his junior colleague to watch his post. He took his radio and checked his gun in his holster.

'Everything alright?' his colleague asked.

'I need to check something,' he replied.

Grant kept his phone up to his left ear, pretending to take a call to obscure his face from the receptionist. It was enough to get him to the stairs. He moved as quickly as he could without arousing suspicion.

Having walked the route with Lagrange on the night of the opera shooting, Grant knew that without her RFID pass card he could only get as far as the entrance to the Antiterrorism Criminal Analysis department.

With more time and prior access to Lagrange's smartcard, the radio-frequency ID tags could have been decrypted and hacked. But her RFID card was smouldering in her microwave. Which meant that Grant would have to rely on the next-best thing: tailgating.

In a research facility or something similar, tailgating

would require a white lab coat or some kind of uniform that made you look like you belonged there. The male Interpol officers commonly kept an informal style such as Grant's dark suit and shirt. The lack of a tie was not uncommon for Lyonnais men in the summer. All Grant had to do was hang around the door, then wait for someone to either enter or exit.

The key was to sweep through without the person realising. Hoping for such an event is risky: they might insist on seeing your pass rather than simply holding the door open. Grant's solution came from a trick taught to him in physical penetration training.

Next to the lifts was a small table where a charity pledge book for the Lyon marathon in October had been left out. Grant took the biro pen from beside the book and placed it between the doorjamb and the door itself. Now, when the door opened from the other side, the pen would fall into the gap. When the door was a pen's-width from closing, it would stop.

While Grant hung around on the balcony, looking like he wanted privacy for a phone call, he heard someone exiting the department. Grant remembered the door being sluggish to close. He counted off three seconds in his head, then noticed the guard who had let him in conferring with the receptionist.

Before Grant could turn for the department door, the guard spotted him. He pointed an accusatory finger at him, then a call of '*Arrêtez-vous!*' reverberated through the lobby.

Grant picked up the fire extinguisher near the door and smashed it into the RFID reader on the wall. With the reader out of action, it would lock the guard out. Grant then removed the pen from the door and slid through before it shut.

The noise had drawn out several members of the Antiterrorism department. Mollifying them with excuses was immaterial. He was in and no one was going to stop him.

He brushed off the protesting officers, including Captain Marcuse, who was foolish enough to try to block Grant's path.

Sensing his staff looking to him to be a hero, Marcuse peacocked forward, his fist pulled back ready to strike. His move couldn't have been more predictable if he had emailed Grant in advance. Grant grabbed the captain's flying fist not even halfway through its journey, then drove it straight back into Marcuse's own face.

The staff could only look from behind their hands, wincing at the destructive power of the blow.

Marcuse flailed on the ground, his nose burst open. Spitting blood, he swore, '*Putain!... Putain!*' then yelled angrily for someone to call for back-up.

Someone shouted that they already had, but no one else was going to mess with Grant.

They took shelter in their offices, locking themselves in, leaving Marcuse sprawled on the corridor floor.

Grant stepped over Marcuse like he was upturned furniture, then headed for Lagrange's office. He announced in French while on the move, 'I'm with British intelligence. I'm working with Detective Lagrange. She's in trouble. I'm not here to steal anything or cause any harm or damage, unless you get in my way.'

One of Lagrange's colleagues tried in vain to lock the

door to their office, but his hands were shaking so hard he couldn't even get the key in the lock.

Grant swatted him aside, and told the others crouching by their desks to get out. They didn't need told a second time.

Having flushed the staff out, Grant barricaded the door by lodging a desk against the handle.

He battered the space bar on Lagrange's computer to bring it to life. The password-entry page appeared.

As he typed in the password, Grant could feel his heart beating with uncommon urgency. If his hunch was wrong about Lagrange having used the same password at home and at work, then his one-man riot had been for nothing.

He hit ENTER, muttering to himself, 'Come on, come on...'

The desktop screen appeared.

He was in.

He couldn't be sure how much time he had, but judging by the yelling and banging outside, the guards weren't making much progress in gaining access through the department door.

Grant navigated through Lagrange's files, filtering them to 'Recently modified'.

The guard who had let him in was suddenly pressed up against the glass pane of the door, trying to force it open. Marcuse had dragged himself along the corridor to let him in, leaving a long trail of blood and snot behind.

Grant didn't allow his concentration to be broken. He trusted that the barrier would hold – though not indefinitely.

What he found on the computer confirmed what he had feared and suspected about Lagrange. One of the files changed most recently related to the Red Notice listing for Henry Marlow.

A message attached to it had been quarantined from the official listing. It was from a member of the public, calling himself Richard Carlton.

Grant knew the name. It had been one of Henry Marlow's many aliases through the years.

"I saw this man in London on 20th September. He was carrying a file marked AC180."

Grant stared at the filename. *AC180.* Just as Marlow had said.

Grant couldn't fathom why Lagrange had quarantined the message, obstructing an obvious lead relating to the death of Claude Pinot.

What Grant found next cleared matters up a great deal.

The next items showed a folder of material that had been collated over multiple months. There were phone records, bank records, emails, surveillance photographs... But not about Claude Pinot. They all related to Édith Lagrange.

The bank records showed cash flowing in on the same day of each month. Two deposits were for the same amount that had appeared in Claude Pinot's bank account. Lagrange had transferred them out and then back in again, to make it look as if Pinot had been paid off.

The other files showed meticulous obstruction of justice: blocking potential sightings of Henry Marlow from reaching British intelligence; removing photographs from Interpol's internal database, which was shared with police forces around the world; deleting messages from Five Eyes intelligence agencies and many other international agencies.

For the past three years, Édith Lagrange had gone out of her way to keep Henry Marlow out of Interpol's circulation, and by extension, almost the entire intelligence community.

Grant took a memory stick from Lagrange's desk and copied the folder onto it.

He was already replaying his conversations with her. How subtle references now appeared much starker in hindsight. But before he could get bogged down in her deception, he first had to get out of Interpol in one piece with the evidence.

As the time on the copied items counter ticked down with aggravating slowness, the guard in the corridor was close to smashing his way in. He had two colleagues with him now, ploughing a larger, heavier desk into the door. Blow by blow, they were getting nearer.

When they finally broke through, the guard pulled his gun on Grant exultantly.

The files now copied, Grant nonchalantly took out the memory stick and pocketed it. As he removed his hand from his trouser pocket the guards formed a semicircle around him, each beckoning him to raise his hands.

Grant did so, whilst holding aloft a navy passport. '*Diplomatique*,' he said, indicating the observation by the Crown that the owner of said passport was immune from arrest.

The barrier guard wasn't interested, and pulled Grant's hands down behind his back.

One of his colleagues lowered his gun. 'Denis,' he said. 'What are you doing?'

He snatched the passport out of Grant's hand. 'I'm holding him until the cops get here,' he said proudly.

Grant could have easily wrestled out of Denis's grip. Instead, he laughed. 'You're going to regret this.'

Denis got right up in Grant's face. He spat, 'Shut it!'

Marcuse, still clutching his bloodied face, pushed his way through. '*Connard*,' he swore, salivating at the prospect of some retaliatory blows.

Grant stopped him in his tracks, repeating his status.

Marcuse gestured that he wanted to see the passport, which he took his time inspecting. After a huff, he handed the passport back to Grant.

Despite the guard's pleas, Marcuse said that it was pointless. 'He has diplomatic cover, birdbrain. Have you any idea how much trouble we'd be in if we handed him over to the *gendarmes*? I don't care if he's walking out with a suitcase full of money. You can't stop him.'

Denis grumbled, 'This is bullshit.'

Marcuse lowered his hand, revealing a nose that was no longer straight. He told Denis, 'Go file a complaint with the United Nations if you've got a problem with it.' Pausing in front of Grant, he said, 'Today's your lucky day, *connard*.'

Grant plucked his passport out of Marcuse's hand and said, '*Merci*.'

He trudged through the debris in the corridor, dodging Marcuse's blood trail. He took out his phone and called Control. 'This is Mobile One. I'm coming in.'

34

The debriefing took place in a windowless seventh-floor conference room, attended only on a need-to-know basis. That meant Winston and his senior staff of Miles, Ryan, and Samantha. Imogen Swann and Justin sat together at the opposite side of the table. On Winston's side, Grant sat farthest away, delivering his report on the events at Place Bellecour.

At the head of the table, Olivia Christie's body language gradually deteriorated as Grant laid out the full scope of Lagrange's intricate deception. He recalled her impassioned opinions about Pinot's deceit, and the strain that comes with living a lie. At the time, Grant had rationalised her insights as a strong sense of empathy from a talented detective. Empathy was one of the most under-rated skills in any police work. Now he realised that her impassioned insights were not about Pinot: they were about herself. In retrospect, it had been the closest she could get to making a confession – something she'd been desperate to do. To unburden herself of the guilt of her double life.

When Grant was through, Christie closed her briefing notes despairingly.

'And nothing has come in on Marlow?' she asked.

Archer was monitoring his laptop for updates from the DGSI. 'It looks like the trail has gone cold, ma'am,' he said.

'That's it,' said Swann with finality. 'He's gone.'

'I doubt that,' Grant retorted. 'He came out of hiding for a reason. He won't stop until we find it.'

To the others in the room, the change in Grant was subtle but notable. He was still wearing Haslitt's shirt. He'd received medical treatment on the flight home – a private plane owned by the Ministry of Defence – then gone straight from the runway at RAF Northolt, six miles outside London, into a car that had pulled into Vauxhall Cross just thirty minutes earlier.

The new darkness of his clothes affected the appearance of Grant's eyes. That was where the real change had happened. It was also why no one could quite pin down exactly what had changed. They knew about his part in Haslitt's death. But what had changed most significantly in Grant couldn't be touched, or seen. It wasn't just *in* his eyes. It was behind them.

Christie said, 'Between these four walls, the President of Interpol is screaming bloody murder about how one of our officers could have been so reckless.' She clicked to a video clip taken from Interpol's security cameras. It showed Grant storming through the Antiterrorism department, then felling Captain Marcuse.

Winston had to suck his lips in to stifle a smile.

If the intention was to embarrass Grant, he didn't show it. He was composed. 'Maybe the Foreign Office can remind the President of Interpol that one of his Internal

Affairs detectives is to blame for our officers being shot in Lyon three nights ago.' He passed down the documents he'd printed on the plane from Lagrange's memory stick. 'Claude Pinot wasn't the mole inside Interpol. Édith Lagrange was. She had files on her computer made by Pinot over the past year, detailing large deposits made to Lagrange from a private off-shore bank account.'

Christie flicked through the evidence. 'For doing what?'

'She had been meticulously removing any intelligence linked to Henry Marlow's whereabouts, deleting leads and suspected sightings of him from all around the world. Not a single thing got through, including our own Grey Notices. She showed them to me the night of the opera shooting as proof that Claude Pinot was working with Marlow.'

Visibly struggling to keep up, Swann tried to clarify, 'So it was *Lagrange* that was working for Marlow?'

'I don't think Marlow has anything to do with this,' answered Grant. 'But someone was paying Lagrange to keep Marlow's name out of circulation.'

Swann turned her face to the ceiling in theatrical frustration. 'For the love of God: *why* would she do that?'

Grant said, 'I think Henry Marlow knows something damaging, and someone needs him silenced. If he's caught by us or some other agency, then he might have a story to tell.' He handed over more of the Lagrange documents. 'These go back over a year. Pinot was building a cast-iron case against her. As you can see, he was meticulous.'

Swann asked, 'If his evidence was so damning, why not take it to Interpol Internal Affairs?'

'*Lagrange* was Internal Affairs! He had nowhere to turn to. Except to us.'

'Which he wanted paid for,' added Swann. 'Always an encouraging trope in a source's integrity.'

Grant conceded, 'Pinot had debts, sure. Flawed? Without a doubt. But the only corrupt detective in that department was Édith Lagrange. And when Pinot found out, he turned to us. He was going to blow Lagrange and her handler's whole operation. They got to Pinot before we could. Then Lagrange framed him. A man with his history, his debts? He was a perfect patsy.'

'Then that means only one thing,' said Winston. 'We have a mole.'

The room was silent.

'It's the only way Lagrange could have found out about Pinot's meet with us. Lagrange's handler has to be inside MI6 somewhere. Someone with access.'

Swann said, 'It's too soon to be throwing around accusations like that.' She turned to Christie in appeal. 'Olivia, really.'

Christie backed her chair away from the table, and paced at the back of the room, contemplating the unthinkable.

Worried that she would shut things down, Grant said, 'Ma'am, if I may. We started this investigation based on an assumption that Henry Marlow was the shooter at the opera. As soon as you remove that assumption, the entire complexion of what happened that night changes everything we thought we knew about that shooting.'

Playing devil's advocate, Winston said, 'All the more reason for Marlow to have killed Pinot: if Pinot shopped Lagrange to us, then the investigation into finding Marlow lights up again.'

Swann added, 'Not to mention the physical evidence at the scene. Only this morning, the French police found a hair on Pinot's clothing. Randall analysed it. It's Marlow's.'

Grant countered, 'We have a fingerprint that Marlow would never have left, on a device he would never have wired so poorly. And a hair that could easily have been left in advance by Lagrange. Not one eyewitness can place Marlow at the scene that night.'

Christie motioned at Marlow's picture on the video wall. 'If he's innocent, why not come in?'

'Because he's on a murder charge, that's why,' Swann sniped. 'Apparently we're not interested in that anymore.'

Grant said, 'He thinks we're out to kill him. Which isn't entirely unfounded.'

'If he's so scared, why did he go out of his way to set up the meet?' Swann picked up the piles of reports and documents and folders in front of her, then let them drop as if they added up to nothing. 'Why would someone go through *all* of this? For *what*?'

Grant could tell it was pointless to persist with Swann, so he turned his attention to Christie. 'Ma'am, I mentioned in my report that Marlow tried to make contact a few days ago.' He opened Marlow's coded message to Interpol, sending it to the wall. 'Twelve hours ago, Lagrange removed this message from a Richard Carlton, sent to Interpol's Red Notice system.'

"I saw this man in London on 20ᵗʰ September. He was carrying a file marked AC180."

Grant explained, 'It's from a hidden IP address. Richard Carlton was an old alias of Marlow's.'

Christie said, 'Lagrange couldn't have known that. Why would she have removed it?'

Swann was conspicuously silent.

'Because she was told to,' said Grant. 'By her handler. And I think Anticorruption and Internal Investigations file one eighty reveals their identity.'

Christie looked at Swann.

'Ma'am,' Swann began, 'this really is beyond the pale. This is what Marlow wants. To dictate this operation and get us side-tracked.'

The fact that Swann was so eager to ignore potential evidence only heightened Christie's intrigue. She told Winston, 'Find it. Open it.'

As he dialled into the relevant database, Swann protested again, 'Ma'am, please...' But Christie wasn't interested.

When the Anticorruption database search appeared on the wall, Swann reached across and closed the laptop lid whilst Winston was still typing. 'Stop,' she said.

Everyone froze.

'You won't find it in there.'

'It's an AC file,' Winston pointed out. 'Why wouldn't it be in the database?'

Somewhere inside Swann, an elastic snapped. She spoke faster now, as if finally released from some long-held secret. 'Because I was told to purge it. Three years ago. It's in the STRAP Two Archives.'

Christie asked, 'Why was a STRAP Two-level file purged without my knowledge, Imogen?'

'Ma'am,' Swann implored. 'I need the room.'

Christie gave a curt flick of her head. 'Everyone with STRAP One clearance wait outside.'

When Grant prepared to get up, Christie said, 'No. You stay.'

Swann leaned forward. 'Ma'am, I really–'

Christie said, 'He stays. It's time we got to the bottom of this.' Once Archer, Samantha, Ryan, and Justin had gone, she gave Winston the nod. 'Open the Archives, Leo.'

35

When Hannibal file AC180 appeared on the wall projector, Winston asked, 'Is this a joke?'

Someone had redacted the entire document. Every line covered with thick black bars.

'Did you redact this?' asked Christie.

Swann replied, 'Redacting and archiving files isn't illegal.'

Christie said, 'That depends very much on what's behind those bars. I can access it on the terminal in my office, Imogen. Or you can save us all a lot of time.'

Swann sniffed resentfully. 'It's an HM Land Registry file purged from the official database. The unredacted file shows a list of properties purchased under a limited company called Thomson Logistics.'

'Why do I recognise that name?' asked Christie.

'It's a shell company we used to control slush funds for the Albion programme. The Land Registry file shows a transfer of various property titles from Thomson Logistics to another shell company.'

'What company?'

Swann closed her eyes for a moment, a darkness coming over her. 'You have to go about a dozen miles down the road, but ultimately it's owned by Crown Prince Mohammad bin Abdul.'

There were a full two seats between Grant and the others, adding to his sense of dislocation – and disillusionment.

Christie could barely comprehend the gravity of what Swann had just disclosed. 'You mean to say that MI6 bought property for the heir to the Saudi throne, by laundering his money through one of our black ops slush funds?'

There was only one answer Swann could give. 'Yes.' After years of evasion and deceit, the truth didn't appear to come as any relief to her. If anything, it only added to the weight on her shoulders. 'The idea was that, because MI6 was legally the source of the purchases, they could never be disclosed on Land Registry. It's a public record. For a few pounds, anyone can access it. AC one eighty ensured that the Crown Prince's property listings can never be declassified.'

For Christie, the deception hit hard. 'This agency has a proud tradition stretching back to nineteen oh nine. We helped to defeat the Nazis. We tracked down Karadžić and Mladic. We recruited Gordievsky who practically won us the Cold War, for Christ's sake. We are not an instrument for private asset-building!'

Winston had never seen Christie run so hot.

In an attempt to bring the discussion back to operations, Grant said, 'If I'm out of line here, then someone please correct me. But doesn't the Prince have more money than our entire operating budget? He must have an army of lawyers and accountants. Why did he need us?'

Winston saw through the deception. 'The Crown Prince needed us to guarantee that we could never make the Land Registry file public. Look at the Panama Papers. Shell companies are no longer a guarantee of confidentiality. For some reason, the Crown Prince wanted to make sure that his father never found out about this deal. Why would that be, Imogen?'

Swann dithered. 'I could only speculate...'

Winston had the bit between his teeth now. 'Who signed the Land Registry file? Was it John Wark?'

'I believe so.'

Winston rubbed his face, then slid his hands down to cover his mouth. He only released them once he was certain there was no other conclusion to come to. 'This could land the Foreign Secretary ten years in jail.'

The more they discussed it, the more the implications seemed to spiral.

Grant asked, 'But how does Marlow fit into this? He would never have had access to this file.' He looked again at the Richard Carlton message. 'Of course... It's Kadir Rashid again. The twentieth of September. The date he was assassinated.'

The mere mention of Rashid's name brought Christie's anxious prowling to a sudden halt.

Unaware of her previous warnings to Winston on the topic of Rashid, Grant ploughed on. 'What if we're coming at this from the wrong side? What if it wasn't Marlow who uncovered the deal? What if it was Rashid?' Grant didn't understand why his line of enquiry was receiving such a cool reception. 'Think about it: an investigative journalist with close ties to Saudi. Marlow doesn't want us to see a motive for setting him up. He wants us to see a motive for killing Rashid.'

Winston knew he should have been pouring ice on the Rashid line – for Grant's sake, as well as his own. But he couldn't resist joining in. 'A deal like this requires a private financier to move the money. It has Lawrence Bloom's fingerprints all over it.'

Grant said, 'The files that Marlow stole from Bloom could be proof of who killed Kadir Rashid and why.'

Countering, Swann suggested, 'Or they could be proof of *Marlow's* involvement in killing Rashid. I know you're too young and arrogant to contemplate this seriously, but have you asked yourself, what if you're seeing exactly what Henry Marlow wants you to see?'

Even Winston had to admit to the possibility. 'It would explain why Marlow was so eager to recover them. And so reluctant to part with them.'

Christie said, 'This still doesn't get us any closer to finding Marlow now. Which, might I remind you, is our sole task. I have five independent reports in my office, all with the same conclusion: the Saudi secret police killed Rashid. Fact. Two hours ago, we were a whisker away from snaring Marlow. We're not going to divert energy and resources to investigating a murder that's nowhere near our jurisdiction, and has already been solved.'

Swann was relieved to hear it. 'I completely agree, ma'am.'

Thinking aloud, Winston said, 'Okay, then. Where does Marlow go? Somewhere familiar. Somewhere he knows.'

'He's not going to hide out anywhere that we have a record of,' said Christie.

That was when it occurred to Grant. 'The hair,' he said to himself, then sprang hurriedly to his feet. 'Madam Director. You said that the French police found a hair belonging to Marlow.'

Swann replied, 'Which you said was planted.'

'What matters is that we still identified it as Marlow's.' He turned to Christie. 'Ma'am, I know how to find him. But I need Randall.'

Christie told him, 'Go.' She turned to Winston and Swann. 'I need to talk to John Wark, anyway. We'll pick this up later.'

Grant's sudden appearance took the rest of the senior staff in the corridor by surprise. He was a coiled spring.

He bounded past, corralling Archer on the way. 'Miles, I need every audio file recovered from Marlow's Estonia deposit box.'

Archer jogged to catch up. 'What am I looking for?'

'Location keywords,' replied Grant.

'I don't understand.'

'You will. Come on…'

36

Randall was on a stool, hunched over a dummy explosive device on a worktable. He had a pair of 25x magnifier eyepieces attached to his glasses, and was making minute adjustments to a pair of wires with some tweezers and a metal pick. He had the Classic FM app playing on his phone – currently Erik Satie's "Gymnopédie No.1", which the DJ had introduced as 'one of the great gentle piano pieces. So, sit back, relax, and enjoy the calming tones of Satie...'

Randall was on the brink of separating the wires – a delicate piece of surgical engineering – when Grant burst in, towing Archer in his slipstream. Randall shot up on the stool. He had jerked the wires with so much force that both of them broke.

Grant took in the sight before him. It looked like an amateur bomb-making facility. 'What the hell are you doing?'

Clutching his chest, Randall gasped, 'I made a replica of the Lyon bomb device.'

'Why?'

Randall removed his glasses along with the magnifiers. 'I was practising. Like you said, we got lucky. I had to check that I had the right solution.' He staggered across the room to the radio and switched off the speaker. There was no music capable of calming him down in his current state.

Grant stopped him from returning to his dummy bomb. 'Randall. This is important. The analysis on Henry Marlow's hair.'

Randall turned to a locked glass cabinet full of trays of centrifuge tubes and specimen vials, all separated by department, then arranged by case file numbers. He took out a vial with a single hair. 'It reached us this morning. It's definitely Marlow's.'

'I'm banking on that,' said Grant. 'What I need to know is, were there any unique chemical traces on it?'

Randall looked almost insulted. 'Grant, I re-ran the tests. Does this look like the lab of a lazy man?'

Other than the scattered pieces of the device on the table, there wasn't so much as a paperclip out of place in the small box room.

Randall said, 'There was nothing in the chemical data that matched with any location in Marlow's file. Most of it is so massively broad you'd be marking out entire countries rather than narrowing down to cities. You're asking me to find a single biological needle in a haystack commonly known as the world.'

Grant asked, 'What about the data that isn't massively broad? Humour me.'

Randall pulled out the binder containing his results and showed them to Grant and Archer as if the answer was obvious.

All they could see was a vast table filled with indecipherable compounds and lists of elements.

Archer was as much at sea as Grant was. 'We're going to need some help here,' he said.

Randall tried not to roll his eyes, forgetting that neither of them had studied forensic science for six years like he had. 'Hair reflects not only the chemicals that are in your body. They also have environmental traces in them. Now, mostly, these are standard and predictable elements like oxygen and calcium and iron that aren't geographically specific in any meaningful way.'

'That's the haystack,' said Grant.

'Yes. But Marlow's hair bears traces of silicon, potassium, phosphorus, and titanium.' Randall opened his arms out as if that were the end of it.

Grant looked at him blankly. 'Randall, the only chemistry I paid attention to in high school was sold in ounce bags and made me want to listen to Pink Floyd.'

Randall said, 'Individually, those elements don't tell you very much. But their combination at the present levels suggest the make-up of lava. I tied it down to a handful of regions...'

The second he presented the findings, Grant snatched them out of Randall's hand.

'These regions are enormous, Grant. The chance that these results will lead to a positive location match on Marlow, statistically, is zero. These areas cover millions of square miles.' As if to hammer the point home, he added, 'I've checked against the files. These are just more parts of the haystack.'

'What if the answer isn't in Marlow's MI6 files?' Grant

showed the results to Archer, pointing to one particular region.

It took Archer's breath away. 'The audio files... How can you be sure, Grant?'

He took out his phone to call Winston. 'I just know. There's something about the way Marlow talked about the place. It's significant to him.' He broke away to talk to Winston, who was still in conference with Christie and Swann. 'Sir, I've got something...' Grant covered the mouthpiece, and pointed at the table as he left. 'Sorry I ruined your thing, Randall.'

He was more interested in what Grant had seen in the results. He grabbed the binder back. 'Where is he going to go?'

Archer pointed to one location that listed chemical traces found in lava near Mount Nyiragongo.

Randall looked at it in surprise. 'Why would Marlow be in the Congo?'

37

Swann's phone rang as she crossed the vestibule outside her office. The number on the caller ID was unlisted, but she knew from the last four digits who was calling.

'Hang on,' she answered, striding towards the sanctuary of her office.

Justin was at his desk, gazing at something on his screen. The moment that Swann appeared in his peripheral vision, he hit the Command+Tab shortcut on his keyboard to change the program he was in.

Not used to seeing him act so cagily, she asked him, 'Everything okay, Justin?'

'Yes, ma'am,' he replied, his gaze unwavering from the screen.

Speaking to Swann without making eye contact was totally out of character for someone who prided himself on an old-fashioned, slavish politeness. He was scared that if she looked into his eyes she'd see right through him.

Swann closed her door behind her and got to her phone

call. 'Sorry, I can talk now. You should expect a visit from C.'

'AC one eighty?'

'Yeah.'

A pause. 'Shit. I gather you told her.'

'I didn't have a choice,' Swann said. 'Marlow told Grant about it.'

'We need to close ranks now. We have no idea what Marlow has planned next. Are all your bases covered?'

Through the gaps in her venetian blinds, Justin was in sight, tapping away on his computer and back on the phone again.

Swann answered, 'Of course.'

Wark went on, 'We can't afford any slip-ups. Not now. Not when we're this close.'

Once she was off the phone, Swann logged into her Anticorruption department system. As director, she could access computer logs from anyone – not just in the building, but in the entire Service. It didn't show the content of emails or documents, but it compiled the metadata on everything that moved: who made what, when, and who they sent it to.

Swann didn't really believe she would find anything when she typed Justin's name into the search window. He'd only ever shown loyalty to her. But she had been aware of Justin spending increasing time with Leo's crew in the European Task Force – their inquisitiveness had apparently rubbed off.

Swann sighed. 'What have you been doing?'

Justin's logs showed that he'd been in contact with someone at GCHQ. After noting their extension, Swann called them.

The GCHQ analyst was used to talking to officers at a similar level. He had never dealt with anyone as senior as the Director of the Hannibals. Their fearsome reputation wasn't confined only to MI6. Swann's authority extended to any matter involving direct communication between a government agency and MI6. Failure to turn over information requests was a severe disciplinary matter.

The analyst was barely out of university. 'Have I done something I shouldn't have?' he asked.

Swann replied, 'I'm following up on a log made earlier by Justin Vern.'

'The spider trace.'

Swann paused. 'Right. That trace contains data pertinent to an ongoing investigation, so I need to see a copy.'

'Of course,' said the analyst. 'I haven't finished collating it all quite yet, but I can send over a copy of what I have so far.'

'Quickly, please,' she said, then hung up.

The second the email with the attachment came through, Swann opened it.

When she began to read, her heart flooded with fear.

A spider trace took a phone number, then analysed all the different phones that had interacted with it. The resultant graphic often resembled a spider's web.

The trace that Justin had requested was on Édith Lagrange's mobile. It was a number that been etched into Swann's brain for the last two years.

She called out, 'Justin. Could I see you a moment?'

He didn't reply. He was no longer at his desk.

38

Foreign Secretary, the Right Honourable John Wark, was surrounded by men just like him: mid-sixties, well-attired, well-fed, and all members of the Portmyron Club for the past twenty years. They were former elected officials of various stripes. That was where Wark exceeded the stature of his company. None of his companions had ever risen to the heights of Foreign Secretary, one of the great pillars of the British Cabinet. As Wark had remarked to his wife when the PM gave him the job, no one ever made history in the Department for Work and Pensions. Foreign Secretaries weren't judged purely on election results. They were measured against history.

Wark's cronies were long out of government and power, now comfortably installed on the boards of various companies, opening doors for their corporate brethren, seeing out the long, slow days of retirement in overly warm, oak-panelled private clubs like the Portmyron.

The Grade II-listed building overlooked Mayfair's Grosvenor Square. Membership costs were publicly undisclosed. They didn't even have a website. Membership was by referral only, and counted ex-Prime Ministers and current British Royalty as members.

It was understood that the criteria for membership selection required applicants to be at least three of the following: male; privately educated; preferably Tory; and who considered Oxford to be 'rather northern'.

Guests could only be allowed with minimum twenty-four hours' notice. So when Olivia Christie showed up unannounced, she had to first get past the floor manager, who was a slightly older version of the waitresses: blonde, wearing a tight black skirt, and heels. The members of the Portmyron were nothing if not predictable in their tastes.

The manager was used to dealing with Establishment figures. She recognised Christie's name, but was steadfast in refusing her entry.

When that became clear, Christie stormed inside anyway. She brushed past a gilt-edged notice on a stand outside the dining room, displaying "Quiet, please". The manager had to grab it to stop it from toppling over.

Christie called out from across the room, 'John.' Her voice pierced the hushed atmosphere of political gossip and chinking cutlery.

Everything stopped.

The waiting staff all looked to the manager for guidance on how to handle the disruption.

She stood behind Christie, gesturing helplessly at Wark and grovelling apologies.

'We need to talk,' Christie announced.

Wark was quick to usher her out to the front steps, smiling uncomfortably as members passed by on their way inside. He tried to alter her angle, pulling her arm.

Christie glared at Wark's hand, his knuckles white. 'Remove your hand unless you want to pull back a stump.'

Wark scolded her, 'Olivia, really. I have a secretary for a reason.'

'This can't wait,' she replied. Out of respect for national security rather than shielding Wark from further embarrassment, she descended the stairs, leading Wark to a quiet corner around a pillar. 'I want to talk about AC one eighty.'

Wark's first instinct was to feign confusion.

'Let's just skip past the denials, shall we. Imogen's told me all about it.'

He rocked on his heels. 'I see.'

'Jesus, John. What the *hell* were you thinking?'

'Well, I don't know, Olivia. Maybe the future safety and prosperity of this country. As is my job. And yours too.'

Christie smiled. 'You don't have an idealistic bone in your body. What did he give you? The great Prince Abdul? Cash? Or an elegant townhouse in St James?'

Wark morphed to his usual routine of attack as a form of self-defence. 'Keep this up, Olivia, and Imogen Swann will have your office before the summer's out.'

'You lobbied hard for Swann to take over as Hannibal Director.'

'God, I wish you lot would stop calling it that...'

'Did you recommend that Imogen take over at Anticorruption to help you hide this property deal?'

'Imogen was the person best-suited for the job. You know that. I would challenge you to name anyone else more qualified than her.'

Christie said, 'Henry Marlow is out there in the field, answerable to no one, on an agenda only he understands. If he were to go public with evidence that MI6 ordered the assassination of a journalist, it would wreck this Service for decades. It's possible that it would never recover. And the minister responsible for the agency at the time would certainly never recover. Still,' she gestured at the building behind them, 'retirement would allow you to spend more time in this place.'

Wark replied, 'Then you'd better make sure that he can't go public.'

Christie paused for a moment. What she wanted to ask next would take guts. 'John, I'm going to ask this once. And I want you to think long and hard before you answer it.'

Wark steeled himself.

'Did you give the order for Henry Marlow to assassinate Kadir Rashid?'

Wark stared at her for a moment, then snorted so lightly it was almost inaudible. 'Olivia, we go back a long way. The PM likes you. You'll be Dame Olivia Christie soon enough if–'

Christie wasn't interested in pay-offs. 'Did we kill Rashid?' she asked.

Wark sighed with irritation. 'No. The Saudis did. As well you know. And if you persist with this Kadir Rashid line... you'll regret it. *Immeasurably.*'

Christie, as a rule, wasn't easily shaken. Especially not in conversation. But never before had she heard an adverb delivered with such eloquent venom.

Wark turned back towards the stairs. 'If you value your job or your future, the next time we speak, I want you to be telling me that Henry Marlow is lying on a slab. If you'll excuse me, I have lunch guests.'

39

Justin took a printout from the spider trace to the Control room. He crouched by Samantha's station, his voice low. He was clearly on edge.

'Can I ask your opinion?' He showed her a list of phone calls, an excerpt from the spider trace. 'What do these look like to you?'

After a few moments, Samantha's brow furrowed slightly. 'These look a lot like calls from a burner.'

'That's what I thought,' he replied.

She pointed out various data clusters. 'These short bursts of activity to only one other number, then the signal disappears.'

Justin asked, 'Is that the phone being switched off?'

'It's most likely the battery being taken out. GCHQ can't track the location without the battery being in.'

Justin took the report back. 'That's what I thought.'

'Are you running that for Imogen?' she asked.

'No, it's... Never mind. It's probably nothing.

. . .

Swann snapped her office blinds shut and locked the door. She went back to the spider trace report, trying to gather her thoughts. She couldn't shake the feeling that some-where, somehow, she had messed up.

The report itself was as complicated as anything she had ever come across. For a non-analyst, finding something pertinent amongst the lists of phone numbers, IMEI numbers, MAC addresses, and lots of technically arcane data, was next to impossible. There was a reason they paid analysts to precis such information.

Swann decided to shortcut it the only way she knew how: by searching for her own work mobile number.

While the results tallied, she tried to swallow, but there was no saliva in her mouth.

There was only slight relief at the confirmation of there being no interaction between Swann's work mobile and any other number associated with Édith Lagrange. But there was a separate heading that caught her attention. It was named "Time proximity overlaps".

Normally for a spider trace, GCHQ analysts report on which numbers have interacted with each other. Unfortu-nately for Swann, Justin's analyst had decided to be much more thorough than that.

The time proximity report showed all the numbers that had registered similar behaviour to any and all of Lagrange's phone numbers – her burner, personal mobile, and Interpol landline extension.

At the top of the list against Lagrange's mobile was the number that matched the most criteria for "similar behaviour": the number of Imogen Swann's work mobile.

'No, no, no,' Swann told herself, 'this is impossible.'

Swann had never taken her work mobile anywhere near Édith Lagrange. And Lagrange would never have been so foolish to bring hers anywhere near Swann.

It didn't make sense.

Then she looked under "Notable activity".

There was one place that all the times and dates had in common: Loyasse Cemetery, near the Gallo-Romain Theatre on the Fourviere hillside, Lyon. The place where she and Lagrange had held their dead drops.

Swann couldn't risk face-to-face meetings, but both women still needed to update one another regularly on their activities. The tidiest solution was a dead drop: a safe spot where they could leave each other instructions or relevant information.

Swann had chosen a marble bench next to the grave of Pierre Bossan – architect of the city's Basilica – securing a memory stick to the underside of it. Neither Lagrange nor Swann would ever come to the spot within two hours of each other, and as long as they kept the phone batteries out of their burners, their mobile signals wouldn't register anywhere.

When visiting the Paris substation – easily excused for someone in Swann's position – Lyon was only a half-day round trip. During the dead drop, Swann would leave her work mobile and the burner she used to contact Lagrange in her hotel room.

The problem was, at the same time of day, for almost the same length of time, Lagrange did the same with her own mobile. Being thorough like Swann, she would remove the battery, cutting the signal completely.

In modern times, switching off a mobile for any length

of time was notable. For two phones to be completely cut off, for almost the same period of time, across dozens of the same days?

Swann almost wilted at her desk.

In trying to avoid a traceable pattern, she had unwittingly created another one.

Once could be a coincidence. Twice would be suspicious. More than three times demonstrated a clear pattern. And GCHQ analysts, above all else, love patterns.

Research had clearly shown that metadata proved much better indicators of behaviour and intent than listening in to phone conversations. In the modern world, where you took your phone, and what you did with it, gave away far more than your actual speech.

Swann and Lagrange's phones had been registered by GCHQ no less than nine times in the past two years.

At first, the pattern seemed to amount to an argument not far removed from 'there's no smoke without fire'. And GCHQ couldn't physically place the pair in the cemetery together. They couldn't identify Swann purely by the burner phone, as nothing tied her to that number. But it was only a matter of time before the behaviour of the burner phone was matched up with her work mobile. Then she'd be fried.

Armed with such evidence, Swann would face a question that would be impossible to answer: why had she been in contact on multiple occasions with a crooked Interpol detective months before she had any reason to?

From that one question, the other dominoes would fall.

What was your business at the Paris substation on those dates?

Where are the records of your business there?

Why are there long periods of unaccounted-for time in your Paris visits, that tie in perfectly with times where Lagrange's location was also unknown?

And those were questions just off the top of Swann's head, thought up in the furnace-like heat of the moment. God only knew what an actual police detective could sink their teeth into over the course of an investigation.

She'd be suspended in no time, and without access to MI6 computers it would be impossible to control the situation.

The decision came to her quickly. Vivid and stunningly clear because her options were so limited. She could empty her rainy-day bank account and disappear, knowing that MI6 would issue a burn notice on her, as well as – ironically – an Interpol arrest warrant. Or she could choose the nuclear option.

The first call she placed was to GCHQ, cancelling the remainder of the spider trace.

The analyst – overworked and already two hours past the end of his shift – was only too glad to hear it.

That left one more piece of the puzzle.

There wasn't time to go out and source another burner phone. She'd have to use one from her safe, which broke a cardinal rule of using burners: single-phone use only. As soon as activity is doubled up, it creates exponential waves and makes it easier to link up activity.

The phone was the same burner she'd used to contact Lagrange. But if she didn't cut off Justin's investigation, then none of her other safeguards mattered anyway.

She tapped out a message to Justin:

"*I know what Swann is up to. Meet me under the trees on River-*

side Walk in twenty minutes. Remove your phone battery before you leave. And tell no one. She has eyes and ears everywhere."

Once she had sent the message, she looked down at her hand. It was trembling.

40

The safest route to enter the Democratic Republic of Congo was to drive through Rwanda from the east. There weren't many places along the Congo's enormous border – the longest in Africa – that could be classed as safe, but the Rwandan side came closest.

The entire Congolese east coast had been mired in a decades-long civil war, costing millions of lives. Estimates ranged anywhere from two- to five million. No one really knew for sure. The fact that the United Nations could lose count of nearly three million people said a lot about the vast empty spaces that made up the country's landscape of sprawling, deep rainforests.

Grant's guide for the mission to Charles Joseph's compound to the north was a nomadic Aussie journalist named Travis Buckley – one of the few white Westerners that called the Congo home, and was routinely mentioned as a fountain of knowledge on the area.

It had been a long time since Travis had been to his native Melbourne. After nine eleven, he'd taken off for the

Middle East where his video reports caught the attention of a major U.S. network. But soon Travis's freewheeling – and dangerous – style of embedded reporting became too reckless for the network executives. Travis went to all the places he was told never to go. Like the "Highway of Death", or to give it its official name, Highway 80: a six-lane highway between Kuwait and Iraq. Home to some of the scenes of greatest devastation in the U.S.-led invasion. There were piles of wrecked cars and buses and bombed-out military vehicles on the highway verge, solidly, for almost one hundred miles. If one had started counting the dead bodies in the sandy ditches by the sides of the road they would soon lose count.

Banditry was rife. Long convoys of jihadis and lawless nihilists – their faces covered with black scarves – roamed the highway, searching for prey. There was nothing they wouldn't steal. Cars. Weapons. Cash.

They also stole people. White Westerners fetched a high price from the well-funded, Saudi-backed forces of Al Qaeda. Such prizes were almost beyond a monetary value in propaganda terms. For jihadists looking for the most valuable content for torture and beheading videos, kidnapping Westerners was a smart investment.

Evading such forces on Highway 80 relied on local knowledge and luck. One day, Travis's luck ran out.

His partner Zach was captured by Al Qaeda, snatched from their van at a fake military checkpoint. Travis had been lucky to escape with his life, aided by a passing military personnel of French soldiers.

Six months later, a video surfaced on the internet showing Zach being beheaded on top of some anonymous dune, along with three European aid workers.

Travis went to the Congo soon after, becoming a tour guide, shepherding wealthy tourists around Eastern Africa.

He had met Grant in early evening in Gisenyi, a city near the border with Rwanda on the banks of Lake Kivu, which became Congolese waters halfway across. Gisenyi had several hotels and numerous beaches, attracting the kind of tourists who felt like they were off the beaten track by coming to Rwanda, while also wanting to be served cocktails on the beach at sunset.

Such customers were Travis's bread and butter. But where Grant and Travis were headed would be no mere safari.

Travis was driving a battered Toyota Landcruiser – the almost indestructible four by four – a vehicle he referred to as 'the tank of Africa'. The jeep of choice from farmers to jihadis.

The inside was littered with wrappers from Ibiraha: a samosa filled with mashed potato. The ashtray was over-flowing with Marlboro Red stubs, one of the harshest smokes on the market and the only brand that Travis had smoked since he was fourteen. Even with both windows down, the car reeked. It was deep in the upholstery. The harshness of the tobacco hadn't just worked overtime on the car. It had turned Travis's voice to gravel.

He had shoulder-length, dirty-blonde surfer hair. He wore a khaki shirt that breathed well in baking heat and also dried quickly after getting wet. Sudden downpours were one of the few certainties in the region.

It had been years since Travis last had a full shave.

Coupled with his thin, lanky frame, he looked weathered, like a piece of furniture left out in the rain for too long.

He could never get used to the heat there. Forty-two degrees and in thin air.

Grant was wearing similarly functional clothing – though his was all dark and almost new.

Over the din of the engine, Travis warned, 'Don't get too used to this.'

'Used to what?' asked Grant.

Travis gestured to the busy surroundings. 'The painted hotels. The markets. Wi-fi. Mobile phone networks. Paved roads. It won't last long, my friend.'

There weren't many good reasons for a tourist to go into the Democratic Republic of Congo, although some still braved the major cities of Kisangani to the north, and Kinshasa to the south. Where Grant was going, he needed a stronger legend than "tourist". He was Doctor Iain Macleod, a geological researcher from Edinburgh University. It was a position that Grant pulled off well, able to talk to Travis about the intricacies of prehistoric mountain ranges and unique rock formations from his native Skye.

The plan was for Travis to get him as far as Goma, a short drive from the border. Grant's cover of geologist had been based on Mount Nyiragongo, the active volcano that loomed over Goma and regularly erupted.

Travis glanced back at Grant's meagre backpack. 'You're a little light on gear, aren't you?'

'I always travel light,' Grant replied.

Travis nodded to himself. He pulled over to the side of the road. Children crowded under his open window, hands outstretched for a few coins or some food: many of them hadn't had a dinner. Travis barely noticed they were there.

He kept the engine running and turned to Grant. 'You don't have to tell me who you're chasing. It's none of my business. You're paying me well – a little too well. But I need to know what we're getting into. Because I take one look at you and I know that the destination is going to be hairy.'

Grant said nothing.

'You're not just going to Goma, are you?'

Once in Goma, the plan was to ditch Travis and improvise the rest of the way. But Travis had not been the sort of guide he'd expected, someone rigid about the dangers of walking straight into a war zone: what several charities had described as one of the most dangerous places in the world. Grant had a feeling that Travis might be valuable.

Grant said, 'I'm headed to Kisangani. I'm looking for someone.'

Travis snorted. 'I thought so.'

'How far can you take me?'

'I can take you *all* the way, brother.'

'I'm headed for the jungle. I can't make any promises about your safety there.'

'Dude, look at where I'm living. Does it seem like I'm worried about my safety?'

'That's what concerns me,' said Grant. 'People who don't care about dying don't make good decisions under pressure.'

Travis threw up his hands. 'Hey, man. Screw it. If it's your time, it's your time. Hey, do you need a weapon? I can get you a weapon.'

'I'm armed,' Grant replied. 'I'm hoping it won't come to that, though. Are we still good?'

'Hell, yeah,' replied Travis. 'Rock and roll.' He

shrugged. 'Hell, I don't *want* to know what you're doing, brother.' He leaned out the window, telling the children in French and then Kinyarwanda – an official language of Rwanda, and Central African dialect – to step back and watch their feet. He handed out some spare coins and pistachio nuts from the glove compartment. He told them to share and to look after each other, then he pulled back out onto the road. 'Kisangani, huh? Shit... Not many people head up there.'

Grant said, 'The back of beyond?'

'Something like that.' Travis took out a cigarette from his shirt pocket and lit it. 'Other people might call it hell.'

The roadside was crammed, people spilling out onto the paved road, the markets still open in the fading light. Women wore variations of *boubou* – traditional gowns and dresses – with matching headdresses made of Kitenge fabric, the colours vibrant and rich, the geometric designs reflecting everything from religious beliefs to marital status. The street throbbed with life and energetic conversation.

'This is us,' said Travis, slowing the jeep as they approached the border.

A rusty sign hung over the road, attached to a flimsy metal rig. It said:

> "SAFE JOURNEY
> BON VOYAGE
> URUGENDO RUHIRE"
> ("*SAFE TRAVELS*" in Kinyarwanda)

On the other side of the Rwandan barrier was the Democratic Republic of Congo. All it took was a glance over the insubstantial border to see the difference between the two countries.

Directly underneath the barrier, the road surface was nothing more than a dirt track. No kerb, no road markings.

After a superficial check of Travis's papers, the guard let them through. The jeep rolled from side to side on the rough surface, absorbing potholes and lumps.

The colours of Rwanda had gone. The *kanga* wrappers around the women's waists were muted in palette, the sarong-like clothing paired with random second-hand tops, mostly Western in design, bearing the logos of recognisable brands.

There were far fewer stalls at the roadsides, and most of them were closed. It wasn't safe after dark.

Houses were little more than huts, held up by strategically placed lengths of rotting timber.

The energy of Rwanda was also gone. There was little conversation, little brightness of character. The locals' faces were turned down. The atmosphere noticeably hostile.

The jeep's headlights became increasingly important, forging a path towards Goma as the sun disappeared. No more than a mile from Rwanda, it felt like a different world.

Now that the façade of Grant's cover had been punctured, Travis relaxed a little more, reaching into the glove compartment for a can of Primus – a popular beer in the area.

After taking a long sip, Travis said, 'Welcome to Congo.'

41

The road didn't improve much even deep into Goma. Black, stiffened lava from a recent eruption at nearby Mount Nyiragongo had raised the ground level of the city by nearly half a metre. The lava had consumed everything in its way, carving a path through what could charitably be referred to as streets. Anything less than four-wheel-drive and the toughest tyres stood no chance of progressing.

As a child, Grant had been fascinated with the biggest blank spaces on maps, and wondered what he would find there. Now, the more he saw of the world, the answer became apparent: devastation. And darkness. As unknowable as the insides of a human heart.

Such places were hard to picture. But when Grant had ever closed his eyes and tried, what he pictured was somewhere like Goma.

It was a city of a million people, most of them starved of work or reason. Schools were rare and poorly attended. Children were left to roam the streets. Some of them threw stones and dried lava chunks at the Toyota, pinging off the bodywork and windows.

'Don't worry,' said Travis. 'They assume if you're white that you must be a rich bastard. Or from the UN.'

The United Nations' off-white helicopters and armoured trucks were everywhere in Goma, the troops doing little but hanging out and smoking. They didn't speak to the locals. Officially, they were peacekeepers, brought in to stem the tide of violence brought about by the civil war. Most of the fighting took place on the outskirts of the city, but when violence erupted the UN were never to be seen. It would take a direct mortar hit before they bothered to intervene.

The only thing that the locals knew the soldiers for were allegations of sexual assault and molestation against minors – crimes that had been rife in the lawless region.

'Aren't there any police?' asked Grant.

Travis laughed. 'You're looking at them.'

He gestured to a group of men in civilian clothes, sitting on plastic garden furniture, drinking Primus, leering at passing women and girls.

There was little reward in attempting to fight crime in such a place. The criminals they did manage to capture were often set free by corrupt senior officers the next day. The men were paid almost no money. They had no means of escape. No way to support their families. Displacement from war was the only way they would ever get out of the Congo.

Those who had truly embraced nihilism controlled the city. Drugs were dealt openly on street corners, driven by cadres of small children wielding knives and guns. By age ten, many already had their first kills under their belts. Taking a life was common practice. Seen from birth.

The roughest places Grant had been to – Haiti, central Mexico, the favelas of Rio – had given him a decent barometer of how dangerous a place felt. The levels of aggression and lawlessness. Goma was the closest he'd ever felt to a perfect ten on his scale. A mix of the old wild west and an outpost on Mars.

Tourism had once been a major draw for the area in the fifties and sixties. Now, the U.K. Foreign Office advised against all but essential travel through areas like Goma, classing it a "yellow zone". The U.S. State Department concurred. Travel anywhere north of Goma was a red zone: "Advise against all travel." A total no-go.

That was where Grant and Travis were heading.

The roads were completely impassable. Travis reckoned they would make it all of half an hour beyond Goma before being murdered. Either shot, or macheted, or clubbed to death. Which left one alternative: flying.

The Aérport de Goma was home to a dozen aircraft that would never fly again, lining the airport perimeter like some kind of aviation scrapyard. The planes either had terminal mechanical issues, or had crashed in one of Congo's many lightning storms.

Having admitted that he didn't have a plan for reaching Kisangani, Grant was fortunate that Travis had an acquaintance that could get them there.

As they pulled up in the gathering darkness outside the tiny terminal building, Travis asked, 'Where are we going after Kisangani?'

Grant reached for his backpack, a substantial sweat now built up on his face and chest, soaking through his shirt. 'The outskirts of Lomami National Park.'

A dense forest on the Congo River.

Travis let out an anxious puff. 'There's at least five rebel groups fighting there. It's proper hairy. Each soldier has a personal stake in the rubber and cobalt mines nearby. Those guys fight to the last man.'

Grant opened his door. 'My kind of people.'

Their transport was a Cessna 206: a propeller bush plane with room for five people that was little more than a tin can.

Grant put his pack over his shoulder and eyed the darkening skies above.

Outside the terminal there was a rotund man with a thick moustache, smoking a cigarette. His shirt had the epaulettes of a pilot.

Travis gestured towards him. 'That's Vlad.'

Almost immediately there was a rumble of thunder overhead.

While pointing at the sky, Vlad said in thick Russian, 'I hope you have life insurance, my friend. We'll be lucky to make it to Kisangani alive.' He broke off with a hearty laugh, which turned into a guttural cough.

Grant recoiled. He could smell booze on Vlad's breath, and it wasn't clear exactly how fresh it was.

Translating, Travis said, 'He says we can leave soon.'

Grant asked, 'What are the chances of rebels shooting at the plane?'

Vlad pointed to the black clouds again and said something to Travis.

Travis translated, 'He says we should worry more about lightning.'

Vlad patted Grant enthusiastically on the top of the arm – right where Haslitt had slashed him. Grant shut his eyes, swallowing the unexpected pain. Vlad then launched into a loud rendition of the *whoa-oa!* chorus from Bon Jovi's 'Livin' on a Prayer'.

Grant said, 'I suppose there's no point in asking if Vlad is the best option we have.'

Travis replied, 'You should have seen his alternate. Vlad's good.' He paused, reconsidering his answer. 'He's *pretty* good... I mean, decent. Very decent.'

Grant stared, deadpan.

Travis said, 'He'll get us there.'

After running through the plane spot-checks – amounting to little more than checking that the wheels were attached to the aircraft – Vlad announced, 'We leave in five minutes.'

Travis was drunk by the time the plane was over Maiko National Park – one of the country's most remote wilder-nesses, a vast sea of green for hundreds of miles, twinkling under the light of the moon.

Travis's six-pack of Primus beer didn't last long. He passed out somewhere over the mountainous jungle and the Congo River.

Grant's only company was the folder on his laptop of Henry Marlow's personnel files, and the remaining audio diaries from the Estonian safe deposit box.

The more he listened, the more he read, the less Grant understood. Not just about Marlow. About himself. Having come so close at Place Bellecour, he felt an urgency, a need to stand in front of Marlow and ask him why. It had no bearing on his mission, yet the compulsion to get answers felt visceral.

The files and audio diaries promised someone much bigger, but even if Grant got to confront him, Marlow would still be just a human. Flesh and bone. There was no way the real man could match the version of Marlow that had taken up residence in Grant's head.

He wasn't flippant about the reality of confronting Marlow in person. Grant's uncertainty about finally meeting him wasn't a fear of being killed, or doubting his resolve in taking definitive action if needed. It was a fear that Marlow might not have any answers to explain his actions.

Grant couldn't pin down what had gone wrong with Marlow to one single thing. It must have been inside him all along. Eating away. Waiting to come out.

He didn't kid himself that having killed Haslitt meant he had every skill required to take down someone like Marlow. If anything, Marlow's state of mind made him less predictable. But as far out as Marlow had strayed and as tenuous as his grasp on reality appeared to be, Grant still retained a belief that he could bring Marlow back some-how. By confronting him, and finding out once and for all what Henry Marlow had become.

42

The Vauxhall Cross exit on the Albert Embankment side consisted of a series of external security barriers that felt like the demilitarized zone between South and North Korea. Only once Justin had cleared the final steel door – solid, giving no through-view – did he feel like he was in the real world again.

After breathing in hours of recycled air under harsh lighting, central London on a warm summer night was like an oasis.

Everyone who worked at Vauxhall Cross had had moments of catching the eye of some passing civilian as they exited the building. Some pretended they were uninterested, but Justin knew that they had a sense of wonder and fascination about them, as if he had just exited Narnia. *Does he know state secrets? Has he just witnessed drone footage of a major assassination? Is he actually a spy?*

In his first few months, Justin had felt a rush of excitement when he felt someone examining him. There was a glamour about it. But glamour soon fades. For Justin, Vauxhall Cross had become a workplace like any other.

The sun had set an hour ago, leaving the riverside dark and muggy.

Justin carried his suit jacket over his forearm. He put his hands in his pockets, feeling the separated parts of his phone: he'd taken out the battery as instructed. He made his way along Riverside Walk, the stretch of pavement directly beside the Thames.

He waited under the gloom of the trees, leaning over the metal barrier at the river's edge, staring at the lights shimmering on the surface. The water may have been peaceful, but Justin was far from at ease. There were protocols to taking meetings like these. Procedures. None of which he'd followed. If Swann had really been up to something, he didn't want her finding out.

If stopping Marlow was the priority, then interfering with the raid team the way she had wasn't playing the percentages anymore. It didn't add up.

Justin had pinned his hopes on the GCHQ spider trace. With Ryan and Samantha's help, he was convinced that they could find something that would explain Swann's behaviour. Without something significant to point to, all he had was circumstantial at best. And he wasn't prepared to take little more than a gut feeling as evidence to Christie. Not against his own boss.

Justin flicked his head left as he heard the sudden footsteps of a jogger. He turned right to check that they had kept on moving. Within seconds, they were around the corner and gone.

He heard Swann's voice behind him. 'Justin.'

She was doing her best to hide her identity by wearing a baseball cap and a long Mackintosh.

When Justin turned to face her, his immediate thoughts were: what is she doing here, and why is she dressed like that? Before he could think of answers, his eyes widened. His neck pulsed forward, a single thrust. He tried to speak. Instead of words, it was blood that came out of his mouth.

He looked down at his stomach where Swann had inserted a pair of scissors. He didn't feel any pain at first, as if his brain couldn't process their appearance in a place where they didn't belong. Then his eyes traced a path along the scissors, to Swann holding the handles with rubber surgical gloves, then up her arm to her shoulder, then her face and eyes.

He couldn't move.

Swann had once heard a field officer describe the nearest thing to an instant kill. It required a strong nerve and a steady hand, but it would give Swann what she required: a quick, silent kill.

She pulled the scissors out of Justin's stomach. Panic took hold of her. It was already too late. She couldn't back out now. She altered her grip on the scissors to overhand, then drove the blades directly through Justin's right eye socket. The immediate sensation in her body was one of amazement, as the blades kept going further and further in. Eventually they could go no further, penetrating the texture of his brain. The scissors were inserted so deep into his eye socket, Swann's fist was right above his cheekbone.

She wanted to throw up, but reminded herself to be strong. *This is what it takes.*

She caught him as he fell, taking the opportunity to

check that no one had seen them. The path was clear in both directions.

It had been a huge risk. But a necessary one.

While Justin's centre of gravity was still relatively high, she pushed him by the shoulders until he tipped over the railing – the scissors still lodged in his face.

His body landed in the water twenty metres down with a soft splash – the slightest of noises in the atmospherics of the city's traffic noise.

She looked around again. With the coast clear, she removed the baseball cap and folded it into her pocket.

She didn't have long to compose herself before reaching the entrance to Vauxhall Cross. It was all she could do not to throw up on the spot. She never knew that nausea could whip up inside a body with such torque. All those warnings she had heard through the years, whispered in senior circles about field officers' first kills and the dreadful toll it can take: she finally understood it now. She felt on the verge of frenzy.

No more than ten seconds after Justin's body hit the water, a jogger huffed and puffed past her, completely oblivious to the ripples on the water below, and what he had narrowly avoided interrupting.

When she rounded the corner, taking her away from the riverside, something shifted in her head. Like some terrible light that couldn't be switched off.

There could be no going back.

43

Grant and Travis landed in Kisangani with a harsh thud, the tiny plane buffeted by a brutal crosswind. Vlad had landed half on potholed concrete, half on grass. The lack of adequate runway lights hadn't helped: a power cut throughout the region had plunged the airport into darkness. But no one had more landings at Kisangani than Vlad. His combination of experience and dutch courage had kept them all in one piece.

Travis stepped off the plane, rubbing his head as a slight hangover kicked in. He said, 'Joseph Conrad called this the "inner station". You wanted the wild country: this is it.'

Grant was relieved to feel solid ground under his feet. But their odyssey would only get more dangerous from there.

The power cut created a glimpse of how the city would have felt in colonial days – when it was still called Stanleyville. The only lights downtown were from motorcycles and scooters, chugging along with a high-pitched whine, carrying as many as three people at a time. Strings of battery-powered bulbs glowed from mobile fast-food stands, serving Congolese barbecue of grilled goat, along with bottles of lukewarm Primus beer.

Before passing out on the plane, Travis had formulated a plan for reaching Joseph's estate. The only mode of travel that didn't guarantee a death sentence: river boat.

At night, the harbour came alive as traders returned from far-away villages. They held pigs by their hind legs, walking them backwards like wheelbarrows down the steamers' rickety gangplanks. Sacks of rice and cages crammed with chickens were thrown around with abandon. Kisangani harbour never slept.

While Travis haggled with potential boat vendors, Grant was immediately swarmed by traders, disarmingly young children, and drug dealers. The more he said no, the more forceful they became.

Travis returned, smoking a cigarette. He pointed at their boat: the Gloria. It had once been used for guided cruises up and down the mighty Congo River, but its best days were clearly long behind it. 'This is us,' he said, leading them to the gangplank.

Absalom, the captain, unhooked their rope from the harbour. Once they were moving, he headed for the cabin, where he would remain for almost the entire length of their journey.

Above the white cabin was a sign painted in black: '*La vie est un combat au Congo.*'

Life is a fight in Congo.

Travis was on board but still involved in a frantic and garbled auction for a bottle of Jack Daniels. He barely

made the exchange of five U.S. dollars before the seller's
hand drifted out of reach.

Travis jiggled the bottle in excitement at Grant. 'Now
we can relax. You should get some sleep,' he advised. 'We'll
be at least four hours upriver.'

He took up a position at the bow, removing a perme-
thrin-treated net from his backpack. He told Grant, 'Make
sure your whole body is under your net. Triatoma – we call
them assassin bugs. They're everywhere around here at
night.'

'What do they do?' asked Grant, taking out his own net.

'Bite you on the face.'

'That doesn't sound so bad.'

Travis chuckled. 'Then they shed faeces over the wound
and rub it in. The faeces enter your bloodstream and make
a new home inside your heart and your liver. Then there's
your tik-tik flies. They deliver Sleeping Sickness. Believe me,
if a tik-tik bites you, you'll know all about it.' He dipped his
baseball cap over his face. 'Sleep tight. The captain will
wake us when we get there.'

Yeah, sweet dreams, thought Grant. He noticed a few
inches of net not covering his feet. He quickly pulled
them in.

Once he heard Travis making light snoring sounds,
Grant took out his .45 calibre Glock 30 with TruGlo fibre-
optic night sights. Entering a property with potentially no
electricity, or in a night-time raid, a crisp, clear laser sight
could be the difference between life and death.

He checked the magazine and the rack slide. Both were
in smooth working order. After putting the gun away, he
noticed that Absalom had been watching him.

A single lightbulb attached to the cabin wall illuminated

his face, which was slick from the river water he'd just splashed on himself: the cheapest fly repellent available. The flies buzzed harmlessly around the lightbulb, oblivious to Absalom's presence.

The captain pushed down an opening in the front window so that he could speak to Grant. He spoke English with a slight French twang – remnants of his third language. 'If you fire that thing on my boat, you can swim the rest of the way.'

Grant showed his palms in deference.

The captain said, 'You're going to Joseph's place, aren't you?'

'What makes you say that?' asked Grant.

'A feeling.'

'What do you know about Joseph?'

'I know that until a few years ago, the area where you're going was not good. A lot of fighting, a lot of shooting. All the time. Then a white guy who looked a lot like you came up this river.'

'The white guy. He killed Charles Joseph?'

Absalom's face gave nothing away. 'That's what I heard.'

'Have you heard anything else about him?'

'I heard that he went into the forest on his own and killed two generals in different militias. He did in a week what the French forces, the African congress, and United Nations couldn't do in five years.'

'Is he there now?'

Absalom shook his head. 'I don't know. I hear that he comes and goes. There are a lot of stories. I'm just glad I don't have to go in there with you.'

44

Winston was on his feet behind his desk, surrounded by cardboard cartons from MI6 Archives. He'd been leafing through them for over an hour. What had started out as an orderly and sensible unpacking of the files had quickly spiralled into a chaotic mess that no one else could understand.

Miles Archer struggled as he backed through the door with another trolley of cartons. It had been four floors with a dozen heavy boxes now. He had his sleeves rolled up, and his fringe was matted with sweat. 'This is the last of it,' he announced with relief.

The cartons were marked "SAUDI ARABIA", along with an associated year for the intelligence inside.

Archer could barely set the trolley down before Winston started pulling off the top cartons.

'Cheers,' Winston said, as if all Archer had done was find him a stapler.

Archer stepped aside for Imogen Swann at the doorway.

She couldn't get more than a few steps into the office. 'You know, we have these computer things now, Leo...'

Winston answered, 'The Archive intranet's down for maintenance for the next few hours. I had to take hard copies. That's the problem with working when everyone else is in bed.'

'What is all this?' she asked.

He barely looked up from the carton he was rummaging through. 'Everything we have on Saudi Arabia from the last five years.'

'What are you looking for?'

'Prince Mohammad bin Abdul.'

'And you need to find it in the next two hours?'

Winston took a single piece of paper from a carton and took it to a stack on his desk. 'Yes, I do. Grant should be reaching the compound soon. I need to be in the Control room when he gets there.' He lifted a full carton of papers from his desk and dropped it on the floor. 'Speaking of staff: I shouldn't have to be chasing up security to find out when senior officers are leaving for the day.'

'What officers?' asked Swann.

'Justin Vern. Security said he left at nine, and Miles says he's not answering his phone...' He was distracted by Swann's pallor. 'Are you feeling alright?'

'A long day, that's all,' she replied.

'I know the feeling.'

Archer appeared behind Swann. 'Your phone's engaged,' he said.

Winston looked towards the handset, then saw that a pile of papers had knocked the phone off the cradle. 'Shit,' he muttered, straining to reach and re-place the handset.

Archer held out his phone. 'Sir, you need to take this. It's the Marine Policing Unit.'

Swann's body went rigid.

'What the hell do *they* want?' asked Winston.

Archer replied, 'They just found Justin.'

'Found Justin? What do you mean?'

'They've found his body, sir.'

The Metropolitan Police's Forensics Service – SCD-4 from the Specialist Crime Directorate unit – had joined the Marine Unit on Albert Embankment, halfway between the Vauxhall and Lambeth bridges.

Given the opportunity for premeditation, a murderer couldn't have picked a worse time to dispose of a body in the River Thames. Justin had entered the water only a few hours short of low tide, which fell at half past eleven at night, when the water was barely a metre high at the river's edge.

The gentle tide had carried him half a mile before beaching his body on the shore close to Albert Embankment.

Low tide was when the Marine unit was busiest, with tourists often finding themselves pinned up against the river wall as the tide quickly rose. Junkies and drinkers were also a problem – which was what the two Marine Policing officers assumed Justin was.

When they had pulled their boat up as close as they could, they noticed that he wasn't reacting to the water lapping at his feet. One officer pointed the spotlight towards the body, catching sight of the scissors sticking out of his face.

. . .

Winston and Swann arrived at the scene together.

When forensics had recovered Justin's ID badge – still attached on retractable elastic on his waistband – they made the call to Vauxhall Cross.

The detective inspector on the scene was first to greet the MI6 pair, a little in awe. He'd met Service personnel before, but not senior spooks at anything near Winston or Swann's level.

To a degree, spies operated on a higher plain on home soil. They had their own department within the Inland Revenue who handled their personal tax matters to keep their real identities safe; if their house was burgled, Counter Terrorism Command (formerly Special Branch) rather than regular CID were called in; they could go pretty much anywhere they liked without a warrant.

The detective inspector had pictured MI6 senior staff with hardened, far-away looks in their eyes. Steely jaws. What he found in Winston and Swann looked more like middle management from a high-street bank.

The pavement was impassable for pedestrians, blocked by multiple black four by fours and people carriers from Counter Terrorism Command: the unit responsible for sensitive national security investigations. There was still an hour left before the tide came in again, giving the numerous forensic investigators in white suits time with Justin's body before having to move him. Being so late at night, there were only a handful of people on Lambeth Bridge pausing to see what was going on.

It was as still and as quiet as the city ever got.

As Justin had been Swann's assistant and she had

seniority, Winston had expected her to take the lead. Instead, she hung back near the black Coroner van that had double-parked on the main road.

The detective inspector held out his hand. 'Mr Winston, DI Kelly.'

Winston paused, keeping his hands at his side. 'I'm sorry. It's a mere formality, but...'

Kelly nodded absentmindedly, then showed Winston and Swann his ID. Even knowing their names and faces required Kelly to sign the Official Secrets Act – the wording of which could put the fear of God into anyone.

Winston took a good look at the ID before committing to a handshake. 'Sorry, Detective Inspector.'

'No problem.' Kelly paused for a moment at the thick scar that stretched down Winston's forearm to his wrist.

Winston quickly retracted his hand.

Kelly could tell that Swann had no interest in a handshake. 'I'm sorry about your man.'

Winston's eyes drifted down towards the shore: the white sheet covering Justin's body was impossible to ignore.

Kelly pointed along the pavement towards Lambeth Bridge. 'We need to take the stairs down to get there.'

Swann spoke up from a few feet back. 'Is that really necessary?'

The two men stopped.

Faltering, she clarified, 'The tide, I mean. Is there time?'

Kelly replied, 'We've got an hour. SCD will be done by then.'

Winston was glad to be moving again, at pace – it distracted him from the sense of dread he was feeling. 'Do you know what happened?' he asked.

'He's been stabbed in the face and stomach.'

Winston recoiled with a grunt of disgust. Swann's reaction was slower, and much dimmer. Her brain was incapable of manufacturing anything else.

Kelly explained, 'He must have been pushed in downstream at Riverside Walk. The water's a little higher there. SCD reckon time of death is only about an hour ago.' Kelly turned back as he breezed rapidly down the stairs towards the shore. 'The forensics are all Specialist Crimes, by the way, so they're all cleared for this.'

When they reached the scene on firm, rocky ground, forensics stepped back, apart from the Crime Scene Manager.

Kelly introduced her, 'This is our CSM.'

She told Winston and Swann, 'You should know that his ID is attached to his trousers, so there's a chance he's been compromised before he was found.'

Kelly asked Winston, 'Do you have any reason to believe you have officers in the field at risk?'

Winston looked at Swann.

'It's too soon to tell,' she replied, looking anywhere but at the white sheet on the ground in front of them.

Kelly didn't need to warn Winston about what he was about to see. From the way the white sheet peaked over Justin's face, it was clear that the murder weapon was underneath.

'Just tell me when,' Kelly said.

Winston nodded.

Kelly crouched over the white sheet, then pulled it back.

Swann turned away immediately. She made it two steps before throwing up.

Winston stared at Justin's face. The colour had drained from it, still holding an expression of shock from the impact of the scissors. It was like a film prop of a dead body. He turned his eyes down towards his feet. 'That's him. That's Justin Vern.' He looked away quickly. 'Could you cover him, please?'

Kelly motioned at the CSM, who covered the body again.

Swann staggered away, wiping her mouth. 'Sorry. I can't...' she said. She walked back towards the stairs, her arms folded in an attempt to keep from trembling.

Winston said, 'I'll inform his family.'

'Will you be my liaison through the night?' asked Kelly.

Winston glanced back at Swann. 'Looks like I'm going to have to be. Is there anything to go on?'

'There aren't any prints so far, but SCD are expecting this to move quickly. This was a risky, impulsive kill. There aren't many places on the riverside you could guarantee that no one would see.'

'What do your instincts say?' asked Winston.

'This was a frenzied attack. An act of panic. The weapon feels improvised to me. It wouldn't be many people's first choice. And it would have been up close.' Kelly considered his language carefully. 'I don't know the ins and outs of Justin Vern's life and what he was working on. But whoever did this is an extremely dangerous individual, and we need to catch them.'

Winston pursed his lips. 'Thank you, Detective Inspector.'

Once he caught up to Swann at street-level, she looked down with a slight shake of her head. 'I'm sorry,' she said. 'It's been a while. And for it to be Justin...'

'I get it,' he replied. 'But we need to act fast on this.'

Swann seemed surprised. 'What's to act on?'

'Justin's phone, for one thing. Security said his stuff was still upstairs. He wasn't leaving for the day, which means he went outside for a reason, and he didn't head to Riverside Walk for something to eat. I'd like to know who he contacted, or who contacted him, before...' He couldn't complete the sentence.

Having had a little time to think up a theory, Swann said, 'There's only one person who can be responsible for this.'

'Who?'

'Henry Marlow.'

Winston said, 'I suppose we can't rule it out. Look, I told Kelly I'd liaise tonight. You should get back.'

'Get back?'

'If Marlow's in the city we need to lockdown Vauxhall Cross. You're probably the only director still on at this time of night.'

Swann nodded rapidly. 'Of course, of course. What are you going to do?'

'I'll tell Olivia,' he said, taking out his phone. 'She needs to know our worst nightmare might be coming true. Henry Marlow in London.'

45

The night air felt cool on Winston as he removed his suit jacket while crossing the river at Lambeth Bridge. His mind was a fog as he entered the King's Arms pub. It was one of the few traditional English pubs remaining in Westminster. Once a mainstay of the political establishment – when spending unprotected time with members of the public was still possible for them – the Arms had become a haven of nostalgia. From the Union Jacks hanging outside above the gilded sign, to the portraits of its illustrious former clientele like Churchill and Dickens.

The barman was shouting for last orders when Winston entered. The bar was quiet, single punters only at such a time midweek. TVs mounted on various walls around the place all showed the same football highlights from a match earlier that night.

The barman said, 'Evening, Leo.' He didn't even have to ask. He pulled the tap on a pint of bitter.

'Evening, Barry,' Winston replied, placing down a ten-pound note. He spread his arms wide, leaning on the bar.

There was something dutiful about how he stood. In observance of a ritual, watching the pint being pulled.

'You know this breaks my heart every time,' said Barry.

'Yeah, I know.'

Barry put the pint down in front of him along with Winston's change, then walked away. He knew that Winston preferred to be left alone.

Winston stared at the pint. Smelling it. God, how he missed that smell. Every time. He thought about how good it would taste sliding down his throat, the soft malty after-taste. Especially on a night like this. He hadn't eaten since earlier that afternoon. Which meant that the gentle light-headedness that would come on somewhere near the bottom of the glass would be particularly warm. But it wasn't just the actual drinking of the pint. It was the way the buzz came on afterwards. Walking home, feeling just the right amount of detachment. Not so drunk that you slurred, or couldn't walk straight. But far enough away from sober that your troubles receded into the background.

Winston also missed the part when you get home. You put on some music, and at that moment it's the only thing you can imagine wanting to listen to, and it's great. You feel so great that you head to the kitchen and grab another can or a bottle. It's still before midnight, and the thought of tomorrow isn't even on the horizon yet. The music is perfect. Then you start finding the slower, sadder songs on an album. You get to thinking about things. Your life. Your past. Things you've lost. People you've lost. People you want. The melancholy makes you feel like smoking a cigarette.

The next thing you know, you're waking up face-down on the living room carpet. There are cans and bottles all around you. The stale alcohol on the carpet is the only thing that smells worse than you. Your head feels like a pigsty.

All of those things were just a taste of what Winston knew would happen if he took so much as a sip of that pint.

He knocked twice on the bar then picked up his change.

When Barry turned around, he found what he always did: a pound tip, and the pint still there, untouched. The door swinging shut. And Winston gone.

As he poured the pint down the sink, Barry shook his head. 'Waste of good beer,' he said.

Winston strode through Pimlico, unable to get the image of Justin out of his mind. He thought through the methodology; the situation surrounding the murder. He'd reached the heart of Belgravia, the terraced, white stucco townhouses giving way to the taller, more grandly ornate buildings of Knightsbridge. Specifically, the red-brick townhouses of Cadogan Square.

Home to Olivia Christie.

A black armoured Rolls-Royce was parked across the street. Unseen in the car, a security officer called in Leo's appearance to Vauxhall Cross – standard procedure whenever anyone so much as approached the Chief's front door.

It reminded Winston just how vulnerable some of the most important government and intelligence figures are in the real world. They can't all live in fortresses like Downing Street. Security-cleared officials screened their mail and delivered it in plain white vans; their internet secured via GCHQ servers; and banking done by unlisted, private entities. Yet physical access was still largely and surprisingly open. A presence would be noted and monitored, but if you knew the address, you could still ring the doorbell of the Chief of the Secret Intelligence Service at close to midnight – as Leo Winston was currently doing.

She answered the door still in her work clothes from earlier. She had only made it as far as removing her blazer.

'I was wondering when you would get here,' she said, standing aside to let him in. She gave a minor wave towards the car across the street.

It had been a while since Winston had last been there. Much like Christie herself, the décor and artwork were stubbornly traditional. There were no Rothko or Pollock abstractions. Christie's was a house of landscape oil paintings, and J.M.W. Turner prints of navy ships (her family came from an impressive line of Navy stock).

Winston said, 'I'm sorry about the late hour.'

'Sit down,' Christie said.

Edward Elgar's "Nimrod from the Enigma Variations" played in stunning clarity from a pair of speakers across the room. Christie turned the volume down on the way to the bar.

A weathered copy of John le Carré's *Tinker Tailor Soldier Spy* sat face-down on the floor, alongside Christie's dinner on a tray: steak and green beans, which she had barely started. The rare glimpse into how Christie spent her evenings would have amused Winston if he hadn't also got the feeling that he was intruding on what was likely to be the solitary half hour she had to herself.

'This can wait,' he said, resistant to sitting down.

'Nonsense,' she replied, pouring herself a whisky. The bar was stocked with every imaginable spirit. 'The steak was cold anyway. Rather a waste of time. I've been on the phone to the Commissioner of the Met.'

Winston finally sat down on the three-seater Chesterfield. 'So, you heard the news.'

'Yes. I'm sorry about Justin. Can I get you water? Lemonade?'

'A water would be great, thanks,' he said. He braced himself. If she was going to ask him, it would be her next question. As articulate as he was when speaking about it, there was little he disliked as much as discussing his sobriety.

Christie handed him a tumbler of sparkling water. 'You realise if it was the sixties, you would have been bounced out of the Service by now. Anyone who didn't drink was viewed as a danger – someone who was scared of slipping up whilst drunk.' Reacting to the lack of laughter, Christie said, 'That was meant to be funny.'

Winston smiled politely.

Christie paused, wondering if he would pull the trigger on whatever he'd come to say or ask, but he evidently needed more time.

The music temporarily filled the lull in conversation.

Christie asked, 'Do you like Elgar?'

Winston held the glass in both hands, looking down into his water. 'I do, ma'am. A throwback to a simpler time.' He gestured at the le Carré on the floor. 'You could say the same about *Tinker*.'

'I don't know. All the great ones ultimately come down to betrayal. It hasn't changed much through the years.'

'Maybe betrayal hasn't,' said Winston. 'But the game has. Don't you feel it out there?'

'Feel what?' she asked.

'I don't know... Like something has broken. All the things we used to control and understand.'

Christie warned him, 'Be careful about romanticising the past, Leo. By the end of the Cold War we were so busy finding evidence of Russia's war games we missed the one thing that really mattered: the entire Communist system was collapsing. It was like we were wandering around a house that was falling down, and we diagnosed the problem as excessive dust and noise. That should have been it for us. Failing to predict the fall of Communism should have been the end for MI6. The whole lot of us. CIA missed nine eleven. We ballsed up Iraq. Now we're just glorified defence. Finding threats and stopping them one at a time.'

Winston took a sip of water. 'That's actually why I'm here. I'm a Task Chief Officer. I'm not used to having late-night conflabs with the Chief of the Service.'

'You can speak frankly here, Leo.'

'On the way over, I asked GCHQ to look into Justin Vern's phone records. He received a call from a burner not long before he was murdered. The phone is untraceable, but I think whoever called him also killed him.'

'You don't think it was Marlow?' asked Christie.

'None of it fits. The weapon. The location. The timing. What would Marlow want with someone like Justin? He was Swann's assistant. An analyst. He didn't run agents. He wouldn't have handed his phone number out. To anyone.'

'It was someone internal.'

'It had to be.' Winston took a beat. 'I came here to request a wiretap.'

'On who?'

'Two people. The first is Imogen Swann.'

Christie drained her glass, then headed straight back to the bar.

Winston added, 'I want to tap her phone and search her office. And I think it needs to happen tonight.'

Christie said, 'I'd better check that's definitely water in your glass, because you certainly sound drunk.'

Unfazed, Winston tried to explain. 'If Édith Lagrange was operating as a mole inside Interpol, who was she working for? Henry Marlow? I don't buy that for a second.'

'You're making a pretty extraordinary accusation against a director, Leo. A RIPA court order might approve electronic surveillance, but intercepts can only be used as a source of intelligence. Not actual evidence.'

'On U.K. soil, yes. But there's a backdoor in RIPA court orders: foreign wiretaps are still admissible.'

'Foreign? You want to send Imogen overseas so you can intercept her phone calls and messages?'

'No,' Winston replied. 'I want to do that to the other person I believe is involved.'

It took Christie a moment or two. 'You're actually serious. I mean, you're actually going to ask me.'

'Henry Marlow knows something about AC one eighty, ma'am. A report that was redacted and classified: that the Foreign Secretary was washing dirty Saudi money through one of our slush funds.'

Christie paused in the centre of the room, reeling. 'You want me to approve a wiretap on the Foreign Secretary? The minister responsible for SIS?'

'Everything that Duncan Grant has found so far points to Henry Marlow being set up in Lyon. I don't think he killed Claude Pinot or any of our people there. Whatever Marlow knows, it involves John Wark and Imogen Swann.'

Christie took her drink to the window, looking out over the immaculate gardens below the balcony. A calmness returned to her voice. 'For your own good, Leo, I'd like you to go home and forget about this. When Grant's done in Congo, he's to return to London for a debrief.'

Winston squinted. 'You're black taping this.'

Christie didn't reply.

He raised his voice, louder than he should have. 'Aren't you? What did Wark tell you? Did he threaten you?'

Christie turned to face him. 'Our first obligation isn't to the truth, Leo.'

'Nor is it to help prop up the government of the day.'

'You're right,' she said. 'Our job is to protect the national interest. Believe me when I tell you that if we don't take Henry Marlow down in the next forty-eight hours, Wark *will* order me to wrap this case in black tape. For all our sakes.'

Winston nodded in resignation, taking a moment to process things.

'Leo,' she said. 'If this is about Wark and you, I need to know.'

'It's nothing personal,' he replied blankly.

'I can't imagine what you went through at the hands of the Chinese.'

'I believe "memorable" is what they aim for.'

'I still blame myself for what happened.'

'I don't blame you. I blame Wark.'

'You should know that if I'd been in the same position as him when he was C, I would have made the same decision. A rescue operation on an MSS facility in the middle of Beijing... it could have ended up a bloodbath.'

Winston gave a wry smile. 'I lied earlier, ma'am. When

you asked about Elgar. I find him sentimental. A throwback to a time that no longer exists. I think that's what you like about him.' He gestured to the framed prints on the wall. 'The same thing you like about Turner. They reflect a different time. A more decent time. It's not just nostalgia for you. It's about decency. And honour. When I was in China, I knew the risks. As Grant does now. Because we believe in *Semper Occultus*…'

Always secret.

'…I know you believe in that too. We can still do this job and be honourable.'

Christie was stunned at Winston's gall, but respected his bravery. 'If you had to live with the decisions I have to make on a daily basis, Leo, I swear you would quite simply break into a thousand pieces. We can aim for honour in this job, but we can't always reach it.'

Winston thought she was done.

She then added, 'You've got to catch Marlow, Leo. Wark wants him dead for a reason. Find that reason. Quickly.'

'Yes, ma'am.' He rose, putting his glass down with a loud chink on the marble coffee table.

Christie said, 'Leo. You lasted six months in the hands of the Chinese and never told them a word. You don't have to convince me that honour still exists.'

His determination revitalised, he said, 'Ma'am.'

46

Crown Prince Mohammad bin Abdul was a man who always got what he wanted. When the Château Louis XIV went on sale, he didn't bat an eye at paying five hundred million euros for it – at the time, a world record for a residential property.

The actual ownership of the private mansion on the outskirts of Paris was shrouded behind dozens of shell companies based in Luxembourg and Montenegro. Companies all owned by one of the Crown Prince's many charitable foundations. The charity element was crucial, as it meant that obscure European financial laws prevented Abdul's ownership ever being proven in a legal sense.

To the untrained eye, the mansion looked like it had been built in the time of Versailles, but it was actually only ten years old. It was set on seventy acres of classically French gardens every bit as jaw-dropping as the mansion itself: there were lush green lawns a half-mile long; flower beds that had been attended to with tweezers; embroidered box hedges; topiary yew trees clipped into small pyramids; a tree-lined maze. There was even a traditional farmhouse with goats and stables, and a dazzling fountain that lit up at night.

Inside, it was hard to quantify the meticulous architectural detailing that had gone into the mansion. There was stonemasonry and ironwork and gilding that had taken years to complete – work that only a handful of people would ever notice. The army of cleaners that worked non-stop to keep the mansion immaculate were the only ones to see many of the rooms.

But none of the Prince's guests were in the mood to notice such artistry. The major political figures in attendance were in France for the G20 Summit, and had been invited for a night-time 'gathering' that was the definition of private. There were no personal aides or secretaries or assistants allowed, and all bodyguards had to remain in a single room for the duration. They didn't mind. The Prince had laid on a banquet for them that would be fit for a world leader.

Upstairs was where the real action was.

As well as the drugs and prostitutes. For their silence, Abdul paid the women tens of thousands of U.S. dollars an hour. Most of the women didn't last longer than six months in the grim and sordid job before the money no longer seemed worth it.

There appeared to be a correlation between politicians' lofty positions and increasingly debased desires, mostly revolving around power games and humiliation – a vile by-product of going most of their adult lives without ever being told 'no'.

For the prostitutes, the cash didn't last long, but the memories lasted a lifetime.

. . .

The lights had been dimmed, and trance music pounded from the speakers in the corner of the room. The Prince had flown in one of Europe's top DJs, paying him six figures to stand in a room on his own while the music was streamed around the mansion.

Four hours in, and the guests had spread out around the first floor.

A ghostly-thin Spanish woman was draped over Foreign Secretary John Wark. His shirt had four buttons open, exposing his hairy chest and drooping pecs.

He was holding a glass of Macallan 1979 Gran Reserva. His sixth. A mere six thousand pounds a bottle.

Abdul handed it out like tap water.

The woman said, 'Today's my birthday.'

'Really?' Wark slurred. He pointed to another girl – woman was over-stating it – across the room. 'She said it was her birthday too.'

'What are the chances...' she purred back.

Wark raised his glass at Abdul, who was sitting across from him on a matching sofa. Abdul was also drinking Macallan, and had a woman on each side who were both wearing luxurious Bordelle lingerie.

Abdul told the women in impeccable English, 'Ladies, please leave us.'

Wark sat up a little, knowing that shop-talk was coming. He now regretted drinking so much so quickly.

Abdul was deadly serious. 'We have to discuss the Henry Marlow situation.'

'I have him under control,' Wark asserted.

'Then why am I hearing that the contents of AC one eighty are now out in the open at MI6?'

Wark raised a defensive hand. 'It's a know-nothing task

chief without a dog in the fight. He's as eager to put down Henry Marlow as we are.' He swirled his whisky. 'MI6 are sending in an operative to take care of it.'

'Ah, yes,' Abdul said. 'Duncan Grant. The Scots know how to make whisky. But I'm not sold on their abilities as assassins.'

'Don't be too hasty on that, Your Highness. He killed Martin Haslitt.'

'I should have been informed about that.'

'Consider yourself informed now.'

'You said that you could control Grant.'

'I can.'

Abdul retorted, 'You said the same about Henry Marlow. We are on the cusp of having a deniability problem. Grant is getting too close.'

'What are you saying?' asked Wark.

'I'm saying that it's not enough just to kill Marlow. Grant has to go as well.'

Wark smiled at his whisky, then drank it all. As soon as he lowered his arm, he poured another. 'There's a reason you came to me for help in the first place. Duncan Grant isn't Kadir Rashid. Another mess like that and we both go down. You need to think of the bigger picture.'

'I am,' said Abdul. 'You thought you were clever having Haslitt place those photos of the Interpol detective in Marlow's deposit box. Thanks to that idea, Grant is in possession of diaries belonging to Marlow. There mentions of operations not in his MI6 records. Operations that Grant shouldn't know about.'

Wark said, 'If you kill my man and it gets out the way the Rashid job got out...' He considered his options, 'politically, it would make British support for your Saudi Vision plan impossible. And let's be frank: any economic plan that revolves around tourism rather than oil needs our support. The tables are turning, Abdul. We don't need you anymore. You need us.' Wark's tongue already loosened, he found it impossible to fasten it again. 'All these people here tonight? The Germans, Japanese, Chinese? The G20? We think the Saudis are a geopolitical joke. You lucked into the most valuable natural resource this planet will ever know, and what have you done with it? You spent trillions escalating a fifteen-hundred-year-old argument between Sunnis and Shias over who Muhammad's rightful successor was.' He gestured at the lavish surroundings. 'You bought tacky imitations of French palaces. Hookers and gold bathtubs and diamond-encrusted Lamborghinis. You're like lottery winners who blow their fortune, and a year later they're back playing the lottery again.' Wark leaned in as if to hammer home his punchline. 'But when the oil dries up in fifty years, Abdul, and the rest of the world gives in to the inevitable and commits to nuclear energy, you'll be right back where the world wants you: a bunch of savages stuck in the middle of the bloody desert. Don't try to make plans. Not for me, and especially for my government. You're bad at it.'

Abdul's eyes narrowed with amusement, as if Wark had played right into his hands. 'Mr Wark, you seem to have me confused with one of my idiot cousins or, worse, my father.' He quoted sarcastically from the PR message the Kingdom had been pressing for months now. 'The Saudi Vision "plan for economic prosperity in the new century" is nonsense. Do you think I don't realise that we cannot replace trillions in oil revenue by turning Saudi Arabia into a tourist hotspot? As if Western tourists are going to come to beach resorts in a country where we behead people in public squares. Where our idea of progress is allowing women to drive. The Saudi Vision plan is the last gasp of a dying kingdom struggling to retain its relevance. But the British know all about that.' Abdul remained composed. 'You don't get it, do you? I have no interest in rebuilding my country. My London property is my parachute: the one investment that won't lose value in my lifetime. Do you know what my father will do if he finds out about it? The secret police work for me. I know their methods. I don't intend on sampling them. But you have just as much to lose as I have.'

'Really,' said Wark, still unconvinced.

'If my father finds out that you backed this deal with me, who do you think he will buy weapons from in future? I have a parachute. Where's yours?'

Wark sat back in his seat.

Abdul stood up and motioned towards a door in the corner of the room. An uncommonly muscle-bound Saudi stood at attention in a suit, with a heavy but tidy beard. Abdul said, 'That's Ghazi, my head of security. He and his men don't make mistakes. They are the best the Mabahith have to offer.'

The Saudi secret police – the most feared agency in the Middle East.

Abdul went on, 'I pray five times a day. I wear my *thobe* and headdress. And I pander to the religious fanatics in my country like everyone else. Because it's the only way to retain power. I look like a Muslim, I sound pious, but inside, it means nothing to me. It's a charade. An act. Do you know how many people I've killed? How many women I've raped? And who is there to stop me? God?' He laughed.

'The only thing I believe in is money. It's why I'll always get away with it.'

'Maybe not in this lifetime,' remarked Wark.

'Wake up, John!' Abdul snapped. 'Look at me and tell me there is justice in this world. This is it. So when I say that Duncan Grant must die, I mean it. I'm not some two-bit emir who thinks that hosting a Formula One Grand Prix makes you a statesman. I'm a goddamn gangster.' Now it was Abdul's turn to lean in aggressively. At just thirty-three years old, he already had the fearsome presence of a Mafia don and warlord rolled into one. 'Marlow dies. And Grant dies.' He gestured at Wark's glass before he left. 'You shouldn't drink so much. You get blinded by pride.'

Wark put his glass down – his thirst had left him.

Abdul conferred with Ghazi as the women returned to the room.

'He's drunk,' Ghazi said.

'And a liability,' added Abdul.

He didn't need to say anything further. Ghazi understood what the Crown Prince wanted.

47

Grant was woken by the sound of Travis peeing over the side of the Gloria.

Travis took the cigarette out of his mouth and said, 'Morning, brother. Or whatever the hell time it is.'

It was still pitch black.

Absalom came out of the cabin, readying an anchor as they pulled in towards a small break in the thick forest.

Grant checked his watch. It was two a.m.

He got straight to his feet. As soon as he got out from under his insect net, there were bugs all over him, drawn to his body heat and odour.

Travis pointed to the narrow clearing. 'We need to head through there.'

'What about Absalom?' asked Grant.

The captain was sitting at the bow with his feet dangling over the side.

'We're paying him a month's salary,' replied Travis. 'He ain't going anywhere.'

Grant picked up his backpack. 'We'd better shift. I want to get there before sunrise.'

They jumped off the boat and headed into the unknown of the forest. The pair could only guess at how far the compound was from there. It was like climbing a mountain, reaching one false summit after another – at each point it seemed impossible that they could go somewhere more isolated, more remote, emptier than where they were.

As Travis explained, swiping through the overgrown shrubbery with a machete, 'You gotta learn to embrace the darkness, brother. It's the only way.'

It was just a feeling that Grant had, but it seemed like they were entering Marlow country.

The pair hacked their way through the thickest vegetation Grant had experienced – even during a six-week survival course in Borneo, in what he was told was some of the most unforgiving jungle terrain in the world. But the Congolian lowland forest was on a whole other level.

There were hundreds of different tree species in a square kilometre. Their canopy low and oppressive. There were constant bird calls from bright-beaked hornbills and toucans. Above was the moonlit silhouette of a solitary black colobus monkey swinging through the trees. Monkeys in each troop took it in turns to stay awake to keep watch for predators. They had learned to appreciate that the sight of humans meant only one thing: destruction.

Grant was concerned about the noise making it easier for anyone following or approaching. But the noise would soon be the least of his concerns.

Travis had told him stories about the militias, and there

was plenty of evidence of their presence. Former presence, at least.

For a few moments, Grant thought they had reached a passage covered in large rocks. Until some of them gave way underfoot, caving in. Grant crouched down for a closer look.

Travis stopped too.

When Grant realised what they were, he shot up again.

They were walking on piles of human skulls, laid like a pathway through the trees. As Grant's eyes adjusted to the darkness, he could see hundreds of them snaking ahead.

He and Travis stepped off the skull track and walked alongside it instead.

The deeper they roamed, the more evidence they found. Shrines covered in skulls, crosses made of bamboo – they appeared like totems of desperation: if there was any kind of god out there, they had left a long time ago.

Travis pointed out a random clearing where the ground had been dug up, the remnants of a mass grave.

'Millions of people have died in these forests,' Travis whispered. 'They've all got to go somewhere.'

There were militia outposts – little more than wooden huts, and shallow trenches – that had burned down. Charred bodies were scattered all around.

Someone somewhere had won, but was now silent and out of sight.

Since they had got off the boat, Grant had felt like they were being watched. They were deeper into militia territory than even UN soldiers had ever dared to go. Few outside the militias really knew what was out there. Like the deepest oceans, it was unmapped territory.

· · ·

After a punishing two-hour hike, the forest eventually thinned. The sun was still a long way off. A vast plain opened out in front of Grant and Travis. Half a mile away, through a layer of mist, was Charles Joseph's compound. Once white, it had taken on a jaundiced tinge. The colour of decay and sickness.

The mansion at the centre of the compound rose above a high perimeter wall. Around it were torches stuck into the ground, the flames at head height.

'Well, someone's in there,' whispered Travis. 'Torches like that don't last more than five, six hours.'

Grant took out a pair of Pulsar Accolade thermal-imaging binoculars. 'It's about three hours until sunrise.' He adjusted his focus. 'You should start heading back now.'

Deliberately ignoring him, Travis asked, 'How many of them are out there?'

Grant lowered the binoculars. 'Whoever's out there, they're hiding, waiting. Bringing you in with me would be a death sentence, Travis.' Grant slid off his pack and took out his gun. He holstered it in the waistband of his trousers. 'I've got a job to do in there. I couldn't promise to protect you.'

Travis chuckled at the absurdity as he saw it. 'Man, you think I care about whether I live or die?'

'I know you don't,' replied Grant. 'But I care.' He sensed in Travis an apprehensiveness to leave. Grant held up his hand.

Travis gripped it. 'Look after yourself, brother.'

Grant replied, 'If I don't get out, do me a favour, Travis. Go home.'

Travis smiled. 'What the hell is home? This is who we *are*, man. We can't be anything else.'

It was a truth Grant couldn't deny.

Overhead, clouds were moving in and starting to open, the smear of heavy rain obscuring the stars.

Travis began, 'If you're captured, I'll–'

'If they capture me, no one is coming. That's the way it is.'

Travis pulled back, getting ready to leave. 'I'll see you at the boat in a few hours.'

Once he was gone, the heavens truly opened. The raindrops were so heavy they felt like pebbles on Grant's head. The rain penetrated his bandage, reawakening the wound on his arm. The weight of his wet shirt pressed down on it, only increasing the pain.

The torches soon went out – the last of the light.

In a way, the storm worked in Grant's favour, reducing visibility to half of what it had been, keeping him out of sight. But it equally reduced Grant's vision. He couldn't tell if he'd been spotted and reinforcements were massing on the perimeter wall or whether he could charge in unseen. As he had done throughout life – the tactic that had served him best – he assumed the worst.

The closer he got, the more the air changed. A rotten smell. Like out-of-date meat. It grew in strength with each step through the overgrowth.

A security light came on inside the compound grounds at the rear, as if triggered by movement inside.

Grant quickly grabbed his Accolades and adjusted the centre dial until the compound came into clear focus.

There were watchtowers at all four corners of the perimeter walls.

'Damn,' muttered Grant.

They had a view of every angle of approach. Then he

noticed that all the windows on the towers had been smashed. The towers were unmanned, and there were large chunks of plaster missing from the walls, blasted out by rifle fire and grenade blasts.

From a distance, the compound looked magnificent. Impregnable. But under closer examination, the mansion was in as much disrepair as the perimeter walls. The concrete balconies were crumbling and there were large holes in the roof.

Whatever happened, it must have been one hell of a fight, thought Grant.

He still hadn't laid eyes on any enemy personnel. It was unthinkable that Marlow could hold down such a property in the middle of militia territory without backup.

Grant crept forward, his progress painstakingly slow through the tall grass. A swirling, gusting wind kept the grass blowing from side to side, keeping him covered. As he closed in a few hundred yards more, the decrepit condition of the compound became even clearer.

It was only as the wind subsided for a moment, followed by a flash of lightning, that Grant realised what was on top of the torches lining the perimeter wall, and what had been set alight.

Human heads.

The stench was so strong, Grant could practically see the malaria between the raindrops. The entire area smelled of disease and death.

When Grant reached a gaping hole in the rear compound wall, he took out his Glock – its polymer frame and Tenifer-treated slide were practically impervious to rain. The peace of mind he needed in such a situation.

There was a TV on inside somewhere, the flickering

glow stretching out into the back garden. It was littered with bodies, strewn over low walls and in the fountain pool. Two males had been stripped, and hung from nooses wrapped around branches of acacia trees near the swimming pool.

The lights in the pool were on, illuminating blood in the water as bodies drifted face-down, shot in the back of the head. Brown water splashed up from the weight of the rain, pounding down on the concrete slabs that were overgrown with weeds.

Grant counted three different militias from the markings and uniforms of the dead. The People's Tigers. Katanga Defence of Congo. Walikale Liberation Front. All had been dispatched without mercy.

As Grant crept through the hole in the wall into the garden, he could make out a slogan painted in white on the inside of the perimeter wall:

"*KILL THEM ALL*"

Grant's immediate thought was of Marlow's memo.

We must kill them all.

Jesus, Henry, thought Grant. *What the hell have you done?*

He re-gripped his gun, adjusting his fingers: he'd been unconsciously tensing them. Tensing his entire body.

No training could prepare an officer for such a scene.

Some of the bodies were old – months? years? – but a lot of them were recent. No more than a few weeks. Grant tried to tell himself that it could have been the work of a militia leader gone mad. Congo wasn't short of them. Child soldiers raised on crack and beer from five years old, initiated into rape and murder by the age of eleven. A child growing into a man like that has little hope of salvation.

But such acts required leadership.

Grant now worried that he had terribly miscalculated Henry Marlow and what he was capable of.

There was a slight motion by one of the open French windows on the ground floor. A short figure. A boy around seven. He was smoking a joint. The smell wafted towards Grant on the wind. It was much stronger than natural cannabis. It was superskunk. Laboratory-made, with chemically altered THC to cause the heaviest, hardest high imaginable. For an experienced dope-smoker it would have been head-twisting shit. For a child? It hinted at dark stuff going on inside.

Grant pointed his weapon towards a first-floor balcony, where another figure wandered out from the gloom. They didn't even seem to notice the rain that was hammering down. More bodies emerged behind them, filling up the balcony.

Then from both sides of the building, too.

Grant whirled around, taking aim at every potential threat as they presented themselves. They had flanked him from behind. Surrounded. But nobody was armed. No one said a word. They just crept towards him.

They had painted their faces with green camo, all wearing black military clothing.

It was as Marlow had described in the Joseph assassination.

Grant called out, 'Henry!'

No one reacted.

He shouted louder, 'Henry!'

Still no reaction.

He moved forward, testing his supposed adversaries. They were holding bottles of beers, cigarettes, joints.

Grant made his way past the swimming pool, eyeing the mansion's interior.

In the living room, the TV glowed with a Hollywood action movie, a crowd of young men and boys sitting on the bare wooden floor around it, entranced. After a brief glance in Grant's direction, they turned back to the screen.

It appeared that little had changed since Marlow first arrived.

Grant was in hunter mode now, working his way stealthily through the vast living room. There had to be one hundred people living in the mansion.

Grant asked them, '*Français? Est-ce que vous parlez français?*'

Still no response.

'Henry,' he shouted again, towards the reception area. 'Henry Marlow!'

A small boy sitting on the armrest of a sofa pointed to the main hallway where there was a grand staircase. The boy next to him swatted his arm back down, mumbling something in Lingala, a local dialect:

'*You'll get us killed, moron.*'

Grant upped his pace, sweeping into the hall.

There were men and women in military fatigues passed out on the floor, surrounded by bottles of Primus beer. There were cigarette butts everywhere.

Grant kept his gun low as he ascended the stairs smoothly and with poise, covering the banister above with his laser sight, the TruGlo red dot landing steadily on any threat zone.

More dead bodies were lying every which way. Draped over the banister. Lying the wrong way up on the stairs. Some had been shot. Others hacked by machetes.

There was still evidence of the building's owner on the walls. Enormous portraits of a stout black man, Charles Joseph. The largest adorned the huge open-plan reception area at the bottom of the stairs, where every visitor would see it. The painting showed Joseph wearing oversize sunglasses, a leopard skin draped over one shoulder, holding a gold AK-47 and smoking a Gurkha Black Dragon cigar – a mere $750 a smoke.

The paintings that lined the stairwell were pocked with bullet holes, remnants of a brutal gunfight. Grant was concentrating so much on any movement at the top of the stairs that he nearly stepped on a bright eastern green mamba working its way down the crumbling marble steps. It hissed at the proximity of Grant's boot, its skinny tongue threatening grave repercussions if he came any closer. The eastern green was one of the most venomous snakes in Africa, with a ferociously wide jaw for its slender shape.

Grant sidestepped it, backing up against the banister to give it the maximum room. Once he was a few more steps clear, the mamba slithered on its way. It seemed uninterested in any of the bodies. Only sudden movements piqued the mamba's interest.

There were dozens of people on the first floor, passed out, or injecting junk into their arms, oblivious to Grant. The beds were stripped, bedding tossed all over the floors. Furniture turned over and broken. How anyone could live in such chaos was beyond Grant's comprehension. Everywhere he looked were signs of madness. Anarchy. Paintings of strange pagan iconography and graffiti on the walls:

"KILL THEM ALL"
"GOD IS DEAD"
"WE KILLED HIM"

The contradictions didn't make sense to him: an army headquarters full of dead bodies, staffed by hundreds of stoned and drunk soldiers. Not one of them willing to raise so much as a fist at Grant's presence.

Grant checked off the rooms one by one, eventually finding the study.

Under the window was a large oak desk, where a computer was set up with a satellite uplink and, thanks to a powerful military-grade wireless router, faster internet than many Western capital cities. The desktop was covered in classified MI6 files and handwritten passages. Grant recognised the handwriting as Marlow's.

A quick scan through the dates showed that he had been there, and for quite some time.

It was Marlow that had been running the place.

Grant swung off his backpack, then took out his satellite phone and dialled Vauxhall Cross. After entering his encryption code, he waited for the signal to get through to the Communications Suite in the basement. He didn't panic, understanding that the rough weather overhead might delay the connection.

While he waited, urging the signal on under his breath, he scanned the walls around the desk, picking through the snippets of intelligence that Marlow had meticulously assembled from sources on the dark web, and a hacked link into an MI6 substation.

One handwritten screed in particular caught Grant's attention:

"I must kill the evildoers. Killing: it's the only language they understand. I have to bury them. Exterminate them. Kill them all, so they can't poison anything else in this broken world. I can't wait to be free of their miserable, corrupt existence. And to be free of myself."

To Grant's relief, the signal connected.

Miles Archer answered. 'Go ahead.'

Grant could barely think where to start. He took a breath and wiped his face with his arm. 'I messed up,' said Grant. 'I messed up, Miles. Marlow's not here but he has gone full Colonel Kurtz. There are bodies everywhere. Severed heads. Swann was right. He's gone totally crazy.'

Winston broke in. 'Are you sure he's not there?'

There was a creak behind Grant, the study door slowly opening.

Grant dropped the phone to take aim with his gun.

Standing in front of him was a man holding a machete. He was completely soaked through. Behind him were a dozen other men, all holding machetes and guns.

Grant peered back at the man in confusion, lowering his gun slightly, then raising it again. 'What is this?' he asked in disbelief.

It wasn't Henry Marlow.

Travis stepped forward, brandishing the machete. 'Hang up the phone, Duncan Grant.'

48

Grant spoke carefully and deliberately. 'Travis... I want you to listen to me. I don't know what you think you're doing. But I want you to put down your weapon. Tell the others behind you to do the same. I *will* shoot.'

Travis appeared unperturbed by the threat, still inching forward. 'I can't let you take him away. From me. From all of us. That's what you came here to do, right? To kill him?'

'Travis,' said Grant. 'Stop... moving.'

He kept coming. 'I know that it's hard to understand. The bodies. The blood. The heads... but it's the only way. Surely you can see that?'

'You're mad. You're all mad.'

'No,' Travis retorted, his voice quivering with rage and disappointment. 'You want to know what *madness* is? You think it's here?' He laughed. 'Look at what you're doing. Coming out to the middle of a civil war to kill one of your own. A great man.'

'A great man?' said Grant. 'All I see is a slaughterhouse.'

'He sees us for what we really are. What the world really

is.' Travis raised his arms. 'Look around and ask yourself, is this place any madder than the place you call home? You have no idea what madness is, brother.' He pointed at himself, his eyes bulging white. 'I know what madness is. I've seen it. All he's done is show us a way out of the darkness. The only way out is *through*. By going deeper than anyone else has ever gone. To embrace the darkness. The blackness.'

Grant wiped his face again, this time with his sleeve. Now it was from sweat rather than rain.

Travis went on, 'One of the militia leaders, Sheka, was running riot around here. He and his men took two hundred villagers, women and children. They spent weeks raping them, torturing them. Until finally they hacked them all to death. News about it eventually got out. The UN envoy knew about it. But Sheka wouldn't stop for anything or anyone. Finally, a government official convinced him to join ceasefire talks with the UN. They met not far from here. On the riverside. The UN sat there with him. With full knowledge of what he had done, and what he would go on to do if unimpeded. All they did was talk. They didn't try to kill him. They didn't even try to arrest him. "Too dangerous", they told the Congolese. They didn't have the authority, they said. It was against the law. The law! Do you know where Sheka is now?'

Grant was afraid to ask. 'Where?'

'He's in the garden. Hanging upside down by his feet. He was alive when he went up there. It takes about eight hours for the blood to really pool inside your brain. Your heart slows down to a handful of beats per minute. Blood floods your heart. It literally fills up. Eventually his eyes fell out. They say he died a few hours after that. Now, isn't that the humane thing to do? Those UN guys had him. All they had to do was point a gun at his head and pull the trigger. But they were too scared to do what's necessary. Marlow isn't scared. He isn't scared of anything, or anyone.' Travis started to lift his machete, the blade now at waist height. 'This is who we really are.'

He was getting within striking distance of Grant.

Grant said, 'You haven't thought this through, Travis. I'm a trained operative with a gun sight pointing right at your heart.'

Travis looked down at the red dot on his chest. It wasn't so much as quivering.

'You're a drunk with about three fully functioning senses, and that gang of stoners behind you aren't in much better shape. Ask yourself if you really want to come at me.'

Travis stopped for a moment.

Grant said, 'I'm going to give you three seconds to put down that machete and back up. Three...'

Travis's eyes filled as he took more steps towards Grant. 'I can't do that, man... If you'd seen what I've seen... you'd understand, man...'

'Two...' Grant warned him.

Travis stopped. But not because of the countdown.

Out in the front garden there was a loud cry, like a frantic warning. It was immediately followed by a blast of white and then orange. The light came first, then the deafening explosion.

Calls in Lingala sprang up around the men: '*Grenade!*'

Men and boys in green military clothing and brightly coloured wigs streamed through the front gates of the mansion, howling and cackling and whooping manically.

The air filled with the insistent cracks of automatic gunfire.

The compound was under an all-out assault.

Travis and the others ran downstairs, desperate to defend their home.

Grant ducked below the window moments before a stray bullet blasted it out. The first of dozens. They were spraying all around the room. The soldiers firing them from the ground were so young and weak they couldn't control the direction of their submachine gunfire.

As plaster and dust spat out from the pock-marked walls, Grant grabbed his sat phone, then braved a brief moment in the firing line to grab a computer hard drive from Marlow's desk. He stuffed it into his bag, along with whatever hardcopy files he could reach from the floor.

Getting in had been a struggle. Getting out was going to be much harder.

The rebels hadn't yet penetrated the mansion interior by the time Grant reached the staircase. It was bedlam all around. Some of Marlow's men simply lay on the ground, either too strung out to fight, or resigned to their fate.

Grant struck with surgical precision at any enemy. He didn't mess around with headshots. He took shots by the numbers, going for chests: the largest target areas, and more than sufficient to take down a threat. No one was wearing bullet-proof vests. The heroin and cocaine speedball combos many of the rebels had taken before their attack made them feel invincible. The commanders had told them that bullets would simply swerve around them, or bounce off them. A theory that was relentlessly proved false as Marlow's men felled them.

The rebels had attacked from the front of the building,

leaving the back mostly clear. With Marlow's men hunkered down against the rebels, Grant swept quickly towards the back garden, only to find a handful of rebels who had strayed from the plan and entered the compound from the rear.

They turned their guns on Grant, but his reactions were twice as fast as theirs. They were on the floor before they even realised what was happening. Single shots were all Grant needed.

Outside, though, was far messier. What looked like an entire platoon of child soldiers were charging in through the large hole in the rear perimeter wall.

There were fifteen of them – all stick-thin, carrying AK-47s that they could barely hold in their hands. The oldest looked around thirteen. They wore baggy camo shorts and oversized shirts, all stolen from militiamen they had recently murdered in a surprise attack.

Grant took cover against the wall next to the French windows. The boys were shooting at anything and every-thing as if they were in a video game.

They kept their triggers pressed, firing constantly. The steady muzzle blast from their AKs created a halo effect around the barrel, deflecting away the pouring rain, which was almost suspended in mid-air by the fire-flash.

There was no way Grant was going to shoot a bunch of kids. It simply wasn't an option. He knew he could pick them off one by one, but as much as he wanted to get out of there alive, he wasn't going to lose himself in the process.

It didn't matter that they would happily execute him then take back his limbs to their commander at breakfast. What they were doing wasn't really them. Their brains had been so twisted by drugs from an early age, groomed and manipulated by powerful men who showered guns and money and attention on a bunch of dirt-poor orphans.

Grant shielded himself as the boys blasted out the last of the glazing in the French windows, turning his back on the shattering glass.

When the fire subsided, he peeked out from behind the windows. If he didn't want to kill any of the boys, his options were limited. That was when he noticed two large propane gas canisters swamped by weeds against the east-side wall.

With the mansion on the verge of being overrun, Grant was about to be caught between the two warring factions.

After one last check, he fired a shot at canister one. The explosion threw the boys to the ground like a hurricane-force wind.

Grant sprinted past the swimming pool and its macabre human detritus, ready to fire at canister two.

Some of the boys recovered faster than others, and turned their weapons on Grant. Dazed and confused, their aim was all over the place, closer to the treeline than to Grant.

Grant fired at canister number two. The explosion rocked the boys even harder than the first, but they were still alive.

Marlow's soldiers spilled out from the patio into the garden, straight into a hail of gunfire as the boys recovered from the twin blasts.

Grant sprinted for the hole in the wall. There was nothing more he could do there. Not for the boys. Not for Travis. Not for anyone.

While the fight raged on, Grant ran for the treeline and the route back towards the Gloria.

He wasn't sure how long he ran for. It could have been an hour, it could have been three. All he knew was that nothing was going to stop him until he saw the Congo River.

Dawn wasn't far away when he got there, the first hints of an imminent sunrise twinkling on the water.

From a distance away, Grant yelled, 'Absalom!'

Already woken by the distance clicks and booms of gunfire and explosions, the captain had been on his feet for a while.

Grant made a whirling motion with his hand in the air. 'We need to go!' he yelled, running at pace into the water to reach the boat.

Absalom lifted the anchor and started the engine. While Grant scrambled aboard, Absalom asked, 'What about Travis?'

Grant collapsed on the deck, heaving for breath. 'Travis is gone. He's not coming back.'

49

The moment the boat was in clear water, Grant opened up his backpack under the light of the cabin.

The captain sneaked a look. He spoke first in Lingala, then in French. '*You moron! I knew you were trouble.*'

Grant took out the computer hard drive, hooking it up to his laptop.

Amongst the trove of documents were surveillance photographs of John Wark and Crown Prince Abdul, as well as maps of central Paris.

What really worried Grant was the collection of high-resolution images Marlow had purchased on the dark web: stolen by hackers directly from the DGSI.

'He's got everything,' Grant said to himself, in awe of the wealth of data Marlow had amassed.

He grabbed his satellite phone and headed for the bow.

Archer answered with relief, 'Thank God! We were–'

Grant cut him off. 'Miles, listen to me. I was wrong about Marlow.'

'What about him?'

'He lied to me at Place Bellecour. He doesn't want out. Quite the opposite.'

'What does he want?'

'He's got the personnel records of DGSI officers in Paris. I think he's going to use them to get to John Wark and Crown Prince Abdul.'

'But what good is the DGSI in getting to them?'

'They're both in Paris for the G20 Summit. Marlow's got surveillance photos of Wark and Abdul. He's going to hit them together.'

The full implications of such an attack knocked Archer sideways. A disavowed MI6 officer assassinating the next King of Saudi Arabia and the British Foreign Secretary would prompt a diplomatic disaster unlike anything the United Kingdom had ever experienced.

Grant could only see one way out. 'Wake up whoever can make it happen: you have to get me to Paris.'

50

It was quarter past five in the morning, and it was obvious that everyone was running on fumes. Winston was wearing the same suit as the previous day – minus a tie. He'd gone straight back to Vauxhall Cross after leaving Christie's house. He had been drinking coffee steadily all night, combing through Justin's computer terminal and phone records for some sort of clue as to what had happened.

The whites of his eyes, normally bright, were bloodshot.

Ryan, Samantha, and Archer were on their feet, picking apart the details that Grant had found at the Joseph compound.

None of the other staffers were in yet, and the room had an atmosphere of being right on the edge. It was a long time to be running such an intense, high-wire operation. There were coffee cups everywhere, and the room smelled of takeaway food and microwave meals.

Winston spun around as Olivia Christie entered the Control room.

'Have you heard?' he asked.

Christie replied, 'You think I usually come into work at half past five?'

'I need you to wake up someone in the Saudi embassy. It has to happen quickly and quietly.'

'I spoke to the ambassador on the way in. They won't take British security personnel. The Prince is too private and too paranoid.'

Winston looked at the ceiling in frustration. He took a moment to think of the bigger picture. 'Why Wark and Abdul? Why now? They're both mentioned in the AC file. But there's still a piece of the puzzle we're missing.'

Christie pointed to the wall. 'What have you got?'

Archer took the lead. 'Marlow has maps of the Quai d'Orsay area, with markings where the French Foreign Ministry is located. It looks like he's going to try to gain access using stolen personnel information on DGSI officers.'

'It's smart,' said Christie. 'On foreign soil, we don't have any options to draft in deeper security in the event of a threat. We'd have to take personnel from the host country. Which means the DGSI. He's trying to force his dirty operatives into our detail.' She inspected Wark's itinerary.

Winston said, 'Wark's already in country, and will be under lock and key at the G20 meeting until fourteen hundred local this afternoon. After that, he's out in the open. We're already turning the DGSI's internal database inside out.'

Christie poured herself a coffee. 'Give me specifics,' she said.

'Marlow's had this planned for a while now. So Samantha is running any new faces from the last six months. Any officers with sudden windfalls in their bank accounts. Miles and Ryan are inside Credit Lapierre, checking classified government salaries. They're looking for anything in bank accounts higher than five figures that didn't come from a salary, online poker, or a lottery ticket. It's still too early for any DGSI officers to call in sick or unexpectedly not show up. Anyone who does is either working with Marlow or already dead. Either way, we'll have names and faces for Grant to check.'

Christie asked, 'Where is he?'

'He's on a UN plane heading for Paris. He should be wheels down in six and a half hours.'

Being careful to lower her voice further, Christie asked, 'Have you told them yet?'

'They know,' said Winston. 'They understand that the best thing they can do for Justin now is to bring Marlow in.'

Back down the corridor, Imogen Swann emerged from the lift. She looked terrible. She may have been wearing fresh clothes and run a brush through her hair, but her face told the deeper truth of a sleepless night.

Winston could see the bags under her eyes from twenty metres away.

Swann said, 'I saw the report on Congo. Is Grant alright?'

'He made it out,' Winston answered. 'Barely.'

'Look, Leo... are you sure he can deal with Paris after this? Maybe we should consider benching him.'

'He can handle it.'

'How do you know?'

'Because I know Grant.' He moved back towards his team. 'Let's get to work.'

51

THREE YEARS AGO

Two women were walking their dogs on a small patch of beach on Skye's Trotternish peninsula, wrapped up heavily with hats and scarves and multiple layers. It was an early December morning, and winter had truly arrived. As was so often the case on the rugged northern part of the island, the wind was howling. Snow had been falling since dawn, turning the beach white.

One of the women paused as her dog bounded into the water. She peered at something coming into shore, riding the wild crest of the waves. 'What is that?' she asked.

Her friend stopped too. 'That's not someone swimming, is it?'

Duncan Grant continued his front crawl until he had cleared the roughest waves. He kept swimming until he sensed the shore rising underneath.

He shook the salty sea water from his head as he rose.

He was wearing neoprene wetsuit bottoms and nothing

else. His upper body was red raw from the freezing water, his muscles were dense and defined, compacted by the cold, and flooded with blood from the exertion of staying on top of the vicious currents driven from the west by the Atlantic Ocean.

One of the women tapped the other. 'Don't stare, Margaret.'

'I wasn't...'

Grant waved to them. 'Good morning,' he called out.

The women waved back, bracing themselves against the falling snow. It was getting heavier.

Grant shook snow from the towel he had left on the beach, then wiped his face. He checked his watch, then nodded in satisfaction. He had lasted an extra two minutes against his last swim, and the water had been two degrees warmer that day.

'Five more months, Dunc,' he said to himself.

The SAS recruiters had never told him why they were dismissing him from the course. They never gave reasons. Until the next selection process started up, he was going to do everything he could to make sure he was ready.

As he threw the towel around his shoulders, already dreaming of his second coffee of the morning, he noticed a dark figure near his cottage. His vision blurred as salt water trickled down into his eyes. When it cleared again, the figure had gone.

The next day, heavy rain had mostly cleared the snow. Grant was on the roof of his traditional white stone cottage, repairing tiles that had been damaged by recent high winds. The cottage was on an exposed hillside.

Each raindrop was like a dart landing on his face. He knew better than to fight the weather. It hurt far less when you just made peace with the pain. He turned up the collar of his wax Filson Aberdeen work coat and accepted the drenching.

His hair was short. Basic. Low maintenance. Only slightly longer than a crop, but long enough to be ruffled around when soaked. He had a thick beard which he had been growing since his exit from SAS selection. He had kept it trimmed and shaped, but he had sworn off shaving it until he finally passed selection.

From the roof, Grant had an unobstructed view of the beach, marked by seaweed-covered rocks that lined the rugged coastline. He could also see the main road – a single-track with passing places.

He wiped rain from his face as a pair of headlights cut a path through the squall. He said to himself, 'Silver Ford Focus again.'

One advantage of the old place was the long farm track that allowed Grant to see anyone approaching from nearly half a mile away.

He watched the Focus enter the driveway. He could make out that the driver was male. Black. Wearing a suit and tie.

As he pulled up outside the cottage, Grant remembered where he'd seen the man before.

The Brecon Beacons.

The driver got out and called to Grant. 'Duncan. I'm Leo Winston. I'd like to talk to you.'

. . .

In the living room, Grant handed Winston a steaming cup of tea. He brought a coffee for himself.

He had dried off for the most part, his hair damp and mussed up. He wore a ribbed sweater with holes, which was too big for him.

Winston surveyed the warped bookshelves groaning under the weight: each shelf was packed out, with books on their sides on top of those spine-on.

There was everything from fiction, to biography, to history.

'Are all these yours?' asked Winston.

Grant sat in the single chair across the room. 'They were my dad's.'

'Have you read them all?'

'Pretty much.'

'Your dad was a farmer, wasn't he?'

Cagily, Grant nodded. 'He was one of those intellectuals who didn't actually do anything with his IQ. Reading was part of growing up around here. It was the same for my parents' generation. Back in the day, there wasn't much else you could do with your spare time if the weather was rough. Hebridean farmers are well read. My dad didn't read as a means to getting away and doing something else. It was to satisfy his mind.'

Winston reached into his leather case and laid out a series of surveillance pictures on the table. They were all of Grant. Doing tractor-tyre flips in the front garden. Doing log lifts on the beach with a trunk that washed up there. 'Do you train every day?'

'Every day,' Grant replied.

'Don't you worry about overtraining?'

Grant smiled. 'It's funny. The only people I've ever

heard talk about overtraining look very far from over-trained. People are too quick to give themselves a rest. Every day I try to do something that's horrible.'

'Why?'

'Because the SAS don't get to look out their window and decide if they want to go on a mission or not. That's the problem these days. Everyone wants to be comfortable. Everyone wants to be happy. They don't realise that in the pain, in the cold, when it's miserable: that's where life really begins. In overcoming.' Grant put down his coffee and leaned forward on his knees. 'Why are you taking photos of me training? It's kind of creepy. Are you here to get me back in?'

'Back in where?' asked Winston.

'SAS selection. I saw you at Brecon Beacons.'

'I'm not from SAS, Duncan. I'm from the Secret Intelligence Service. I'm the reason they took you out of selection.'

'Why?'

'To start the background check. It takes a while. It's still not done yet.'

Grant paused. 'I don't understand.'

Winston sipped his tea, drawing out the moment. 'Duncan, I want you to be a field officer in the British Secret Intelligence Service.' While Grant tried to get his head around what he'd just been told, Winston explained, 'I'm not interested in team players, Duncan. I don't want my fastest or strongest guy held back by the slowest and weakest. We don't all cross the line together. If you do this, it's to excel. The things that made you imperfect for SAS make you an ideal candidate for what we need.'

'What do you need?' asked Grant.

'Someone who will walk into fire. First: I need to know that you're ready.'

Grant went to the old bureau against the wall and took out a worn notebook. He turned it to the most recent pages, then handed it to Winston.

The pages were full of observations – a diary or journal of sorts. What made Winston smile was what Grant had entered the previous day:

"*Ford Focus again. Rental? Too clean. Telephoto lens on cloudy day.*"

Grant had logged each time Winston had taken a covert photo of him.

Winston said, 'I was sure you hadn't seen me.'

A satisfied look flashed across Grant's face.

Winston dropped the notebook on the table. 'I know you're tough, Duncan. You've also got a brilliant mind, but no one to drive it. This is the start of a two-year process. There are no guarantees at the end of it.'

Grant asked, 'How many other candidates are there?'

'Candidates?'

'Yeah. How many people am I up against?'

Winston pointed at him. 'You're it.'

Grant was still clearly struggling. 'Why me?'

Winston took another sip of tea. 'A guy gets sent into a hedge maze. All he knows is that he has to get to the centre, and he has a map that shows him how to get there. He walks for hours, following the map. He avoids all the dead-ends. It seems easy. Eventually, he bumps into someone else who doesn't have a map and says they've been in there for years. "Lucky you met me," the guy says, "I've got a map." The other one replies, "No. You're the lucky one. I had that same map and it doesn't go where you think it does."

I'll be with you every step of the way, Duncan. You know why?'

Grant said, 'Because you know where the map goes.'

'Exactly. You want to know why you? Because SAS takes only the top one per cent of the country. From that, ninety per cent fail. Me? I take only one per cent of that one per cent. That's where you are, Duncan. You're uncommon amongst rare people. You might not feel ready now, but you will. And it all starts today. If you want it.'

Grant looked up. 'I want it.'

52

Grant was two hours out from Paris, working through Henry Marlow's hard drive files on his laptop when his satellite phone started ringing. The United Nations cargo plane was noisy as hell. Grant had to cover one ear to hear Winston on the other end.

Winston was standing behind his desk, surrounded by the cartons of Saudi Arabia intel. 'Did you get my message?' he asked.

Grant replied, 'Yes, sir. There's nothing in Marlow's files that shows Swann has any connection with this Wark property deal.'

'What about Marlow? He's going to a lot of trouble to pursue Wark and Abdul.'

'Sir, all the evidence at the Joseph compound demonstrates that he has gone totally, utterly insane.' In a way, what Grant had seen had been so extreme he simply couldn't entertain the imagery at all. He completely blanked it out.

Winston asked, 'What are we dealing with?'

Grant said, 'I think that when he went there and killed Joseph, something happened to him. He must have been coming apart for a while, but something about the job made him snap. There were hundreds there. Some no more than boys. My contact was one of them. They've been slaughtering rebel forces there. There were hangings. Beheadings. There's no way any of it could have happened without Marlow's say so. I was in his study. There are diaries, essays. He's been living there as recently as a few weeks ago.' Grant dug out a few of the diaries from his bag. 'He talks about waging a war unlike any other. That the only way to defeat the real enemies is a display of, quote, brutal force.'

'Christ,' said Winston. 'We really did a number on this guy, didn't we.'

'He goes on for pages and pages about nullifying the militias by turning them into drug fiends. Purging them of their idealism. It's a game to him. Toying with them, controlling them. All he wants is to create chaos. It's like a cult.'

Winston puffed. 'The only thing worse than a zealot is someone who believes in nothing. We pushed him to a place so bleak, so nihilistic... He could be capable of anything.'

Grant said, 'I hate to say it, sir. But neutralising Marlow might be our only option to contain him.'

Winston was worried he was going to say that. 'Grant, listen to me. If you kill Marlow, we lose our last chance to find out why Justin was killed, and to build a case against Wark. I need Marlow alive.'

Grant scrolled through the file directory he'd found.

'Has Randall made any progress on that file I sent through?'

'He's working on it,' said Winston.

'It's the one file on the hard drive that's encrypted. It makes me wonder if it's the Rashid file he stole from Lawrence Bloom's safe. We know that he stole something from Bloom, but we haven't found it yet.'

'Randall's working as fast as he can.'

Grant said, 'I checked the logs on the hard drive. It was the last thing Marlow worked on.'

Winston paused, remembering one piece of paper he'd looked at hours ago.

'Sir?' said Grant. 'Are you there?'

Winston replied, 'Grant, I'll call you back.'

Once he'd hung up, Winston quickly moved aside the piles of intel from his desk until he found the document he was looking for: a printout of Justin's computer logs that showed a report request to GCHQ.

He checked the name of the analyst that Justin had been emailing: Colin Yorke. Once he was patched through to Cheltenham, Winston asked what Justin had been looking into.

After Yorke summarised the report on Édith Lagrange's phone records, he explained, 'I didn't get very far. Director Swann pulled the plug on–'

'Imogen Swann?' asked Winston. 'From Anticorruption?'

Worried that he was in trouble, Yorke said, 'I assumed that because the trace was an Interpol detective that some kind of mistake had been made.'

Winston's head raised, tantalised. 'Why a mistake?'

'Because of the dead drops.' Yorke pulled up his interim report. 'I found a clear pattern with Lagrange's personal mobile and another number. A burner.'

Winston closed his eyes, concentrating. 'Walk me through it.'

'Lagrange's mobile signal went dead for nearly identical periods of time as this burner. That in itself isn't strange. What's strange is that the pattern repeats across multiple months. If it had just been switching off, that would be one thing. But these are completely dead signals. Batteries being removed. Classic dead drop behaviour. I can't identify who owns the burner, but whoever does, they met Lagrange dozens of times. Now, almost everyone has a phone on them, so whoever owns the burner, they probably ditched their regular phone in the same way.'

Winston's mouth hung open for a moment. 'Are you saying you can work out who owns the burner?'

'Yeah,' replied Yorke.

Winston said, 'Run it. And send me what you sent Justin Vern. Now.'

In the Control room, Swann's mobile rang. She moved to a quiet corner before answering it.

The voice at the other end said, 'Ma'am, it's Security downstairs. You asked to be alerted if Mr Winston left the property.'

As Director of Anticorruption, Swann was granted certain control privileges that no one else had – like knowing the movements of any of MI6's two and a half thousand employees.

Security went on, 'Would you like to be contacted when he returns?'

'No,' Swann said, a little too swiftly. 'Thank you.' The senior staff were too busy with their Paris work to notice her sneaking out.

53

Winston had his jacket off when he got out the taxi at Eaton Place in the heart of Belgravia. It was still morning, but the air was already warm, promising another scorching day.

Eaton Place was among the grand terraces of Georgian white stucco houses. The area was home to dozens of embassies and prestigious scientific establishments, each identified by huge flags that protruded from their first-floor balconies.

It was only as Winston ascended the stairs of Swann's building that it hit him: *how the hell can she afford to live here?*

He wasn't living on a pittance himself, but he knew roughly what kind of money Swann made, and it wasn't enough for Belgravia prices.

While attempting to pick Swann's front door, Winston was interrupted by a pale Eastern European woman wearing a cleaner's smock and carrying a bucket filled with cloths and sponges.

Winston altered his grip on the lock pick to make it

seem like he was turning a key. 'Hot already,' he said to the woman.

She smiled politely.

As soon as she reached the next landing, Winston resumed picking and got the door open.

If he'd been impressed by the neighbourhood and the three-storey building, that was nothing compared to the interior. The design was sharp and contemporary. Not that Swann had played any part in choosing it. It had been like that since she'd moved in. She didn't care about modern dark-oak walls and pillars, leather furnishings, or bleakly minimalist art. Living there felt to her like an extended stay in a boutique hotel – never really hers, never settling in. She fretted about leaving rooms messy, and still found herself opening the wrong cupboards for things a year after moving in.

After a quick scan of the various rooms, Winston put on his latex gloves and set to work.

He knew that Swann wouldn't have been so stupid as to burn clothes. Attempting such a thing indoors risked setting off smoke alarms on the landing, and the gardens were overlooked by dozens of neighbouring windows.

Clothes were the key, he decided.

He checked the washing machine in the kitchen, his heart sinking when he found damp clothes inside. A quick sniff of the drum told him that Swann had used bleach. He rummaged through cupboards under the sink and found a bottle of Dettol washing machine cleaner. He began to smile.

It was a chlorine-based bleach.

Swann had assumed that because the bleach killed

bacteria that it would be sufficient to remove DNA-trace evidence. Namely, blood spatters.

The bleach certainly cleaned any visible stains, but Randall had once told Winston that applying luminol to clothing made haemoglobin light up bright blue, meaning that DNA evidence remained.

Winston knew he was onto something - the only clothing in the drum was the outfit that Swann had been wearing the previous day.

He quickly shook out a bin bag to open it up, and stuffed the clothes inside. He then opened up the kitchen bin. Swann hadn't been so reckless as to dispose of gloves inside her home. The bin only contained empty microwave-dinner packaging and chocolate wrappers.

He was about to check the other rooms when his phone started ringing. In the circumstances, it seemed much louder than usual.

He answered as quickly as he could, trying to keep his voice down. 'Yeah?'

'It's me, sir,' said Archer. 'Where are you?'

Winston took the phone to the living room in case someone heard his voice on the landing.

It was sensible. But it also meant that he didn't hear a key being slid out of the lock with the most precise move-ment, followed by the front door opening.

Winston said to Archer, 'I had to step out. What's the matter?'

'I got your message about checking out Grant's source in Congo,' Archer replied. He had an entire file on Travis Buckley on his screen. 'There's source material on Buckley that goes back to Henry Marlow's days in Albion. Marlow was running him as an agent in Uganda.'

Winston, aware of a distinct lack of time, pressed him, 'Miles, I need the short version of whatever this is.'

'It's the sign-offs for surveillance on Buckley. They're all signed by Director Swann. It just seems a little...' Archer waited for Winston to say something.

Instead, there was a thud from Winston's end, then nothing.

Archer said, 'Sir? Hello?'

Winston could only mumble, his answer inaudible. 'Grant...'

He blacked out on Swann's living room floor.

Swann stood over him with a cast iron ornament in her hand. She put it down, then ended Winston's call by taking the battery out.

She took out a clean burner and texted an unofficial asset:

"I need a two-man clean-up at my house."

54

Grant was grateful as he landed in Paris-Le Bourget Airport, half an hour earlier than planned thanks to a generous south-easterly wind. He needed every spare minute he could get, as intel from the G20 Summit said that proceedings were wrapping up sooner than expected.

The airport was a vital fifteen minutes closer to central Paris than Charles de Gaulle, and was only used for private business operations and air shows, giving MI6 greater and necessary privacy.

Grant was on the phone to Samantha while he enjoyed his favourite part of flying on diplomatic planes: being able to walk off without having to wait for baggage or customs. Veteran officers had assured Grant that such minor pleasures would wear off, but for the moment it was all about saving time.

Samantha said, 'I've got three DGSI personnel who have called in sick today. One of them checks out: his wife is in hospital. But the other two are question marks: no answer on their home phones. I have an asset on the ground if need be.'

'Don't bother,' Grant said. 'Those men are already dead. Get word to the RaSP officers with the Foreign Sec. Find out which men are using those stolen identities.'

Across the Control room, Ryan said, 'Abdul is using the DGSI for extra cover. We tried to tell the Saudi embassy but they're not interested.'

Samantha relayed the message to Grant.

'Not interested?' Grant complained. 'They're about to get the next King of Saudi Arabia assassinated.'

MI6's Head of Station for Paris, Nicholas Warrington, waited at the bottom of the plane's stairs. He consulted his watch with exaggerated disdain, then folded his arms huffily.

Grant did a double-take as Warrington appeared to be wearing motorcycle leathers. In the background, beside a plain white Citroën saloon, was a wasp-coloured BMW K1200S. The son of three generations of aristocratic stock, Warrington's reputation as a playboy wasn't entirely baseless. He was in Paris for good reason: he was widely considered one of the Service's most brilliant station chiefs. He was also flam-boyantly handsome–tanned faced and silver fox appearance– with expensive appetites that put Italian politicians to shame.

As Grant reached the bottom of the stairs, he held up a finger, asking for Warrington's patience.

That only aggravated him further.

Samantha told Grant, 'We've told RaSP to stand the DGSI officers down. They've agreed. But Abdul is still in the firing line.'

Grant hung up. He couldn't understand why the Saudis

would accept extra security from a source MI6 told them was a potential threat.

Sensing Warrington's impatience, Grant apologised.

Warrington didn't take kindly to the presence of a younger, more rugged version of himself. 'That's alright, Grant,' he sniped, handing him a metal box with a Glock pistol inside. 'I'm just a lowly station chief to the most important city in Europe, with fifty officers assembled around a G20 Summit with absolutely no idea what to expect.'

'I don't have much time, sir,' said Grant, taking out the gun and sticking it into his back waistband. 'I was told you would organise transport.'

Warrington gestured to the Citroën saloon. 'The keys are in the ignition.' He turned to leave, as if that was the end of it. 'If you'll excuse me...'

Grant jogged a few steps to catch up with Warrington. 'Sir, the Foreign Secretary's life has been threatened.'

'And that's RaSP's problem,' said Warrington. 'Not ours. You know how they get when we try to interfere on security.'

'Sir, I have half an hour to get to Quai d'Orsay and I'd be better off walking than driving that thing.' Grant pointed accusingly at the Citroën.

'What do you suggest?' asked Warrington.

All it took was one look from Grant at the BMW bike for Warrington to say, 'No way. *Absolutely* no way!'

Grant beseeched him, 'I'm out of time, sir. What station do you think they'll send you to if the Foreign Sec is killed on your watch? Minsk? Warsaw?'

Warrington looked back at the bike like it was going off

to war. He extended a finger at Grant's face. 'If there's one scratch, one dent in her...'

Grant reached into Warrington's hands to take the key, then ran towards the bike before he could change his mind.

Warrington set off after him, looking at Grant's clothes: his mud-spattered Congo gear. 'You can't ride in that.'

'I don't have much choice,' said Grant without turning back. He tried the helmet that was resting on the seat, but couldn't get it past his forehead. He tossed it to Warrington.

'You can't ride without a helmet.'

'What are they going to do, pull me over?' Grant started the engine and revved it hard. 'I doubt that,' he said with a smirk.

Warrington put out his hand. 'Okay, you have to be very soft on the—'

Grant spun the back wheel, taking off like a rocket.

Grant was soon on the four-lane A1, the busiest Autoroute in Paris. He made rapid progress, zigzagging from lane to lane as needed. His clothes were too loose for motorcycle riding, flapping violently in the wind. The humidity and heat parched the exposed parts of his skin, feeling both hot and cold at the same time.

He felt consumed by his singular task: to stop Marlow at all costs. He was insistent to himself to remain calm. It was a common mistake in rookies to artificially inflate the pressure of a situation in order to focus better. Grant understood from his many years of wild swimming that there were diminishing returns for physical performance if you allowed your heart rate to exceed a certain point. Somewhere around one seventy-five was what Grant liked to limit himself to. Anything beyond that impaired motor function.

Congestion built as the road swooped down into the entrance to the Tunnel du Landy. Searing straight between lanes was Grant's only option. If anyone so much as opened a door he would be completely poleaxed. But the sense of gained time only encouraged him to turn the throttle harder, to squeeze every extra second from the road.

He was relieved to emerge onto the Boulevard Périphérique, a four-lane road leading straight into central Paris. As usual, it was clogged. Unwilling to sacrifice any time, Grant weaved through every available gap, spaces that only seemed to exist in his fearless anticipation of the flow of traffic. At least three times, he felt the front chassis of cars brush against his lower leg as he squeezed through. Each time he told himself not to take such a risk again, but within seconds he was pushing even harder. His brain had shifted into a flow-state, a mix of instincts, lightning reactions across the play of brake and throttle, and total concentration on everything moving around him. He could feel it in his bones: a sweet spot heart rate no faster than one-fifty.

Startled commuters on the other side of the road watched in horror as Grant climbed north of seventy miles per hour, while everyone else around him puttered along at twenty.

The road ahead climbed gently, seemingly never-ending. Then a long sweeping left into another tunnel plunged him into almost total darkness. There were no overhead lights. In the gloom, and not used to the set-up on the bars, Grant couldn't find the lights. He had to rely on the red rear lights of cars in front of him to lead the way. A perilous task. Especially when a truck suddenly decided to switch lanes without indicating.

Grant slammed on the rear brake with his right foot and slid left. He shouted, 'Muppet!' as he came almost to a standstill. He got right back on the throttle, twisting it hard. He was relieved to feel the sunlight beating down on him once more.

The road straightened at the huge roundabout at Porte Dauphine onto Avenue Foch. Held up by overly cautious tourists in rented cars, awed by the hulking presence of the Arc de Triomphe at the end of the avenue, there was no space for Grant to plough down the centre of the road.

He threw the bike to the right, then pulled the front of the bike up as if doing a wheelie, stomping down hard on the foot pegs to compress the suspension. When the back wheel bounced up, Grant rose to a stand in harmony with the momentum of the bike. The rear wheel lifted off the ground in a bunny hop, mounting the wide sandy pavement. There were only a few people sitting on the benches lining the avenue, leaving Grant free to get back up to speed – terrifying speed.

Relying on memory from the plane where he last checked a map, Grant launched himself around the Arc de Triomphe – by quite some margin the fastest-moving vehicle there. It was typical French-traffic anarchy. No road markings. A free-for-all. Only a slide at high speed stopped him from taking out a food-delivery cyclist.

Some people have got a death wish, thought Grant.

On the narrower Avenue Marceau, low overhanging trees ahead restricted his view.

He was looking for flashing police lights, and listening for sirens. Indications of a nearby convoy.

As he ran red lights all the way through to the Pont de l'Alma bridge, he saw dozens of police lights through the horse chestnut trees on the Quai d'Orsay on the other side of the Seine river.

A long line of black Mercedes and Range Rovers, followed by an ambulance, and yet more police cars were in motion.

'Shit,' Grant cursed to himself.

The Foreign Secretary and Crown Prince were already leaving.

55

Without any radio communication with Vauxhall Cross, Grant was flying blind, looking for the U.K.-registration plates on black Range Rovers that identified John Wark's vehicle. Two of Wark's security officers from Royalty and Specialist Protection – RaSP – rode with him, along with three more in their own Range Rover directly ahead. In London, that would have been the extent of Wark's convoy, which would have relied on skilful, nimble rerouting through central London's packed roads. But the French police opted for the American method of convoy management: sheer size. There were police cars and motorbikes and ambulances and unmarked security saloons everywhere.

There were so many that the entire area had come to a standstill, as multiple foreign leaders' convoys attempted to access the site of the G20 Summit in the French Foreign Ministry further along the road.

Grant cursed the flawed thinking behind the French system. Thanks to a convoy twenty vehicles long, John Wark was now a sitting duck in stationary traffic. Nothing increased the danger to a high-risk individual's safety more than coming to a stop on a public road.

As traffic slowed to a crawl, Grant took out his Bluetooth earphones and dialled Vauxhall Cross on his satellite phone.

Archer was relieved to hear Grant's voice: the entire Control room had been glued to live surveillance from MI6 officers on the ground.

He could see Grant's location flashing on the map, closing in on the beacons for Wark's cars. 'Mobile One, he's about a hundred yards in front of you.'

'I see him,' Grant said.

As they had planned, Archer said, 'I'm patching you through to him now...'

After a brief delay, Grant was connected to Wark.

Grant said, 'Sir, this is Mobile One. I believe you're expecting me.'

Wark was audibly anxious. 'That's right.' Struggling to hear over the din of nearby sirens, he put Grant on speaker and turned the volume up.

Grant said, 'Sir, I have concerns about some DGSI personnel that may be in this convoy.'

Wark's regular body-man, Leitch, sitting across from his principal, nudged his secondary beside him. 'Typical Six. Give them a tailored suit and a pair of sunglasses and they think they're James Bond.'

His secondary remarked, 'Arseholes.'

Leitch considered RaSP, not MI6, to be at the business end of things. If RaSP were the action men, MI6 were the thinkers, the analysts, safely tucked up in surveillance trucks watching monitors.

Grant said, 'Sir, I need to get you out of this traffic and into the British embassy as soon as possible.'

The embassy was only five minutes away on the illustrious Rue du Faubourg Saint-Honoré, home to almost every major fashion house, as well as the French President's Élysée Palace. In the current traffic crisis, it might as well have been an hour away.

The road blockage wasn't clearing because of one of the DGSI's Mercedes – guarding the Crown Prince's monstrously long convoy – that had beached itself on a kerb attempting a three-point turn. When the driver pressed the accelerator, the wheels turned impotently in mid-air.

Ahead, Bravo team had had enough. 'Leitch, we need to help clear this vehicle. Permission to exit?'

Leitch replied, 'Do it, Bravo.'

Grant heard the order via Wark's phone. He craned his neck, seeing four of Bravo team's RaSP officers emerge from their Range Rover. 'No,' Grant called out, 'tell them to get back inside!'

Wark didn't know what to do, tied between following his main body-man or some rookie MI6 officer whose name he didn't even know.

Bravo team rushed to the aid of the stricken DGSI vehicle.

Grant could get no closer on the bike, so he climbed off, ditching it at the side of the road. He took out his weapon, keeping it low as he ran through the stalled traffic.

Wark complained, 'What a bloody mess. First you bring in a new RaSP unit, then you replace my best officers with–'

Grant pressed in his earpiece, thinking he'd misheard. 'What new unit, sir?'

'Bravo team. MI6 told the Foreign Office to arrange extra back-up. So we did. They came in this morning. You said the French had been compromised!'

Grant's run turned to a sprint. He knew what was about to happen now. And what he and MI6 had got wrong. 'Sir,' he explained. 'Marlow hasn't put his men into the DGSI. They're in RaSP!'

Wark's heart jolted.

'He *wanted* us to stand the DGSI officers down so you would be left with only British RaSP officers for your back-up.'

Leitch was looking through the front window, watching Bravo team approaching the DGSI car, when they suddenly pulled their weapons.

Realising that Grant was right, Leitch muttered, 'Oh, no...'

The French officers inside and around the car were helpless. Bravo team took them out with single shots.

The civilians, caught in the middle, fled their cars, leaving their doors flapping open.

Grant bobbed his head in and out of cover, unable to sight a clear shot. He gestured rapidly at the terrified commuters fleeing from their cars. '*Ne sortez pas!*' – '*Don't get out!*'

After felling the DGSI, the fake RaSP officers of Bravo team now had a clear path towards the Crown Prince. The Saudi security officers were quick to face the challenge, but Bravo team dispatched them with mercenary efficiency.

Grant told Wark, 'Hang tight, sir. I'm coming to you. I need to get past the Saudis first...'

Leitch reached for Wark's head, pushing him down. 'The windows are bullet proof, sir. Just stay down. Stay calm.'

Bravo had the Crown Prince's car surrounded.

The French police fired back as best they could, highlighting the stark difference between soldiers and police constables in a gunfight.

In their plain suits, the DGSI officers on the fringes of the assault had no idea what was going on, or who was an enemy.

'Do not get out of your car,' Grant warned Wark on the phone. 'Stay with your body-man. No matter what happens. Don't trust anyone you don't recognise. I'm on my way.' He was still fifty metres from the Crown Prince's car. It wasn't close enough.

While members of Bravo team defended their position, their point man opened the back door of the Crown Prince's car, then fired three swift shots inside. Two to the chest, the last one to the head.

The air was punctured by gunfire. For the uninitiated nearby, the shots were louder than anything they'd ever heard.

Grant halted his charge. He could see Abdul's blood-stained white *thobe*.

Bravo team bolted through the traffic, covering each other like the soldiers they were. Despite their numerical advantage, the French could barely defend themselves from the onslaught, let alone get on the offensive.

Bravo ran to a line of scooters that had riders waiting for them in the bicycle lane, one for each of Marlow's men. They each raced away unimpeded on the pavement. They had executed their plan to perfection. But it was far from over.

Grant sprinted to the Crown Prince's car, while Abdul's remaining officers scrambled to check his vitals.

Grant watched as they turned his body over.

It was Abdul's *thobe*, and Abdul's headdress. But it wasn't Abdul's face.

Grant immediately looked beyond to Wark's car, where a secondary team of mercenaries had moved in – men in black military clothing and bullet-proof vests. They'd been sitting in civilian cars behind Wark's convoy, waiting to pounce.

Grant was about to run to Wark when he noticed a phone in the hand of a Saudi officer: it had a picture of Grant's face on it.

The Saudi turned his gun on Grant, who barely had time to react. He threw himself across the bonnet of a car, sliding to safety on the other side, while the Saudis' bullets sparked and pinged against the bodywork.

As the secondary team surrounded Wark's car, Leitch pulled his weapon: staying inside was no longer an option.

'No matter what happens, you stay in here,' said Leitch.

Wark was frozen with fear.

Leitch growled, 'Answer me!'

The aggression snapped Wark out of his shock. 'Yes, yes!' he replied.

On the Saudis' blindside, Grant scrambled along the row of abandoned cars, keeping his head low. He fired on the mercenaries every chance he got, giving Leitch the cover he needed to go on the attack. It was a risk for Grant to reveal his position, but even with his help, Leitch didn't stand a chance.

They flanked him from both sides. There was nowhere to go.

Leitch went down fighting, taking out two of the mercenaries. Once he was on the ground, the mercenaries riddled him with bullets.

Wark looked on in terror, realising he was next.

Eager to avenge Leitch's death, Grant moved out from behind the car, his finger pressed on the trigger, firing until his clip was empty. He took down another three mercenaries, while the others easily took cover.

While Grant reloaded, Wark was grabbed by the neck and dragged outside. Just as Grant was to about to launch another offensive, he was pinned back by advancing Saudi officers.

Grant cursed. He was stuck.

The mercenaries took Wark to their getaway saloon, busting clear of the traffic by mounting the pavement.

Grant sat up against the front of a car, trying to plan an escape. Warrington's bike was tantalisingly near, but there was a lot of open ground to cover in order to reach it.

The Saudis yelled at each other, followed by a flurry of aggressive French.

Grant peeked out from behind the car.

Back-up from the French security services had finally appeared. The Saudis raised their hands, obeying French demands.

Grant decided to make a run for the motorbike, but as soon as he broke cover, DGSI officers yelled at him to drop his weapon.

He didn't have a choice. It was either drop his gun, or be shot in the back.

As he dropped the gun, he kicked the tyre of the car

next to him in frustration. Every second lost, the mercenaries got farther away.

'I'm British intelligence,' Grant shouted, fighting off the DGSI's attempts to restrain him. 'MI6.'

The French weren't interested in his claims. They believed they had caught one of the shooters of a terrifying siege outside their own Foreign Ministry.

Grant demanded they check his passport.

An officer found it, then showed it to his superior.

The officer said, '*Merde*.'

The second they released him, Grant ran for Warrington's motorcycle.

Having been cut off from Wark's phone, Grant's earpiece had been relaying the sound of the attack back to Vauxhall Cross. As he got the bike up to speed, Grant shouted into the mic, 'This is Mobile One. I am code black. Repeat, I am code black. Target One has been taken...'

Far from the mayhem on Quai d'Orsay, several streets away on Quai Voltaire, moving swiftly and unnoticed through the traffic, Crown Prince Abdul was in the back seat of an anonymous white minivan that had escaped the French ministry from a service exit with no convoy, no following vehicles.

Abdul was totally calm, scrolling through pornographic pictures on his phone while he spoke to Ghazi. 'Is Grant dead?'

Ghazi replied, 'He escaped. He'll likely go to the British embassy.'

Abdul showed no signs of the rage he felt inside.

'We still have assets in the city,' Ghazi offered. 'The embassy is well protected, but we could still get to him.'

'No,' Abdul replied. 'They'll want Grant back in London. You can kill him there.'

'What about Wark?' asked Ghazi.

'Marlow will take care of him for us. He doesn't want a ransom. He wants blood. You concentrate on Duncan Grant.'

Ghazi replied with reverence, 'Consider it done, Your Highness.'

Swann had to shout to control the pandemonium in the Control room. In Winston's absence, Christie had put her in charge. Archer listened on headphones to the replayed audio from Grant's call. Eyewitness statements flooded in from the scene. Contradictory accounts and references to casualties were already accumulating on social media.

Swann begged for quiet as she got Grant on the phone.

'What's Wark's status?' she asked.

Grant was going full gas across Pont Alexandre III bridge. Surprised to hear Swann rather than Winston, Grant shouted into the mic to be heard. 'Kidnapped. Five guys. Silver Audi, a French registration. All I could get was Charlie Echo six eight. I think the regional code on the side was two three.'

Ryan and Samantha started work on it.

Swann stepped forward with eagerness. 'Was Marlow there?'

'Negative,' Grant replied. 'But there were two crews. One tried to kill Abdul, but he'd sent in a body double. The double's dead and I had no visual on Abdul. They want

Wark alive. Marlow's crew could have killed Wark, but they didn't.' The essential information relayed, Grant asked, 'Where's Leo?'

Swann looked worriedly towards Christie, who was listening beside her. 'He's not here right now, Mobile One,' said Swann. 'I'm running the room in the meantime. Where are you?'

Grant answered, 'I'm heading to the embassy. You've got to tell DGSI to drop the net. If they do it in the next five minutes, we can still stop them leaving the city.'

'Wish us luck with that,' Christie said, trying various French contacts on her phone. 'I can't even get them on the phone right now. It's bedlam over there.'

Tell me about it, thought Grant, navigating the crowded French streets at speed.

Archer threw his headphones off and shot to his feet. 'Ma'am! Marlow's phone just appeared on the grid.'

Swann raced over to see.

Archer said, 'It's a SIM from one of his old ops. It must be four years old at least.'

On the move, Swann told Grant, 'Mobile One, hang on. I think we might have Marlow for you. Stand by...'

'No,' Archer said. 'He's not in Paris. He's in London.'

Swann pointed at the video wall. 'Get it up! Where is he?'

Archer projected his tracker onto the wall, showing a beacon on the phone's location.

'God help us,' mumbled Swann.

He was five streets away.

Christie picked up an internal phone and called the Security suite. 'This is Olivia Christie. Authorisation code: alpha foxtrot three three one zero bravo. This is a code four national security emergency. We have an imminent threat. Initiate full code four procedures on the building.'

Within a few seconds, a shrill alarm went off all through the building, a pre-recorded voice informing all staff of the emergency status.

In the Control room, everyone fixed their eyes on the beacon of Henry Marlow's phone, moving ever closer to Vauxhall Cross.

56

Everyone on Rue du Faubourg Saint-Honoré had heard the gunshots, but they hadn't sounded so close that the shoppers with their Burberry and Hermès bags took any urgent action. Some were rooted to the spot, checking their phones for news, while others took their first quickened steps towards finding shelter.

Every few seconds more sirens joined the already crowded chorus. Any illusion of the exclusive surroundings being safer than elsewhere in the city had been shattered. A point emphasised by the sudden appearance of Grant, who charged down the street before coming to a skidding halt outside the British embassy.

Anticipating panicked *gendarmes* outside, Grant showed his passport as he climbed off the bike, not even bothering to kick out the stand. The bike fell to one side with a crash.

Prompted by the sight of a wild-eyed six-foot-three man marching towards them – his shirt spattered with dried mud and blood, torn open to the midriff – the *gendarmes* pulled their weapons on him.

'*Arrêtez-vous!*' they yelled. ('*Stop!*')

'*Diplomatique,*' Grant called out, holding the blue passport out, familiar to the guards.

They lowered their guns and stepped aside for the British Deputy Ambassador, who appeared behind them. Expecting Grant, he said, 'There's a secure line waiting for you upstairs.'

Grant marched straight up the marble staircase. He was shown to an office on the second floor, which had to be cleared out: two secretaries and an intern who had been watching live news footage from France 24.

Once Grant was alone he muted the TV, leaving the sound of not-so-distant police sirens in the background. Relying on a mental checklist of processes for such a situation, he picked up a landline phone.

Before he started dialling, he shut his eyes for a moment and took a deep breath in and out. Two seconds was all he could afford.

Once connected, he was put through to the Control room. With Christie fielding calls from Scotland Yard, Miles Archer was the only who noticed Imogen Swann slipping out the office, heading for the lifts at speed.

As soon as Archer answered, Grant asked, 'Where's Marlow?'

Archer replied, 'He was only a couple of streets away when the signal disappeared. We've got SO15 canvassing the area right now.'

'Marlow will see them a mile away. He wants us to know he's there.'

'Why?'

'Whatever's next, I don't think he's planning on getting

out of it alive. Miles, listen: Marlow didn't infiltrate the DGSI. He infiltrated RasP.'

Archer turned his focus back to his screen. 'We know. We just got word from the Paris station: four RasP officers have been found dead in their hotel rooms. Marlow faked that trail to the DGSI. He wanted you to find it.'

Grant put a hand to his head in anguish. 'Knowing that we would request further back-up from RaSP instead. We walked right into his trap, Miles.'

Archer was distracted for a moment by Randall rushing along the corridor clutching a manila file. Randall went straight to Christie, who seemed shocked by something he was showing her.

At the corner of Archer's screen, a small window confirmed the ongoing recording of the conversation for the official registry: a procedure for every phone call taken in the Control room. Archer hovered the cursor over the "PAUSE" button for a moment, then he clicked it. Shielding the mouthpiece, he said, 'Mobile One, I've just switched off the registry recording.'

'What? Why?'

'Because if I'm wrong about this, I don't want it on record with the Hannibals.'

'Want what on record?'

Archer gulped. 'I think Swann set you up with Travis Buckley. He was listed in Henry Marlow's old mission files. Swann signed them. I was in the middle of telling Leo when his phone went dead.'

'Was she in the Control room at the time?'

'No, she wasn't in the building. Your op had already started by the time she got back.'

'Where is she now?'

'She just ran out,' Archer said.

Grant paused. 'Miles... what if she's working with Marlow? He's in London. He could have Leo right now.'

Christie shouted from across the room, 'Miles! Get over here. And bring your phone. Grant needs to hear this too.'

Archer took the phone across the room, telling Grant, 'Mobile One, you're on speaker with C and Randall.'

Christie told Randall, 'Tell them what you just told me.'

'I decrypted the file that Grant sent.' Randall showed Archer the file. 'It was hard to crack, but not too hard, if you know what I mean. Like Marlow wanted us to read it.'

'What is it?'

Randall said, 'Proof of who ordered the assassination of Kadir Rashid, and the attempt to cover it up. Bloom must have been keeping them as insurance.'

Grant cut in. 'Insurance against who?'

Randall answered, 'John Wark and Imogen Swann.'

Archer said, 'Ma'am, Mobile One and I believe there may be a problem with Director Swann.'

'That's becoming clear to me now,' Christie said. She leaned down to speak into Archer's phone. 'Mobile One, I'm sending this to you right now. You need to see it.'

'What about Wark, ma'am?' asked Grant.

Christie said, 'Nicholas Warrington is heading up the search for Wark. I need you back here. And so does Leo.'

57

FIVE YEARS AGO

Kadir Rashid rushed through the airport terminal. His leather messenger bag was tucked under his arm, the broken strap hanging limply. There was no time to fix it. A wildcat strike in Lebanon had delayed his flight by half an hour. There was every chance his source would already have left.

He was wearing a beige linen suit and denim shirt, both creased. In the last three days he had been to Moscow, to Rome, to Beirut, and now Geneva. It had been almost a week since he had slept more than three hours at a time. The many plane flights should have afforded him all the opportunity he needed to catch up on sleep, but Rashid had been working the entire time, putting together the last pieces of a story he had been working on for eighteen months.

Finding his source had been lucky, but getting him to go on the record was bordering on the miraculous. Now all of his work could have been undone by some Lebanese baggage handlers.

On the move, he scanned the café customers' faces from a distance. It was only once he reached the café that he noticed his source hidden away at the back corner, far from prying eyes.

'I'm sorry,' Rashid said, out of breath, taking a seat.

His source looked nervous, sipping fussily from a tiny espresso cup. His second. He was a Saudi national, dressed like a Western financier. And a well-paid one. He had small, frameless glasses, and a three-piece Brioni suit. He had spent a full three minutes perfecting his tie dimple and ensuring his silk pocket square was in a neat classic fold.

Rashid felt like a slob in comparison. After rubbing at his two-day stubble, he reached into his busted messenger bag and took out a voice recorder, hiding it under a copy of an international edition of *Le Monde* that he had scribbled notes on.

The source shuffled awkwardly in his seat. 'Is that really necessary?' He had a soft voice, speaking in his native Arabic.

Rashid's voice was harder. 'I can't take blind quotes to my editor. Not on something like this.'

The source kept stealing glances at the queue, worried about who might be watching.

Rashid looked back in the same direction. 'It's no one,' he said. 'Just families. We're safe here.'

The source wiped his hands carefully with a napkin. 'What do you want to know?'

'Would you mind if we did this in English? Otherwise I have to translate every time my American editors want to listen.' Rashid took out his notes, pointing to a page of three circled names, all linked by arrows:

"*Lawrence Bloom, Prince Abdul, Imogen Swann*".

Rashid said, 'You're the only one who knows.'

'Do you have any idea what they would do to me if they knew I was talking to you?'

Rashid replied, 'The same things they would do to me. I need confirmation. If I were to print these names, would I be right?'

The source bowed his head, thinking things through one last time. He finished his espresso, sliding it carefully next to the other one. 'Yes. You would be right.' He took a cleansing sip of water, then picked up his bag. 'I never want to hear from you again.' Before he left, he added in Arabic, '*Fi Amanillah.*'

Stay in the protection of God.

Rashid stayed at the table, glowing, excitedly writing up his notes of the meeting. His source would be anonymous, for deep background only. Not even his editors at *The New York Times* would learn his name. What mattered was that he had him on the record.

When he was done, Rashid put his notes into his bag, feeling the kind of rush that no caffeine or drugs can replicate: that of knowing you were onto a big story. The sort of story on which careers were built.

Across the café, sitting at a table with two small children, a man in a plain polo shirt helped mop up a cup of milk that had been spilled.

'Don't worry,' he said in French, consoling his son. 'It was an accident.' While the father stood up, his wife took over the cleaning.

She looked tensely at Rashid's source making his way through the crowd into the terminal.

The man told her, 'Don't worry. I see him.'

Finding a quiet spot by the enormous windows that overlooked the runway, the man made a phone call.

Now speaking English with a French accent, he said, 'He just left. The source is our friend from Credit Lapierre.'

There was no response at the other end.

'Should I call Mr Bloom, or—'

'No,' came the reply.

'We must move quickly. Rashid has confirmation now.'

'I'll tell Bloom. He prefers to hear bad news only from me.'

Lawrence Bloom arrived at the New York Stock Exchange on Wall Street in his customary Rolls-Royce Phantom. The car had been designed to eliminate nearly all outside noise. When Bloom's driver opened the door, the volume of the city came as a shock.

Bloom's favourite part was getting out of the luxurious car. Onlookers rarely recognised him. As billionaires went, he was one of the most secretive and mysterious.

His bodyguards ensured that Bloom's short walk to the trader's entrance on the corner of Wall Street and New Street was an uneventful one. Anyone who got close – even accidentally – found themselves blocked off at least six feet away from Bloom.

The chairman had been waiting outside in freezing conditions for the last thirty-five minutes in case Bloom showed up early. He shook Bloom's hand like he was his long-lost brother, unleashing a torrent of vacuous compliments and appreciation. In return, Bloom barely looked him in the eye. He didn't trust compliments. The only thing he trusted was the market.

For many celebrities or company executives, ringing the opening bell at the 'Big Board' was a symbol of a lifetime's achievement. Doing it once is considered an honour. It was to be Lawrence Bloom's fifth time.

The chairman checked his watch twice on the way across the lobby to the elevators, mindful of being short of time.

When Bloom's phone rang, he halted when he saw the caller ID. 'I need to take this.'

The chairman tried not to grimace. He appealed to Bloom's assistant, who had arrived in a separate car with the bodyguards behind the Phantom. 'We *really* need to watch the time,' the chairman said. 'We have to start at nine thirty sharp.'

The assistant's eyes were deadened from years of Bloom's demands. He always answered as if Bloom was standing right beside him. 'Trading can start when Mr Bloom is ready.'

'The financial press—'

'Do you want a bet that no one is going to blame Mr Bloom for a delay?'

The chairman pulled the arm of his coat down over his watch. It was the last he would speak of time.

Bloom walked to a quiet spot, away from the barely restrained murmur of excitement that had sprung up from his presence.

'Are you absolutely sure?' he asked.

At the other end, Imogen Swann replied, 'We don't

have a choice, Lawrence. Rashid's not going to stay silent on this. He has confirmation now.'

'It has to be kept quiet,' said Bloom. 'I mean silent.'

'Silent?' asked Swann.

'I financed this deal for Abdul, Imogen. I'm not having some Marxist reporter killing it. I won't accept anything less than silence.'

Silence. It almost amused her. In a career etched in paperwork and blood, it was the kind of euphemism that had come to define her career. *Loose ends. Deprioritize. Disincentivize. Permanent stand-down.* This was how assassination worked.

Swann said, 'I know the man for the job. Someone I trust.'

'Your man will have to be silent as well.'

Swann paused, unsure if Bloom really meant what he was suggesting.

He clarified, 'We can't have any loose ends.'

'He's a good man, Lawrence. One of my best.'

'Then he would understand the position you're in. And what the repercussions of failure would mean.' Bloom concluded by saying, 'I'll let you decide how you want to let him go once the job is done.'

That day, the opening bell on Wall Street rang thirty-seven seconds late. A fact that went unremarked in the financial press.

58

SCO19, the Specialist Firearms Command of the Metropolitan Police, moved in on Imogen Swann's residence on Eaton Place. Previously known as the blue berets when they still wore them during operations, they now wore blue baseball caps or, as was the case on the Swann raid, combat helmets.

They approached rapidly, silently, in single file, their H&K MP5 submachine guns covering the front door, balcony, and any threats on the street. Their instructions were clear: deadly force, if necessary, had been approved by Command.

Behind their balaclavas, every one of the twelve officers was laser-focussed with concentration. There was no misplaced ego or bravado in their movements. It didn't matter who was first through the door or who brought in a suspect. What mattered was successfully executing the raid and keeping everyone safe. Nothing stiffens the resolve, or brings people together like following someone into a potentially deadly crime scene. Each officer would die to protect the person next to them.

The lead officers assembled outside Swann's door, parting for the arrival of the officer with what was regarded by many in the Met to be the scariest job in all of Specialist Operations: the breach leader – the officer responsible for breaking down a door. Because of the weight of the red steel 'Enforcer' door ram they carried, the breach leader only had a sidearm. If anyone was waiting on the other side with a loaded weapon, the breach leader wouldn't stand a chance. Breach leaders require two things: strong arms, and total trust in their colleagues for cover.

All eyes turned to the point woman, who raised an arm, then counted off fingers.

One.

Two.

The breach leader swung the ram back...

Three.

The point woman made a fist.

The breach leader made light work of the door. He turned in profile as his colleagues flooded into the property.

The unit was no longer silent. Cries of 'Armed police!' went up as each room was shouted off – declaring them safe.

In the living room, there was a bloodstain on the cream carpet next to Leo Winston's mobile phone. The battery lying next to it.

The point woman called in to Command. 'This is Unit One. The property's empty, sir. Over.'

'Hold tight, Alpha,' came the reply. 'SIS have their people coming over.'

'Received.' The point woman told her crew, 'Touch nothing. Spooks are on their way.'

59

The period buildings around Berkeley Square in Chelsea had largely been converted for the offices of upmarket businesses, wealth management companies, and some of the City's smaller hedge funds. The last residential property had been sold as long ago as the fifties. Now the entire area was owned by various pension funds and private asset managers.

One of which was Number Three. The seven-storey block had been sitting vacant for years – not that you could tell from street level. There were curtains in many of the windows, and flowers in the first-floor balcony baskets.

Inside, all twenty flats were bare to the floorboards. They were owned by a company called Rolt Gewiss: a Lichtenstein banking firm. And one of the many shell companies that housed Crown Prince Abdul's foreign assets.

There were only two people in London who had keys for Number Three. One of whom was Imogen Swann.

She had nothing to fear from her echoing footsteps as

she climbed the interior staircase. The only person who could hear her was tied to a wooden chair on the first floor.

All the window shutters were closed.

Winston, bound and gagged in the centre of the room, could see the tension on Swann's face as soon as she burst in. This wasn't the composed Swann he was used to. She looked manic. Sweaty. Maybe even out of control.

She went straight to the kitchen. The units had been ripped out, leaving only an old steel sink and a tap. The water still ran, refreshingly cool on her hand. She dipped her head into the flow and took a much-needed drink. She could feel the chilly water working its way down through her chest, cooling her blood.

Before she went to Winston, she pulled up a floorboard, revealing a metal box.

Winston looked on in despair as Swann checked the magazine in the gun, then tightened the suppressor that was already attached.

'I want you to know I take no pleasure in doing this,' she said.

She strode towards him. There was no hesitancy or dallying. It was simply a job that needed done. There would be no eulogising or speechifying. There was too much else to get on with. Like her imminent extraction from London.

Winston tried to talk through the rag in his mouth, his voice coming out as a muffled noise.

Swann assumed it to be the last desperate pleas of a man who knew he was about to die. Then she noticed that his eyes were fixed not on her, but on something just beyond her.

When she turned around, she saw Henry Marlow

pointing a gun at her. 'You're rusty, Imogen,' he said. 'I've been on you since Green Park.'

Swann started to raise her gun.

Marlow smiled. 'I know what you're thinking: this seems so much easier at the range. With the paper targets, and the headphones and protective glasses. Feels like you can draw your gun faster than the Man with No Name. Then you end up standing in front of someone like me, and it's all a bit too real.' He took a step forward, landing on a creaking floorboard. 'Can you feel it? That tension in your trigger finger? How easily it spreads through your hand, into your wrist and up your arm? Before you know it, your whole arm's shaking. It feels like you couldn't hit a barn door if it was right in front of you.'

Swann could feel all those things happening as Marlow described them. She knew that he was right. She didn't stand a chance. She lowered her weapon, gently placing it on the floor.

Marlow gestured with his free hand. 'Kick it towards me.'

She did so.

Once Marlow pocketed it, he took a supporting grip of his gun handle again. He might have doubted Swann's abilities, but he'd waited too long to risk any silly mistakes.

A thin shaft of light from the window landed across his body. He was wearing a smart suit, overly formal to fit in with the area. He looked strange in it. His wild eyes and messy hair betraying his true self.

There was a part of Winston that was mesmerised by Marlow's presence. After all the confidential files and reports, the mythology, the fleeting encounters and close shaves, now that Henry Marlow was actually standing in front of him, he was everything Winston had expected.

Marlow motioned with his gun. 'On the floor. Sit on your hands.'

Swann didn't argue. There was nothing she could say that would allow her to leave the room alive. Not after everything she'd done to him. 'For someone who should know better than to take business personally, you seem to be taking this very personally, Henry.'

'Quite the opposite,' he replied. 'If all I wanted to do was kill you, I could have done that years ago. Killing you is the easy part. A bullet. Arson. Maybe a car bomb?' Marlow looked at Winston. 'Did she tell you about that? I'll bet she didn't...'

60

FIVE YEARS AGO

Marlow had arrived in Geneva that evening, having been on standby for the past three weeks. That meant sitting around in a hotel room waiting for a phone call on a burner. As preparation for a job went, it wasn't ideal. You couldn't work out in a gym, go running, dine in a restaurant. Everything about your life revolved around the phone call, and being somewhere quiet and far away from possible observation or surveillance.

The job should have been routine. Gain access to the target's residence unseen, administer the poison, then exit unseen. Documents for extraction were waiting in a bus station locker nearby, along with the keys to an objectionably average car, and directions to a decrepit cottage on the edge of the Bavarian Forest where he would sit out the next fortnight in solitude.

That had been the plan, at least. Until Marlow picked

the lock on Kadir Rashid's apartment in the Old Town and found his study.

The desk was a riot of paper and books with multiple bookmarks in them. Sticky notes plastered the wall above the computer monitor, as well as the edge of the monitor itself. It gave Marlow a headache just looking at it.

Marlow was curious as to how a Saudi-born journalist, working for an American publication, ended up becoming a Russian agent – as Swann had detailed in her dossier on Rashid. It was a tangle of allegiances that didn't sit right with Marlow.

After a gentle rummage through, Marlow put together the pieces of what Rashid was working on.

On the wall behind the computer, a series of notes had been stuck in a meaningful order. At one side was a rare picture of Lawrence Bloom. Next to that was a picture of Crown Prince Abdul.

The picture showed Abdul coming down the steps of his private Learjet at Riyadh airport, surrounded by bodyguards.

Beside him: a surveillance picture of Imogen Swann striding along Albert Embankment in London.

Marlow stared at the photo. He felt like he'd been punched in the gut.

He was a twenty-year veteran of MI6. The best Albion operative they'd ever had. He didn't need to see anything more to know that Rashid was no Russian agent.

Swann was playing him.

There were more photos across the wall, a series of London properties: everything from extravagant Holland Park mansions to Georgian townhouses and south London retail outlets.

Marlow removed a few of the pictures to see if anything had been written on the back, but they were blank.

He was about to gather up the information and make an escape when he heard keys being dropped in a plate in the hall, then the rustle of a paper bag.

Marlow had no more than a few seconds to decide what to do: execute, or stall.

Rashid pushed open the door to his study, clutching a brown bag of groceries. When Rashid reached for the light, still oblivious to the stranger in the dark, Marlow called out, 'Don't!'

Rashid dropped the groceries.

An apple gently rolled towards Marlow's feet.

Rashid put up his hands. He was no fool. He knew that his work had made him a lot of enemies over the years, and he had a good idea what Marlow was there to do. He just didn't know yet if it was to kill or merely intimidate.

'What do you want?' Rashid asked shakily.

As Marlow stepped forward, he realised he had never had a conversation with a target before. It had never been his place to execute any kind of judgement until now. They did not assign his jobs to him for appraisal. They were given to him with an expectation of certainty.

Marlow said, 'I want to know if it's true.'

'If what's true?' asked Rashid, hands still raised.

Marlow pointed at the desk. 'Your story.'

'My source confirmed it yesterday.'

'Swann?'

'She's up to her neck.'

Marlow seethed. This wasn't what he was for. He was supposed to be taking out threats to civilised society. Threats that the judicial process or military action couldn't neutralise. What he brought was concentrated targeting. Not personal vengeance.

Marlow said, 'Pack a bag and leave. Do you have somewhere safe you can go?'

Rashid looked at the floor, eyes darting all over the place.

Marlow didn't have time to deal with shock. He took hold of Rashid's shoulders. 'Are you listening to me?'

'I... I think so,' Rashid whimpered.

'Go somewhere safe. Don't come back here if you can avoid it.'

There was nothing else to do except leave. Marlow ambled towards the study room door with a panther-like gait.

Rashid lowered his hands, finally convinced that Marlow meant him no harm. He turned around. 'Thank you,' he managed to say, trembling.

Marlow stopped in the doorway, lit by the single bulb in the hallway.

'You were here to kill me, weren't you?' asked Rashid. 'Why didn't you?'

Marlow spoke over his shoulder. 'That's what she wants.'

Once he'd gone, Rashid collapsed to the floor in tears. He rubbed his hands on the floor, savouring still being alive.

The decision to flee came quickly. The cobbled, snaking streets of Geneva's Old Town felt charmingly anachronistic in the daytime, but claustrophobic and haunting at night. Marlow hadn't survived so many years with the Service by not having an easily implemented 'out' – an escape plan – and he wasn't going to take any chances.

He dismantled his burner phone on the move, distributing the various parts to different sections of the Rhône river.

61

ONE WEEK LATER

Marlow had known many safe houses over the years, across many continents. The one that he cherished most was a tiny apartment in a fishing village in the rugged Cinque Terre coastal region of north-west Italy. The five towns were known for their brightly coloured buildings of pinks, reds, and yellows, built into steep banks overlooking the most picturesque of harbours.

Cinque Terre was synonymous with blazing sunshine and azure skies, but Marlow had arrived in deep winter.

In a rare occurrence for the region, the coastline was covered in snow and the tourists were largely gone. The few souls braving the exterior seating of bars and restaurants were wrapped up in heavy coats and scarves.

Marlow's apartment was buried in the middle of town, with elderly couples above and below him. Their hearing was so bad they didn't even realise Marlow was there most of the time.

Marlow had waited a week before making contact with Swann from a payphone on the outskirts of town.

She was angry, she admitted, and wanted him to come in.

The call lasted barely a minute.

Once Marlow returned to his apartment, he sat on the end of his bed, turning over the conversation in his mind. It didn't make sense. Swann had asked him what went wrong, and seemed to accept his answer that he'd blown his cover at the apartment and Rashid had taken off soon after.

But Swann hadn't pressed him on whether he'd seen where Rashid was going. It was as if she already knew where he was.

Marlow packed his toothbrush and a t-shirt and headed downstairs with his go bag.

Swann was one of the few people who knew about his Cinque Terre safe house. He didn't actually believe she would try to harm him, but he wasn't going to wait around to find out.

The cold weather had got to his little Fiat, though, and he couldn't get the car to start. The sound of the engine turning over and over without luck was drawing attention in the quiet square. It wasn't long before an offer of help came his way – a polite young man in his twenties named Silvio. He explained that he fixed up old cars at his grandfather's yard and surely would be able to get it going.

Marlow, not in the mood to stick around, acquiesced. He handed Silvio the keys, then remembered that he had hidden away a clean phone behind a bathroom tile. Even if Silvio got the car going, there was a chance it could break down again. As someone who had driven many miles up the north coast of Italy, Marlow knew that the many blind

corners near sheer drops was not the place to have a break-
down in the snow without a phone.

Marlow told Silvio, '*Un minuto...*' while he dashed
upstairs.

After retrieving the phone from the bathroom, Marlow
heard the familiar churn of the engine. It was still going
when he reached the courtyard, where his eye caught something on the ground.

A folded copy of *Corriere della Sera* on a ground-floor
neighbour's front doormat. It had been left with the bottom
half of the front page showing. The headline was small, but
the accompanying photograph was what caught Marlow's
eye.

It was Kadir Rashid.

Marlow took the newspaper out of its wrapper. The
headline said, "*Journalist Kadir Rashid assassinated.*"

The gallery of photographs inside with the full story
showed CCTV images of various Saudi men captured in
different areas of a hotel.

The caption below named them as "*The journalist's assassins – a hit squad from Saudi Arabia.*"

Over at the car, Silvio had the driver's door open, one
foot on the ground, the other massaging the accelerator.

Just when Marlow dropped the newspaper, the engine
suddenly took. Silvio's face lit up, and he revved the accelerator, giving Marlow a thumbs up.

Marlow had made it another half step when the car
lifted clean off the ground. Silvio was engulfed by a bright
fireball that mushroomed up into the air.

The blast blew Marlow back off his feet, glass flying in
all directions. By the time the car landed in a smashed,
melting heap there was little left of it – or Silvio.

Such a sound hadn't been heard there since cannon fire during the Battle of the Ligurian Sea in the Second World War. Residents ran to their balconies and to the courtyard, watching in disbelief as black smoke billowed out of the car. There was nothing anyone could do.

Marlow struggled to his feet. There was too much adrenaline in his body to know yet if he'd been hurt. His face was speckled with broken glass. He did the only thing he could in the circumstances.

He ran.

He ran until his heart pounded.

Until he could taste blood.

He ran so hard for so long he could smell the iron in his bleeding wounds.

He felt like a wild animal, finally uncaged.

While he ran, he distracted himself from the burning agony in his leg muscles and cardiovascular system by thinking up a plan.

First, he would disappear. He would hide.

Then, he would figure out how to make them pay.

62

Marlow asked Swann, 'Sound familiar?'

'Get it over with, Henry,' she said, her head hanging forlornly.

'Like I said,' explained Marlow. 'I didn't come here just to kill you, Imogen. That's what the Rashid job taught me: the madness of it all. I want out.'

When you live a lie for as long as Imogen Swann had, it becomes hard to stop. With Winston present, there was still a part of her brain that wanted to mount a defence.

Swann said, 'You don't get to just walk away after going rogue, Henry. I was prepared to take whatever action was necessary to bring you in. Alive or dead.'

Marlow laughed. 'That's good,' he said. 'I think you'll have a harder time arguing about the contents of Bloom's safe. He protected himself well. He documented your entire arrangement about me, and Rashid. I made sure that Grant would find the files in Congo. I don't expect they took long to decrypt. It's over Imogen.' He stood over her, gun barrel pressed so hard into her forehead that it left a circular indentation when he pulled it away. 'I don't want to kill you, though.'

'What do you want?' she asked.

'I want out. For good. I don't want any money. I want to be left alone. No more Lyons. No more set-ups.'

'Okay,' said Swann, trying not to get her hopes up. 'You want out? You're out.'

'No. You're going away for a long time. I want to hear it from someone who still has a future.' Marlow turned to Winston, taking the rag out of his mouth.

Winston gasped, sucking in air.

'Can you promise that?' Marlow asked.

Winston nodded. 'I can. What I can't promise is that we'll let everything else slide.'

'And why is that?'

'Congo, Henry. Grant told me what he saw there. I don't know what happened to you. The Saudis killed Rashid, and Lyon might have been Haslitt's work, but you don't get to walk away from everything else. From *this*. I think you're broken, Henry. You need help.'

'Broken,' Marlow said to himself, as if he had never heard the word before. 'I'm walking away, alright. I'm going to walk back to where all this started.' He turned towards the front door.

Swann didn't allow herself to believe that Marlow was really going to let her live.

But he opened the front door and didn't look back as he closed it behind him.

Swann could barely believe her luck. Then she realised the glorious opportunity that Marlow had left her with.

Winston was still tied up. He shouted, 'Henry! Get back here! She's going to kill me!'

Swann stood up. 'He doesn't care, Leo.'

'He's got your gun,' he spat with disdain. 'If you want to kill me, you're going to have to do it with your bare hands.'

Swann loomed over him, hands reaching for his neck. 'Trust me. After Justin, this will be a walk in the park...'

Winston was shocked by how strong her grip was. And how fragile a windpipe is when being squeezed. He was sure it would collapse at any moment.

After a minute, his vision turned dark, his limbs weakening, going limp as he summoned everything he could to loosen his restraints and fight back.

Swann looked into Winston's eyes for a second, then quickly looked off to the side. It was taking much longer than she'd thought.

She grimaced, begging internally for him to black out before she lost strength.

His head fell to one side, dark clouds descending on his vision, when there was a sudden break of light in front of him.

The front door was kicked in, immediately followed by shouts of 'Armed police!'

Swann's grip loosened only slightly in response, looking over her shoulder where her eyes met SCO19's dazzlingly bright torches.

She only released her hands from Winston when an officer tackled her, hauling her away by the waist.

Within seconds, they had cuffed her – her rights read.

Another officer tended to Winston, tapping him gently on the cheek.

Winston reoriented himself to the room, which was suddenly much busier. The officers were covered from head to toe, balaclavas under their helmets, grey fatigues, bullet-proof vests, and gloves.

'It's okay, Mr Winston,' the officer said, untying him.

Winston garbled, 'Henry... Henry Marlow... He's–'

'We know. We got him.'

Winston closed his eyes in relief.

Finally.

It was over.

He felt at the rope burns around his wrists. 'How did you find me?' he asked.

The officer helped him to his feet. 'Someone on your team gave us a list of potential properties you might have been taken to. I don't know the full details, sir.'

Winston flashed his eyebrows up. It was certainly fortunate. The last he could remember, there was somewhere north of thirty properties on the list of Prince Abdul's buildings.

Two officers led Swann away.

'Can I see him?' asked Winston.

'Sir?'

'Henry Marlow.'

'I'm sorry, sir. Not until he's booked in.'

Winston glanced at the officer's ID patch on his upper sleeve.

Underneath "METROPOLITAN POLICE" there was a number "3". Then under that, "CTSFO" – Counter Terrorist Specialist Firearms Officer – with a coloured triangle in the bottom corner of the patch. The officer with Winston had a purple triangle. The other officers had yellow.

The officer registered Winston's interest but didn't say anything. He holstered his Glock 17.

'Must be quite a few teams for a raid like this,' said Winston. 'Two? Three?'

He led Winston towards the front door, placing a hand on the small of his back. 'Just us, sir.'

'That's impressive,' said Winston.

He didn't show it, but inside he was on fire. He knew he didn't have long to act.

He glanced at the officer's Glock. Before he could organise his thoughts, he grabbed it. He backed up quickly, taking aim at the officer who stopped dead in his tracks.

The officer's colleagues turned their guns on Winston, yelling at him to drop his.

'Don't fire,' the officer told his colleagues. He showed Winston his palms. 'Mr Winston... I don't know if you understand what's happening right now. My name's Matt Carling. And I'm here to help you. We all are.'

Winston sucked his lips tight together and shook his head defiantly. 'Bullshit. You're not SFO.'

Carling took tentative steps forward. 'Mr Winston... you were being strangled. Listen to me carefully. Your brain was oxygen-deprived. When oxygen rushes back in, it can cause confusion.'

'How many teams are there, Carling?' Winston asked, blinking hard and backing up towards the shuttered windows.

'I told you, Mr Winston. It's just us.'

'Then why have your colleagues got different triangles on their patches? Different units get different patches.'

Carling's colleagues looked at Winston like he'd lost his mind. So much so, Winston began to question his theory. Was Carling right? Was he delusional? Had the patch system changed? Was he about to shoot a perfectly innocent police officer who had just saved his life?

Winston shouted, 'Stop! Don't think I won't shoot. I've got two kills in my file. I'll make you the third.'

'I believe you,' said Carling. Then his caring expression vanished. Without turning, he said, 'Somebody shoot this prick.'

One of them fired a single shot into Winston's right leg, sending him straight to the ground. He howled in agony and dropped the gun.

Carling reclaimed his gun, then stared at Winston nonchalantly. 'Henry said to let you live. Swann and Wark won't be so lucky. Keep pressure on it. SCO nineteen are on their way.'

Winston shut his eyes. He couldn't stand the pain. Out of nowhere, he was seeing things that only visited him in nightmares. A dank basement cell in Beijing. A Ministry of State Security prison. An interrogator shouting at him for the location of his handler. Then the vision faded. And he was left with the pain again.

Somewhere at the back of his mind Winston was aware of the front door closing as Marlow's men left.

A few streets away, Swann kicked and fought in the back of a black unmarked van. She tried to scream, realising that she wasn't being arrested. What she was about to face was far, far worse.

63

Winston wasn't sure he could hang on for much longer without passing out, when he heard heavy footsteps storming up the stairs.

'Please be real,' he wheezed. 'Please be real...'

The SCO19 point woman called for a paramedic as soon as she saw Winston on the floor.

'You're going to be alright,' she told Winston, tending to the wound. 'There's no exit wound. That's good.' She turned to the door. 'Get that paramedic!'

Archer had followed close behind the firearms officers. He wanted to get through, but was told he'd have to wait until the rest of the building had been swept and cleared.

'That's my boss in there,' he protested, fighting his way past three men twice his size.

Winston was glad to see a familiar face. 'Miles... how did you find me?'

'Someone called Scotland Yard with an anonymous tip,' he explained.

'Marlow was here,' said Winston. 'He's got a crew. They took Swann.'

'We dropped the net, sir. Marlow's got John Wark too. Did he say anything about him?'

Winston grimaced as the point woman pressed harder on his leg. 'He said something about going "where it all started". It's got to be somewhere in the city. Get Grant on it. He knows Marlow inside out.'

Grant was in the back of a Metropolitan Police Armed Response Vehicle, the siren and lights going, racing through heavy traffic on the M4 outside Heathrow.

As soon as Archer relayed the Marlow quote, Grant's eyes lit up. He asked the driver, 'How quickly can you get me to Vauxhall Cross?'

'Very,' said the driver. He floored the accelerator, sharking out to the hard shoulder where they remained for the next five miles, the speedometer reaching one hundred miles per hour.

64

'You didn't really think it would be that easy, did you?' asked Marlow.

Swann recoiled as he whipped off her hood, revealing to her a dark, long space. She couldn't see far.

It was cold.

Underground? she wondered. She was secured to a chair, her hands behind her back.

Marlow powered on a set of construction lights dotted around the ground. What Swann could now see in front of her sent a wave of anguish through her body.

She tried to wriggle free, in vain.

A few feet away was a gun secured to a metal rig, pointing at her face.

Beside her was an identical setup, the rigs facing each other. On both, there was a metal step on the ground hooked up to the rig, connected to the trigger. Swann followed the connection from the step at her feet, realising that it was connected to the trigger for the gun next to her.

Marlow crouched behind Swann's rig, checking that he had aimed the gun correctly. For a moment, their eyes met. He flashed her a wicked smile. She tried to wriggle again, but Marlow had secured her to the chair with heavy-duty straps around her neck, waist, and legs. She couldn't move in any direction. There would be no escaping the path of a bullet.

'We're going to try a little experiment,' said Marlow. 'It's something I call "Taking What You Give."'

'Please,' Swann whimpered. 'I have money, Henry. A lot of it. Hidden away...'

He shushed her, moving towards a staircase at the back of the room.

It was behind Swann, out of sight. But she could hear multiple footsteps descending the stairs.

Swann's eyes were adjusting more to the light, revealing little details about the space: old, decaying tiles on the walls. Pipes running along the ground. Tiled pillars.

Two of Marlow's London crew brought a man with a hood down the stairs, then secured him to the other seating rig.

Swann could hardly look.

One of the goons removed the man's hood, revealing John Wark. It was the first light he'd seen since being bundled into an Audi on Quai d'Orsay.

The two goons stood off to the side, keeping a close watch.

'I'm afraid I must apologise,' said Marlow, walking slowly, deliberately around the edge of the room until he was in the eyeline of both of his kidnap victims. 'Imogen here has had a little more time to acclimatise herself with the set-up, John. As you've no doubt identified, you both have guns pointing at your heads. I'll now also draw your attention to the pedals at your feet. They are linked not to the triggers of the guns facing you. But the gun next to you. As you may also have noticed, the guns pointing at you are quite large. Smith and Wesson five hundreds. Press your pedal, and Forensic Services will be jumping straight to dental records.'

'You're mad,' Wark ventured, still firmly in denial of the reality. He'd already concluded that Marlow wanted him purely as a bargaining chip. Now that those goalposts had dramatically shifted, he couldn't adjust.

'I'm mad...' Marlow said to himself, considering the term. He pointed to the ceiling. 'Look at what's happening out there. It's all falling apart. A world of chaos. Or had you not noticed?' It wasn't anger in his voice. It was desperation: he wanted them to understand. 'We can't control it any longer. This is all that's left.'

Swann tried to interrupt. 'Henry, listen to me. You're unwell. You don't have to do this.'

'Have to? Of course I don't *have to*! I *want* to. Can't you see that?' An eerie calm came over him. There was no talking him out of it. He had decided long ago. 'It was when you sent me to him. To Joseph. The file made him sound like a madman. A typical arms dealer, lusting after money and power. When I got there, it was...' He shook his head in wonder, as if picturing a memory of something beautiful, moving. 'When the Allies liberated the concentration camps, the soldiers couldn't believe what they were seeing. That such cruelty and horror could exist. The only food the soldiers had with them were these army-issue chocolate bars. Being decent and humane, the soldiers handed them out. The only problem was, the prisoners were so malnourished their bodies had completely shut down. They were in starvation mode. So when they ate the chocolate, they went into shock. Dozens of them died this way.' Marlow laughed in dismay, and horror. 'They survived an entire industry of death. And what killed them? A soldier with a kind heart and a chocolate bar. When I heard that story, I thought, *of course*. How perfect!' Marlow took out a gun and fired single shots at both of his goons. He didn't even flinch. His expression placid. Then, without missing a beat, he continued like nothing had happened. 'Listen to that story and then tell me this is a sane world. Tell me it makes sense.'

'It doesn't, Henry,' said Swann. 'And neither does this.'

'The only way to win,' Marlow explained, 'the only way to get out of this, is to believe in nothing. Because once you believe in nothing, everything is permitted. Everything is possible. Our morality is what holds us back.' He ran his hand over his mussed-up hair with increasing belligerence. 'The jihadists send disabled children into markets with bombs.' He spluttered into laughter. 'Do you not see how *brilliant* that is? To believe in something so absolutely... that you could do that? Not just thinking, but *knowing* that it was right? That's what Charles Joseph understood: you win when you become capable of doing whatever is necessary to survive.' Marlow stood up and backed away. 'That's why I'm giving you one hour to decide between yourselves: who lives; who dies. Feel free to talk about it. Or, of course, you can just press your pedal and be done with the whole thing.'

Wark asked, 'What if neither of us does it?'

'That's simple.' Marlow showed them a remote control with a plunger button. 'I release this and both your guns go off.' He set a digital timer on the ground showing an hour, then he started the countdown. 'It's time to decide how much you really want to live.'

65

Against the advice of the paramedics, Winston had demanded they take him to Vauxhall Cross. Everyone in the Control room stood up when he returned, hobbling in on a bandaged leg with a crutch.

Winston accepted the applause with typical style. 'If you're clapping then you're not doing your job.'

Silence.

Having punctured the triumphant air, Winston caught himself, switching to a more conciliatory tone. 'Look, guys... In the last twenty-four hours we have lost Justin. The Foreign Secretary and Director Swann have been kidnapped. We have no demands and we don't know where they are. On top of that, we now have to bring in both Director Swann and Henry Marlow. Let's not lose sight of what's still on the line here. We have one lead from Marlow: quote, where it all began. I want all eyes on Marlow's personnel files from his rookie year. Any safe houses, contacts, training sites. Anywhere he could be hiding out.' He paused, waiting for action. 'Okay,' he gestured urgently, making a loop in the air with his hand. 'Let's get after it.' Noticing Olivia Christie waiting for him, Winston told her, 'I don't know what I want more: to stop Marlow, or bring in Swann and Wark.'

'I'm glad you kept that out of your little motivational speech,' she said.

Winston was unashamed of his caustic comment. 'John Wark ordered the murder of Kadir Rashid to cover up the fact that he laundered a tyrant's dirty money, to buy property worth close to five billion pounds. Imogen killed one of our own to hide her part in the same deal, and she would have killed me as well. If they get out of this alive, I'm going to see that they spend the rest of their lives in jail.'

Christie laid a hand on Winston's shoulder on the way past, suggesting a reticence on her part. As if Winston was going down a path she wished he wouldn't.

With a phone clamped against his cheek, Ryan spoke up to get Winston's attention. 'Sir, I have NADOC on the line...'

The National Air Defence Operations Centre.

'An hour ago, they tracked an HH sixty Pave Hawk helicopter entering British airspace.'

'I don't know helicopters,' said Winston.

'It's military, sir. And exceedingly fast. Seems that it landed near Beckton. A police patrol car just found it. It's empty.'

'How did a military helicopter get inside London without us knowing about it?'

'It was following the same route as the high-speed train line from Dover, sir. The operator saw a blip on the radar but was told to ignore it.' Ryan's frustration was evident. 'They saw what they expected to see.'

Winston said, 'Wark could have been on that chopper. Get GCHQ. Tell them we need every camera they have in Beckton. If it was Wark, they'd have needed more than a few guys. That means anything in a saloon or bigger. Likely a van without windows.'

Archer brought a phone over to Winston. 'It's Grant, sir.'

Winston slammed the console button to put him on speaker. 'You're with the room, Grant. Go ahead.'

Grant sounded buoyant, speaking over the noise of the car engine. 'I think I've got it, sir.' He was reading Marlow's files from a laptop. 'I don't think Marlow was talking about his first years in the Service. This is personal to him. He's taken Swann for a reason. We shouldn't be looking in Marlow's files. We should be looking in Swann's.'

Winston's posture straightened, then he snapped his finger frantically at Archer, Ryan, and Samantha. 'You three. Get me any known training grounds or cover locations used by Imogen. Anywhere decommissioned but that the Service still has on lease.' Winston stood behind them, eyes scanning for whoever got the result quickest.

Ryan and Samantha announced, 'Got it!', at the same time.

Samantha said, 'Down Street. A disused underground station.'

Ryan added, 'She used it as part of Marlow's cover. An address for an exporter business.'

Winston asked Grant, 'Did you get that?'

'Got it,' he confirmed, seeing the address come through on his phone's map. He showed it to the driver. 'Get me there.'

66

Down Street underground station had once been part of what would become the famous Piccadilly line. The wealth of the local residents meant that it suffered low passenger numbers and closed in nineteen thirty-two, a mere twenty-five years after opening. Its history didn't end, though. During the Second World War the platforms were bricked over and the station became home to Churchill's War Cabinet, while the official Cabinet War Rooms were completed in basement offices in Whitehall.

Down Street station had been empty ever since.

The Met Police driver let Grant out on Piccadilly near the Wellington monument. The station entrance at Down Street Mews was around the corner, and Grant didn't want to draw any unwanted attention.

The narrow one-way street was quiet, as the bottom end had been closed off while extensive renovations were carried out on a residential building covered in scaffolding.

Grant took a long look at the white van parked in front. The back doors were open, showing plenty of hardware and construction equipment. What he didn't see was the faces of the two Saudi men in high-vis vests in the front seat, running their final checks on their handguns.

Tahir and Umar were Mabahith agents, run by Ghazi from the Saudi secret police. Bringing in outside talent was risky and slow, so Ghazi kept a number of trusted operatives based full-time in foreign countries. When the time came, he had men who were acclimatised, spoke the language well, knew the geography, and could act fast. Tahir and Umar's skills were wide-ranging, with a specialty in targeted kills and street grabs: rarely requested on British soil, but when it was necessary, Tahir and Umar were Ghazi's most reliable men.

Tahir was the senior of the two. 'Five minutes,' he said. 'Then we go in.'

Umar nodded.

The entrance to the station was through a boarded-up door just off the courtyard that led to the rear of the building. It looked secure, then Grant discovered the padlock was broken, hanging open on the latch.

He took out his gun, borrowed from the secure box in the police car: a trusted Glock 17 – the standard sidearm of Met Specialist Firearms Officers. He pushed the door open gently, covering his blind spots as soon as he was through the door. It was almost entirely black inside.

He took a deep breath, holding his weapon out in front of him, then headed through the old turnstiles towards the stairs – into the darkness.

Back at the builder's van, Tahir and Umar removed their high-vis vests and stripped off their loose, paint-stained denim shirts, revealing black long-sleeved baselayer tops. Their tight fit accentuated their muscular physiques.

They were focussed, determined. Assets of the Saudi secret police weren't eager to disappoint the Crown Prince. Al-Haa'ir, the maximum-security Mabahith prison near Riyadh, housed plenty of ex-agents who had.

Umar took one last look at his phone, which showed the faces of their two targets: Henry Marlow and Duncan Grant.

67

The timer was already down to ten minutes remaining, and both Wark and Swann were still alive.

Marlow stood in silence, listening to their conversation with amusement.

'I have a family,' Wark pleaded. 'Children.'

'Congratulations,' replied Swann. 'You clearly have every right to shoot me.'

'If you had children, you would understand.'

'This whole thing was your idea to begin with. I was just following orders.'

Wark scoffed. 'Oh, bollocks, Imogen.'

Marlow tilted his head, asking Wark, 'Do you really think you can trust her not to do it? She's already got blood on her hands.'

Wark asked Swann, 'What is he talking about?'

Marlow answered for her. 'She killed Justin Vern last night.'

'Justin?' said Wark. 'Tell me he's lying, Imogen.'

'I had to,' she asserted. 'It wasn't just for me. It was for both of us. He found out about my dead drops with Édith Lagrange. It was only a matter of time before the rest of our story crumbled.'

'But...' Wark could barely summon the words. 'One of our own.'

'And what was I?' asked Marlow, oozing contempt.

The air grew colder the farther Grant descended the single staircase. His eyes adjusted to the darkness, aided by the faintest traces of sunlight leaking in from the floor above. He felt like he was deep-sea diving, the light fading with each step down into the belly of the city.

Decades of dirt and moist air had left a layer of mould on everything. With each ninety-degree turn downstairs, the air grew thicker. And colder.

Although both ends of the tunnel had been sealed where they met the platform, one of the walls had fallen down twenty years earlier. It was still connected to the current underground network – through a labyrinthine system of adjoining tunnels and passageways. It took a while to get there, but a swirling breeze created by a far-off train reached Down Street. The metallic screech from the rails was little more than a few decibels, but whenever Grant paused on a landing he could hear it.

Each storey down was a step into the unknown. Grant didn't know if he would find dead bodies or a bomb or an ambush. Considering Henry Marlow's state of mind, anything seemed possible.

Three storeys down, the darkness was punctured by the construction lights. Grant could hear muffled voices.

One male. One female.

They're still alive, he thought.

He just didn't know for how long.

'Seven minutes left,' Marlow warned. 'Apparently, life is not that important to either of you. Pitiful, really.'

Unseen in the darkness, Grant crept down the stairs, crouching behind the crumbling stone banister. He needed a moment to assess the geography of the platform. The blind spots.

Marlow had set up his twisted game where the train tracks had been covered over. Tiled pillars stood all the way along the platform, the only available cover to hide behind.

There was a pile of bricks a few feet high at the open end of the tunnel, the faint noise of the underground system so near and yet so far.

Grant had to move with deft, careful steps as there was so much debris underfoot. Marlow would be able to hear the slightest scrape on the concrete.

At first, Grant couldn't believe what had been set up. It was unclear whether Marlow was in control of both guns. Grant had to proceed on that assumption, and that the slightest sound would be a critical mistake. He would have to move fast, though. The timer was ticking down, and he didn't want to find out what happened when it reached zero.

The major obstacle he faced was the way the construction lights illuminated the bottom of the staircase. Any break in the light would cause a noticeable flicker. If Marlow suspected someone had got in, he might execute Wark and Swann on the spot.

Wark declared, 'I won't do it, Henry. I won't let you turn me into... *whatever* it is you've become.'

Marlow closed his eyes, as if in deep concentration. 'What I've become?'

Grant seized his chance. He jumped down the last three steps, then tucked himself up behind one of the pillars. He waited several seconds, holding his breath. If Marlow had heard him the first Grant would know about it would likely be a bullet in the head. Then he heard Marlow continue talking, still a healthy distance away.

'You still don't get it,' Marlow said. 'You *made me* what I am. Through all my career, your greatest fear has been the ideologues. Fascists. Communists. Islamists. But actually, the most dangerous enemy is someone who doesn't believe in anything. Who embraces the meaningless. Who can stare into that black abyss, and smile at it.' He raised a finger. '*That* person is capable of anything. That person is capable of walking straight into hell.'

Wark said, 'I was on the ground after Srebrenica in ninety-five. You think you know hell?'

Marlow got up close enough for spittle to land on Wark's face. 'I've seen hell,' he said. 'I've been there. I used to wonder: how do you get someone to walk into hell? The answer is quite simple, actually. You do it one step at a time. It starts with a little push. You push them just to the point where they want to stop. Then you back off. Then you push a little more. And back off. You keep doing this, inch by inch, day by day, mission by mission. One betrayal at a time. Until they look around and realise, "I'm in hell."' Marlow's voice was brimming with emotion. He wasn't anywhere close to tears, but it was clear that he felt what he was saying with uncommon intensity. 'That's not the worst part. The worst part is when they realise that they're in hell and they never put up a fight. They never protested. You know why? Because they were following orders.' Marlow backed away, taking a moment to compose himself. 'I've spent a lot of time thinking about orders the last few years. Have either of you heard of Reserve Police Battalion one oh one?'

Wark and Swann were no longer really hearing him, lost in their own private hells.

Marlow said, 'They were a group of middle-aged German reserve policemen sent to control a Jewish village during the Second World War. These were ordinary men. They weren't ideologues, or even anti-Semites for the most part. Hardly any of them had even fired their weapons before. Within a few weeks, the battalion had killed eighteen hundred Jews. A massacre. Six months later, they'd murdered tens of thousands – no one really knows for sure. When I read about this, the scale of it took my breath away. How you could get ordinary men to do that. Then I realised, if you could get people to quit their beliefs, their ideologies, imagine if you could get them to believe in nothing. How powerful that would be.' Marlow stepped into Wark and Swann's eyeline. 'If I had even a tenth of that strength...'

Grant peeked out from behind the pillar, trying to see the timer which was now out of view. His primary concern was now the device he had spotted in Marlow's left hand – and what it controlled.

Grant's options were limited: he could shoot Marlow and hope that it wouldn't cause Wark and Swann to be killed in the process. But if he wanted answers, he needed Marlow alive.

Then Marlow made the choice for him. He shouted, 'Are you going to hide behind that pillar all day, Duncan? I put those lights at the bottom of the stairs for a reason.'

Grant swallowed hard. 'Henry,' he called back. 'You don't have to do this.'

'I *am* aware of that,' Marlow replied. 'The fact that it's my choice is sort of the point. The poetry of it will be more powerful if you work it out for yourself, Duncan. Honestly...'

'Let them go. Take me instead. You wanted me dead when I was in the Congo. Now's the chance to do it properly. Yourself.'

'No,' said Marlow. 'I've worked too hard to get in a room with these two after all these years.' He stared at the timer. 'The thing is, Duncan. I don't think you can see how long is left from where you are. Is it two minutes or thirty seconds?'

Grant tried again to see it but he couldn't get an angle on it. 'There's enough time for you to do the right thing.'

'You see,' Marlow wagged a finger in the direction of Grant's voice. 'That answer confirms to me that you don't know. I'll tell you what I'm going to do. I'll give you a choice of who to save. Swann or Wark. You put a bullet in either of their heads, and the other one gets to walk out of here.'

Grant leaned his head back against the pillar and closed his eyes. He cursed under his breath.

'What will it be, Duncan?' Marlow boomed. 'Justin Vern's killer, or the man who let your precious handler be tortured by the Chinese for six months?' He paused. 'Judging by your silence, I'll bet that that's news to you. Yes, the Right

Honourable John Wark here knew about Rashid and did nothing, *and* when he was Chief, he let your daddy dearest dangle until the Chinese offered a prisoner swap.' Marlow turned to Wark. 'Remind me, John. How many years were you willing to let Leo rot in Beijing? Ten? Twenty?'

Mentally, Wark had checked out. He now simply stared at the ground, waiting for it to be over.

Swann spoke up. 'Duncan, don't listen to him. He's lying.'

'Said the liar,' Marlow retorted. 'Tick tock, tick tock, Duncan! Is it ten seconds left?'

'It's a minute!' Swann shouted. 'Hurry up, Grant. What the hell are you waiting for?'

'In case you're wondering,' said Marlow. 'I am indeed holding a suicide button. Killing me is off the table unless you want Wark and Swann to die. Which is fine by me...'

Grant peeked out from behind the pillar again, keeping a mental countdown from a minute.

'This is your problem, Duncan,' said Marlow. 'Don't confuse other people's weakness for your strength. Look at how weak, how ineffectual you are when there's a rational choice to be made. Even knowing that Swann killed Justin Vern, you still can't pull the trigger. Come on. Do it! Do it and join me. We've got so much work to do after this.'

Grant called out, 'You want me to be like you, Henry. To give in. To stop fighting for good. I won't do it.'

'You tell yourself that. But we both know I'm right. These two deserve to die. You just don't have the strength to do it yourself. I don't want you to stop fighting, I want you to start! But the real enemy, not the one you've been taught to fight. Did they tell you I went crazy? Is that it?'

Grant replied, 'I thought that if we talked, I might be able to make sense of it. That was before the Congo.'

'I'm not ashamed of the things I did there. You just can't understand them yet.'

'I don't see much to understand, Henry. I don't know where you think you're heading, but you're not even on the map anymore. The map you have is empty.'

'You *do* think I'm crazy.'

Grant paused to consider the term. 'I'm not sure that there's a word for what you are.'

Swann got breathless watching the timer. 'Ten seconds, Grant, for Christ's sake!'

Grant could already see what was going to happen. Swann had butchered Justin just to cover her tracks. She wasn't about to sit there and let Marlow defeat her.

Forced to face each other, Wark and Swann simultaneously felt like they were looking into the eyes of their potential victim and assassin. With the timer now down to mere seconds, something shunted in Swann's head.

Seven seconds left...

She began to sob. 'I can't do it...'

For a moment, Wark thought that she had finally come around to his thinking: that they couldn't let Marlow win by playing his game.

'What's it going to be, Duncan?' asked Marlow.

Grant's choice was clear: he couldn't shoot Marlow. But he also couldn't bring himself to shoot Swann or Wark.

He leaned out from the pillar on Marlow's blindside and took aim at the front left leg on Wark's wooden chair.

He fired at it: a direct hit.

Five seconds left...

The leg folded, lowering Wark's height the few inches necessary to escape the bullet.

Swann looked in horror. 'No!' she cried.

She stamped her foot on the pedal, firing the gun that was no longer aiming at Wark's head.

Seeing what Swann was trying to do, Wark fought with everything he could to move out of the way. But Grant had done enough.

Wark shut his eyes in a wince as the bullet flashed excruciatingly, but harmlessly, close to his head.

Swann yelled out in anguish at Wark's escape.

Marlow laughed. 'Three seconds left, Imogen...'

Swann stamped on the pedal again, firing another bullet. She grimaced with effort, stamping again. And again. In the enclosed space, the shots sounded like bombs.

She kept firing until the chamber was empty. But there was nothing she could do. Wark was out of the firing line.

The platform turned silent.

Marlow locked eyes with Swann, holding the remote out. 'Time's up, Imogen.'

'No,' she begged, eyes wide. 'Please, Henry!'

Grant took aim at one of her chair legs, attempting the same shot.

Voice trembling, Marlow said to Swann, 'You deserve so much worse than this. But if it's any consolation, there's absolutely nothing waiting for you.' Marlow dropped the remote, triggering the mechanism on the gun pointed at her.

Grant fired twice at Swann's chair leg – both shots missed. Then he hit it with the third.

It was one bullet too late.

68

Wark was stricken, still tied to his lopsided chair. He heaved for breath, still processing the speed of what had just happened. Shock had already taken hold of him. It didn't get any better when he looked to one side, seeing Swann's face pointing to the ceiling, a blood-filled hole in her forehead.

Both hands now free, Marlow pulled out a sidearm and fired in Grant's direction.

Grant dived back behind the pillar, covering his head from the tile shards showering him. Marlow was in open space just ten metres away, but Grant couldn't get a shot at him.

Marlow took cover behind the nearest pillar.

'It's over, Henry,' Grant told him.

Marlow smirked as he considered his options. There weren't many. He could drop his gun and let Grant take him in, where a long process of black site interrogations beckoned. Or he could try to shoot his way out.

In the end, the choice was made for him by the sight of

Tahir and Umar breaking the light at the bottom of the stairs. Something primal in Marlow's synapses fired, the old reflexes kicking in.

Grant leaned out from the pillar and saw Marlow's gaze turning from him to the stairs.

Marlow yelled, 'Down!'

Both Umar and Tahir fired at Grant, but Marlow's warning had come in time. Grant ducked, diving around to the other side of the pillar.

Marlow had clear shots on the Mabahith agents now, who were on the run and had nowhere to hide.

Tahir turned in profile, succeeding only in clearing a path for a bullet towards Umar behind. Tahir ran towards the nearest pillar while Umar clutched his stomach.

He knew the seriousness of his wound and cried for help.

Tahir put a finger to his lips – he couldn't hear where Marlow and Grant were.

Tahir, Grant, and Marlow were all temporarily sheltered behind pillars.

Recognising their shared enemy, Grant whispered to Marlow, 'Lights.'

Marlow nodded at the suggestion, and shot out the bulbs of the construction lights.

Suddenly shrouded in darkness, no one dared to move.

Grant still felt in danger from Marlow, who was lurking somewhere behind him. How close, he wasn't sure. One pillar away? Two? Grant decided to focus all his efforts on Tahir.

Firing blindly into the dark was a waste of ammunition, as well as a fast way of giving his position away: the muzzle flash of a gun in such a setting would light up like a firework.

Grant cursed internally at his lack of a suppressor.

As Tahir sneaked along the platform, one step every few seconds, Grant opted for a different tactic. He crouched down and slid his shoes off. Staying low, he crept out from the cover of the pillar.

What he had planned was high-risk, but the only alternative was blind hope. Which never had been, and never would be, a strategy of his.

The only sound was Umar's whimpering at the foot of the stairs. There was something about Wark's close brush with death, and the timbre of Umar's cries in the dark, that made Wark panic. He fought against his restraints, trying to get free.

Somewhere over Grant's shoulder was a scraping sound followed by rapid footsteps.

Marlow, using his familiarity with the platform layout, had made a run for the tunnel opening.

Grant was prepared to let him go for the moment. He didn't want to move until he had located Tahir.

Hearing Marlow's footsteps, Tahir stepped out from behind his pillar, willing to take a few shots into the dark.

As soon as Tahir racked the slide, the sound sent a fresh wave of panic through Wark. Fearing he was about to be shot, he unconsciously kicked out a foot, triggering a second shot from the gun facing Swann.

From Grant's vantage point, the light from the muzzle flash illuminated the outline of Tahir's outstretched arm. Without even thinking, Grant took his shot, striking Tahir on the inside of his elbow.

The bullet shattered the joint instantly. His forearm

hung at an irregular angle, unable to do what Tahir's brain wanted it to.

Grant took his opportunity and set off after Marlow.

Tahir fell to his knees. Following the noise, he fired blindly, using his weak hand, striking the surrounding masonry.

Grant kept low until Tahir ran out of bullets, then he scrambled over the pile of bricks at the mouth of the tunnel, hearing Marlow's footsteps echoing farther down the line.

Back to one-on-one, Marlow's charity had come to an end. He fired twice at Grant. Warning shots more than anything. The slight bend in the tunnel had robbed him of a clear shot.

As Grant and Marlow ventured deeper into the abandoned tunnel, Tahir struggled on, reduced to a one-armed crawl. The pain might have slowed him down, but death was the only thing that would stop him.

Marlow reached the existing London Underground network. Light bulbs attached to the ceiling to aid maintenance works became more frequent, extending his shadow back towards Grant. Marlow had stopped running.

Grant followed suit, not wanting to run straight into a bullet.

Up ahead, Marlow laughed bitterly, then rattled the stainless-steel gate in front of him. It was locked and bolted. There was no way out.

Grant upped his pace again. 'Let me take you in, Henry. Winston and I... we know what Wark and Swann did. We've got the Lawrence Bloom file. I'll find a way to get you leniency. I promise.'

'I believe you, Duncan,' Marlow called out. 'It's not up to you, though.'

Grant emerged around a long bend in the track, then got his first glimpse of Marlow since the lights had gone out on the platform.

He was slouched against the gate – the posture of a man resigned to his fate. 'It seems appropriate. The two of us, both destined to end up in the same place. You must have thought about it.'

Grant said nothing. He raised his gun, ready to fire.

Marlow did the same.

There were no escape routes. Nothing to hide behind. Just two men, finally face to face.

'Drop it, Henry,' said Grant. He wasn't about to squander the chance or hesitate. He'd already survived too much to let that happen.

But before he could fire, a shot came from behind him.

Marlow kept his gun pointed at Grant, but was too shocked to pull the trigger.

Grant looked down at where the bullet had exited at his right clavicle. The impact spun him half a turn to face Tahir, who was slumped against the wall. Firing the shot had taken up the last of his reserves. It was all he could do now just to remain upright. He didn't stay there long.

Grant returned fire, landing a fatal shot in Tahir's chest. Grant then fell to his knees. He clutched the wound with his left hand but could still feel the blood pouring through his fingers.

Marlow walked casually towards him, seeing the approaching torchlights of the Met Police's Counter Terror Specialised Firearms Officers.

Marlow dropped to his knees at Grant's side. 'I know what you're feeling,' he said. 'Not sure if you'll live or die...'

The officers shouted warnings as Marlow put the gun to his temple.

Grant felt on the verge of passing out, but still summoned the strength to lift his hand from his wound.

Marlow said, 'Remember, Duncan. Words no longer matter. Only action.'

With the trigger held but not quite pressed yet, Grant tried to knock Marlow's arm away. But he missed.

The last thing Grant saw before passing out was Marlow being almost catapulted backwards. A bullet had hit him in the torso.

Then Grant's vision narrowed, turning black until it was all he could see.

EPILOGUE

FIVE DAYS LATER

The extent of Grant's injuries were largely dependent on luck: Tahir's bullet had caused a minor flesh wound. Four days after his entry- and exit wounds were patched up, Grant was back on his feet. A few inches either way, and he would have been talked of as one of the Service's great lost talents.

Instead, he returned to Vauxhall Cross with a heavily bandaged chest beneath his suit – a black one, with a white shirt underneath.

Christie and Winston led the applause when he entered the Control room. Grant raised a hand – not out of appreciation, but in the hope of halting the public show of admiration as quickly as possible.

'Right, that's enough,' announced Winston, sympathising with Grant's discomfort. 'He's getting a medal, he doesn't need a standing ovation as well. Back to work.'

The staff smiled as they returned to their keyboards

and phones.

Christie and Winston took Grant aside.

'How are you feeling?' Christie asked.

Grant could tell that it was but a precursor to what she really wanted to ask. 'Fine,' he replied.

'I thought you'd want to know: he's asked for you.'

Grant turned to Winston. 'What do you think?'

Winston paused to consider it. 'The interrogators are getting nowhere. We have two more days before we have to hand him over to the Met.'

Grant asked Christie, 'Is there time before...?'

'We have time,' she replied.

The five basement holding cells were set up in a row, with bulletproof glass on the front instead of bars. Concrete dividers separated each cell. It was rare for there to be more than one detainee present at any time, but on the occasions there were, MI6 didn't want detainees to be able to communicate with each other – whether by hand signals or mouthing words.

The ceilings had microphones built into them, and cameras were pointed into each cell, recording constantly. There was no telling what details they might capture during a detention.

The cells weren't intended to replace the Met's existing facilities for terror suspects and other high-profile arrests. The refurbished Charing Cross Police Station's high-security cell suite had become the go-to destination for such criminals. And MI6 officers – like MI5 – had no powers of arrest. But every so often a case like Henry Marlow's necessitated that time be given for MI6 to uncover any further threats, and interrogate suspects explicitly about matters involving national security and classified intelligence. Conversations that couldn't happen with regular detectives in the room.

The chest injuries Marlow sustained from the gunshot wound to the chest had ended up largely superficial thanks to a covert ballistic vest. When the news had been relayed to Grant as he recovered in a private room at St Thomas' Hospital, he wondered why Marlow had put on a Kevlar bulletproof vest then held a gun to his own head. Winston had put it down to Marlow wanting to go out on his own terms. Grant wasn't nearly as convinced.

Marlow's cell was at the end of the row.

Grant wasn't sure what he'd find until he got there. It was a scene of paranoid security: Marlow had been deprived of such basic items as shoe laces, and pillow or duvet cases.

He sat on the floor next to his bed, which consisted of a mattress laid on top of a concrete block. He was dressed in a white jumpsuit, and had on white canvas slip-on shoes. 'I knew you'd live,' he said.

Grant sat on the plastic chair placed a few metres back from the glass. 'I was particularly touched at the part where you did nothing at all.'

Marlow scoffed. 'Is that why you came here? To complain? The interrogators have done plenty of that already. They get frustrated so quickly these days.'

'Have you been mistreated?' asked Grant.

Marlow pulled an ironic expression. 'I think we both know how well they react to stubborn silence.'

'Another forty-eight hours and you'll be in the safe hands of the Met.'

'Don't be naïve, Grant,' he said. 'I won't be seeing a police station any more than I will a courtroom. I'll be shuttled around from black site to black site so that MI6 and CIA and everyone else can all get their licks in. To find out everything I know. How many people I sold secrets to.'

Grant said, 'There's no evidence you sold secrets.'

'Like that matters. What matters is keeping all this quiet. What are they saying about Swann? No, wait. Let me guess.'

Grant gave him a moment.

Marlow said, 'Shot during a home invasion. They can use it as an excuse to beef up the security budgets on senior MPs.'

'Close,' said Grant. 'But the Met Commissioner was worried that headlines of murder in Belgravia would put off high-stakes property investors.'

Marlow shook his head at their predictability. 'What did they go with? Car accident, followed by a hasty cremation?'

'She was in an urn within twenty-four hours,' Grant confirmed.

'They really have no imagination,' Marlow muttered.

'The Saudis weren't nearly as credulous about Tahir and Umar.'

'They were Saudis?'

'Mabahith assets. We flew Tahir's body back. Umar begged to be sent to jail here instead.'

'Deportation is a death sentence for someone like him.'

Grant said, 'I'm sure the Crown Prince will take care of him.'

Marlow smiled.

'What is it?' asked Grant.

'No... it's just, that phrase means something very

different to people like you and I.' The smile disappeared
from Marlow's face, which turned introspective. 'Why did
you try to stop me?'

The question took Grant by surprise. 'Protecting British
interests. You're more valuable alive than dead.'

Marlow peered at him, evaluating each micro-expres-
sion of his body language. 'You think you won, don't you?
Because you preserved life. You think that's the answer to
everything. Let me guess: a dead parent before adolescence.
I'd be surprised if the other one's still alive. See, there's also
a time to strike, Duncan. For decisiveness. You don't understand that yet. But you will.'

Grant didn't want to let Marlow see him shaken by his
observations. 'Why didn't you kill Swann and Wark straight
away?' he asked.

Marlow answered, 'I wanted to make them suffer.'

'That wasn't about suffering,' said Grant. 'That was
playing.'

Marlow looked away.

'Tell me about the Congo, Henry.'

'What's to talk about?'

'I was there. You didn't just use that compound to hide
out. I saw the severed heads. The doped-up kids. You were
running a militia.' Grant leaned forward, thinking about
everything that had happened. And where they each found
themselves now. 'This is what you wanted all along, isn't it?
Helping me escape the Hole with the recordings you left
there. The fake DGSI leads in the Congo. The lazily
encrypted Lawrence Bloom file. Acting suicidal while taking
precautions to stay alive. Why so much work to lead to this
moment? You in a box.'

Marlow dipped his head. For a moment, he considered

answering honestly. Then he said 'No,' walking to the back of his cell. 'I thought you were ready. Come back to me when you are.'

The ceremony was conducted in an anonymous, windowless room on the fourth floor. Present were John Wark, Olivia Christie, Winston, and Grant. Wark still had healing scrape marks down one side of his face, and bruising around his neck.

Christie stood next to Grant against a backdrop with an oversized Union Jack flag and the Royal coat of arms. She held out an open blue box to Wark, who took out a bronze medal with a red- and black-striped ribbon.

He said, 'Duncan Grant, I hereby award you the Paul Dukes Medal, for extraordinary valour in the line of service.'

'Thank you, sir,' said Grant.

He held the medal aloft just long enough for a photographer to come in and take two quick snaps, before being ushered back out the door again.

Wark shook Grant's hand. 'The Service owes you a great debt, Duncan. As do I.'

Grant shook Wark's hand without expression.

While he held on to Grant's hand, he pulled Grant closer. 'My door will always be open to you, Duncan,' Wark whispered. As if to hammer home the point, he lifted his eyebrows as he pulled back, making sure Grant read between the lines.

The insinuation couldn't have been clearer if Wark had hired a plane banner to fly over the Thames: '*Keep quiet and you'll be rewarded.*'

The formalities dispensed with, Christie opened the door and stood to one side, inviting Grant and Winston to leave the room. There were delicate matters to discuss.

On his way out, Grant wiped his hand against his trouser leg. Trying to wipe off the sensation of Wark's touch.

As soon as the door closed behind them, Winston tried to soften the abruptness of the moment. 'You survived all that, Grant. Tell me you at least learned something.'

'Who to trust,' said Grant.

'And who would that be?'

'No one.'

'I know what happened,' said Winston. 'I've been there. You spent one evening with Lagrange and you thought she understood who you really are, what you'll have to live with. And I warned you about letting Marlow get inside your head.'

Grant was too embarrassed to comment. 'I shouldn't have believed him,' he said. 'He played me. He knew when I listened to those diaries that I would want to believe him. To fight for him. It was a mistake. It won't happen again.'

'I listened to them as well, Duncan,' said Winston. 'I think I know what you heard in them. And I promise you, what happened to him will never happen to you. I won't permit it.' He turned to leave, then backtracked. 'The lesson isn't trust no one, Grant. The lesson is trust *me*.'

'Yes, sir,' Grant replied.

'Enjoy your leave. We'll see you in a fortnight.'

As Winston turned, Grant said, 'I can still feel him. Haslitt. In my fingers.'

'Don't wait for it to go away,' Winston said. 'Remember it. Hold onto it.'

'Is that for your benefit, or mine?' asked Grant.

Winston didn't answer.

On his own in the lift downstairs, Grant looked at the medal in his hand, then put it in his pocket along with his spare change.

In the windowless room, Christie and Wark were alone.

'What a bloody mess,' said Wark, wiping the tiredness from his face.

'Marlow won't be a problem,' Christie confirmed. 'Langley have already asked if we'll share him. Last I checked, they still have an impressive list of black sites. Or, you could say, property portfolio.'

Wark lifted his head, unsure of what would come next.

Christie said, 'Don't worry, John. I have already expunged AC one eighty and all the other files on national security grounds. No one will be able to read them for another fifty years, and even then they'll be classified STRAP Three. There will be all of twenty people in the country who have the authority to know the files even exist. There will be no testimony to the Joint Intelligence Committee. No Hannibal investigation.'

'Thank you.'

'I didn't do it for you. I did it to protect this agency.'

He enthused with even greater gratitude, 'Thank you, Olivia. You won't regret this.'

She grinned. 'You think that's it? Will you seriously stand there and tell me that at no point in those numerous transactions with Abdul, there was no payoff for you? A million here, a million there? Buried across dozens of offshore accounts?'

Wark's gratitude turned to fear. 'What do you want?'

Christie didn't have to think about it. 'I want the Albion programme reinstated. And I want Leo Winston running it. Reporting directly to me.'

'What about the JIC? The Treasury? And the PM will never sign it off. Not after Marlow.'

Christie said, 'A man like you with everything to lose can be very persuasive.'

Against the height of the Union Jack behind him, Wark suddenly appeared very small. 'So it's about blackmail, then.'

On her way to the door, Christie said, 'No. It's about betrayal. It so often is in this game. I told someone that recently.'

Walking to Waterloo train station, fighting his way through the crowded streets at lunchtime, Grant couldn't believe that he'd just been handed a medal by the Foreign Secretary in recognition of service for MI6. It didn't feel real.

He thought of the line from his training days: *your entire life has been leading up to this point.* Through all of his gruelling physical training, as well as everything else he'd had to contend with growing up, the one thing that had kept him going was the thought of achieving some kind of recognition that all his hard work and toil would be worth it. It would serve something greater than his own life. Now that they had given him what he wanted, he was surprised at how little he felt. He was just another man in a suit amongst hundreds of others.

A successful career and escaping his childhood were supposed to be the things that fixed him. Recognition, achievements, medals... Those were meant to confirm that he'd made it. He'd overcome. He'd survived.

Sitting on the train heading for Glasgow on his own, tie loosened, a single can of lager in front of him, he didn't feel fixed.

* * *

ONE WEEK LATER

The cemetery was on a cliff at the northernmost point of the Isle of Skye, the Trotternish peninsula. Beyond the cliff were the wild waters of Tulm Bay. Like most days on Skye, it was windy – visibility clear enough to see the Isle of Harris thirty miles away.

Grant stood silently in front of the grave for several minutes. There were only one hundred plots on the site, and they were rarely visited. Most relatives of the deceased there had long since moved to the mainland, or passed on themselves.

Grant's only company was a smattering of sheep, whose only interest was in chewing the lush, buttercup-filled grass in the neighbouring field.

The grave headstone showed the names ALASDAIR GRANT and MAIRI GRANT. Duncan's dad had been proud of the surname's meaning: "great" or "large". Duncan had once said that it was a pity his dad had shown such little evidence of being either.

Mairi Grant had died so long ago that Duncan could barely remember her face, or a conversation between them. Things weren't quite so ambiguous with his dad.

Duncan had lived through Alasdair's deterioration, his

increasing alcoholism, and refusal to get help – or at least help himself.

In his teens, Duncan had gone out with a local girl who had been almost pathologically incapable of cruelty or selfishness. When Duncan asked her how she did it, she told him that it was simple. She imagined trying to walk in the other person's shoes. The phrase had meant little to him at the time, but it had stayed with him.

Walking in someone else's shoes.

It was something Duncan had never really tried to do when it came to his dad. Duncan had never lived through losing a wife, a stoic Scottish shepherd struggling to raise a child on his own. Could he swear that in the same circumstances as his dad, he wouldn't have fallen apart in the same way? He wasn't sure why it had never occurred to him before.

His moment of reflection was interrupted by the sound of a car starting down the narrow, twisting track towards the cemetery. It was a Ford Focus. A definite city car.

Grant turned back to his parents' grave. He already knew who was coming.

Winston parked up on the grass verge and joined Grant. He said, 'There was no answer at the cottage, so I thought I'd try here.'

'I'm in the middle of nowhere on a fairly large island,' said Grant. 'I don't mind you telling me that you had GCHQ ping my phone.'

Winston stuffed his hands into his trouser pockets. It might have been peak summer, but there was still a distinct chill by the coast.

Grant, in a loose black t-shirt, seemed unaffected. 'Are your parents still alive?' he asked.

'No,' Winston replied.

'It makes you wonder,' said Grant. 'Why you're supposed to care so much. I mean, what does family even mean? They're just people. No different to strangers when you think about it. They don't really know you – not the real you, anyway. Not who you really are. The person you are when you're alone, or that looks back at you from the mirror. They never *see* that person. So what the hell does it matter?'

Winston replied, 'I think it's something to do with blood. You don't have to love them. You don't even have to like them. But it's your blood. They matter because they're who you are as well.'

Grant said, 'It's horrible to say, but sometimes I'm glad they're gone. I mean, I'd rather they were still here, but there's a bit of me that's relieved to have got it all out of the way. Because it's either sudden and tragic, or a slow, drawn-out decline.'

Winston agreed, 'There is a kind of freedom about it.'

'It's you and the world. You were as alone when they were here. You just didn't realise it.'

Neither of them had been looking at each other, opting instead for the neutral ground of the headstone. It felt like they could be more honest with each other that way. Without judgement.

Grant said, 'Is it true about what happened to you? With the Chinese?'

'Yeah,' Winston replied.

'You must have known what would happen when they captured you. How did you know you could take it? Being tortured.'

'You don't. You can't know. Not until it's happening.'

'What was it like, when you got back?'

Something about the surroundings, the wide-open space, the sound of the sea, the sharp gusts of wind, made it easier for Winston to talk about it. That Chinese cell couldn't have felt further away in that moment.

'I drank a lot,' Winston replied. 'It got pretty ugly for a time. I took myself right to the edge. Right to the limit of wanting to kill myself. Luckily, someone helped me. It was like, I couldn't stop drinking until I'd looked over that cliff edge, and seen what was waiting below.'

'What was there?' asked Grant.

Winston exhaled. 'Nothing. A total void. I looked right into it. That was when I realised, this is it. This is all we get. I might be wrong about that, but it seems to me that the best way to live my life is to act like this is all we get. I don't care if you believe in God, the afterlife, or Arsenal Football Club. As long as you believe in something.'

'Is that what stops you?' asked Grant. 'From drinking again?'

Winston couldn't help but let a glimmer of a smile show. 'I do this thing sometimes... I go to a pub and ask for a pint. But I don't drink it. I just stand there, staring at it. Staring it down. Like I'm telling it, you don't control me anymore. Look how strong I am, to stand here and not even flinch. I can take it. There's nothing the world can throw at me that I can't take. Because I know what I've lived through. And if I can survive that, I can survive anything. I think that's an instinct we share.'

'You worked me out in the last week?' asked Grant.

Winston chuckled. 'Week? Grant, I figured that out after five minutes with your file three years ago. I was in the car with Forrester when you were running up and down

Jacob's Ladder for six hours. I saw it. I never want you to forget that place.'

Grant knew that Winston hadn't driven all that way to talk about mortality.

Winston fetched a blue file from the car. It was a light shade of blue that Grant had only seen once before on an MI6 file.

Winston said, 'C is reopening Albion, Grant. And not before time, it would seem.' He handed Grant a series of crime scene photographs from the file. 'We've got a problem.'

Grant flicked through the pictures of the dead. 'Who are they?'

'Station chiefs. A few of our own. CIA. Mossad. FSB. You name it. Not many agencies were spared.'

'How could this happen?' asked Grant. 'Didn't the first three send up a flare?'

'That's the thing,' said Winston. 'They were all killed at the same time. Synchronised assassinations. Fifteen in total across four different continents. That's not the worst of it.' He handed over one more picture.

It was from a substation CCTV, showing a man fleeing one of the murder scenes.

Grant knew the face well. When he'd last seen it, it had been on a towering painting inside a mansion he would never forget. It was Charles Joseph.

Winston said, 'You were right about Marlow playing us. Joseph's alive. C has asked me to run the Albion programme to track him down. I want you to be my Albion.'

Grant looked up from the file to meet Winston's eyes.

'I know you've read up on the old operatives,' said

Winston.

'The Treasury hasn't had to worry much about pension payments. Most Albions don't make it that long.'

'We're going to do it right this time. I'm running things, Grant. I'm not Imogen Swann and you're not Henry Marlow. Since your SAS days, you've always worked best on your own. Christie and I agree: you're the only one we want for this. But I don't know where the map goes on this, Duncan. Only you know that.'

'I've had my entire life to prepare for this.' Grant handed Winston the Albion file back. 'I'm ready.'

Walking to Winston's car, Grant looked back at his parents' headstone. When he looked at their names, his thoughts turned to Marlow's diary, when he talked about his first kill.

"I'll never forget that day. No one ever does... I walked into that room one man, and left it a totally different one…"

As Winston reversed the car slowly along the bumpy track to a place that he could turn, Grant didn't take his eyes off the headstone. Eventually, Winston backed up until Grant could no longer read the names on the headstone.

What it made him feel, he wasn't quite sure. Not yet, at least. He had walked into that cemetery as Duncan Grant…

"…I knew I would never be the same again."

…and would leave it an Albion.

THE END

Duncan Grant will return will *Dead Flags*, coming in winter 2021.

ENJOY KILL DAY?

YOU CAN HELP WITH JUST A MINUTE OF YOUR TIME...

If you enjoyed *Kill Day*, it would be a great help to me if you left a rating or a brief review on Amazon.

Most major publishers spend a huge amount of money on marketing, and to get books into the hands of reviewers. I might not have that ability, but with a minute of your time, you can get something that money cannot buy: word-of-mouth support.

Many thanks,

- Andrew

ACKNOWLEDGMENTS

This book is dedicated to the memory of Del Swan. My best man. The best man.

Thank you:

To my tireless editor and beloved wife, Emma.

To DW, who read a late draft and made invaluable suggestions.

Julien Virlogeux who advised on all things French.

James: my fabulous cover designer. And Louise: my accountant.

To my wonderful Facebook fans, whose lovely comments keep me going, make me laugh, and make this the best job I can imagine. Your support is much appreciated.

The following books were invaluable for research, and I highly recommend reading for pleasure as well as insight:

Safe by Chris Ryan

Calum's Road by Roger Hutchinson (stunning memoir of the man who built a road on the tiny island of Raasay next to Skye in Scotland)

Inside the Kingdom by Robert Lacey (history of Saudi Arabia)

The History Thieves by Ian Cobain (history of British classified intelligence)

On Intelligence: A History of Espionage and the Secret World by John Hughes-Wilson

MI6: Life and Death in the British Secret Service by Gordon Corera (BBC Security Correspondent who writes with real insight about the most secret of agencies)

Legacy of Ashes - A History of the CIA by Tim Weiner

Outliers by Malcolm Gladwell (a few of Duncan Grant's traits were discovered in this wonderful, highly readable book about extraordinary people you've likely never heard of)

The Ultimate Art of War by Antony Cummins (lovely illustrated edition of the classic book)

See No Evil by Robert Baer (CIA agent's memoir; blistering stuff)

The Perfect Kill by Robert Baer (how assassins work)

The History of MI5 by Christopher Andrew

There were many, many more books that helped me along the way, but the ones above are some of my favourites. If you liked *Kill Day*, I think you'd get a kick out of them.

* * *

There are a lot of sacrifices required in order to write a book. It might be a gloriously sunny day and all you want is to get on your bike and ride out into the countryside. You also often need to stay up long into the night with work first thing the next morning. Or you have too much to do to finish that damn chapter, so you can't spend the weekend with your family.

To all the people in my life who are willing to make these sacrifices with me, thank you.

Finally, to anyone reading this: thank you for buying this book. It took a lot of long hours and hard work to complete, but every new reader that discovers it makes it all worth it. I hope you'll come back and join Duncan Grant for his next adventure, coming later this year.

- Andrew
Glasgow, Scotland

Printed in Great Britain
by Amazon

62780532R00270